CORIN BURNSIDE grew up in a house full of books and has been scribbling stories for as long as she can remember. A passion for history, travel and the natural environment colours her writing and provides inspiration for her storytelling.

She divides her time between her family in the UK, and her home in the heart of the French Pyrenees, where she lives with her husband and The Princess, a demanding Hungarian Vizsla who helps with plot holes in exchange for cheese.

Her Forgotten Promise

CORIN BURNSIDE

ONE PLACE. MANY STORIES

HQ
An imprint of HarperCollins*Publishers* Ltd
1 London Bridge Street
London SE1 9GF

www.harpercollins.co.uk

HarperCollins*Publishers*
Macken House, 39/40 Mayor Street Upper,
Dublin 1 D01 C9W8
Ireland

This paperback edition 2023

1

First published in Great Britain by
HQ, an imprint of HarperCollins*Publishers* Ltd 2023

For John, Gemma and Michael.

Prologue

Margaret

1944

Four bodies were pulled out of the rubble. Four neighbours I had passed on the stairs and said good morning to countless times. The rest of us, whose flats survived the blast, had to stand and watch as our homes were pulled down. Then we were allowed in to salvage anything worth saving.

I spent a dispiriting day dredging through dust-covered bits and pieces, some so broken I barely recognised them. Amazingly, my bed and bedside table survived. A girder had fallen and got caught on a bit of wall, shielding them from other debris.

The table drawer hung open, and inside, covered in dust and wrinkled with water damage, was the book of Tennyson poetry.

In the end it was the only thing worth saving.

I left without looking back. Agnes was gone and if I had been at home, I might be dead by now.

It was time to move on and try to rebuild my life.

Chapter 1

Claire

ENGLAND – 2014

When I found Aunt M on that Friday afternoon, she was in the middle of the road outside the railway station, standing on a mini-island halfway over a pedestrian crossing. She seemed as oblivious of the cold February rain as she was of the gawpers on the pavement. All she wore was a pair of bedroom slippers, and a pale mauve dressing gown.

I'd been driving around for hours, after a frantic call from the manager of the residential home where Aunt M lived. Distracted for a moment by a flash from my phone lying on the passenger seat next to me, I almost missed her. Andrew again. Disappearing from the veterinary surgery without telling him why I'd left early did me no favours, and not answering my phone would undoubtedly add to his annoyance and frustration.

And there she was: my poor aunt in nothing but her nightwear, a spectacle for the gathering onlookers. To my horror one or two were even taking photos.

Without thinking, I swerved across two lanes of traffic and stopped on a double yellow. Ignoring irate drivers, I jumped out and pushed through the crowd, dodging a cyclist as I ran into the road. I reached the island as the lights changed and four lanes of traffic rumbled forward. Aunt M stood there, hanging on to a bollard as if it would save her from drowning. A middle-aged couple in cagoules and hiking shoes were talking to her but she seemed as unaware of them as she was of the weather.

Words fell out of my mouth as I reached her.

'Bloody hell, Aunt M, thank God I've found you. Where are your clothes? You're frozen; come on, let's get you off the road to somewhere dry.'

Giving the couple a quick nod and smile, I put a hand on her cold, clammy arm, then pulled off my jacket and threw it around her bowed shoulders. Her scalp showed through thin white hair pulled tight around pink plastic rollers, and fragile bones dug into my side. Shivers rocked her body as I hugged her to me, hoping she'd stay on her feet until we could get to the side of the road.

'Do you know this poor lady?' said cagoule woman. 'I think it's disgusting she's allowed to wander around in such a state. She should be in a home being looked after, not left to her own devices so she can walk the streets. You should be ashamed of yourself.'

'She's my aunt,' I said, bluntly. 'Thank you for your concern. I'm not her carer, but I will most certainly be speaking to those who are.' I turned back to Aunt M. 'Come on, let's get you out of here.'

She looked up at me out of clouded blue eyes, the skin around them puffy and bruised-looking. There was fear there, like you might see in a terrified animal, but not a flicker of recognition. She felt rigid, as if on the point of flight. I patted her arm, whispering soft, reassuring words, and her body slackened, almost catching me off-guard. I took her weight, but she pushed feebly against me, intent, it seemed, on getting away.

'Who are you? Leave me alone – I must find Agnes.' Her voice rose.

'You're all interfering, do-gooders. I'm perfectly capable of walking into town on my own, thank you very much. Why don't you all just fuck off and leave me alone?'

Cagoule couple tutted, and a stifled giggle came from those still watching from the roadside.

'Do you think we can make it to the pavement? The green man's on go,' I said, trying not to alarm her again and cursing myself for using that slightly too loud, slightly too slow, ever so cheery tone.

She looked at me as if I were something unpleasant on her shoe.

'Why have you brought me here? This isn't my coat. I would never wear something so vulgar,' she said, trying to drag my top-of-the-range waxed jacket off her shoulders. 'Where's Agnes? She promised to bring chocolates and champagne.' Then she smiled, seeming to have forgotten I was there for a second, before glancing up at me. 'We're celebrating,' she whispered. 'Nobody else knows. We haven't told them.' Shaking her head, she put her finger up to her blue-tinged lips. Her eyes sharpened, and a flush crept up her face. She pulled my coat closer around her shivering body. 'Get me out of here. It'll be blackout in an hour or two and we must be indoors by then.' Her chin trembled. 'I wish I knew where Agnes was.'

What had brought her to such a state? The last time I'd seen her, she had recently moved into a private residential home in a converted manor house. There'd been an incident at her home in Richmond, where a pan had caught fire and she'd needed rescuing through her bedroom window by the fire brigade. To my shame, I'd let other things get in the way of going to see her, even though the residential home was only twenty minutes' drive away. I realised it must have been at least six months since my last visit and I had no idea she'd become so confused.

I persuaded her to step down off the island. It seemed an age until we made it to the pavement, her pace no more than a shuffle, the slippers soggy from the rain and sliding off her feet with each achingly slow step. Reaching the side of the road at last, Aunt M stopped again and leant against me. Shudders racked her thin frame and I fought my anxiety. She needed to be in a hospital as soon as possible. What if she fainted or had a heart attack? I couldn't take her in my car; it was now blocked in by the commuter traffic, and an ambulance would take too long to get to us. Looking frantically around I saw a taxi pulling in and waved. Thankfully, he stopped beside us and I bundled Aunt M into the back, then ran and locked my car, leaving the hazard lights flashing.

Back in the taxi I asked the driver to take us to the nearest hospital as quickly as he could. He nodded, pushed his shirtsleeves up to his elbows, twisted his baseball cap around backwards and pulled out in front of the other vehicles to a blaring of horns.

Aunt M had sunk onto the seat and closed her eyes, my coat and the soaking dressing gown falling open and revealing crepe-like, white skin. I tried to cover her up – under normal circumstances she would be horrified to be seen in such a state. She looked at me, very much in the present now, the blue eyes clear and wary.

'Claire? What are you doing here? Are you taking me home?'

I breathed a silent *thank God*.

'Yes, it's me, Aunt M. You'd gone for a bit of a walk and got stuck, remember?' I said. 'Of course, I'll take you home, but I think it's best if we pop into the hospital, first. I don't want you getting a chill. Let's have a doctor check you over, and then if they're happy, I'll take you home. Will that do?'

She nodded and looked down at the wet coat. 'Why am I wearing this? I'm cold. Who took all my clothes? It's not decent, going around in just my dressing gown and slippers.' She coughed, a rattle that seemed to come from deep in her chest, and dragged the coat more tightly around her. Then, as if a light had gone out, her eyes lost focus and she stared at me like I was a stranger. 'Agnes will be so worried if she comes back and I'm not there. I need to get home before she returns.'

Whoever this Agnes was, I couldn't remember ever hearing the name before. She'd mentioned the blackout – did she think she was back in the war? Was she remembering someone from her time in the WAAFs, perhaps?

'Who is Agnes, Aunt M? Is she a friend?'

'I might wear my blue frock, tonight. Agnes says it goes with my eyes.'

And she slid down lower on the seat and fell asleep.

At the hospital, I left Aunt M in the taxi for a few moments while I ran into the reception area of Accident and Emergency to find a wheelchair. Her face had lost even more colour during the fifteen-minute journey and turned chalk-white. I doubted she was fit enough to make the short walk inside. Passing through the automatic doors, I stopped and stared at a confusion of signs pointing in different directions. A nurse came through a door and turned to walk away from me.

'Excuse me,' I said, hurrying to catch her.

'Can I help you?' she said.

I gabbled an explanation and she jumped into action, finding a wheelchair and following me out to where the driver had parked on a yellow criss-cross area reserved for ambulances. Aunt M was still dozing, and the nurse sat beside her for a moment, holding her wrist and looking at her watch.

'This lady needs to be seen as soon as possible. I'll get a porter to help lift her and we'll get her inside.' She was efficient and business-like, and I'd never been so happy to pass on a task to someone else. Within a minute or two, Aunt M was wheeled into the building. Ignoring protests from the taxi driver, I thrust a twenty-pound note through the window as he began to pull away, then followed the others back into the reception area. The nurse was waiting for me.

'I need to take some details. Your name, please, and that of the lady. She's your aunt, did you say?'

'My name is Claire McRory, and yes, she's my aunt. Her name is Margaret Scott, and she lives at Stanbury Hall Residential Home. I'm sorry, I can't remember the exact address . . .'

I slumped onto a chair, trying not to cry. What was wrong with me? I'm a fifty-year-old professional woman who is used to dealing with emergencies – but in that moment I felt completely overwhelmed. Andrew, with impeccable timing, chose that moment to fire off another text, and I hastily muted the phone. The nurse frowned.

'I'm afraid you'll need to turn that off while you're in the hospital,' she said.

I did as she asked. At least it gave me an excuse to avoid him for a while longer. Taking a few breaths, I tried to calm myself enough to answer her questions. I filled in as much as I could of Aunt M's personal details, embarrassed about how little I knew of her life nowadays. How easy it had been to forget about my only relative and allow my own troubles to take up all my time and thoughts. I should have kept in touch, made sure she was well.

I hadn't even known I was down as her next of kin until the manager of the residential home rang me after she'd gone missing. Aunt M was the one who'd made the decision to go into a home and had organised everything, including shutting up her house. I'd only visited her when it was her birthday, at the end of the previous summer. After all, ninety is a milestone. And she was fine then – at least, she'd seemed fine. Chatty, in that slightly eccentric way she had, and dressed to the nines, with her hair and make-up immaculate, as always.

How had she come to this in such a short time?

Chapter 2

Agnes

LONDON – February 1943

The cellar below the streets of the city of London was as cold and uninviting as a morgue. Agnes Kerr shivered, from nerves as much as the temperature. Beside her, the sergeant seemed impatient to get on with the business of the day, as if Agnes was one more thing getting in her way. A blast of even colder air blew into the room as the door onto the street above opened and then clanged shut. Agnes heard the clatter of heels as someone ran down the stairs and a tall blonde girl arrived, shaking the rain off her gamp.

'Corporal Scott, you're late. Not for the first time. I do not want to tell you again,' Sergeant Atkins said, her voice clipped. She huffed out an exasperated breath. 'We have a new recruit. Show her the ropes will you, tell her who's who – you know the kind of thing. And get that coat off; you're a WAAF not a flaming barrow boy.'

'Yes, Sergeant; sorry, Sergeant.'

9

Agnes was that new recruit, like the new girl in school, as out of place as the ill-fitting uniform that hung off her small frame. The blonde hurriedly divested herself of the offending coat and stood in front of her, her hand held out.

'Hello. I'm Margaret Scott. There's a spare seat next to mine – you'd better nab it before someone else does. What's your name?'

Her voice reminded Agnes of summer. Light and sunny, as if she were about to share a joke and was on the verge of a giggle.

'Agnes. Agnes Kerr.' She looked up at the taller girl, shyly, and shook her hand. 'I'm pleased to meet you, Margaret.'

Heat prickled through her hair as she stumbled over the English name.

Margaret showed her to the bank of radios and patted the chair next to hers. They sat, and Agnes picked up her headphones, fiddling with the connection on one side, glad to have a familiar piece of equipment to concentrate on. Her fingers fumbled with the wires and she blew on them.

'Ugh, I didn't think it would be so cold.'

'Oh, it never gets warm. I always wear a woolly vest. Sergeant Atkins is a stickler for correct uniform, but at least she doesn't check what's underneath.' The blonde girl winked and grinned. 'I hope you don't think me rude, but you don't sound like you're from around here. Where's home?'

Embarrassment chased its way up Agnes's spine. She kept her eyes on her task, hating being different. When she glanced up, Margaret smiled, and she couldn't help but smile back.

'Is it that obvious? My mother is French, and I grew up there until the Germans invaded. Papa is English and he brought us all here when Paris fell.'

The smile was replaced by a look of horror.

'That must have been awful for you,' she said. 'I dread Britain being invaded.' Her blue eyes became serious. 'I can't imagine how terrifying it would be. Do you still have family over there?'

'No.' How could she begin to explain? 'Maman's parents died

when I was very young; I don't really remember them. We lived in their house while Papa worked in Paris.'

Agnes lapsed into silence, not wanting to think of those days. Margaret's voice broke into her reverie.

'How much training did they put you through? You probably know as much as I do about this job,' she said, the English habit of small talk coming naturally to her, it seemed. 'I've only been here a couple of months, and I'm not sure I'm an asset to the WAAFs. Sergeant Atkins tells me off so often, I'm amazed I haven't been sacked.'

She laughed, a low chuckle that lifted Agnes's spirits and made her grateful for the other girl's tact.

'I learnt the basics of radio transmitting and receiving,' she said. 'It seems straightforward enough.'

Margaret regarded her with her head on one side. Agnes dropped her gaze. She probably thought she was terribly dull. And she was. She couldn't remember the last time she had laughed at something frivolous and silly.

'Where are you staying? Do you live close by?'

She smiled in a lopsided way, white teeth – not quite straight – peeping between her lips.

'At a boarding house near here.' Agnes grimaced. 'It's awful – the landlady is a dragon. I thought I'd explore and try to find somewhere of my own, once I know the area a bit better.'

Margaret made a sympathetic face.

'What about parties? All work and no play, you know – there's a good scene here. I could show you around if you like?'

'You're very kind. I'd like that, Margaret.' Agnes paused. 'Sorry. May I call you Maggie? Would you mind?'

She pronounced it *Maggee* with the inflection on the ending, the name falling naturally into her French accent, so much easier to say than Margaret. Margaret laughed and said she didn't mind at all, and for a moment it felt as if the sun had come out in the cold dungeon below the streets of the capital.

They settled down to work, Agnes relaxing into the familiar routines she had been taught in training. Once or twice, she felt Margaret's eyes on her, but concentrated on what she was doing, needing to get used to the equipment, aware that the lives of others depended on her skills as a radio operator. By the end of the busy shift, she was confident she could cope with anything that came up. It felt good to be doing something essential to the war effort.

Agnes was tired and cold by the time she and Margaret, along with the rest of the shift workers, climbed up the steep stairs out of the cellar and reached street level. The other girls gossiped and giggled as they left, but all she wanted was to get back to the boarding house and sink into bed. Pulling her scarf closer around her neck to block the thin wind sneaking under her coat collar, she said a quiet goodnight to Margaret and walked away.

Later, dropping with fatigue, she shovelled a few mouthfuls of the landlady's watery soup down her throat before dragging herself upstairs. Lying in the uncomfortable, narrow bed in her dismal room, sleep evaded her. Her mind spun with the events of the day.

It was the first time she had mentioned France and her childhood to anyone, never mind a complete stranger, and memories she thought she had buried resurfaced like a noxious gas bubbling and popping on the surface of a lake.

Her father, Christopher Kerr, an English diplomat based in Paris after the Great War, was a distant parent, who lodged his family well away from his working life. They lived in the home Agnes's mother had grown up in, the old farmhouse sitting in the heart of the French countryside, warm and filled with the love her mother wrapped her and her brothers in.

When Papa came home, Maman spent hours with their cook, planning meals for friends and neighbours; elaborate dinners that went on until the early hours, the guests sitting out on the

12

terrace beneath Agnes's window, drinking Armagnac, chatting and keeping her awake.

Jeanne Kerr became a different person while her husband was at home; she dressed up, styled her thick, wavy hair into a chignon, put on make-up and tottered round in high heels. Gone was the mother Agnes adored, replaced by an impatient, inattentive woman, who had no time for her children. Her eyes were only for her husband, and even at a young age Agnes picked up on the desperation in her behaviour while Christopher was at home.

He would coach Edward and Pierre in cricket and rugby, take them out on the lazy river to practise rowing, and play tennis with them on the bumpy gravel court in the garden. Agnes stood on the sidelines, ignored, yearning to join in. Like her mother, she would do anything to gain his attention, showing him pictures she had painted, dances she made up, piano pieces she tried to master, only to stumble over the chords in her nervousness. Her father would lose interest in a few moments and take her brothers to the boules court in the village.

Jealousy soured her, its taste bitter in her mouth so she became mean to the boys and avoided their games. Only her mother had time for her, it seemed – as long as *Papa* was not there.

At the age of eleven, she was sent to the international school in Paris, a place she hated with every fibre of her body. Once a month her father picked her up on a Saturday afternoon, and took her to places she had only read about – the Louvre, Notre Dame, the Eiffel Tower. Occasionally, he had a woman with him, whom he introduced as a friend from the embassy. The lady was English, beautifully dressed, and smoked cigarettes in a long ivory holder. Her name was Katherine and Agnes disliked everything about her, recognising her as a competitor for her father's attention, even though the day was meant to be for her.

The only subjects Agnes excelled at were languages and drama. She was a student who went unnoticed by everyone except the drama teacher, Miss Brown, a wild-haired young woman who put on productions of Shakespeare plays twice a year. On the stage she could be anyone but herself and for the first time in her life Agnes forgot her crippling shyness for the few hours when she was someone else.

The start of the war barely came to Agnes's attention, until one day after lunch, she was summoned to the headmistress's office and found her father pacing up and down the room.

'We have to leave. Today. Paris is too unsafe,' he said, as soon as she entered.

Agnes's spirits lifted. Any excuse to leave school was fine, even though the prospect of being over-run by the Nazis was terrifying.

'Are we going home?'

Papa shook his head.

'I've arranged for Maman and your brothers to travel to Caen. We'll meet them there and take a boat to England.'

She stared at him, not quite believing what he was saying, panic rising inside her.

'But I don't want to go. Why can't we stay at home, in France?'

'Agnes, it's too dangerous,' her father snapped. 'Mme Payan has just told me they are shutting the school at the end of the week, and moving any students who can't go home to Bordeaux. You're coming with me. Go and pack, quickly. We must leave within the hour or we'll miss the boat.'

Desperation tightened in her chest.

'But all my things are at home. I can't go in my school uniform.'

'There's no time. Don't you understand, you stupid child?' Her father's voice rose, his face reddening. 'This is serious. The Germans will be marching into Paris any day now. If we don't leave, we'll be trapped. I don't want to spend the war in a German labour camp, do you?'

He took her by the shoulders and shook her. Agnes had never seen him like this, so angry, treating her as if she were an idiot. Tears pricked her eyes. She shook her head, hoping he wouldn't notice.

'I'll go and pack,' she whispered, wanting to run away and hide her hurt and humiliation.

'Be quick – we haven't got long,' he said again, turning his back on her and resuming his pacing.

Agnes stood for a moment, wanting to scream at him that she wasn't stupid, wasn't a child.

But instead, she turned and ran; one day she would show him what she was capable of. The tears she'd withheld ran down her cheeks as she made her way to the dorms. She slowed to a walk, sobs shaking her until she stopped and sank down on a bench in the corridor. Miss Brown, passing on her way to a class, stopped in front of her.

'My dear, what is the matter? You look as if the world has fallen in around you.' She sat beside Agnes and took her hand. 'You know what they say about a trouble shared being a trouble halved.' She lifted her chin and looked at her with a small smile, softness in her eyes.

Agnes tried to control the sobs and wiped her eyes on her sleeve. Her nose ran and she patted her pockets for a handkerchief. The teacher put one in her hand and waited till the outpouring had reduced to the odd gulp.

'I have to leave.' Tears pricked at the backs of her eyes again, and she dragged in a breath to steady herself. 'Papa's here to collect me and we're going to England.' She grabbed the teacher's hand. 'But I don't want to leave France. England is so far away, and is cold and wet, and the food is horrible, by all accounts.' She sobbed again. 'Papa thinks I'm just a stupid, ignorant little girl. He never listens to me.'

Miss Brown laughed.

'But, my dear, of course you must go. Your father is right to get you out of here, while you can still leave,' she said. 'And while I would never think of you as ignorant, you are still very young and perhaps being a little silly, don't you think?'

Agnes stared at her.

'You don't understand. Nobody does.' She gave the teacher her handkerchief back, wiped her eyes on her sleeves once more and rose. 'Papa might be English, but Maman is French, and I'm French and I know this is where we should be.' Raising her chin, she brushed down her skirt. 'Goodbye, Miss Brown.'

Chapter 3

Claire

I found Aunt M in a curtained-off cubicle, lying on a narrow bed with rails pulled up each side, as if she were a toddler in a cot. She'd been given a hospital gown to cover her nakedness and a thin hospital blanket to warm her. My coat, the dressing gown and soggy slippers were set tidily on a plastic chair. She lay on her side, eyes closed, like a discarded doll, her limbs at odd angles and her mouth half open. For one awful moment I thought she was dead. Then an eyelid twitched, she gave a small cough, and I let out a long breath of relief. I turfed the things off the chair and pulled it over to the bed, sat down and gently took her hand, all the while watching her face.

She had been beautiful in her day, and even now the bone structure so evident in her gaunt features had a symmetry, the cheekbones prominent, the nose straight, the brow high and sloping back to the ridiculous pink curlers. The skin, too big for those bones, hung in gentle folds and wrinkles but was unblemished. I always thought of her as a true English rose, blonde hair curled around her face, blue eyes full of laughter. She was my mother's sister, and the perfect auntie. When I was very young and she came to see us, she'd insist on taking me out, on what she called 'a jolly'. It might be a day at the seaside, or an afternoon in the city to see a show and have tea at a posh hotel, where the sandwiches and cakes were served on a silver tiered stand. She never seemed to mind when I only wanted to eat the cakes.

'Who wants to eat boring cucumber sandwiches, anyway?' she'd say. 'Let's have more cakes, shall we?'

And she'd wink and put her finger to her perfect lips and remind me not to tell my parents what we'd been up to. As if they would have cared less.

When I was twelve or thereabouts, I remember dreaming about Aunt M being my mother and how much more fun it would be than living with my own parents. To them, I was something to be shunted around from boarding school to whichever relatives would have me in the holidays. Being encumbered with a child in their mid-thirties was not something they'd planned for.

Aunt M's voice dragged me out of my memories. 'Who are you and why are you staring at me?' Awake and confused, a frown harrowed lines into her forehead. Her voice could have cut crystal and it rose as her agitation grew. 'Where's Agnes? Why isn't she here? I must see her.'

I tried to calm her, but she wasn't having any of it.

'Aunt M, it's Claire. Remember, I found you wandering in the road? I was worried about you, so I brought you to the hospital.'

There I was again, talking in that too loud, too slow voice, as if she were an idiot. She was confused, not stupid.

'But where is Agnes? She'll be worried about me. The bombs, you know.'

She struggled to sit up, a tear escaping the corner of one eye and running down the crevice beside her nose.

'Don't be afraid. There are no bombs here, Aunt M.' I stroked her hand, wondering how to take her out of her past, back to the present. 'Who is Agnes? Can I call her?'

'I don't know where she went,' she whimpered. 'She disappeared.'

At that moment she seemed very much in the present, looking at me with grief-filled eyes. How had I never heard of this woman? True, we'd been out of touch for a while, but Aunt M had been a great one for telling stories about her life and the people she'd known, especially the authors she'd worked with and met, during her days as a publisher.

All I knew was she was suffering and I couldn't help her. Having come this far today, I couldn't abandon her again. Reconnecting with Aunt M had struck a chord in me – it wasn't only the guilt I felt, after it had taken a near tragedy for me to recognise how neglectful I'd been. It was how lost she seemed and how I empathised with her confusion and fear. It didn't matter if I was from a different generation, a different time; in my own way I was just as lost and afraid as she was.

A doctor came and examined Aunt M after I'd waited with her for over an hour. I was relieved when he said he wanted to keep her in for observation. She rallied once they'd managed to find a vein and pump some fluids into her, but I could see she was exhausted. She was still not lucid, still back in the Second World War, her memories more real than the present day.

I left her sleeping in a ward full of other elderly people, the air full of grunts, snores, and whimpers. Deafness must have its advantages in those circumstances. Although I was reluctant to go, dreading something would happen to her overnight, I couldn't wait to leave that room full of the living dead.

I rang Stanbury Hall and spoke to a woman who answered after multiple rings, sounding flustered, and then relieved when I told her my name, and where their errant resident was. The growing anger I'd been bottling up was in danger of spilling over, even though I had no doubt the person on the other end of the phone was not to blame for Aunt M's absconding. I was put through to the manager and, after some pointed comments about the lack of security and care at the place, made an appointment with her for the next day, saying I would bring Aunt M back with me, should the medical staff think she was fit to leave hospital.

After retrieving my car – a parking ticket plastered to the windscreen – I finally reached home after eleven o'clock. I was met with disgruntled meows from Betty, the ginger and white cat I'd rescued three years earlier. Putting down some food for her, I realised I hadn't eaten since noon, hunger making me glance in the fridge for a quick snack before I fell into bed. The half-empty bottle of Chablis in the door offered a better option and invited oblivion. Pouring a large glassful, I drank it leaning against the warmth of the Rayburn in the quiet dark of the kitchen, while munching on a chunk of stale cheddar.

Fatigue dragged at me, but I was too wired to sleep, and turned my phone back on. Andrew had left four voicemails and the same number of text messages:

– *Where are you? Please call me.*

– *You're late. Why did you leave without telling me? Our meeting should have been an hour ago. I need to talk to you.*

– *I can't believe you're ignoring me. Call me! It's important.*

– *ANSWER YOUR BLOODY PHONE!*

The man was impossible. We might still share the business, but the bond we once had was gone, now we no longer shared a bed. He could wait until the morning. I threw the phone across the kitchen table, watching it skitter off the end and almost hit Betty, who had finished eating and was curled up on a chair. She hissed at me, jumped down and stalked off. I ransacked a drawer for some sleeping tablets, and dragged myself upstairs to bed.

Waking the following morning with an aching head, I called Andrew before he could gain the upper hand by phoning first. Our relationship had become distant since the divorce, though we still worked together. Being co-owners of a veterinary practice, we would have damaged both our careers and financial security if we had split it up. When I explained why I'd left in such a hurry, he was furious I'd not bothered to let him know where I was at some point during the evening.

'I was worried you'd had an accident, or done something stupid.'

He sounded tired and tetchy.

'What do you mean – stupid? It was an emergency, and I was anxious about Aunt M.'

'Claire, you've been as stressed lately as you were during the divorce, and let's face it, you have form when you're upset . . .'

He let the words hang for a second.

Heat ran up my neck. My past history was just that – old ground – and it was unfair of him to throw it in my face. I ignored the jibe.

'She's my only living relative. I couldn't just abandon her.' Guilt caught me unawares. Tears pricked behind my eyes as I pictured Aunt M as I'd first seen her, a lost soul standing in the road. My words came out as a whisper, almost to myself. 'She might have died, for God's sake.'

'I'm sorry,' he said. 'It's just . . . well . . . there's something I need to tell you. I don't want you to hear about it from someone else. I'm on call and will be at the surgery all day. Can you come and see me there? Please?'

He sounded almost embarrassed. Curiosity made me relent and I promised to meet him later.

Chapter 4

Agnes

By the end of her first week, Agnes had lost her nerves and looked forward to being at work more than anything she had done since coming to England. It was a good feeling to be helping in the fight against the Germans, and she loved the challenge of deciphering messages of gobbledegook and unearthing the words within. The next day though, she had a day off and dreaded it, having no idea what she would do all day by herself.

She had been at work for half an hour when Margaret finally arrived, blowing in like a warm wind to the freezing temperature in the cellar. Sergeant Atkins told her she was on a final warning in front of the whole room; if she was late again, disciplinary measures would be taken.

Clarice and Pat, two of the other girls, thought it was hilarious and teased Margaret mercilessly throughout the morning. For once, she didn't rise to their bait, keeping her head down and barely saying a word. Agnes kept quiet; if Maggie wanted to talk, she would. It seemed as if she had something on her mind, and occasionally she noticed her muttering to herself with a glint of tears in her eyes.

Eventually, Agnes took off her headphones and stood up, stretching the kinks out of her back.

'It's lunchtime. Shall we go over to the café across the road?' she said, nudging Margaret. 'It looks like you could do with a break from them.'

She nodded across the room to where Clarice and Pat were giggling over some nonsense. Sergeant Atkins bore down on the pair and berated them for not taking the job seriously enough, ordering them to work over lunchtime to catch up. Agnes's lips twitched.

Margaret gave her a grateful look.

'I'd like that, thank you,' she said.

'Those two girls, are they always like that?' Agnes said, as they climbed up to the street. 'They seem . . . childish, if you don't mind me saying.'

Margaret stopped for a moment, a frown crossing her face, as if she was considering the question.

'We all handle our fear and worry in different ways, don't you think?' she said, eventually, walking on and crossing the busy road quickly in front of a slow-moving wagon, Agnes hurrying to keep up. 'Those two have their demons, believe me. It's their way of dealing with everything this shitty war throws at us. They mean no harm and are good friends.'

Agnes shrugged.

'You don't seem to find their teasing funny, today. Is everything all right?'

Margaret pushed open the door to the Lyons café without answering. By the time they were shown to a table and had given their order, she seemed more inclined to talk. Agnes breathed a quiet sigh, glad she wouldn't have to be the one trying to keep the conversation going.

'Sorry, I've been a bit of a sourpuss this morning,' said Margaret. 'The sarge really put the wind up me, giving me that warning. I suppose I deserve it; I know I've been awfully lackadaisical about the job.' Fiddling with the spoon in the sugar bowl, her eyes cast down, she continued. 'Trouble is, you see, I find the whole thing so damned difficult. But I can't keep on asking others to help me; you've all got your own work to do. It's embarrassing.' She looked up at Agnes. 'You put me to shame. You're so quick and efficient, and I'm horribly slow and stupid.'

Agnes stared at her. That this funny, smart and beautiful young woman thought *she* was better at the job astounded her.

A flash of a memory: her father's voice and how much it had hurt when he said the same words to her.

'Don't say that. Don't ever say that about yourself.' She gripped Margaret's hand, squeezing it until the other girl winced. 'You're not stupid, do you hear me? None of us is ever stupid.' Margaret looked taken aback by her vehemence, and Agnes dropped her hand, flushing that she had let her guard down. What was it about this girl that had got under her skin? 'Sorry. But it's true. And perhaps this job is not best suited for you, but please don't bring yourself down.' She smiled at her, seeing the surprise in her eyes. 'We need to believe in ourselves, don't you think? There are plenty of people in this world who won't do it for us.'

Margaret laughed. 'Agnes Kerr, you're right. Thank you for the pep talk. I shall just have to try harder.' She raised a hand to attract the waitress. 'Now, I'm starving. Let's see what delicacy they have on the lunch menu, today, shall we?'

When their food arrived, they both looked at what passed for a meat pie and mashed potato and burst out laughing. A week ago, it would have been the last thing Agnes would have thought amusing, but Margaret's laugh was infectious, and they giggled like a pair of schoolgirls until they were breathless. A table of four middle-aged ladies next to them scowled and muttered their displeasure.

They managed to pull themselves together but when Margaret took a tentative bite of the pie Agnes had to stuff a napkin against her mouth to stop herself laughing again at her expression. She nibbled a corner of her own pie, pulled a face and put it back on her plate, wiping grease off her fingers.

'God, that's awful.'

They battled their way through as much of the food as they could manage without talking. The silence was comfortable, the quiet only broken when they finished their meal with a cup of tea.

'Do you have any friends or family in London who you'll visit on your day off?' Margaret said.

Agnes shook her head.

'My family live out in the countryside and I haven't made friends with anyone since we've been in England.'

Margaret frowned. 'Well, that won't do. I have a day off tomorrow, too. What say we go and do something together? We could go up to the heath and have a walk. I need some fresh air after being cooped up in the Dungeon all week.'

She was right. A good dose of cold London air would be a tonic.

Agnes grinned. 'I would like that very much. Thank you.'

'And while we're on the subject, I hope you'll think of me as your first friend in London.'

Agnes smiled again, her spirits lifting. 'I would like you to be my first friend here,' she said. Her cheeks grew hot at the thought that this wonderful person seemed to like her. She swallowed the dregs of her weak tea and pulled a face. 'I wish there was something nice to eat, though. I miss French food.'

'It's not always so bad, though I doubt you would ever think English food is as good as French,' Margaret said with a laugh. 'I hear all French people think we only eat boiled beef and suet pudding.'

She grinned in response. 'You may be right, and I know I should be grateful. There are plenty of people who would kill to eat something like this.' Her eyes lost focus for a moment. 'What I would give for a plate of *coq au vin et pommes de terre, rôties*, though.'

'Oh, don't – that sounds wonderful. You're making my mouth water.' Margaret put her elbows on the table and leant on her hands, a wistful expression on her face. 'My wish would be for fresh eggs, scrambled lightly, with two rashers of crispy bacon and fried tomatoes. Followed by hot toast covered in lashings of butter and my mother's marmalade, and as many cups of proper coffee as I can drink.'

'Ah, the English breakfast. I've never tried it.'

'Well, when this is all over, I shall personally make you a breakfast fit for a king.'

'And I'll cook coq au vin for you.'

Agnes held out her hand across the table.

Margaret took it, and they shook.

'It's a deal.'

Chapter 5

Claire

Aunt M was allowed to leave hospital after her overnight stay, and I collected her after lunch to take her back to Stanbury Hall. It was one of those Victorian piles that are either pulled down to make way for something more modern or converted into a hotel, private school or, as in this case, a retirement home for those who could afford it.

The gardens wrapped around the red-brick building, softening its square, forbidding façade. Spring colour was waking up everywhere as early daffodils bloomed and shrubs and trees changed from winter drabness to bursting buds of lime green, and the catkins of hazel. With low afternoon sunshine casting long shadows, the place had an air of peace and calm. Some of the residents were sitting in sheltered corners, woollen rugs around their knees and shoulders. Staff members in pale green uniform sat with them or helped the less able to hobble on paths criss-crossing the well-tended sward of lawn.

The only time I'd been there was for Aunt M's party and I'd taken little notice of the surroundings. I was prepared to dislike the place; how could they have allowed an old lady to wander away with almost nothing on, and not realise she was gone?

The original grand entrance hall had been turned into a reception area, with a business-like desk, behind which sat a receptionist. I settled Aunt M down on one of the smart, uncomfortable chairs, looking like a badly dressed bag lady in an odd assortment of my clothes. She had insisted on bringing the ruined slippers and dressing gown back with her, and clung on to the carrier bag containing them, her head drooping onto her chest. She might have been deemed fit to go home, but the short journey had drained her reserves.

The young woman manning the desk hurried over, greeting Aunt M like her own long-lost relative. She called for another member of staff who came quickly and ushered my aunt away, saying I was welcome to come too. Hesitating, I checked my watch, not wanting to be late for my meeting with the manager – there were things I needed to say face to face.

As Aunt M disappeared into a lift beside a grand staircase, I noticed a woman marching over to me. Striking and elegant, her shiny, pointed stilettoes tapped a staccato beat on the black and white tiles. I went to meet her, relieved I'd dressed smartly in a pair of tailored wool trousers and my good coat, and not in the jeans and sweater I'd picked out initially.

'Ms McRory? Please, come this way and we can talk in my office.' She sounded harassed and spoke with a slight accent; mid-European, perhaps?

'Good afternoon – Ms Schwartz,' I said, making a show of reading the name plate pinned to her white, linen shirt – Greta Schwartz. I held out my hand and she took it briefly in a nominal handshake, then turned and strode back the way she'd come, and I had no choice but to follow her. She took me along a light and airy corridor to a large, high-ceilinged room with a bay window looking out onto the gardens at the side of the building. She showed me to one of a pair of leather armchairs on either side of a low table.

I remained standing.

'Ms Schwartz, perhaps you'd like to explain to me how a frail, elderly lady could wander away from here and not be missed for so long?'

'I'm sorry about what happened, but I can't tell you much until our own investigation is complete,' she said, bristling like a cat backed into a corner. 'Please believe me, Ms McRory, I want to get to the bottom of this episode as much as you do. It's something that's never happened before, and I hope will never happen again.'

Her eyes had tiny lines radiating from them, and dark shadows beneath spoke of sleepless nights.

'It could have ended in tragedy,' I said.

'You don't need to tell me. I'm so relieved Margaret is okay.' She spread her hands in front of her. 'Please – I need to know what happened when you found her. Would you like a cup of tea?'

The façade slipped, and she looked exhausted and anxious.

I nodded and sat down. She went over to her desk, picked up a phone and ordered a pot of tea, then came and dropped into the second chair, smoothing her skirt across her knees in a nervous manner.

'I told the receptionist on the phone where she was,' I said. 'She must have walked at least a mile and a half, because I found her at the railway station. She was standing in the middle of the road when I saw her, soaked to the skin and exhausted, poor thing. God knows what would have happened if I hadn't seen her.' I closed my eyes for a moment, remembering Aunt M's white face, the vacant expression. 'She didn't know who I was,' I whispered.

It terrified me to think that the woman who had raised me from the age of fourteen as if she were my mother, when her sister fell far short in the role, and who had been independent and capable in everything she had ever done now needed full-time care. It was a hard thing to admit – that my loving aunt no longer recognised me. Was this the beginning of dementia?

29

The brightest soul I'd ever known might end up not knowing where she was or who she was? I wanted to weep for her.

Greta Schwartz watched me with a sympathetic expression. I'm sure she was used to seeing residents descend into frailty, but how she could do such a job I had no idea. It was tough enough dealing with people grieving over their sick animals.

'Is my aunt becoming more than forgetful? I mean, does she have Alzheimer's or something like that?'

She evaded the question and asked one of her own. 'When was the last time you saw your aunt, Ms McRory?'

Prickles of guilt made me uncomfortable under her gaze. I sagged into the chair.

'It's been too long,' I admitted. 'The last time I saw her, she was the life and soul of her own birthday party.'

'Ah, yes. That was not long after she came to live here. A party for her ninetieth birthday she organised herself.' Greta Schwartz eyed me, appraisingly. 'Margaret was still very competent then, if a little forgetful – but then, we can all be a little forgetful, can't we, when things get in the way?' I shifted in my chair as she continued. 'What you need to appreciate, is that in the past few months she gets confused more often, believes it's the 1940s and she's in her twenties. She's still lucid most of the time, but the spells when she is disorientated are becoming more frequent.'

I stared at her. It seemed too hard to believe that my vibrant, loving aunt had gone downhill so quickly. But nobody in their right mind would go for a walk in their dressing gown, especially in February.

'In that case, surely you must have been keeping more of an eye on her?' I said. 'I just can't understand how she wasn't missed. It must have taken her ages to walk as far as she did. Why someone else didn't stop and help her is beyond me, but that's a whole different matter. I need to know it won't happen again.'

The manager dropped her gaze, fiddling with a pen she'd picked up off the table. After a moment she raised her eyes and met mine.

'We had a bit of a crisis going on, yesterday,' she admitted. 'Two of our residents were taken seriously ill at almost the same time. The illnesses were unrelated – not food poisoning or anything like that,' she said. 'Margaret had just had her hair set after taking her morning bath and was in her dressing gown and slippers; it was not long after half past eleven. Her carer left her to go and help with one of the sick residents. When she returned, no more than a few minutes later, she couldn't find Margaret. The carer assumed – wrongly – that she had got herself dressed and gone out to the gardens. She loves it there,' she added.

'By the time we realised she wasn't anywhere on-site it was past lunchtime. I phoned the police to report her missing, as well as yourself. With other residents sick, we didn't have enough staff to go looking for her, even though we wanted to, of course. We were so relieved when you rang to say you'd taken her to hospital.' The manager shook her head and sighed. 'Up until a month ago, she did everything for herself and we helped only if she asked us. Now she needs care most of the time. We never know if she's going to be in the present or living in the past.'

'It's your job to keep her safe. Surely, she's not an unusual case?'

'The speed with which she's deteriorated is uncommon. But you're right. We should have kept her safe.'

'Does anyone come to visit her? Old friends? Why didn't you let me know how she was? I would have been here like a shot; she's been like a mother to me.' I rubbed a hand over my eyes, blinking hard.

'She was adamant she didn't want to bother you, Ms McRory. Said you had a busy life and an important career.' She paused. 'I suppose she thought it wasn't necessary. The only other name I have is that of her solicitor.'

That would be right. Aunt M had never bothered anyone with her problems. She just got on with things on her own – never married, always totally independent and self-sufficient. Why would she think she needed help from anybody else?

'Can I go and see her, please?'

'Of course. I'll show you the way.'

Greta Schwartz rose, smoothing the creases out of the front of her pencil skirt, again, and I followed her to Aunt M's room on the first floor. She knocked on the closed door of number 17 and entered the room.

Aunt M sat in a high-backed armchair beside a large window that faced out onto the gardens. She didn't seem to notice we were there, just kept staring out of the window, her head nodding slightly. I went over to her and crouched down, taking her hand, hoping she recognised me.

'Hello, Aunt M. You look better now you're back home. How are you feeling?'

Her eyes searched my face, and she put her hand up to my cheek.

'Claire, dear, how nice to see you. I'm fine, thank you, it's nice to be home. I couldn't sleep with all those old people making so much racket, last night,' she said. 'You look tired; that husband of yours is working you too hard. You should take a holiday.' She gazed out of the window again. 'I thought Agnes would have been home by now. Have you seen her?'

'No, I'm sorry, I haven't,' I said, inwardly cringing that I hadn't told her about my divorce from Andrew. Something else I'd allowed to slide. I put on a bright smile. 'I don't think I've met Agnes, have I?'

'You'd like her – she's great fun.' Aunt M's face brightened, her eyes shining. 'You should come to supper. She makes a wonderful rabbit stew.'

I could have cried. She was still so confused. Her eyes took on the same blank expression again, and she had gone away from me. Her head dropped and within a moment she was asleep. I left her dozing in her chair and returned to find Greta Schwartz in her office.

'May I visit my aunt again, tomorrow? I hope after a good

night's sleep she'll be a bit stronger and we can talk for longer. Tell me, Ms Schwartz, has she ever mentioned someone called Agnes?'

'Please, call me Greta. Yes, of course, you can come again whenever you like. We don't restrict visits,' she said. 'Agnes? No, not to my knowledge. Although some of the other staff might have heard that name. Who is she – an old friend, or a relative?'

'I don't know. But she kept talking about her yesterday and mentioned her again just now. That was why she was out on the street – looking for Agnes.'

She shrugged, a small frown creasing her brow. I stood up and she followed suit. Leaving the building, I looked back at the first-floor window behind which my aunt might still be snoozing. I wished I knew what was going through her mind.

In the meantime, I had a meeting with Andrew to get through.

The veterinary surgery was closed by the time I arrived. Saturday mornings were always busy, but we kept the afternoons for emergencies only, so most of the staff could have something of the weekend to themselves. Lights blazed out over the yard at the back, illuminating the recovery boxes and small-animal wards. On-call auxiliary staff were doing evening rounds – checking patients, cleaning out pens and looseboxes, and feeding the animals: the everyday tasks of a busy veterinary practice.

Andrew was already in the office, going through some papers he'd spread out on the desk. I poured two mugs of strong coffee from the machine in the corner, passed him one and sat down on the opposite side of the desk. Since our divorce we'd kept our relationship as professional as possible, only meeting at work. He said nothing for a moment or two, staring at the sheets scattered in front of him. I could see they were the notes from a sick dog he'd been seeing for the past few months. Lifting the coffee and blowing across the top of it, he looked up at me.

'How's your aunt?'

'Improving. She's been allowed out of hospital, thank goodness.'

Andrew nodded and took a sip of coffee. 'Sorry, if I seemed uncaring on the phone yesterday.' He cleared his throat and dropped his gaze back to the papers in front of him.

'What's going on, Andrew? What's so important you had to tell me on my weekend off?' Time off at a weekend was sacrosanct; we'd always made it a rule to leave work at the office when we were married. Since he'd been seeing Helen, our practice manager, I tried to spend as little time as I could in his company. Thank God she wasn't there. 'Has there been a complaint or something?'

He shook his head. 'It's nothing to do with the business.'

A flush bloomed on his face, and he rubbed the back of his neck, a gesture I knew well. He was embarrassed, or at least, uncomfortable.

'For heaven's sake, I've better things to do than play a guessing game with you.' I stood up.

'Claire, wait. Sit down. Please,' he said. His next words came out so quietly I almost didn't catch them. 'Helen's pregnant.'

I sank onto the chair, staring at him.

So.

No wonder he didn't want me finding out from the practice gossipmongers. Two small words, capable of blowing my world apart.

Andrew had never been the one at fault in our failure to get pregnant, and now the look he gave me was more than I could stand. We'd been a good team, but eventually were broken by my body's inability to produce a child. Pity, coupled with the spark of excitement in his eyes was too much to bear.

'Congratulations,' I managed, before the need to get out of there became too much and I fled.

In the car, ignition key in my shaking hand, I let grief take over, put my head on the steering wheel and wept.

Chapter 6

Agnes

Margaret infiltrated her way into Agnes's life in the same way spring slid its way into the tail end of winter. One moment it seemed as if the sun would never shine again, and the next it appeared, bringing light and warmth, where there had been darkness and cold. Agnes didn't realise how lonely she was until they met and became friends.

Over the next few weeks Agnes offered to help Margaret whenever something flummoxed her, and she gradually grew in confidence and was less anxious about messing the job up. Even Sergeant Atkins noticed the change and stopped haranguing her for every tiny step out of place.

On the day of the spring solstice, it was Clarice's birthday. She loved to dance and had persuaded them to go out together for the evening. After finishing their shift, the four girls climbed out of the cold, fuggy atmosphere of the Dungeon to the street. There was still a little daylight left and a residue of warmth that promised summer and lifted their spirits. Agnes stopped, tilted her head back and laughed, her mouth wide, grateful for the better weather warming her bones.

Clarice and Pat were in the middle of a heated discussion about where to go that night.

'What do you think we should do?' Pat said, turning to Margaret, who was gazing at Agnes.

Margaret spun round. 'Depends what you want, I suppose,' she said. 'Dancing to a band, or smooching to some jazz in a club? It's your birthday, Clarice, so you choose.'

'Where will the Yank flyboys be? That's the important thing,' Pat said with a giggle.

'Pat!' Clarice pretended to be shocked, but they looked at each other and burst out laughing. They began sashaying down the street, arm in arm, singing 'Yankee Doodle'.

Agnes laughed at them and she and Margaret wandered on behind.

'Are you going out with them tonight?' she said.

Margaret nodded. 'Of course. Any excuse for a night out,' she said. 'I've got to work the weekend, but that's not going to stop me enjoying myself.' She grabbed Agnes's hand and dragged her into a run. 'Say you'll come too. We need to have some fun.'

Agnes's immediate reaction was to refuse, but Margaret's enthusiasm was infectious and she nodded. 'I'd love to,' she said, laughing again as they raced along the broken pavement, jumping over rubble from a bombed-out house.

'The Palais, then. It's the best around here.'

Agnes agreed, though she had no idea what or where the Palais was. They caught up with the others and Clarice liked Margaret's suggestion. They would meet outside the doors at eight o'clock.

Later, Agnes dithered, her stomach in knots at the prospect of the evening ahead. It was the first time she had been invited out as part of the group; the first time it seemed important to fit in, wear the right clothes, drink the right drink, say the right things. She had no idea what to expect. The more she thought about it the more she felt out of her depth and terrified. Maybe she should just stay at home, invent a sore throat or a tummy bug when Maggie called for her.

In the end she forced herself into getting ready and wore the only decent frock she possessed: black silk with a white collar and three-quarter-length sleeves, the full skirt finishing just below her knees.

Clarice and Pat were already there when she and Margaret arrived, slightly out of breath due to her being in such a panic and Margaret having to help her with her hair. Agnes's feet hurt from the shoes she had chosen, which were too tight and had a heel. Good for dancing, but totally unsuitable for running along the street from the station. They left their coats with the cloakroom attendant, then made for the huge ballroom downstairs, Agnes in awe of the sky-blue frock that matched Margaret's eyes and seemed moulded to her slim frame.

The noise and heat hit Agnes with a physical force. The band on the raised dais was playing something loud and fast, the dancers spinning around the floor. She stood and stared at the sight in wonder. So many people, the music battering her eardrums, the lead singer's face sweat-covered, his hair slicked back. He had stripped down to his shirt, with sleeves rolled up above his elbows, his mouth so close to the microphone he almost kissed it, using the stand as an extension of his body, twisting and swaying in time to the rhythm of the music as he sang. Pat and Clarice immediately flung themselves into the fray. Waving to someone on the dance floor, they joined a group of other girls and boys, some of them in uniform, both British and American.

Agnes and Margaret climbed the worn, carpeted stairs to the gallery where they could watch the dancers below, managing to grab a table as another couple left. Agnes marvelled at how Margaret caught the eye of a passing waiter without turning a hair, and ordered gin for the four of them. Even the thought of doing such a thing made her sweat.

They sat watching the writhing mass of humanity below them, saying nothing. This place was so outside of her experience that Agnes felt awkward, as tongue-tied as a gauche teenager and glad the noise prevented conversation. She had only been for drinks at the local with the rest of the girls after work, before, and still found it hard to relax in their company. She sipped the foul-tasting liquor, the gin burning her throat and making her cough.

Her mood dipped. Her first instinct had been right: it was a mistake to come. This was no place for her. She noticed two GIs eyeing them up from where they stood, holding up the bar, and prayed they wouldn't approach them. Margaret sat opposite her, gazing down at the dance floor, her foot tapping to the music, unaware of the Americans' increasing interest. Agnes's stomach churned from the strong drink and she pushed her chair back, feeling the need for some air.

The song ended, bringing relief to her ears, and one of the GIs chose that moment to weave a path through the tables towards them, bumping the chair of a soldier sitting with a red-headed girl. Some of the soldier's drink spilled as he took a pull and he yelled abuse, rising with a damp patch on the front of his uniform.

'Fuckin' Yank,' he cursed, but the drunk American was oblivious and continued his meander towards the girls' table.

'Oh Lord, let's get out of here,' Agnes said, grabbing her bag.

Margaret looked confused. 'Why? Don't you like this music?' she said. 'I thought you wanted to dance tonight.'

Before Agnes could say anything, it was too late; the American stopped at their table, swaying slightly as if he were a sapling caught by the breeze. A sheen of sweat plastered his hair to his forehead.

Margaret gaped, the beginnings of a blush colouring her cheeks.

'Ladies, may I buy you both a drink?' the American slurred, his eyes seeming to have difficulty in focusing on them.

'That's terribly kind of you, sir, but we have our own drinks, thank you,' Margaret said, in her best cut-glass accent. Agnes kept her eyes averted, hoping she would go unnoticed.

The GI pressed his case. 'Well, wouldn't ya like another one? Ya seem like nice gals, and me 'n' my pal, Chuck, over there, we jus' want some company.' He pointed in a vague way towards the bar.

'Well, the gentlemen we came with this evening might not take kindly to you stealing us away, so I suggest you go and find some other nice gals. There are plenty to go round, don't you think?'

Agnes sat up and stared at her friend. What did she mean, *gentlemen friends*? Margaret glanced across, caught her eye, and dropped a slow wink.

'Aw, c'mon gals. I can't see any gen'lemen here, and I've heard about you Londoners. Y'all love a good time, eh?' He slurred the words and winked himself, or tried to, but the drink was having a disastrous effect and his face paled as he stood in front of them. ''Scuse me, a moment,' he said, turning sharply with a hand up to his mouth, and lurching towards the lavatories, knocking chairs and tables as he tried to reach them before losing his stomach.

Agnes and Margaret looked at each other and burst out laughing.

'Men. They're all the same. Let's go and have that dance, shall we?' Margaret said, as the band started up again, and Agnes nodded, relieved to have a chance to get away from the unwanted attention.

After half an hour of being jostled by sweating bodies and held too tightly by semi-drunk servicemen, she had had enough. Margaret seemed to spend most of the time in a clinch with a young man in RAF uniform, their arms around each other, talking as if they had known each other for years.

Agnes jostled her elbow to catch her attention and pointed to the door. 'I'm going home,' she mouthed.

Margaret frowned and excused herself, planting a quick peck on the young pilot's cheek. She followed Agnes to the quiet of the foyer.

'What's the matter? Are you all right, Agnes?'

'Yes, I've just got a bit of a headache. Too much gin and loud music, I suppose.' She pulled a face. 'I'm not used to it.'

'I'll come with you, then.'

'No, don't spoil your evening. You and that chap seemed to be getting on like a house on fire.' She tried to smile. 'I'll be fine.' She said the words, knowing they were a lie.

Margaret put a cool hand on her cheek. 'Who, Tom? He's an old friend I haven't seen for months,' she said. 'You do look flushed. I don't like the idea of you going home alone.'

'Maggie, don't fuss. I'm perfectly capable of getting back on my own. Go and enjoy yourself.'

'If you're sure you're okay.'

'I'm sure. I'll see you at work.'

'Goodnight, then.'

Margaret leant in and gave her a feather-light peck on the cheek then turned and re-entered the ballroom without looking back. Agnes stood for a moment, the palm of her hand against her cheek, as if it would protect the kiss and keep it safe.

Chapter 7

Agnes

Agnes woke to a knock on her door, her head heavy and a ringing in her ears from the music the night before. It took her a moment to comprehend what it was and where the sound came from. Nobody had ever come to her door so early.

Her landlady stood with a fist raised as if she was about to knock again, when Agnes finally opened the door. She stepped back, a hand to her mouth, damming the squeak of fright erupting from her throat, the other pulling her gaping dressing gown together.

'This came for you. Thought it must be important.'

The woman thrust a brown envelope into her hands, turned without a word and click-clacked down the bare wooden stairs.

Agnes stared at the telegram, heart up in her throat somewhere. The only people who knew where she lived were Margaret, and Edward, her brother.

With shaking hands, she ripped open the envelope and read the short message.

MAMAN EST MORTE STOP TU DOIS RENTRER À LA MAISON STOP EDWARD

Disbelief made her read the telegram again, and then she dropped it as if the paper was on fire. There must be a mistake. Or Teddy was playing some kind of sick joke in an effort to get her to go back home. Her mother couldn't be dead – how stupid did he think she was? She picked up the flimsy sheet again and read it for a third time, terror now mounting until it ripped a howl from the depths of her gut.

Her legs buckled under her, and she collapsed, grief and horror fighting inside her. She had no idea how long she lay on the floor, sobs wrenching their way out of her until her ribs ached. At one point she was aware of a voice asking if she was all right, and telling them to go away.

Eventually, she dragged herself up and lay on her bed, exhausted, colder and lonelier than she had ever been in her life. How could her mother be dead? It was unthinkable, a mistake. How dare she die when she, Agnes, still needed her?

A kernel of guilt wormed its way into her thoughts. It was weeks since she had written, months since she had been home. Had Maman been sick? Was there an accident? A stray bomb hitting the house? Her mind became a vortex of images, accusations, and memories, racing so fast she thought she would go mad. She screwed her eyes shut and tried to block everything out, but still they came, bringing more tears as she recalled how much her mother had hated coming to England and missed her homeland. She prayed she hadn't died alone and clung on to that hope as being the one thing that made the thought of her mother's death remotely bearable.

At last, she rose, her mind scoured as if a sandstorm had blown through it.

She must go, then. In truth, the last thing she wanted to do was see her father, but Teddy and Pierre would need her, and she needed them. Now, as never before.

She washed the salty streaks from her face, red and swollen eyes staring back at her in the mirror as she dragged a comb through her hair. After dressing quickly and throwing a few things into a small bag, she locked the door behind her, ran down the stairs and out onto the street. At the corner she entered the telephone box and scrabbled for some coins, her fingers so stiff and clumsy she dropped her purse and the change bounced onto the filthy floor, rolling around her feet.

Fuck. Fuck. Fuck.

She bit back a sob and took a shaky breath. She mustn't fall apart again, had to control herself.

Retrieving the coins, she fumbled a couple into the slot and rang the number. One of the corporals answered and Agnes left a message, only saying she had a family emergency and would be away for a few days. She would probably get the sack for not following regulations, but she didn't give a damn. She had no time to do anything else.

Replacing the handset on its cradle, she strode down the street to the nearest Underground station. Dread dogged her steps, but she pushed the darkness away. Now, she just had to get to the house and face the reality of never seeing her mother again. She hadn't been there since a row with her father, six months previously.

Arriving at the small cottage in the countryside outside London, which he had rented when they came to England, she saw her father's large black car parked on the road outside the gate and shivered. It was a gloomy place with towering trees around the perimeter and a tiny garden. Nothing like the rambling, sunny farmhouse she remembered in France.

As dusk lengthened the shadows of the great pines and cast darkness over the run-down house, Agnes wanted nothing more than to run away as if nothing had happened; pretend she wasn't needed and could go on with the life she had built for herself without her family. It had been Maman who was the lynchpin that bound them. Without her, there was nothing to hold them together.

She shook the thoughts from her head and opened the wicket gate, shoving it wide across the gravel path, overgrown with moss. The hinges creaked and a head appeared through the door of the open porch straight ahead. Edward ran down the path, stopped in front of her and for a moment Agnes thought he was about to hug her. She steeled herself for the unfamiliar gesture, but something in her face or the way she held herself stopped him, and he merely put a hand on her shoulder and greeted her with a kiss on either cheek.

'Hello, Agnes. You came.'

'Of course I came.'

His face was in shadow, but she caught the glitter of his eyes. She should be able to comfort him, now as never before, yet still there was that barrier between them, created by Papa, and she stepped back.

He took her bag and led her into the cottage. It had always been cold, but now, at the end of winter, it was glacial, though there was a fire in the sitting room. Agnes kept her coat on and stared at her father, who sat in the chair closest to the struggling flames, poking them.

What should she say? She suspected that once she opened her mouth, she would be unable to control what came out of it and she would hurt her brothers even more than they hurt already. The sight of Christopher Kerr sitting in her mother's place, looking for all the world as if he deserved to be there caused a rage so hot, Agnes had to turn away.

In the end, she asked the one thing she needed to know.

'What happened? How did Maman die?'

Uttering the words almost undid the small composure she had carefully built.

Edward choked on a sob and left the room without saying anything. Pierre, the youngest of the three of them, sat like a stone in the window seat looking out at the growing darkness. Her father cleared his throat and rose from the chair. His face was blank, his eyes hooded, the only light from the few flames of the fire doing nothing to illuminate them. Agnes waited, saying nothing more.

At last, he spoke. 'She killed herself.'

Agnes feared her heart had stopped. The shock of his words washed over her in waves of horror.

Suicide? No, it was not possible – her mother would never go against her religion like that. Of all the ways she might have died, suicide had never crossed Agnes's mind. Jeanne Kerr was a staunch Catholic; she would not do such a thing.

She shook her head.

'No, no, no, she couldn't have, she would never do that.' She glared at her father. 'Who found her? They must have been mistaken. It was an accident. Maman would never kill herself; it went against everything she believed in.'

'I'm sorry, Agnes, I wish it wasn't true, but there is no mistake. A neighbour found her. She'd hanged herself.'

Christopher came over to her and attempted to put his arms around her but she stepped aside, batting his hands away, fury coursing through her blood.

'Don't! Don't you dare try and touch me.' She spun round, pointing an accusing finger at his chest. 'You made her life a living hell. How dare you come into this house and act as if none of this is your fault.' Her voice rose, and now the brakes were off she couldn't stop the words if she wanted to. 'You killed her, as surely as if you'd stuck a knife in her ribs. I hate you and that bitch you've shacked up with. I bet she's happy, now you're free and can make a respectable woman of her.'

'Don't bring Katherine into this. None of it is her fault.'

Her father's reply was sharp and angry. There was no regret, no sorrow, no grief at what he had driven his wife to. If Agnes had had a gun on her at that moment, she would have put a bullet in him without thinking twice.

45

She picked up her bag from a chair by the door, where Edward had left it.

'You know the worst thing?' she said. 'You don't even care. You don't care that we – Teddy, Pierre and I – no longer have a mother. You don't care that she was so miserable she had no other recourse but to end her life.' She stepped right up to her father and glared at him. 'You, Christopher Kerr, are the most arrogant, selfish bastard I have ever met, and I never want to see you again. I'm ashamed to be your daughter.'

He blanched at her words and she was glad she had wounded him. It was little enough, and too late, but it was all she had. Turning to leave, a voice stopped her.

'What about us? Are you ashamed of us too?' Pierre stepped out of the shadows and caught her hand. 'Don't go, yet, Agnes, please. Come with me.'

They left Christopher standing where he was, and Pierre led her through the narrow hall to the kitchen at the back of the house, where the ancient range gave off a little more heat. The only light came from an oil lamp on the table at which Edward sat, his head in his hands.

He looked up as Pierre pushed Agnes into a chair, and then dropped down next to her. Agnes looked at the grief and sorrow on the faces of her brothers, and reached out a hand to each one. They sat in silence for a few moments, holding on to one another, closer than they had ever been during all the years of their childhood.

'I'm sorry you had to hear that, Pierre,' Agnes said, after a while. 'I'm not sorry I said it, though. I hate him.'

Pierre, who, now she looked at him, seemed to have grown by half a foot since the last time they met, put his free hand over hers.

'He has a lot to answer for, and someone had to say it,' he said. 'But, please don't run away. Stay tonight, at least.'

Tears pricked against the backs of Agnes's eyes. In truth she had nowhere else to go. There wouldn't be another train to London until the morning and she couldn't face walking the two miles back to the nearest village and trying to find somewhere to stay. Exhaustion hit her like a fog enveloping her mind, but still she baulked at the idea.

'I can't stay in the same house as him.'

Pierre gripped her hand. 'You don't need to. He's not staying tonight. Says he will come back for the funeral.'

'He's a fucking heartless coward.' Edward's words fell like shards of glass. 'He can't even face us.'

'Oh, Teddy.'

Agnes pulled both her brothers close and they sat, huddled together, arms around shoulders, heads close, taking comfort from each other.

A few moments later, she heard the front door slam.

The funeral, such as it was, was the most dreadful day of Agnes's life. She couldn't bear to think of it as she took a slow train back to London afterwards. All she wanted to do was forget. Which was impossible.

The next day, Agnes returned to work. She was exhausted, did her job like an automaton, spoke to no one. Sitting next to her, Margaret respected her silence, but Agnes felt her eyes on her and turned away, not wanting her pity, or for her to see her tears. At the end of the shift, Margaret followed her up the stairs and out onto the street. Agnes felt dazed, the weak spring sunlight almost dazzling after the dimness inside. Her head spun and she tripped up the final step, almost falling. Margaret caught her arm and picked up the handbag she had dropped, dusted it off and gave it back with a tiny smile.

'Thank you,' Agnes croaked.

'Is there anything I can do?' Margaret asked. Agnes shook her head. 'Would you like to go and have a cup of tea at Lyons? If you want to talk, I'm a good listener. It might help.'

She didn't want sympathy.

'Nothing can help,' she said, a tear escaping before she could stop it. 'It's my fault. If I'd stayed at home, she'd still be alive.'

She walked on slowly, the guilt almost too heavy to bear. Margaret stood where she was. Agnes continued, and was surprised when Margaret caught up and walked beside her, not saying anything, but a comfort all the same.

It was only a fifteen-minute walk from the Dungeon to her digs in the middle of the dingy street. Agnes stopped in front of it.

'God, I hate this place,' she said. 'Thank you for walking with me – you're very kind. It's put you out of your way for the station.'

Her voice sounded rusty in her ears, and she cleared her throat. It seemed an age since Clarice's birthday.

'Will you be all right?' Margaret's words were softly spoken.

'I don't know.' Agnes paused and cleared her throat again, looking at her shoes. 'My mother's dead – how do I get over such a thing?'

'Oh, Agnes, I'm so sorry. That's tragic. Was she sick?' Margaret sounded shocked, then stopped. 'Sorry, it's none of my business.'

'Not physically. She is – was – fragile, though.' A sob escaped before Agnes could prevent it. 'My father's fault.' She spat the last words with venom. 'He treated her appallingly. I think she got tired of pretending her life was fine.'

Choking on the words, Agnes put her hands over her face. Margaret pulled her into her arms and held her while she cried, the two of them standing in the busy street with strangers pushing past, tutting at the obstacle in their path. She was past caring – her mother's death was just another wartime tragedy after all, and they could think what they liked.

Chapter 8

Claire

The prospect of continuing to work alongside Helen didn't bear thinking about. Speaking to Andrew again was out of the question, so I emailed and told him I wanted some time off and would be away for a fortnight. Let Helen sort out the mess of my client list for the next couple of weeks.

Was I being a bitter ex-wife? Possibly, though I hoped it didn't appear that way – and our divorce had been a mutual decision. Did I feel guilty? A little, mostly for letting down my clients. What would I do with two weeks of kicking my heels? I had no inclination to go on holiday, but at least I could spend more time with Aunt M. Guilt still niggled at my neglect of her, when she had spent so much time in the past watching out for me.

I had let my own troubles overwhelm me to the point where there was no space left for anyone else.

The weather had returned to the damp, raw greyness that seemed to be its default setting over the past few weeks. It suited my mood as I returned to Stanbury Hall, but I put on a smile and a forced cheeriness as I entered Aunt M's sitting room. She was waiting in the same chair as yesterday, gazing out onto the gardens.

'Hello, Claire dear. The blackbirds are beginning their squabbles over territory; it means spring is on its way,' she said, putting her cheek up to mine for a kiss. 'I do like this room in the afternoon. The light is so much better on this side, don't you think?'

'It doesn't feel very spring-like today, Aunt M, but you have a lovely view of the gardens.' I pulled another chair over to the window and sat beside her. 'You sound much brighter. I was worried about you yesterday.'

'Oh, you don't need to worry about me, dear. I'm a tough old bird, don't you know,' she said, with a wide smile. Someone had done her hair and she was wearing lipstick. She took my hand and I noticed pale pink polish perfectly applied to her manicured nails. Aunt M was back. I lifted her hand and kissed the back of it.

'I've a long-overdue apology to make. I've been terribly neglectful over the past year or two – have hardly come to see you at all. It's unforgivable, and I'm so sorry. I want to make it up to you.' I had to pause for a moment, my throat tight. 'I would understand if you didn't want anything to do with me, after the way I've treated you.'

'What are you talking about, you silly girl?' Her reply came as a sharp rebuke. 'What's there to forgive you for? You have your own life to live – why should you feel you need to come and visit an old biddy like me?' She turned and took my chin in her hand and lifted it, so I was facing her. I felt like the child who'd have done anything for her adored aunt. 'We two will always mean the world to each other, won't we? And if we don't meet for a month, a year, a decade, what does it matter? You were there when I needed you.'

I put my arms around her, and we hugged. If I hadn't seen how confused she'd been, I would have believed she was just the same as always. She would be ninety-one in a few months and I vowed to help make the rest of her time as easy and comfortable as possible, just as she had done for me when I was fourteen and my newly divorced mother disappeared to the other side of the world on a whim, leaving me with nowhere to call home. It had been Aunt M who took me in, made me feel that her home was my home. She had been my rock for as long as I could remember. And I knew I had let her down over the past few years, even if she was too kind to say so.

A vague idea I'd had the previous evening took root.

'I happened to be in the right place at the right time, on Friday. Thank goodness I could help.' I searched her face, trying to gauge her memory of that day. 'When I found you, you were looking for someone. You kept asking me if I'd seen Agnes – do you remember? I didn't know who you meant. Is she one of your friends here at Stanbury Hall?'

Aunt M frowned, her eyes losing focus. She turned and gazed out of the window again.

'Agnes Kerr was someone I knew during the war,' she said. 'I sometimes get confused, you know, forget where I am and what day it is. Old age catching up with me, I suppose.'

'Why were you looking for her?'

I could have kicked myself as tears filled her eyes. They brimmed onto the sagging lower lids and ran down her cheeks, but she didn't appear to notice, lost in her memories. Then she came back to the present and brusquely wiped her face with her hand, took a deep breath and blew her nose on a scrap of lace-edged fine lawn.

'I'm sorry, forget I said anything,' I said.

'It's not your fault, Claire – I'm just a silly old woman.' Drawing another ragged breath, she glanced across at the other side of the room. 'There's a photo in the top drawer of the sideboard, dear. Would you bring it over for me, please?'

I found the print inside a cardboard cover and looked at a photograph I'd not seen before, of two young women wearing what I presumed were WAAF uniforms, sitting on a bench, their arms around each other's shoulders. One was my aunt, blonde and beautiful, laughing at the other girl, who was much shorter, and dark against Aunt M's fairness. Thinking how happy they looked, I felt a pang of something like envy – here was a friendship I'd never managed to find with anyone, not even Andrew. Giving it to Aunt M, I watched as she stroked the faces. Another tear escaped from the corner of one eye.

'This is Agnes and me during the war,' she said, shakily. 'We were very young, and I've never felt as alive as I did at that time. It was horrific and terrifying and wonderful, all mixed up together.'

'Did you meet in the WAAFs?'

She nodded, still gazing at the photo, her expression far away again. She closed her eyes, her face drawn, and looking every one of her ninety years.

'We shared a flat,' she whispered.

It was difficult to imagine her so young, living through such terrifying times. There must have been people she'd known who didn't make it to the end of the war. Perhaps this friend was one of them.

'What happened, Aunt M?'

'We . . . lost touch. It was impossible to keep track of people. You have to understand, London was a chaotic place back then.'

Sad resignation crossed her face. I gently squeezed her hand.

'But surely someone must have known what happened to her?'

'I don't know,' she admitted. 'I wish we'd stayed in touch, though. There are only so many people in one's life who truly matter.' Now she smiled at me again. 'Thank goodness I have you. You've always meant the world to me, you know that, don't you?'

My heart twisted. I put my arm around her thin shoulders and gave her a gentle hug. Whoever Agnes was, she and Aunt M must have been close. Seeing her sadness, I made my mind up. I would help if I could.

'What if I tried to find out what happened to her, for you?'

'Oh, I couldn't possibly expect you to do that, dear. It would be impossible after so long,' she said quickly. 'You're busy with your work, and I expect Andrew will complain if you start a wild-goose chase on my behalf. But thank you. Agnes has been gone for a very long time, and she's not coming back now.'

A prickle of guilt ran up my back. I must tell her about the divorce, but it would have to wait a little longer.

'I've got a couple of weeks of annual leave to take, which starts tomorrow,' I said. 'So, I'm not busy with work. To be honest, I need something to take my mind off what's happening there, but I won't bore you with that just now. Andrew will be fine with it. You and I have a lot of catching up to do, and there's nothing I would like more than to spend my holiday helping you – if you'll let me.'

She eyed me just as sharply as she had years ago, when I thought dying my hair bright red and dressing like Ziggy Stardust was a good idea, knowing it would annoy my parents because image was everything to them.

'I have no idea how you'll discover what happened to Agnes. She's probably dead by now. But if it'll make you happy, and we get to spend some time together, then why not?' She looked down at the backs of her liver-spotted hands, and her voice dropped to a whisper. 'I would like to know what became of her. It would put my mind at rest.'

Chapter 9

Agnes

A month after the funeral, during which Agnes worked herself to exhaustion, trying to find some way of getting over the loss of her mother, she, Margaret, Clarice and Pat climbed out of the Dungeon into a sunny late afternoon. They had been in the gloom for eight hours and Agnes blinked as her eyes grew accustomed to the brightness. Clarice and Pat hurried off in the opposite direction to meet their boyfriends. Agnes and Margaret wandered along the street towards the station in silence, as had become the norm. At the corner opposite the Lyons tea shop, Agnes halted.

'Do you want to get a cup of tea and a bun, if they have any?' She wasn't quite sure what made her suggest it, only knew she needed someone to talk to. Margaret seemed taken aback by her words, and stared at her without answering for a minute or so. Suddenly, it felt like an awful idea. What was she thinking, wanting to unload her misery onto someone as nice as her only friend? She shuffled her feet, wondering if she could take the words back. 'Only if you have time – and want to, of course,' she said, her face on fire.

'Yes. Yes, I'd love a cuppa.' Margaret stumbled over the words.

They found a table by the window and sat, waiting to be served. Once they were inside, Agnes worried at a sore on the corner of her bottom lip, not knowing where to start.

'I'm glad you suggested this,' Margaret said. 'I've missed coming here with you.'

Agnes tried to smile. 'You've been so kind since Maman died.' She sighed. 'I don't know what I would have done if you hadn't been sitting beside me every day, Maggie.'

Margaret blushed, her blue eyes glinting. 'What are friends for?' she said, lightly.

Agnes took her hand. 'You've been more than a friend – you've kept me sane.'

Margaret seemed lost for words, just smiled her sweet smile, her head on one side.

Abruptly, Agnes let go of her hand. 'Can I tell you what happened to my mother?' It came out as a plea. 'I need to tell someone and you're the best person I know – the only person I know, who I want to talk to about it.'

At that moment, the Nippy sauntered over, pad in hand, and Margaret gave their order.

'Two cups of tea and two buns, please.'

'Only one bun left,' she said, pencil hovering over her pad, bored gaze looking out of the window.

Agnes and Margaret glanced at each other.

'That'll be fine. Can you bring two plates though?'

The waitress nodded and scribbled something, walking away as she wrote.

Agnes fiddled with the edge of the tablecloth, pleating and unpleating it repeatedly while they waited. After a moment, Margaret put a hand across the table, staying the relentless movement.

'You don't have to tell me anything, you know, but I'm a good listener if you want to talk.'

'I need to tell someone. Rage is eating me up. It's gnawing at me until I can't think of anything else,' Agnes said. 'I can't even grieve for my poor mother because of it.' She stared out of the window, not seeing the traffic passing along the busy road. 'If I saw my father walking down that street, I would push him under a bus. I dream of killing him – isn't that a terrible admission?'

She glanced across the table and saw shock flit across Margaret's face.

'What did he do?'

Agnes fought to control her emotions, unable to speak. The tea arrived, breaking the tension. She poured it into the two cups, added milk, and cut the bun in half, passing Margaret her share. She took a sip, licked her dry lips, chewing at the sore corner again. It was hard to know where to start, but once she began, she poured out all the misery that had been bottled up for weeks.

'Before we came to England, my father worked as a diplomat in Paris. Maman, me, and my brothers, Teddy and Pierre, lived in a small village in the countryside where she grew up. Papa would come home every few weeks for the weekend.' She took another sip of tea. 'I was sent to school in Paris when I was eleven and Papa sometimes came and took me out for an afternoon. Once, an Englishwoman came too. He said she was a work colleague, but I could tell there was more to it than that.' Her tea grew cold and she forgot about the bun as she recalled her life in France before the war. 'And then everything changed. The Germans invaded and Papa dragged us away from all we knew and planted us in the depths of the English countryside, while he went back to work in London. I was enrolled in a girls' boarding school in Somerset – God it was the worst two years of my life.'

She stopped for a moment, remembering how much she detested the school, unable to meet Margaret's eye.

'Your mother must have found it very difficult too.'

She nodded, and pulled the bun into pieces on her plate.

'Maman hated it as much as my brothers and I did. She was a devout Catholic but there was no church near enough to join, so she couldn't go to Mass and confession. It ate away at her, I think. Her religion was everything to her.' She sighed, looking at the mess on her plate but miles away, remembering how much her mother changed over that time. 'The house was cold, damp and isolated, she knew nobody, and we'd been packed off to school, so she was on her own most of the time. Papa was hardly ever there. I even heard her beg him to come home, when he telephoned once to say he was too busy to come and see us.' Bitterness lent her voice a steely edge. 'Now I know it was because *she* was in London too – his lover, the woman I met in Paris.' She stabbed the eviscerated bun viciously with her knife. 'He told Maman he wouldn't be coming back – ever – and she had to get on with things by herself, as he wanted a divorce. He conveniently forgot that it's against the law for Catholics.'

She stared at Margaret, fighting tears. 'She didn't tell us, her children, what was happening. Two days later she was found hanging from a tree in the garden by a passing farmer.' Placing the knife carefully beside her plate with a shaking hand, she finished her story. 'They wouldn't even give her a Christian funeral or burial. I will never, ever forgive him for what he did to her.' Angrily, she swiped a hand across her face. 'I hope he burns in hell.'

Agnes glanced up at her friend. Margaret looked dazed, as if she had weathered a storm. She said nothing, but sympathy and pity were in her eyes, and Agnes was relieved she didn't try to judge her for her harsh words.

They sat for a few minutes in silence, for which Agnes was grateful. Telling Margaret had been cathartic and made her feel a tiny bit lighter inside.

'Would you like to come and stay with me for a while?' Margaret's words seemed to come out of nowhere. Agnes's head snapped up, and she regarded her with a frown. 'I have a spare room,' she hastily added, her cheeks turning pink.

Agnes considered the offer. It was tempting, yet how could she accept? It was bound to end in disaster; her emotions were all over the place, and she thought too much of Maggie to risk ruining their friendship.

'You're so kind, but I couldn't impose myself on you – for one thing, I'm not sleeping at all and spend most of the night wandering about. It would be awfully disturbing for anyone trying to sleep in the next room.' She managed a small smile. 'But thank you, I'm very grateful.'

'Oh, you don't need to worry about me being disturbed,' came back the reply. 'With all the different shifts we have to work I find I can sleep through anything. Even bombs don't wake me up, nowadays.' Margaret pressed her point. 'Do you really want to go back to that dreary place? You said you wanted to move out as soon as you found somewhere better. We could try it for a few days and see how we get on – what do you think? If it suits us both, then perhaps we could be flatmates?'

It was easy to give in.

Agnes did hate her digs, she did want to move, they did get on well together. So much of it made sense, and yet, a small part of her recognised the danger of becoming too close to Margaret. Her kindness, the way she smiled, her joy in simple things all drew Agnes to her. She told herself she must never again become too fond of anyone – the pain of losing them was unbearable. They would be friends, but she would keep a distance between them.

She managed a small smile.

'All right then,' she said. 'Yes please, I can't wait to get out of that place. If you let me stay for a few nights I would be most grateful.'

'Let's go then.'

The first couple of nights at Margaret's flat Agnes found strange and unsettling. She was acutely aware of the girl on the other side of the wall and imagined she could hear her breathing. They tiptoed around each other, being overly polite about who should use the bathroom first and which chair to sit in. She knew she was being monosyllabic and withdrawn, but was unwilling to be too familiar, and still wasn't sleeping. On the second night, she gave up trying, and sat in the dark living room holding the only photograph of her mother she possessed, overcome with grief. She woke with a stiff neck to find Margaret creeping around, trying not to disturb her.

A few days later, she decided she had used up enough of her friend's goodwill and generosity and packed away the few things she had brought with her. Margaret came in just as she was closing the small suitcase.

'Don't you want to stay?'

The disappointment in her voice took Agnes by surprise. She paused for a moment.

'I can't take advantage of your kindness and generosity any longer,' she said. 'You've helped me too much, already. It's time I went back and got on with things.'

Margaret looked baffled. 'When I asked you to stay, we agreed it would be a trial, to see how we got on together, didn't we?'

She shrugged, not looking up.

'And we've rubbed along well, haven't we? You can't deny it. We could make it official, if you prefer. Share all the bills – put your name on the rental lease. I think my landlord would be happy to do that.'

Agnes lifted the case off the bed.

'Maggie, do you think it's a good idea for us to work side by side every day, and live in the same flat?' She walked through to the living room with Margaret following her. 'We're very different – our views on some things are poles apart. We've learnt that already about each other. I don't want to spoil our friendship by arguing over whose turn it is to put the rubbish out.'

'But our differences are what makes our friendship work, don't you think? We're not children – can't we agree to disagree on some things?' She sounded desperate. 'Stay for another week, and see how you feel. Please. You can't honestly tell me you want to go back to that awful bedsit?'

'Of course I don't want to go back to that place, but what else can I do?'

'Stay here, you stubborn thing.' Margaret grabbed her arms and shook her, gently. 'You hate it there, I'm lonely here – I admit it. It doesn't have to be forever, but surely it makes sense for now?'

Agnes stood in front of her, looking at the floor, trying to think of something to say. The silence stretched, and Margaret glared at her, waiting for her to speak. At last, she nodded and put the case down.

'Don't blame me when I drive you mad with my terrible habits.'

Margaret laughed, and hugged her. 'We should celebrate. Tea?'

'God, you English and your tea. Don't you have champagne in this establishment?'

'Sorry, mademoiselle, the butler stole it all when he left last week.'

They looked at each other and started giggling. Agnes felt a little giddy. No more lonely nights, sitting by herself, feeling sick with fear when the bombing started. Having Maggie as her flatmate filled a gaping hole that she hadn't acknowledged before. She just prayed they both wouldn't regret it, one day.

Chapter 10

Agnes

Once Agnes accepted the fact that she and Margaret could be both work colleagues and flatmates without jeopardising their growing friendship, she allowed herself to mourn. She had to accept she would never see her mother again and get on with her life. The guilt she carried that she should have stayed and tried to help her didn't diminish. Yet, she couldn't change what happened, so boxed it up and buried it deep inside.

The rage she harboured against her father also didn't diminish, though she said nothing to Margaret about the flames of hate she fanned during sleepless nights when she paced the floor of her room.

Spring moved into summer, and working in the Dungeon each day continued to give Agnes the mental stimulation she needed to block out the sorrow and hurt. She became so absorbed in her work Maggie said it could have rained pigs and she would have carried on decoding and sending messages. Even through her self-absorption she recognised that her friend was less happy. Margaret craved sunlight and fresh air, and had grown to hate being cooped up in the dim atmosphere underground each day.

On their way home on a Friday evening, with the sun still warm and the fumes of London choking, they discussed plans for the weekend – the first one they'd both had off for weeks. Agnes wanted nothing more than to bury her head in a book and sleep, but Margaret had other ideas.

'It's my sister's birthday tomorrow. Do you want to come home with me? My parents are having a family dinner for her – she's sixteen,' she said. 'I haven't been home for months, and my mother's letters are full of pleas for me to go.'

The prospect of a weekend with Margaret's family was the last thing Agnes wanted, but how could she say so without upsetting her friend, who continued chattering, unaware of the turmoil she had created?

'Jessica is an annoying brat. We have absolutely nothing in common, and she behaves like a princess. You would think she would grow out of it, but I swear she's getting worse.' She huffed a sigh and eyed Agnes hopefully, making her squirm. The sisters' relationship sounded awful, but how could she say no? Margaret pressed her case, perhaps sensing Agnes's reluctance. 'I can't get out of it, but at least it's a break from London, and home cooking and fresh air will be a nice change.' She put her hands up in mock prayer. 'Please say you'll come. It's going to be so boring otherwise.'

Agnes frowned, stung by her flippant words. 'You're lucky to have a family who obviously love and miss you, Maggie.'

'Oh Lord, I'm so sorry. That was tactless of me.' Margaret's cheeks flushed. They walked on in silence for a few moments, before she tried again. 'Won't you come? Please? Mummy wants to meet you. I've told her all about my new flatmate, and she's desperate to practise her French. She's also a marvel with potatoes and cabbage.'

She looked at Agnes, a tentative smile lighting her face.

Agnes caught the look and knew she couldn't say no. She dragged in a ragged breath.

'Well, it would be rude to disappoint your *maman*, wouldn't it? And potatoes and cabbage are my favourite vegetables.' She smiled. A small, sad smile. 'Thank you, I'd like to come.'

The following day they walked the mile from the station and arrived at Margaret's family home in time for lunch. The house was a well-built stone farmhouse, with a huge rambler rose climbing up the outside of the front, wrapping the doorway in fragrant yellow blooms. It made Agnes ache for her own home in France; if this one had shutters on the windows it could easily pass for a French house. Beyond the wide gravel drive she noticed a post and rail fenced meadow full of vegetables. No doubt it had been home to the pony Maggie had told her about so often, and which she still mourned.

'Margaret!'

An older version of Maggie ran out of the front door and wrapped her daughter in a hug, then pulled a handkerchief out of the sleeve of her pale blue cardigan and dabbed at her eyes. Stepping back, she surveyed her from head to toe at arm's length.

'London suits you, darling. You look so elegant with your hair done like that. You're turning into such a sophisticated young lady.' She patted her cheek, then looked at Agnes. 'And you must be Agnes. It's a pleasure to meet you, mademoiselle,' she said, almost shyly. 'Come in, come in.'

She opened the door wide and ushered them inside.

Margaret looked a trifle embarrassed by her mother's enthusiasm, but Agnes lost her reservations about the weekend; she felt welcome and knew she would like Maggie's family.

'James. Look who's here.'

A tall, rather stooped man with wispy blond hair shuffled down the hall. He wore corduroy trousers and a tatty checked shirt. On his feet was the worst pair of carpet slippers Agnes had seen. Margaret ran to meet him, and flung her arms around his neck. He swung her round as if she were a small child, while she

63

squealed in delight. Agnes looked on, realising the desert of her own family life compared to this happy scene. Margaret planted a kiss on his cheek and tucked her arm under his.

'Come and meet my friend Agnes, Daddy.'

Glancing down the hall as a door slammed, Agnes saw a pair of heels disappearing upstairs. Another door slammed even more loudly. That must be Jessica, who didn't seem too happy that her big sister was home. She might be sixteen, but apparently Margaret had been right when she said her younger sister was a brat.

Mrs Scott chivvied them through to the kitchen. She looked flustered, chiding Margaret as she told her to help serve lunch.

'I wish you'd let me know you were coming a bit sooner,' she said, doling out thin soup into bowls, while Agnes and Dr Scott sat at the long, scrubbed-pine kitchen table. 'At least the hens are laying. I'll make a soufflé. That piece of cheese you brought is perfect for it.'

'Sorry, Mummy. We never know when we're getting time off from work. It was a last-minute thing. And now you've got us to feed, as well as yourselves. I wish we had brought something else to help you out.' She put her arms around her and kissed her cheek. Agnes's heart ached at the affectionate gesture and she looked away. 'Soufflé will be wonderful. Your cooking is always so tasty, and anything is better than my efforts.'

Her mother brushed away her compliments. 'Oh, it's no matter, we're just thrilled to see you. Take those before the soup gets cold.'

Dr Scott ignored his womenfolk, fixing his gaze on Agnes with eyes disconcertingly like his daughter's. He asked her where she was from, and soon she found herself chatting as if she had known him for years. He had that ability, like most country doctors, of putting people at ease, she supposed. She imagined he always took an interest in what his patients had to say, and could find some common ground with them. After a few moments of small talk, he confided that his passion was for French art and that he had visited the Louvre before the war.

'My father took me, when I was at school in Paris,' she said, trying to keep a smile on her face. 'Wouldn't it be funny if we had passed each other there?'

Dr Scott laughed. 'Indeed, it would. What a coincidence that would be. So, tell me, Agnes . . .' he pronounced it the French way, *Agnès*, with a soft 'g' '. . . who is your favourite French master?'

'Cézanne,' she said, immediately, glancing up and smiling her thanks as Margaret placed a bowl of soup in front of her.

Dr Scott nodded, and blew over his soup. 'His work certainly has appeal. I prefer Toulouse Lautrec personally. He has something of the common people about him. I particularly enjoy his early work.'

'Oh, yes,' Agnes agreed. 'His sketches of horses and working people are wonderful.'

'Indeed.'

Jessica appeared after her mother yelled up the stairs that she would go hungry if she didn't come down in two minutes. She sat opposite Agnes, glowering over her soup. Margaret sat beside her.

'How's school, Jess?' she said.

Her younger sister shrugged. 'You know, school's school,' she said, not looking up. 'It's the same as when you were there. Except the food is worse, and we have to dig our own potatoes and feed the pigs. It's disgusting.'

Margaret laughed and sympathised.

Mrs Scott frowned. 'Jessica, it might be your birthday but where are your manners? Take your elbows off the table, dear, and sit up straight. We have guests.'

'It's Margaret. She's not a guest.'

'Agnes is a guest, and you'll not answer back, young lady.'

Jessica reddened and scowled, but sat straighter. Agnes kept her eyes on her food as the atmosphere became chilly. Dr Scott, with a few quiet words, calmed the choppy waters of his family.

'Anne, don't we have a bottle of something put by for a special occasion?' he said, his eyebrows disappearing into his receding hairline. 'It's in the pantry. I'll get it while you put the glasses out.'

Mrs Scott smiled her thanks and jumped up to find glasses while the good doctor left the table for a moment and returned with a dusty bottle. After popping the cork, he poured the cool champagne and gave everyone a glass, even Jess.

'To Jessica, on your birthday,' he said, raising his glass to her.

Jess smiled and Agnes saw the resemblance to her older sister when her face lit up. She wanted to tell her how pretty she looked when she wasn't sulking, but said nothing, merely raising her glass and smiling when she caught her eye. She sipped the delicious wine and grinned at Margaret who looked across at her, raising her glass a little. Agnes pushed her chair back and stood up.

'Dr and Mrs Scott, I can't thank you enough for making me feel so welcome. It's a pleasure to meet you and Jessica.'

She raised her glass to them and Mrs Scott beamed.

'It's so nice to meet one of Margaret's friends from London,' the doctor said. 'I hope you can come again.'

'Thank you, I'd like that,' she said, sitting down again.

Margaret lifted a slim package out of her handbag and handed it to her sister.

'Happy birthday, Jess. I hope you have a lovely day.'

Her sister took the gift, gazing at it and then at Margaret, with a surprised smile.

'Thank you.' She looked at it for another second, then tore off the brown paper, squealing when she found the nylon stockings and tiny bottle of perfume inside. 'Margaret, you are the best!' she said, hugging her.

'You're welcome.'

Dr Scott harrumphed and looked less than pleased, muttering about girls growing up far too fast these days.

Mrs Scott let out a high-pitched squeak. 'The soufflé,' she cried, leaping up and rushing to the range.

* * *

After lunch, Agnes and Margaret offered to clear away and wash up. They finished drying the dishes and hung the damp tea towels over the rail on the ancient Aga to dry.

'Come on, I've got something to show you,' Margaret said, grabbing Agnes's hand.

She was brimming with excitement and led the way around the back of the house to the old stables, where Agnes supposed Margaret's pony had been kept. There was no remnant of those childhood days that she could see, only the smell of mouldy hay. Leaning against the back wall of one of the looseboxes was some kind of machine covered in a dust sheet. Curious, Agnes wondered what it was, and why Margaret was so excited. She watched her pull off the sheet and stroke her hand along the sleek lines of the engine and the leather seat.

Agnes's eyes widened. 'Is this yours? How on earth did you come by such a beauty and learn to ride it?'

'Yes. It's a Silver Hawk motorcycle. Isn't she gorgeous? Grandpa taught me to ride her a couple of years ago, when he came to live with us after Granny died.' Her face fell for a moment. 'He passed away over a year ago, and bequeathed her to me. I can't believe it's almost a year since I last rode his pride and joy, and I can't wait to take her out again.' Margaret's eyes lit up as she fell over her words. 'I'm going to make sure she's roadworthy and then we're going to ride her back to London, tomorrow.' She turned to her. 'Are you game?'

Agnes nodded, too amazed at Margaret's hidden talent to say anything. She grinned and put her hand on the seat, taking in the lines of the motorcycle, wondering what it felt like to sit astride such a powerful machine.

She looked up to find Margaret watching her, a wide smile on her face, and heat ran up her neck into her face. Covering her confusion, she coughed, clearing her throat.

'What do you have to do before we can take it out?'

'Check everything is working. Brakes, tyres, that kind of thing. Come on, she weighs a ton; help me push her outside.'

Between them they wheeled the motorcycle out of the stable onto the cobbled yard. The cover had kept the bike pristine and the chrome shone in the sun. Dr Scott appeared and watched while Margaret carefully looked over the tyres, checked their pressure, and squeezed the brake on the handlebars.

'Everything seems in working order,' she said. 'I don't suppose you have a can of petrol squirrelled away, Daddy?'

'There's some in the garage, I think.' He frowned. 'It's not easy to find, nowadays, you know. Are you taking this monster out?'

'I'm taking her back to London. And don't call her a monster; she was Grandpa's dearest possession, and she's mine too.'

'Hmph, your mother won't be happy. She always worries when you get on that thing,' he said. 'And there won't be enough fuel to get you to London. How will you get hold of ration coupons? Civilians aren't allowed to buy petrol.'

'Daddy, don't be such a wet blanket.' She was cross he was spoiling their fun, but Agnes knew he was right. She had the same concerns. 'Come on, Agnes, let's take her for a spin, make sure she's going okay before we set off tomorrow.'

Donning coats, caps and goggles, they were soon ready to go. Margaret climbed astride the bike and Agnes watched her trying to get it going. Kickstarting looked hard work and soon had her sweating, but finally, after half a dozen attempts, it spluttered and the engine caught. Revving until it ran smoothly, she shuffled forward and yelled at Agnes to climb on behind her.

It took a while for Agnes to relax into the ride and enjoy the sensation of speed and freedom. She kept her arms wrapped around Margaret's waist, the intimate feel of her muscles tensing and relaxing as she controlled the powerful machine something she had not experienced before. At the top of a hill, they pulled off the road and Margaret left the engine idling for a moment. Agnes gazed at the countryside spread out below them in all its summer glory.

'Let's have a break,' Margaret said, pushing down the kickstand and switching off the engine.

They dismounted, and pulled off their caps and goggles. Agnes shook her hair loose, letting the breeze cool her head. She dropped onto the grass verge, her feet hanging over the bank, and pulled off her jacket. Margaret flopped down beside her and a gust of wind caught their hair – the blonde and the dark – entangling them for a moment. Agnes lay back, enjoying the feel of the sun on her bare arms, thinking how far away London and the Dungeon seemed.

Margaret picked a daisy and twirled it around, then leant over her and tickled her chin with it. Agnes smiled and closed her eyes, aware of the other girl's light perfume as they lay side by side. It would be so easy to pretend everything was normal, that they weren't in the middle of a war, with millions of people dead or misplaced, their homes in ruins or occupied by the Third Reich. The prospect of returning to work was a depressing thought.

Why had she been so reluctant to accept Margaret's invitation?

'Your parents are nice people,' she said. 'You're very lucky to have such a kind family.'

'Is this difficult for you to bear, so soon after everything?'

Agnes didn't answer for a while, wondering if she would ever get over the guilt. Finally, she shook her head. 'I feel more peaceful here than I have for a long time.' She pushed herself up onto her elbows and gazed at the countryside in front of them. 'I've tried to keep from thinking about Maman; working hard, making myself exhausted so I can sleep.' She sighed. 'This reminds me a little of home. Your parents' house makes me think of France.'

Margaret sat up and put an arm around her shoulders.

Agnes leant into her for a moment, breathing in the fragrance of her. 'It's okay, I don't mean in a sad way. It's comforting. I'm glad I came.'

Margaret's skin against hers felt like silk. Warmth that had nothing to do with the sun shot through her, and the hairs on her arm rose.

'I'm glad you came, too. Gosh, is that the time?' Margaret jumped up and brushed down her skirt. She grabbed her hand

and pulled her up. 'Come on, we should get back. I have to help Mummy with dinner. Some family friends are coming to celebrate Jess's birthday.'

Agnes wondered if she had felt it too . . . whatever 'it' was . . .

Margaret's confidence on the bike seemed to grow as they sped along the quiet lanes. On the final straight back to the house she opened the engine right up, Agnes yelling in her ear, and by the time they arrived they were both high on adrenaline, every nerve tingling. With the engine switched off they sat, catching their breath, listening to the metal tick as it cooled. Agnes hugged Margaret hard around the middle, pressing her cheek into her back, before dismounting.

'That was wonderful.' She couldn't keep the grin off her face, exhilaration thrumming through her veins.

'Isn't it exciting? I can't wait to get her back to London.'

They put the motorcycle away and walked back to the house arm in arm. Her limbs were heavy with fatigue, but Agnes was closer to being happy than she had been for as long as she could remember.

Being back in the Dungeon after the fun of riding the motorcycle back to London reminded Agnes of returning to school after the summer holidays. A day later, though, and she was once more fully immersed in the business of decoding messages from all over the battlefields of Europe. The work wasn't easy but she loved the challenge of deciphering lines of complete nonsense until the true message revealed itself.

She knew the same could not be said for Margaret, who had lost what little confidence she'd gained and grew more anxious with every shift. She constantly worried she would make a mistake – or worse – not recognise that a radio had been captured and the Nazis were sending false messages. She told Agnes she would never get used to it and dreaded the Dungeon more every day.

With the spell of warm weather continuing, they sat in the park beside the river to eat their lunchtime sandwiches, making the most of the sun while they could. Nearly all of the space had been dug up and planted in neat rows with potatoes, spinach, peas, carrots and beans. Agnes loved the continuous hum from bees feasting on the bean and pea flowers – a poignant reminder of her mother's garden.

'I wish there was another job I could transfer to,' Margaret said, her voice gloomy. 'One I'd be more suited to. Outdoors, not cooped up in the Dungeon. Something less stressful.'

'I'm sure there are jobs like that, aren't there?' Agnes lay back and shaded her eyes. 'Why? Don't you like working with me, Pat and Clarice?'

'I love working with you, and the others. You know that.' She lay beside her, twirling a daisy in her fingers, reminding Agnes of the weekend just past. 'I hate the Dungeon though, and I'm not cut out to be a radio operator. I'm not nearly clever enough.'

'Of course, you are, Maggie. It's confidence you need in your own abilities.' She sat up. 'You are good at your job – and it's vital, you know that.'

Margaret shrugged. 'I don't feel like I do a good job. I'm too slow and make too many mistakes – which you always have to correct.' She fell silent for a moment. 'I want to work outdoors, feel the wind in my hair, breathe fresh air. Maybe I could be a land girl.' She nodded towards three women bent double in the middle of the rows of vegetables.

Agnes snorted.

'What's so funny?'

'You? With your perfect hair, make-up and polished nails? I can't see it.'

Margaret pulled a face but couldn't deny the truth in her words. She grew quiet again and Agnes racked her brain for something she could suggest that might suit her.

Suddenly, she sat up.

'I know what you would be good at.' She caught Margaret's hand and dragged her to her feet. 'Come with me. If you're serious,

I've got just the thing.' She led her to the WAAF offices, two doors down from the Dungeon. 'I had to deliver a message here last week and saw something on the noticeboard.'

She stopped in front of it and pointed to a sheet of paper with various positions that needed filling.

DESPATCH RIDERS

Experienced motorcyclists required to carry documents and messages from London to airfields around the country. Must be proficient at motorcycle maintenance.

Margaret stared at the notice, a smile spreading across her face. She turned, her eyes sparkling.

'Oh, this is perfect. Where do I apply?' Agnes grinned and pointed to a corporal sitting at the desk, who looked up as Margaret approached. 'Can I see the recruitment officer, please, Corporal.'

She checked a large diary and told her to come back in two hours for an interview. They were now late for the afternoon shift and Sergeant Atkins would give them a roasting, but Agnes didn't care. She crossed her fingers and prayed Margaret would be given a job doing what she loved and it wouldn't be long until she was roving the countryside on two wheels.

Margaret passed the motorcycle test without a problem, and Agnes and the others took her out for the night after she finished her last shift. They decided to go back to the Palais.

'We'll still see each other all the time, won't we?' she begged, looking at the three girls sitting around the table they had bagged. 'I'm based in the London pool, and Agnes can keep me in touch with you.'

'You two have been joined at the hip since Agnes arrived,' said Pat. 'It's going to be strange not having you doing all the work.'

'Yes,' Clarice piped up. 'I think it's jolly unfair that you're making our jobs much harder. I can't believe you can ride a motorcycle, though. You kept that quiet, you dark horse.' She jumped up and grabbed her by the arm, swinging her around. 'Come on, we've all got to dance. Who knows when we'll get together, again.'

They ran downstairs and joined the crowd on the dance floor. It was much quieter than the last time they were there, and there were more girls than boys, so they partnered up with each other. After a couple of dances, Agnes and Margaret agreed to sit one out. They got a drink and found their table was still free up in the gallery.

They watched Pat and Clarice doing the Jitterbug, perfectly in time with each other.

'It's all very well Clarice teasing us for being joined at the hip as she calls it, but those two are the terrible twins.' Margaret laughed. 'They're inseparable – look at them. They must practise, surely?'

'They're very good, aren't they?'

The drinks arrived and they sat in comfortable silence, fanning themselves. Agnes thought how strange it would be not to work alongside Maggie every day. She was glad they shared the flat; couldn't imagine not seeing her.

'Come on, let's down these and get back on the dance floor – those two are having far too much fun.'

Agnes swigged her drink, screwing her face up at the rough spirit. Margaret followed suit, choking as the liquor hit the back of her throat. She wiped her eyes and Agnes laughed. 'Come here. You look like a panda.'

Taking a handkerchief out of her bag, she did her best to undo the damage. Their eyes met for a moment, and she caught the scent of Maggie's perfume, bringing a warmth that ran through her body, making her head swim.

'Thanks.'

'You're welcome.'

They ran down the stairs back to the dance floor just in time for the band to finish one tune and start a slow jazz number. Margaret led, and they swayed in time to the music. Agnes's head swam from the effects of the gin, and she closed her eyes for a moment, trying to regain her equilibrium. She was very aware of their bodies lightly touching as they danced. She stepped in closer and it was as if they were melded together, their bodies responding to every movement of the other, until it seemed they were the only people on the floor.

Later, they wandered home through the near-dark, warm summer streets, bare arms occasionally brushing. They walked in silence, Agnes's mind a riot of thoughts and emotions. Something happened there, on the dance floor. She was certain Margaret felt it just as she had, and now she didn't know what to think or do.

She had spent the evening floating on air, yet now was filled with doubt. Was it just her who was so confused, or did Maggie feel the same?

Chapter 11

Claire

Aunt M looked up when I walked into her room. It was a relief and pleasure to see her back in form. Her hair and make-up were immaculate, she was dressed in a perfect twinset and tweed skirt with a set of pearl earrings, and I caught the subtle scent of the perfume that was so much a part of her.

'Hello, dear,' she said, smiling at me as I came over and bent to kiss her cheek.

'You look well,' I said, feeling very scruffy in my jeans and old cardigan. 'You put me to shame, Aunt M.'

'Pah, don't be such a ninny. You're a busy professional woman, and when you're on holiday you should dress exactly how you want to.' She patted her hair. 'My problem is that I'm far too vain. Always have been. Agnes laughs at me, because I take so long to get ready and am always late.'

She mentioned Agnes as if she had seen her yesterday, not seventy years ago. My heart hurt for her.

Still, it gave me the opportunity to talk about her.

'Do you remember you told me about Agnes the other day?

75

I would love to hear more about her. If I'm going to find out what happened to her, I'll need as much information as you can give me.'

She blinked and looked sideways at me. 'I told you about Agnes? Did I?' Confusion clouded her face for a moment and she blushed. 'Oh, I did – after my little escapade. I remember now. Do you really want to waste your holiday looking for her?' Aunt M put her head back against the chair and closed her eyes. 'It will be a fool's errand, I'm afraid. How on earth can you find her after all this time?'

'There's so much information on the internet, Aunt M, including personnel records from the war. Even if Agnes is dead, there's a good chance I can find something about her and why she disappeared.'

Aunt M gave me a withering stare. 'And if she simply got fed up of me? London was a big place, even then. It was easy to get lost, if that's what one wanted to do.'

'Is that what you believe she did?'

She shrugged. 'I don't know. I didn't think so, at the time.'

'Well then. Maybe she got posted somewhere else, or was hurt in an accident or a bombing?'

Looking as if she was miles away, Aunt M gazed out at the gardens, and I hoped she hadn't slipped back to the past again. I needed her memory, but I needed her mind in the present too. When she turned away from staring out of the window, I sighed – she looked as sharp as ever.

'Do you mind if I quiz you a bit, on what you remember about Agnes?'

'Not at all. Ask away – just don't be surprised if I can't remember things clearly – my memory isn't what it was, you know,' she said, seemingly oblivious to the irony in her words.

'I'd like to record our conversation if that's okay?' I said, taking out my mobile and showing it to her. 'Then I can go back and listen to it when I get home and won't have to bother you again.'

She took the phone and turned it over and over in her hands, examining it from top to bottom.

'I wish we'd had these in my day,' she said. 'When I think of all the paraphernalia we had to carry around, just to interview someone. This is so small; how does it work? And can it do everything at once? Where does the tape go?'

I smiled at her. I couldn't quite believe she was the same confused soul I'd rescued a week ago.

'It doesn't need tape, Aunt M. It records everything digitally – and don't ask me how because I've no idea,' I said. 'All I know is that when I press this, here, it records our voices. I can also take photographs with it. Look.' I activated the camera and showed her how it worked.

She took the phone again, and inadvertently took a selfie, dropping it in shock when the flash went off. We both laughed, and I showed her the image she'd taken – most of her chin and one ear.

'You can't keep that,' she said, giggling. 'Will you take one of us together, for me? How do you develop the film – is it a film? I'd like to have a photograph of you and me, so I can frame it and put it on my shelf.'

'Of course,' I said. 'We need to sit together so we're both in the shot. If you move over a little, I can sit on the edge of the chair, like this.' I perched with my arm around her shoulders, held the phone up and told her to look at it and smile, then took three shots in quick succession. 'There, all done. I'll print these off at home later and get the best of them framed for you.'

'You have a studio at your home?'

'Only a printer. It's all you need nowadays.'

'Goodness,' she said. 'Things are much easier now, aren't they?'

'In some ways they are,' I said, shutting down the camera and changing the setting to begin recording. 'Are you ready? We'll stop whenever you've had enough. We can talk some more tomorrow; there's no rush.'

For as long as I could remember, Aunt M always loved telling stories and had a talent for making people laugh. It was one of the things I adored about her. She could keep me entertained for hours with outrageous tales, mostly – I suspect – fabricated on the spot, a product of her agile brain and a love of anything mischievous.

Once she began talking it was hard to get her to stop. Hesitant at first, she was like a bottle of gassy lemonade with the pressure released; the words flowed out of her. Not that a lot of what she said was much help. She wandered off into her thoughts and memories, half-telling a story and then changing to something else as she was reminded of another tale by a word or name.

Her eyes lost focus as she went back to her life during the war. The fear that was part of everyday life, the comradeship of her friends and co-workers. When she spoke of Agnes, it was clear to see the depth of friendship the two of them had shared.

The war was terrifying, like living on the edge of a crumbling precipice; never knowing if your turn had come, whether the next bomb might have your name on it. But we were young, and it was a grand excuse to live as if there was no tomorrow.

Oh and how we lived, my friends and I. We worked hard, sometimes in the toughest of conditions, and we played even harder. As if we had to condense our youth into a tiny capsule of time. We'd go dancing until dawn then go home, sleep for an hour or two and turn up for our shift the next day as normal.

Everyone knew about tragedy. Everyone had lost someone they loved. Who could tell when they would be next? We lived in the moment and tried our damnedest to shut out the horror.

Agnes and I met in the WAAFs, when I'd been there for a couple of months. Agnes was given the radio next to mine on her first day. She had the sweetest smile, and was so clever, you know. Intelligent, diligent, all the things I wasn't, and never would be. She was noticed by the brass, after a very short time.

I was intrigued, and asked her why.

Why? Well, because she could decode so quickly, you see; just had a knack for it. I was hopeless – no, dear, honestly, I was – so slow, had to keep referring to the books to remember it all. Agnes looked at something for five minutes and had it deciphered in no time. She was given all the most complicated messages.

We worked side by side and became good friends. Then her mother died – it almost destroyed her, but she bottled everything up and just got on with things. I knew she was grieving terribly and asked her to be my flatmate, so I could keep an eye on her, help if I could. It brought us even closer.

What to say about her? That she was tiny? And spoke the most beautifully accented English? She'd grown up in France, before the war. Her mother was French and her father English, so she spoke both languages perfectly. She could make me laugh until I had to hold my sides. Beauty was within her and shone out of every pore of her body. She was the strongest person I've ever known.

And now, my dear, you want to try and find Agnes. It's very kind of you, but I don't hold out much hope that you'll succeed – it's been seventy years, for heaven's sake. I suspect you see me as a good project to focus on. You might think I'm your batty old auntie, and perhaps I am, but I can see you're keeping something from me. I'm not so dotty I don't recognise the signs of worry and stress. You were always an open book and I get the impression something's bothering you and I wish you'd tell me. Is it something at work? It seems a little too convenient you can take so much time off to help me, on a whim.

Where was I? Agnes. Who never called me Margaret, only Maggie.

I remember everything about her, of course. Like the day the photograph of us I showed you was taken. How could I forget?

By that time, I had left the Dungeon, as we called the cellar where we worked. I hated being cooped up all the time, and was hopeless at being a radio operator. I became a motorcycle courier, which I loved.

'What? Aunt M, you rode motorbikes? How did I not know that?'

I vaguely remembered an old bike covered with a tarp in the garage at the Chimneys. It never crossed my mind it had been hers.

'Well, dear, it was a very long time ago. Yes, I loved my motorcycle. It had belonged to my grandfather, and he taught me to ride it, and left it to me when he died.' Her eyes softened for a moment and a smile played on her lips. 'Where was I?'

The photo of her and Agnes lay on the small table beside her chair, and she lifted it, gazing at the image with a smile.

Oh, yes, this photograph. When it was warm, if I wasn't away on a run, I would pop over and we would take our sandwiches to the park by the river, and sit in the sunshine, pretending life was normal. Wanting not to feel frightened for a change, you know? One of the chaps had a camera and he took a photograph of us.

I suppose we were a bit like chalk and cheese and yet we hit it off straight away. We shared the same sense of humour, but nothing else really. She was quiet and shy whereas I was a party girl. I introduced her to people I knew, showed her around. She came home to meet my parents – your grandparents – for a weekend, when it was your mother's birthday. They adored her, and even Jessica thought she was all right, I think.

We shared a flat for six months or so. There was never enough of anything – food, drink, cigarettes – we had to scrounge for everything. But we were young and loved life, so it didn't seem to matter.

Then one day she disappeared and I never saw her again.

Aunt M looked exhausted by the time she finished talking, her words coming more slowly, in more of a ramble as she reminisced about life. Considering how confused she became at the slightest thing, I was astounded at her powers of recall. It was as if she were talking about yesterday, not seventy years ago.

'I've tired you out,' I said.

She shook her head. 'This has been the best morning I've spent in a very long time,' she said, patting my hand. 'I've talked about things I've not spoken about for years. There are so few of us left who lived through the war, you know, dear.'

'I can't begin to understand how awful it was, living during the Blitz, and all the deprivations you had to go through.'

'They were terrible times,' she said. 'But I felt more alive than I ever have since. It's so hard to explain.' She closed her eyes for a moment. When she opened them, there was a shine to them. 'I just wish we could have come out of it together, Agnes and I.'

I sighed. For all she had told me, there was nothing in Aunt M's reminiscences that was much help. I racked my brains to try and think of something that might give me a clue as to where Agnes had gone. I couldn't imagine someone just walking out of their home without saying anything. To my mind, that was her own memory playing tricks on her. It seemed far more likely that she had been sent somewhere else. As far as I could remember from my scant knowledge of Second World War history, servicemen and women were always being moved around from one place to another.

'Do you think she might have been posted somewhere else? If she was so good at operating radios, perhaps your superiors sent her somewhere like Bletchley Park.'

Aunt M shrugged. She slumped back into her chair, gazing sightlessly out of the window. I knew she had had enough for one morning.

'Maybe, dear. I don't know, and even if she did, why didn't she tell me? She wasn't thoughtless; she was caring and kind.'

She shook her head. 'If she wanted to let me know where she was going, she would have. So why didn't she?'

'I don't know, but I'm going to do my best to find out. There will be records of where she went and who she served with. I just have to track them down.'

She dropped her head and drew in a shaky breath. 'It's kind of you to try. I would like to know what happened to her. She was very special.'

Chapter 12

Agnes

Margaret had been in her new role as a motorcycle courier for three weeks, and Agnes was used to seeing much less of her. Their shifts were often different, but they made a pact to try and eat at least one meal together each day, if time allowed. Mostly, it was supper, and the one who finished work first would cook whatever they had managed to find in the local markets and grocer's shop.

Agnes arrived back at the flat with a parcel of meat that would make a good stew and set to preparing it and the few vegetables they had in the larder, hoping Margaret wouldn't be too late.

It was almost dark by the time she heard the key in the door and Margaret appeared, looking drawn and tired. She joined Agnes in the kitchen.

'Hello,' Agnes said, with a smile. 'You look exhausted, you poor thing. Where did you have to go, today? You're very late – I was worried you'd crashed or broken down or something.'

'No, nothing to worry about. I had to go to bloody Norfolk, though, and hit a storm on the way there. It took hours.' Margaret lifted the lid on the stew and put her nose over the pot, taking a deep sniff. Her eyes brightened. 'That smells divine. What is it?'

'Rabbit. At least I think it's rabbit.' Agnes winked and grinned. 'There was a man at the market selling it. I couldn't resist – it's been ages since we had a good feed of meat. I managed to get potatoes and onions. And carrots.' She turned to her, laughing. 'It's not exactly coq au vin, but we're having a feast, and it's only Tuesday. Imagine that.'

Margaret laughed at her enthusiasm. 'I'm so hungry I don't care if it's rat,' she said. 'Is there any hot water? I'm dying for a bath. My shoulders feel like I've been run over by a steamroller.'

Agnes nodded. 'This needs another half-hour, so go and have a soak. I'll shout when it's ready.'

Agnes pottered around the living room, tidying cushions, putting away newspapers and watering the dusty houseplant they had managed not to kill since Dr Scott had given it to them. After half an hour, the stew was cooked but there was no sign of Margaret, so she tapped gently on the bathroom door. It swung half open and revealed her flatmate fast asleep in the rapidly cooling, lavender-scented bathwater.

Embarrassment chased its way up her back at seeing her friend naked, and she half-turned away, but then let her eyes wander over Margaret's body, drinking in the sight of her. She was so beautiful, Agnes couldn't help staring. Tiptoeing in, she gently put her hands on the sleeping girl's shoulders and began to massage the tight knots along the base of her neck and across the muscles in her back.

Margaret shifted and groaned, letting her head fall forward under Agnes's insistent fingers and she continued for a minute or two, enjoying the pleasure she was giving.

'God, that's wonderful. Thank you, you're an angel,' Margaret mumbled.

Agnes chuckled. 'Glad to be of service, madam. Right. That's enough luxuriating. Supper is ready.'

She was tempted to say, never mind supper, just let me keep on doing this. She wanted to run her hands down to her trim waist and beyond, discover everything about her.

Yet how could she ever admit such a thing to her friend? A girl who had given her a home and taken her under her wing, when she, Agnes, had no one she could turn to. How could she betray that friendship? Margaret would be horrified and repulsed if she knew what her flatmate dreamt about. She would just have to keep her confusing thoughts and emotions to herself and carry on as she had done since Maggie invited her to share the flat.

'Agnes?'

She jumped and almost slipped on the wet floor, having heard not one word of what Maggie had said. She caught her balance and stood up.

'Sorry. Must be nearly as tired as you are. What did you say?'

'Do you want to jump in here after me? It seems a shame to waste all this hot water.'

Suddenly, she just needed to get out of the bathroom and collect her thoughts, get her breath and act as if everything were normal.

'That's okay, leave it for now. I'll bathe after we've eaten.'

She couldn't resist pausing in the doorway as Margaret stood up.

'Pass me the towel, please. I'll be there in a tick.'

Throwing it to her, Agnes watched her wrap it around her nakedness, then fled.

Over supper, they talked about their day.

'Rosemary seems to be settling in.'

Agnes had taken Margaret's replacement under her wing and liked her. She was bright and quick to learn, getting on well with the rest of the team.

'How are the Terrible Twins?'

'Who? Oh, Clarice and Pat? They're just the same. Driving Sergeant Atkins up the wall.' She chewed on a piece of meat. 'It's not the same without you, though. I miss you sitting beside me.'

Warmth ran through her at the thought of her hands on Maggie's skin, bringing a flush that travelled the length of her body. She rose from the table, unable to bear the thought of Maggie guessing what was going through her mind. She brought the stewpot over to the table and offered another spoonful. Margaret nodded.

'Thanks.' She grinned at her. 'It's nice to be missed, you know, but you're all much better off without me. Sergeant Atkins must be a happy soul now I'm not being a thorn in her side.' She took another mouthful of the stew. 'This rabbit or whatever it is tastes incredible. I can't believe you can produce something so good out of such mundane ingredients.'

'Throw everything into the pot and let it stew. Nothing clever about it,' Agnes said. 'The wild marjoram I found on the heath last week makes a big difference to the flavour.' They ate in silence for a moment. 'Tell me about your day,' she prompted. 'I've never been to Norfolk. What's it like?'

'Flat. Lots of water. Boring. Give me woods and hills any day.' Margaret put down her fork, resting her chin on her hand, her eyes unfocused. 'At the base I bumped into someone I knew when I was at school. I'm amazed he recognised me – the last time we met was at a ball, and I was in evening dress.' She laughed. 'Today I looked like a drowned rat.'

'No one would forget you, once they'd met you,' Agnes murmured.

'Really? Hmm, I don't know about that. Anyway, he asked after Tom.'

'The boy you were talking to half the night when we went to the Palais for Clarice's birthday?'

'I'm surprised you remember him,' Margaret said. 'Apparently, he's gone AWOL. I can't believe I didn't notice something was wrong when I saw him, that night.'

Agnes eyed her sharply. 'Why should you have?' she said. 'Do you know why he's run? Is he a coward?'

'No! That's the last thing one could say about him,' Margaret snapped. 'He's been flying since he joined up in 1940. Do you have any conception of the attrition rate in fighter pilots?'

Agnes shook her head, kicking herself for not realising that Margaret was so upset.

'Well, the fact he's still alive is extraordinary in itself. He's very good at what he does, but it's taken its toll. He's lost too many friends and seen too much death. They call it battle fatigue.'

'It must be the same for many, many fellows. They don't all run away.'

'No, they don't. But we ought to find a little compassion for those who've given everything, and have nothing left.' She jumped up, and began clearing the table, slamming plates into the washing-up bowl. She placed her hands on either side of the sink and leant on them, her head hanging.

Agnes rose and put an arm around her waist, leaning into her. 'Tom's desertion is not your fault,' she said. 'I'm sorry if my words upset you. You're right. There's a limit to a person's endurance, and only so much anyone can give.' She berated herself for being so unsympathetic. In truth, she was a little jealous of this Tom, and of Margaret's friendship over the years with him. 'You look exhausted. Why don't I do the washing up and you go to bed early. I've no doubt you'll have another long day tomorrow. You need your sleep.'

'If you don't mind?' Margaret said. 'I am very tired.' She turned and made her way towards her room, halting with her hand on the doorknob. 'Thank you for tonight – and for caring. I know there is nothing I can do, but I hate the thought of him being out there, somewhere, his nerves in shreds.'

'You're welcome. He's lucky he has a friend like you thinking of him. Goodnight.'

'Night-night. Sleep well, Agnes.'

Tired as she was, sleep eluded Agnes far into the night. When she finally dropped off, her head was full of confusing dreams that involved Margaret and her in a perpetual game of hide-and-seek within a huge, dark and empty house. Whenever she thought she had found her, she discovered a bare cupboard, and a distant ripple of laughter, which she doggedly followed, never quite catching up, only ever spying a naked shoulder, or the scent of perfume on the air.

She woke with a heavy ache in the pit of her belly, acutely aware of who lay on the other side of the thin bedroom wall.

Rising early with a dull head, Agnes moved quietly around the flat in her nightgown and dressing gown, not wanting to disturb Margaret as she put the kettle on and gathered crockery for breakfast. Watching the clock on the mantelpiece, she poured a cup of tea, picked it up and tapped on Margaret's door.

'You've got half an hour before you need to leave,' she said. 'I've got a cup of tea here for you.'

Margaret answered in a strange, strangled voice. 'I'll be there in a minute.'

Agnes frowned and opened the door. Margaret sat on the end of her bed, still in her nightgown.

'Are you all right? You look pretty seedy; do you feel ill?'

She shook her head. 'No, I'm perfectly well, but I couldn't sleep a wink for worrying about Tom, wondering if he's okay. It's silly. We've hardly seen each other since we were children, but I hate to think what might happen to him.'

Agnes put the tea on the bedside table and sat on the bed next to her. 'It's not silly at all. You're a compassionate, loving woman, worried about your friend.' They sat in silence for a moment. 'You're very special, Maggie. I'm sure Tom would come to you with his problems if he could.'

Margaret searched her face and Agnes forced herself to hold her gaze, hoping her words brought some comfort. Being friends with her was enough; she must bury the other, confusing feelings that kept her awake at night. She valued what they had too much to jeopardise it.

She rose, but Margaret took her hand and drew her down onto the bed again, leant in and kissed her. Shock almost paralysed Agnes. Margaret pulled away slightly, looked at her with a question in her eyes, and she nodded. Their lips met again and she was lost in their soft warmth and the sweet taste of her mouth. Maggie pushed her back onto the pillows and slid a hand under her nightdress, caressing with a silken touch, almost sending her mad with desire.

'I've wanted to do this since the first day we met,' she whispered.

Agnes gasped as her fingers moved lower. 'What took you so long?'

Chapter 13

Agnes

They say absence makes the heart grow fonder, and being apart each day made the time Agnes and Margaret spent together more precious. If they had continued working alongside each other Agnes was sure they would have remained close friends – would they have become lovers? Who knew? She was just over the moon it had happened.

The confusing thoughts and emotions that had plagued her were gone. Being with Maggie felt so right, loving her made her whole. As if a part of her had been missing and she didn't even know it. They kept up the pretence of being close friends because it was nobody else's business. She just hoped others wouldn't judge them too harshly if they did discover the truth.

It was Margaret's twentieth birthday. Joy of joys, the two of them had managed to wangle the same day off. Sergeant Atkins took some persuading, but Agnes made up an excuse about visiting a sick friend outside the city. She would probably be given all the worst night shifts for the next few weeks, but it was worth it to have the day together.

She got up to make tea, leaving Maggie lounging in bed watching her through the half-open door as she moved around the tiny kitchenette. The sun shone through the window, catching dust motes in its rays until it looked as if it were raining glitter, promising another warm day. All Agnes had on was a sheer nightgown, which she knew left nothing to the imagination, showing off every curve of her body, enjoying the feel of her lover's eyes on her. When she brought the tea tray into the bedroom, Maggie lay on her side, head supported on one hand. Agnes paused in the doorway, tray held in front of her.

'What?'

Maggie grinned in a lopsided way. 'Nothing. I like watching you – especially when you make me breakfast. Thank you, by the way. It's such a luxury to be able to lie in bed for a while.'

Agnes put the tray on the bedside table and sat on the edge of the bed. They kissed – long and sweet, and the tea was forgotten. By the time they came back down to earth it had gone cold and they lay in the narrow bed, drowsy with lovemaking, their naked bodies curled like spoons around each other.

An hour or more passed, and Agnes had never felt more content, known such deep-seated happiness. She could lie there forever with Margaret's silky skin against her body, breathing in the scent of her, kissing her, caressing her. The war forgotten while they were in their little haven.

Eventually, she stirred, kissed her neck, and sat up.

'Don't move,' she said and got out of bed, relishing the warm rays on her body. Leaving the room, she soon returned, her hands behind her back. Kneeling over Maggie, she kissed her again. 'Happy birthday, my love.'

She held out a brown paper bag. Inside was a slim book, a tiny box of chocolates and a bottle of champagne.

Maggie stared at the treasures as if she couldn't quite believe they were real. 'How? How did you get these?' she said.

Agnes shrugged, a flutter in her belly and a throaty chuckle escaping her lips.

'They're wonderful – you're a marvel.'

Opening the book – the collected works of Tennyson – Maggie read what Agnes had written. *'To my darling Maggie. My one and only true love, my saviour, my soulmate. I will love you until the end of time. A.'*

She held it to her heart, her face glowing.

'I mean it, you know,' Agnes said. 'You are my one love. There'll never be another – I want you to know that.' Maggie put a hand up to her cheek and she moved it to her lips and kissed it. 'Whatever happens with this shitty war, whether we somehow can't be together, or one of us doesn't make it through . . .'

Her words were stopped with a finger, Maggie's eyes bright with unshed tears.

'Don't. Please, don't. Can't we forget what else is happening, just for today?' She cleared her throat. 'Now. Are we going to drink this champagne, or just look at it?'

Agnes kissed her, went to fetch some glasses and they opened the bubbly. The rest of the morning was spent in bed, getting drunk, eating chocolates, and reciting poetry to each other while making love. It was a day Agnes knew she would cherish for the rest of her life, a memory that would shine brightly in the darkest of times.

Going back to work the next day with a hangover was a drag. Agnes's train was delayed by an unexploded bomb on the line, and as the sun climbed higher the temperature of the carriage rose until the people jammed in with her made her feel like they were sardines in a canning factory. She arrived two hours late, having given up waiting for the train to move, and walking the rest of the way.

Sergeant Atkins looked sceptical when she apologised and told her the reason.

'That seems a very convenient excuse, Corporal, especially as you look like something the cat dragged in,' she said.

'Sorry, Sarge. It really is the truth.' Agnes kept her eyes on her shoes, her head hammering behind her eyes.

'Hmm, well you had better get to work, now you're here. And while I remember, the section officer wants to see you at ten past six, after your shift finishes. Make sure you are *not* late this time.'

The sergeant dismissed her, and Agnes fled to her radio position, glad to be out from under her eye. A frisson of worry nagged at her, wondering what the SO could possibly want her for, but she had no time to consider it as she tried to catch up on her work over the morning. When she had a moment to relax, she pictured Maggie drinking champagne and reading Tennyson to her, which more than made up for her thumping headache.

When she had a break at lunchtime, she couldn't wait to leave the gloom of the Dungeon. Wandering over to the small park across the road, she lay back in the shade of a willow tree on the dusty patch of grass beside the river, dozing in the sunshine.

She woke to something tickling her face and waved away the annoyance, not wanting to be disturbed.

'Wake up sleepyhead.'

A giggle made her open her eyes, and she sat up, grinning.

'Well, this is a nice surprise,' she said, as Maggie flopped down beside her.

Others were already spread out, enjoying the sunshine while they ate their Spam sandwiches. Pat came and joined them and they ate, smoked, and chatted about what they would do at the weekend. The Americans Pat and Clarice had been walking out with had gone back to their units and were currently busy dropping bombs over German factories. Agnes could see the anxiety in Pat's eyes, and she and Maggie exchanged a look. She put an arm around Pat, who had a little cry on her shoulder. They moved on to safer ground and discussed whether they could still find sausages with real meat in them.

'What I would give for a proper fillet steak,' Agnes said, sighing.

'But I suppose sausages will have to do. Pat, didn't you mention a butcher you know near here who can get them?'

'He's a pretty shady character,' she replied, nodding and wiping her eyes. 'I think he has contacts with the Americans and gets hold of them on the black market sometimes. I've heard they cost a fortune though.' She pulled a pencil out of her bag and tore a corner off her sandwich paper. 'Here's the address if you want to go and ask.'

'Can you go on your way home after work?' Agnes said to Margaret. 'I might be a bit later than usual.'

She had pushed the prospect of the interview out of her mind. Now it resurfaced and her stomach clenched.

'Yes, of course,' Maggie said. 'Why do you have to stay late?'

'I've been ordered to go and see the SO,' she said, and changed the subject back to sausages and what they would eat with them.

Something told her it was not an ordinary meeting, but thinking about it made her pulse race, so she tried to put it out of her mind again. She wiped her hands down her thighs, palms suddenly damp.

Agnes gazed out across the river at the peaceful scene around them. If only they could stay like this; she could lie on the grass with the sun on her face and forget all the fear and misery. Her attention was caught by Walter, one of the chaps who worked in the Dungeon. He was taking photos of the ducks on the water, and she could see he was trying to catch the reflections of them as they glided past. Maggie threw the birds the crusts from her sandwiches and he didn't look too pleased as they came bustling over to the bank, cackling like a load of gossips arguing over the food.

'Thanks for nothing,' he said, packing away the camera.

'Oops, sorry, Walter.'

Maggie flashed him a smile and he grunted.

Agnes asked him if he would take a photo of her and Maggie together. He grumbled that he didn't see why he should after they had spoilt his chances with the ducks.

'Oh, come on Walter,' she said. 'It's such a perfect afternoon, and who knows where we'll be a little while from now.' She smiled, hoping to win him round. 'And I'll pay for the development, of course. I might even stand you a beer if the photo's good enough.'

She winked and grinned, and he smiled reluctantly.

'Come on then,' he said. 'But we need to be quick. I'm due back on duty in ten minutes.' He looked around, then pointed to a bench by the riverbank. 'That should do. Sit there.'

They did as they were told, their heads close and arms across the back of the bench, smiling and laughing at the camera. Walter took three shots in quick succession.

'I'll develop these once I've finished this roll of film and let you have the prints,' he said. 'I'd better get back – there'll be hell if I'm late.'

'Lawks, I'd better get moving too,' Maggie said, glancing at her watch.

'Thank you, Walter, you're a champ,' Agnes said.

They packed up their lunch boxes and said goodbye. Pat and Walter had already crossed the road, but Margaret stopped Agnes with a hand on her arm.

'You seem anxious about your meeting, later. What's it about?'

'I don't know.' She grimaced. 'God, what can I have done so wrong that I'm being hauled up in front of the SO?'

'It's probably just some boring administrative thing that needs sorting out,' Margaret said. 'You're their top radio operator. There's no way you've done anything wrong.'

Agnes wanted to believe her, but still her stomach knotted at the thought of it.

'Don't wait supper for me, if I'm not back. I've no idea how long I'll be.' She tried to smile. 'And don't forget about the sausages.'

'I promise.'

* * *

95

Arriving at the SO's office after her shift finished, with a minute to spare, Agnes knocked on the polished wood of the door and waited to be called in.

Section Officer Johnson opened the door herself, standing back so Agnes could enter first.

'Come in, Corporal Kerr, sit down,' she said, indicating a chair in front of a large desk for Agnes to take. Section Officer Johnson was a stocky, red-haired woman with a strong Scottish accent. Known for having the ability to flay the skin off a recruit's back with the lash of her tongue, Agnes had always managed to stay on the right side of her and knew her to be a fair and forthright officer, who didn't suffer fools lightly. Still, she found her stomach churning and wished she hadn't eaten a Spam sandwich at lunchtime.

'Corporal, there's someone who wants to talk to you. Not here – you must go to this address,' she said, handing Agnes a slip of paper. 'Seven o'clock sharp.'

Agnes stared at her superior officer, her mind a jumble of confusion.

She gave herself a mental shake and looked at the address.

'There's no name, ma'am. Who am I supposed to ask for, when I get there?'

'Don't worry about that. They know you're coming and who you are. It will all be explained to you when you arrive.'

'Have I done something wrong? Is this the police or something? I don't understand what it's all about.'

'You've been selected based on your skills and your background. That's all I can say, Corporal.' The SO went across and opened the door again. 'Good luck. You'll do very well, I have no doubt.'

She smiled, and Agnes saluted as she left the office, no clearer than when she'd entered.

The address the SO had given Agnes wasn't anything like the buildings where she worked in the centre of the city. She stopped outside the shabby-looking block of flats and checked the piece of paper again. Surely this wasn't the place? But it was correct, so she rang the bell for the flat she required. A tinny voice answered immediately, and she gave her name. A moment later the front door was opened by a small man with a limp who said nothing, just ushered her inside and up the grimy stairs to a small flat on the second floor. It was sparsely furnished with two desks, some chairs and a couple of telephones. The man smiled briefly then left through a different door.

Behind one desk sat a woman in civilian clothing, who spoke with an American accent.

'Corporal Kerr, how nice to meet you,' she said, shaking Agnes's hand. 'Please, sit down. Cigarette?'

Agnes sat, shook her head at the offered cigarette, and wondered what the hell was going on.

Why had she been ordered to come here? It was almost clandestine – was this woman a spy or something? She had heard rumours of an organisation that recruited people for some kind of secret work, but she knew nothing about it, or even if the rumours were true. Her head spun, trying to make sense of what was happening.

The woman sat across the desk and perused her, as if she were inspecting her for defects. Heat ran up Agnes's back and prickled along her hairline. She shifted in the chair, wishing she didn't feel so out of sorts. It was obvious she needed to be on her best form – and she was far from that.

'Corporal Kerr,' the woman said. 'What I am going to talk to you about is top secret. You must not say anything to anyone, whatever the outcome of this meeting. Do you understand me?'

Agnes nodded.

'Ye . . .' Her throat dried up; she swallowed and tried again. 'Yes, ma'am.'

'Good.' The woman tapped the end of her cigarette on the edge of an overflowing ashtray. 'Have you heard of an organisation called the Special Operations Executive – the SOE?'

'No, though I think everyone has heard rumours of an outfit who recruit people for some kind of secret work. I know nothing else about it.'

The woman nodded. 'Those rumours are true. The SOE recruits agents to go behind enemy lines, liaise with local Resistance groups and help them fight the Germans. It's vitally important work. It's also extremely dangerous.' She looked straight at Agnes, her eyes searching her face. 'We look for people who can blend in to an area as if they're locals, who can operate a radio efficiently, and who are fit and healthy.' She smiled. 'Your name came to our attention. You're half French, I believe?'

'My mother was French, and I grew up there, before the Germans invaded.'

'Perfect. You are also a radio operator and somewhat of a whizz at deciphering. True?'

'Yes, ma'am, at least I can decipher; not sure about the whizz part.'

'Let us be the judge of that. You are exactly the sort of person we're looking for. I think you could potentially be a great asset to us.' The woman put her hand up, as if to stop Agnes replying, though in fact she was so dumbstruck by what she had heard that she could say nothing. 'Do not make a decision now, today. Go home, think about it and come back in two days and we will talk some more. I know you'll have a hundred questions by then, and I'll be more than happy to answer them.'

Agnes stared at her, not knowing what to think or say. Her brain seemed to have shut down and refused to process half of what the woman had told her.

'Can I ask one thing, please?'

'Of course.'

'You said it's top secret. Is there anyone I can talk to?'

'You can tell one person in your immediate family. Someone you trust implicitly.'

'Not a friend I trust more than anyone else?'

She shook her head. 'Family only.' The woman rose and came around the desk. 'Until we meet again, Corporal Kerr.'

She put her hand out and Agnes took it, automatically. She was ushered through the door and stood in the dingy hallway, for a moment, trying to think.

What had just happened?

And what would she tell Maggie?

Agnes arrived home as the sun dropped behind the church spire opposite. She was exhausted and didn't want to talk, her head swimming with everything she had heard. Maggie made her a cup of tea and began cooking supper while she changed and sipped at the hot drink.

While they ate the omelette and greens, Maggie apologised for not being able to find the sausages, although Agnes had completely forgotten about them. She noticed Maggie's furtive glances and knew she was desperate to hear what had happened. It came as no surprise when she asked, in a carefully casual way, why she had been ordered to see the SO.

'Oh, it was just about some more deciphering stuff they want me to do,' she said, having prepared the words earlier, hoping they would be enough. 'It was at another office across the river – it took ages to get there, and then all the trains were packed and slow.' She shrugged. 'Nothing exciting, really. I have to go again in a couple of days. I won't really know any more until the brass gives me new orders.'

It seemed to satisfy her, though Agnes noted the frown, quickly gone, at her offhand answer.

'Are they transferring you, then?' The question was asked in a deadpan tone, Maggie's eyes on her plate.

'Oh, no, nothing like that,' Agnes said at once. Too quickly? 'Look, can we not talk about work any more tonight? I'm so tired. All I want to do is curl up and read. Do you mind, awfully?'

'Of course not.' Maggie seemed relieved and rose to put the plates in the sink. 'Shall we read the Tennyson together in bed? Then you can fall asleep by the second poem if you want.'

She planted a kiss on the side of Agnes's mouth and pulled her up out of her chair.

Arm in arm they walked into the bedroom and as she undressed, Maggie kissed her neck and shoulders. Agnes lay in bed, her body cupped by Maggie's, reading the book of poetry, so tired she could barely see, her mind going back over the words of the American woman.

The poem mirrored her thoughts . . . intriguing and tempting her, unwilling though she was . . .

> Come into the garden, Maud,
> For the black bat, night, has flown,
> Come into the garden, Maud,
> I am here at the gate alone;
> And the woodbine spices are wafted abroad,
> And the musk of the rose is blown.
>
> For a breeze of morning moves,
> And the planet of Love is on high,
> Beginning to faint in the light that she loves
> In a bed of daffodil sky,
> To faint in the light of the sun she loves,
> To faint in his light and to die.
>
> All night have the roses heard
> The flute, violin, bassoon;
> All night has the casement jessamine stirr'd
> To the dancers dancing in tune;
> Till a silence fell with the waking bird,
> And a hush with the setting moon.

I said to the lily, "There is but one
With whom she has heart to be gay.
When will the dancers leave her alone?
She is weary of dance and play."
Now half to the setting moon are gone,
And half to the rising day;
Low on the sand and loud on the stone
The last wheel echoes away.

I said to the rose, "The brief night goes
In babble and revel and wine.
O young lord-lover, what sighs are those,
For one that will never be thine?
But mine, but mine," so I sware to the rose,
"For ever and ever, mine."

The poem, which they had read together the previous day in the warmth of sunshine, drunk on love and champagne, now seemed full of pathos and she couldn't finish it. A spike of dread filled her with despair.

She knew she was going to break her love's heart, and there was nothing she could do about it.

Chapter 14

Agnes

Two days later Agnes made her way back to the SOE recruitment office. She hadn't slept since the first interview, grief and dread growing within her knowing what she had to do. The office hadn't changed, except that the ashtray was even fuller than the first time she had gone there. The American woman had been joined by the man with a limp, who sat to one side and said nothing.

'I expect you have some questions you'd like answers to,' the woman said, after Agnes sat down opposite her, in the same chair as before. 'Don't be afraid to ask anything; nothing is too small, if it helps you come to a decision.'

'I only have one question,' Agnes said. 'How long would it be before I started? Would I have time to put my affairs in order, so to speak?'

'You would join the next batch of recruits within two weeks.' The American looked her squarely in the eye, her head on one side, as if considering something about her. 'We have dire need of more potential agents with your radio skills and language expertise. Good men and women are being killed every day, especially radio operators. The Germans are becoming experts at tracking them down; the attrition rate, I'm sad to say, is extremely high, but we must keep on helping the Resistance groups; it's imperative. If you decide to join us, as soon as your training is finished, you would be sent to a group who has lost their radio operator.' She lit up a cigarette, took a long drag and blew the smoke up towards the discoloured ceiling, then looked at Agnes again. 'You should know that many groups are infiltrated by spies and collaborators working for the Nazis. One of your most important tasks would be to identify any potential traitors who could give you away.'

Agnes sat back in the chair, trying to take in the woman's words. It was obviously dangerous work, but then, wasn't that what she already knew?

In truth, only the first sentence stuck in her brain, the rest had washed over her, for her mind was already made up.

Two weeks until she must leave Maggie.

So soon ...

She dragged in a breath, cigarette smoke bitter on her tongue.

'If you think I can be of use in freeing my mother country from the Nazis, then I want to help.'

The woman seemed a little taken aback. 'Are you sure you don't want to know more about the job and what it entails? Most people do.'

She shook her head. 'Ma'am, if it wasn't for the Germans, my mother would still be alive. There is nothing I want more than to help kick the bastards out of France.' She paused for a moment. 'To be honest, if I discovered all the awful things I'll be involved in, I would probably lose my nerve, so better not to know too much, don't you think?'

The woman narrowed her eyes and fixed Agnes with a look, as if she were weighing up whether she had what it took.

'Very well,' she said. 'You sound very certain, and that's good. My colleague here will take your details and give you all the information you need about joining your training batch.' She stood up, holding out her hand. 'Welcome to the Special Operations Executive, Corporal Kerr. You have a lot of work to get through before you're sent to France. I hope you're prepared for it.'

'Ready for anything, ma'am,' said Agnes, with a confidence that was the opposite of how she felt at that moment.

She took the outstretched hand and shook it, hoping her palm wasn't sweating too badly.

The man, who had said nothing so far, took her through the forms she needed to fill in, and where and when she would start her training. She left half an hour later, a kernel of excitement and anticipation in her belly, sitting side by side with dread and guilt at the thought of abandoning Maggie.

She wasn't sure how she managed to act normally that evening. Maggie didn't seem to notice anything amiss, and Agnes did her best to join in her delight that the long-awaited sausages had finally been tracked down. She conjured up a mockery of a cassoulet, with some overgrown broad beans and a carrot. It wasn't anything like the delicious dish she remembered her mother making when she was a child, but it made Maggie happy, which was all she cared about.

When they went to bed, their lovemaking took on a whole new level of passion, Agnes clinging to her long after Maggie fell into an exhausted sleep.

How could she do it?

Never mind the war.

Never mind the Germans and what they had done to her country.

She couldn't leave; not when she had just found the happiness she'd never thought would be hers.

She owed Maggie everything; her love deserved so much more from her than this.

How could she be so cruel?

So selfish?

And so on, through the long, dark hours that night, and every night, until the end of the week, when her shifts changed and she was due to go on night duty. Maggie worked day shifts, so they would only see each other in passing, when she arrived home in the early morning as Maggie got ready for work.

Sergeant Atkins had been made aware of her leaving, and said she was sorry to see her go. The change of shift was engineered so that she wouldn't be working alongside the rest of her usual team, avoiding awkward questions about where she was going. It all seemed very clandestine and outlandish, but she supposed being an agent meant nobody could know what she was up to. She would miss Pat and Clarice, and even Walter and Sergeant Atkins had grown in her affections over the months she had worked with them.

A seed of doubt made her wonder if it was worth it. After all, what difference could she possibly make in the grand scheme of things? Her work with the WAAF was important – she was damn good at her job and people relied on her.

Too late to turn back now, you fool.

She had made her bed, burnt her bridges, leapt in without thinking it through. Every cliché she had ever heard swam round her head, driving her crazy. The sooner she left, the better; the waiting was killing her, and she wasn't sure how long she could keep up the pretence of normality before she fell in a heap and admitted everything to Maggie.

When the day finally dawned, she came back from her last shift as it was growing light, and found Maggie sitting on a stool in the hallway pulling on her boots, ready to make her way out to the garage where she kept her motorcycle.

Agnes leant in and kissed her, long and deep, memorising the feel of warm lips and sweet breath on her mouth, not able to speak, grief a massive rock in her throat.

'Well, this is a nice way to start the day,' Maggie said, clasping Agnes's waist and drawing her down.

They kissed again, then Maggie rose and took Agnes by the hand, dragging her into the bedroom, where their kisses became more urgent, clothing was ripped off and they sank onto the bed, their bodies wrapped around each other.

For Agnes it was almost unbearable: passion laced with grief and guilt knowing that this was the last time she would lie in Maggie's arms and be loved. Afterwards they lay for a while, holding each other, not saying anything, until Maggie sat up.

'Sergeant Billings is going to have my hide,' she said, a smile lifting one side of her mouth. 'It's worth it, though.'

She bent and kissed Agnes on her bare shoulder, her hand sliding down and caressing the taut skin of one hip, then slipping lower until Agnes groaned. Her mouth moved from shoulder to breast, and Agnes pulled her back down and wrapped a leg around her middle, trapping her. Maggie chuckled, deep in her throat. She kissed her mouth once more, then pulled away. Within five minutes, she had dressed. 'See you tonight. Sleep well, my love,' she said, and then was gone.

As soon as she left, Agnes was bereft, an aching space inside her. She put her face into the pillow, the scent of Maggie's perfume still on it, and gave her grief free rein until she had no tears left.

She couldn't just leave, not without saying anything, or at least giving Maggie a clue as to why she had disappeared.

She must get up; she dragged herself out of the bed, dressed, and packed the few things she would need. She had been told not to take anything of a personal nature that could potentially give her away. The one thing she took, hidden in the bottom of her small case, was the photograph Walter had taken of them at the river. He had developed the film and given her two copies a few days earlier. She left the second on the mantelpiece for Maggie. It was a risk she was prepared to take, to remind her of her love.

Then she sat at the table and composed a short note. It didn't give anything away that could jeopardise her new role, but she couldn't go without giving Maggie something to cling on to. At the end, she made a promise to come back safely, that they would meet again and she mustn't worry.

Where to put it though, where it would be out of sight, but Maggie was sure to find it?

Her eye fell on the book of Tennyson poetry, lying on the bedside table. Folding the note in three and writing Maggie's name on the front, she placed it in the page they had been reading. She knew it was the perfect place; could imagine her opening the book, trying to find some comfort in her distress and the note being there, letting her know she hadn't been spurned or abandoned.

She lifted her case, took her coat from the back of the door, and with tears threatening, cast a final look around at the place where she had been happier than at any time in her life. Walking out, she closed the door quietly, and then left.

Chapter 15

Claire

On my way home from visiting Aunt M, I passed the local library, and on a whim parked the car and went inside. I had no idea where to search for anything to do with missing persons during the war, but it had to be a good place to start. A lady at the reception desk looked up and smiled.

'Can I help you?'

I explained what I wanted to find out, and she typed something into the desktop computer in front of her.

'This might be helpful,' she said, turning the screen so I could see what she'd found. 'The National Archives at Kew would be the best place, I think.' She typed in another question. 'Their records are available online, but if you have queries you might find it more useful to visit the archives yourself. And we have a small section in our reference area where you may find something to help you in your search. Our archivist is very knowledgeable on the Second World War; I'm sure he would be happy to talk to you. He's on his lunch break, but he'll be back later.'

I thanked her and promised to come back if I needed more help.

As soon as I got home, I replayed the recording I'd made of Aunt M telling me her story, noting down anything I thought I could use in the search. I thanked God for the internet. Surely, I would find something about Agnes, even if it was only her date of birth.

I looked up the National Archives and spent some time searching through their Second World War catalogue for anything relating to women in the forces. The records didn't have much information – I found both Agnes and Margaret there, from their WAAF days. Only the name and dates of service. Agnes Kerr served until the end of the war, which meant she survived – that at least, was something. Now if only I could discover where she served . . .

Late in the afternoon I went back to the library and asked if I could see the archivist. A small, slim man with a clipped moustache, who must have been in his seventies, came to meet me. I could imagine him in the army. He walked as if he were marching on a parade ground; I almost expected him to salute. He introduced himself as Harry Bowden and asked what I was looking for.

'Do you have any information on a woman called Agnes Kerr? She was a WAAF in London during the Second World War. She seems to have dropped off the radar around autumn 1943.'

'That isn't much to go on,' he said. 'What did she do in the WAAFs, do you know?'

'Radio operator and decipherer. She was a friend of my aunt's and she went missing around that time. They worked together in London, decoding messages from Europe. She was half French, if that's any use. My aunt never discovered what happened to her, though I've found her service record in the National Archives and she served until the end of the war.'

'Hmm. Half French and a radio operator, you say? That's interesting. Perhaps she was sent to Bletchley,' he said, almost to himself. 'Follow me. If she was transferred from radio operating, there are a couple of things she might have been sent to do. I'll take a guess – might be wrong, but might not.'

He trotted off towards the back of the library. I followed him down a flight of stairs to a large basement with a faint musty smell. It was dimly lit, with a row of desks that had lights above them. At this late stage of the day, it was almost deserted. Mr Bowden took me to a shelf full of books on the far side against the wall. Running his finger along the line of spines, he stopped at one and picked it out. Leading me to one of the desks, he switched on the lamp, sat, and pulled up another chair beside him. Taking the book, he placed it on the desk and put his hand over it in an almost protective gesture.

'This book tells the tales of all the women who were sent to serve in France.' Noticing my confusion, he paused. 'Have you ever heard of the SOE?'

I frowned. The acronym was familiar, but I couldn't place it. I shook my head. 'What does it stand for?'

'Special Operations Executive,' he said. 'It was a secret organisation, made up of men and women who were sent to France and other occupied countries to help the local Resistance groups fight the Nazis.'

'What has that to do with Agnes Kerr?'

'Those who were recruited had to sign the Official Secrets Act. Apart from their families, they couldn't tell anyone where they were going or what they were doing.'

My head spun. If he had guessed right, my search might already be over and I could let Aunt M know what happened to her friend straight away. It all seemed too easy.

Something clicked in my head. 'So perhaps she would have been someone of interest to this Special Operations Executive?'

Harry Bowden nodded. 'If she spoke fluent French and was a radio operator, she would certainly be the kind of person they'd be looking for.' He dropped his eyes to the cover of the book. 'If Agnes Kerr was recruited by the SOE, she will be in here. But I must warn you, many of them did not come home – and some of their stories are horrifying.'

I nodded; the atmosphere in the cavernous room was so quiet and Mr Bowden's voice so grave that I was a little spooked. Did I really want to open the book and discover that Agnes had come to some ghastly end? I had to clear my throat before I could speak. 'Agnes Kerr did not come home after the war, as far as I know, though her record shows her serving until the end, as I said. My aunt has always wondered what happened to her. It would put her mind at rest if I can find out the truth about her.'

'Very well. Let's check the list of those who are in this book.'

I opened the slim volume and scanned down the list of chapters, each one headed with the name of a woman. And she was there – Agnes Kerr in plain black typeface. The hairs on the back of my neck rose and a chill draught blew across my face. I didn't want to be in that dim, musty room when I discovered what had happened to her. This was too private, too personal. It was more than a distraction from my own problems; it was the life – the lives – of two women who had been friends and then lost each other. They deserved my undivided attention.

'I'd like to borrow this, if I may?' I said, closing the book before Mr Bowden's curiosity and enthusiasm got the better of him.

He seemed disappointed, but nodded and we went back up to the reception area. While the librarian checked out the book, we chatted for a moment.

'You should go and ask for her wartime records at Kew,' he said, as I shook his hand and thanked him for his help. 'Some records have been lost, but you might be lucky and find what you're looking for.'

'I'll do that. Thanks again.'

The next day I phoned the National Archive office and asked if I could look at Agnes's record from her time in the SOE. I was given a time slot for someone to supervise me while I read them. The thing I'd dreaded discovering in the library book – that she'd been tortured or executed by the Gestapo – didn't seem to have been her fate. Her chapter was short on facts compared to some of the other women and I was curious to know why. There was no reference on what happened to her after the war, so the mystery remained.

I became engrossed in reading about the SOE, hoping to find some other small clue that might help. It was hard to believe what ordinary people were expected to do, and the level of physical training recruits went through. The deprivations of their time in the Scottish training camp made me shudder, but I supposed it made sense – considering what some of them had to go through once they were in the field, they had to be tough. It made me sit back and re-evaluate the picture I had of Agnes in my head; Aunt M might remember her as a sweet young thing, but she must have had a core of steel running through her just to have been good enough to become an agent.

The secrecy surrounding the organisation made it clear Agnes couldn't tell Aunt M what she was doing, once she'd been accepted as a recruit. Only immediate family could be told where she was going and Aunt M was her flatmate, nothing more.

I sat back and digested the information, trying to put myself in Agnes's shoes. How difficult had it been for her? It was evident recruits were chosen based on their knowledge and skills, and their ability to speak foreign languages. She must have been an obvious choice, going by what Aunt M told me about her decoding and radio expertise, and her French background. It seemed extraordinary that someone so young was involved in such a clandestine and dangerous organisation, and yet there must have been hundreds of young men and women like her over the war years. When I thought of the term 'secret agent' I pictured films like James Bond or *Casablanca* – tough, middle-aged men with rugged looks and gravelly voices – not a twenty-year-old French girl.

I was early for my appointment at the National Archives, and spent an impatient twenty minutes wandering around the exhibitions and displays on view. The place was a surprise – I'd imagined it to be an old, fusty building, with Doric columns and dark corridors leading to silent rooms. Its light, bright style was welcoming, and the lovely grounds around it set it off well. I'd ordered Agnes's records when I made the appointment, and after I'd proved my identity and registered, a smartly dressed young woman led me to one of the reading rooms and brought the documents to me.

I'd passed off the shivers I had experienced when seeing Agnes's name in the library book as nothing more than me being over-wrought. The original records of her wartime exploits brought just as visceral a reaction, though. Agnes felt so close she could have been looking over my shoulder. I have never believed in ghosts but at that moment I wouldn't have been surprised to see her standing behind me. Yet, this was no dim basement in an old building, but a modern construction with every hi-tech resource anyone could wish for.

The supervisor looked at me enquiringly, wondering no doubt, why I stood like a dummy, staring at the file. The documents were yellowed, some torn and watermarked, some with words blacked out. I carefully began to examine the papers. In truth, there seemed little of use to me. Dates of when she was recruited, the start and finish of her training, when she was posted to France. Nothing about the end of the war, of her coming back to Britain. Or of her death at the hands of her enemy.

Thankfully, the information I most needed to find was on the final sheet. She had been posted to a town in the Pyrenees called St Jean Layrisse. The name jumped off the page at me – there was the shiver again, rippling through me, making the hairs on my arms rise.

I swear I touched nothing, but at that moment the papers slid off the table and on to the floor. The supervisor quickly gathered them up, muttering about careless handling and didn't I know how fragile they were?

I apologised. How did it even happen? I was so clumsy. I hoped nothing was damaged. I bent to help her, but she'd picked them all up and carefully checked each piece before putting them back in the file.

'Can I help you with anything else?' Her voice clipped, grudging.

I shook my head, apologised again, wanting to leave, my skin clammy though the room wasn't cold.

Out in the fresh air, I couldn't believe I'd allowed myself to be spooked for a second time. What was wrong with me? But, for all the strangeness, my search had moved forward – I knew where Agnes had been based. Now, perhaps, I was on my way to solving the mystery of her disappearance.

Chapter 16

Claire

The following day I took Aunt M back to her old house, which had been closed up since she moved into Stanbury Hall. The closer we got, the tenser she became. She shrank into the front passenger seat of the car, fiddling with the buttons on her coat, a frown cutting deep trenches in her forehead.

'We don't have to do this, you know,' I said. 'I just thought you might like to visit your old home. Are you happy to go back? Just say if it brings up too many painful memories.'

I glanced at her then kept my eyes on the road, concentrating on my driving; the traffic around Richmond was busy, and I didn't want to miss the turn-off into Cherry Lane, where the Chimneys sat on a large corner plot.

'Oh no, I've no sad memories of this house, Claire, dear. I bought it years after the war, and it was a happy place – don't you remember coming to stay when you were a child?'

'Of course, I do. I loved staying here for school holidays, but that was as much to do with it being your home as the house itself. And of course, it became my home too when you

115

took me in after Mother left, though to be honest I wouldn't have cared where you lived, it was being a part of your life that mattered to me. But I want to see the old place. You seem anxious, though.'

'I am,' she admitted. 'I'm worried once I go inside, I won't want to go back to Stanbury Hall. This is my home. I hated having to leave, you know.' She sighed.

Why didn't I consider how she might react to going back where she'd been happy and independent? I pulled the car over into a bus stop.

'Oh God – sorry, Aunt M,' I said. 'Let's go and have a cup of tea somewhere, and I'll take you back to Stanbury Hall afterwards.'

'No. This is something I must do, and if I don't do it today, I'll have to do it another,' she said, her jaw tightening. 'I left almost all my things in that house, you know. Everything happened so quickly when I moved, and packing up seemed too much after my little accident, when the fire brigade had to rescue me. I locked the door and walked away – I was frightened something really dreadful might happen if I stayed. I couldn't trust myself anymore, you see. But there are so many of my things still inside and I need to sort them out. Especially my books. The poor things, they'll be covered in dust and spiders by now, I should think. Let's go and rescue them, shall we?' She smiled and sat up, squaring her shoulders. 'Come on, dear. A bus will be along in a moment. What are you waiting for?'

I grinned at her, returned to the traffic and continued until we reached the Chimneys. Driving through the wrought-iron gates and up to the front door, it felt as if the outside world had disappeared – the mature hornbeams and red-brick wall surrounding the grounds shut out the noise of traffic.

The house backed onto woods that were part of a large estate and led down, eventually, to the Thames. Seeing it again I remembered running wild in the garden with some of the local kids, climbing over the wall to explore the woods, pretending we were hiding from unspecified 'baddies' and having to live off the land. This place not only held memories for Aunt M. I found it difficult to shut out my own thoughts of those happy days.

I helped her out of the car, and she gave me the keys to the front door. The building always made me smile: a beautifully balanced five-bedroomed Georgian house, the front door set in the centre, with two large windows on either side, and six more above. To one side was a later addition that housed the modern kitchen and boot room.

I'd come home.

I opened the door with shaking hands. Aunt M walked slowly up the two shallow steps into the large hallway and stopped to look around. Everything was in shadowy darkness; shutters and heavy curtains kept out the light and prying eyes, and it gave the impression of the house holding its breath.

Leaving the front door open to let in a little daylight, I went up to the first landing of the wide staircase and pulled back the deep green velvet curtains covering the window. Low, spring sunshine fought past the grime on the outside of the glass and helped to illuminate the hall below. I rubbed at the lowest pane and gazed down at the gardens, where I remembered playing in and out of the rose beds and under the pergola with its swathes of wisteria and clematis. Now it looked like a jungle, with shrubs and trees growing into one another, and dead, straw-like grasses bent into a thick mat where the lawns should be. I made a note to myself to find a gardener who could come and keep things tidy. Aunt M would hate to see it in such a state.

She'd wandered into the large sitting room to the left of the front door; again, all the windows were shuttered, and I hurried to open them up. The last thing I wanted was for her to trip over something and break a leg. Once there was enough light to see, it was plain all the furniture was covered with dust sheets. There was a musty, unlived-in smell about the room, with a back-note of something long dead. My nose led me to the fireplace, where I found a baby pigeon – or the remnants of one – which must have fallen down the chimney and broken its neck. I picked it up with a pair of coal tongs and took it outside, dumping it under a bush.

Returning to the room, I found Aunt M had removed a sheet from a large glass-fronted bookcase, opened the doors and was gazing at the titles intently. She drew her fingers along the line of spines, stopping at one or two, as if reintroducing herself to old friends. A small, distant smile lit her face, and she mouthed the titles as she went. No spectacles were required, I realised – she knew each book and its place on the shelf, by heart.

'Do you want to take them with you when we go?' I asked.

'Yes,' she said, not taking her eyes off the books. 'There are a few other things I want to take, too, but my books are the most important.'

'I have some boxes in the back of the car,' I said. 'I'll go and fetch them.'

I collected the boxes and pulled an armchair across in front of the bookcase for Aunt M, tucking a plaid rug around her to ward off the chill. I began taking the books out and packing them up, according to her instructions. The final few were slim volumes of poetry, something I'd not read for years. Aunt M was flagging, her shoulders drooping with tiredness.

'Do you want any of this poetry, or shall I leave these books behind? There's a collection of Tennyson, some Keats . . .' I checked the titles '. . . and one with a selection by several poets.' I held them up for her to see. One slid out of my hand and landed on its spine on the floor, the pages opening in clumps. 'Oh, damn. Sorry, I hope it's not damaged.'

I picked up the Tennyson and checked the cover, which must have been damp at some time going by the large water stain on the front. Inside the flyleaf was a handwritten inscription, the ink smudged in places.

"To my darling Maggie. My one and only true love, my saviour, my soulmate. I will love you until the end of time. A."

I swallowed a lump in my throat. What a romantic thing to write. Of course, Aunt M must have had her share of lovers during her lifetime. What man wouldn't fall in love with her? I wondered who A was, and what happened to him.

Feeling like a voyeur, I dusted the book off, sad that some of the pages had stuck together from being damp. A folded sheet of paper dropped out of it on to the floor.

'Not that one, dear. I simply can't bear to read those beautiful poems anymore,' Aunt M said, a catch in her voice. 'I'd almost forgotten that book was there.'

'Something's fallen out of it,' I said, picking up the paper and looking at the faded writing on the front of it, crinkled at the edge, where it too must have got wet. 'This was inside the book, Aunt M. I think it's a letter or a note or something.'

'What's that you said? A letter? Why would there be a letter inside my book?' She seemed genuinely bewildered.

'Perhaps you left it there and then forgot about it,' I suggested. 'Do you want to look at it?'

'I can't imagine it's of any importance, now,' she said. 'It's probably just an old bill or something. Throw it in the bin.'

I looked at the folded piece of paper again; like the inscription the ink had run a little, but the writing was perfectly legible. *Maggie*, written in the same beautiful, elegant hand; a shiver ran down my back, as if a ghost had walked over my grave.

'I don't think it's a bill. Shall I take a quick look for you?'

'If you like, dear.'

It was strange opening something that probably hadn't been looked at for decades. Taking the single sheet of paper out and going over to the window where the light was better, I scanned the short letter. As I read it, I caught my breath at the realisation of what I held.

The note was dated October 1943.

Dearest Maggie,

By the time you read this I'll be gone. I feel wretched leaving without being able to tell you why, but please believe me when I say I have no choice, my love.

I've been recruited by a different outfit and after training they're sending me away. I wish I could tell you more, but I'm not allowed to. They've made me sign the Official Secrets Act. It could be dangerous work, but if I can help my mother country, I must do it.

So, I'm leaving you for a few months, my darling. I'm sorry I couldn't tell you before. I know you thought I was being beastly; it hurt so much not to be allowed to say anything and you've been wonderful in not complaining, even though I could tell you knew I was up to something. It was all to do with this job, but I wouldn't have blamed you if you had shown me the door.

Please don't worry about me, I will be perfectly fine and back before you know. I promise you we will see each other when this awful war is over.

All my love and always in my thoughts,
Agnes

Glancing down the letter, I felt something do a swan dive in my stomach. Talk about a shock – the words leapt off the page at me, turning everything I thought I knew about my aunt on its head. Questions jostled for space, but I said nothing for a moment, thinking about the effect the letter might have on Aunt M. It was plain this was not just a letter to a friend – these two had been much, much more to each other. No wonder my poor aunt had never forgotten Agnes; she was the love of her life.

I crouched down in front of her.

'It's not a bill,' I said. 'Maggie is the name on the front. I'm guessing it's for you. Are you sure you didn't just forget it was there?'

She looked at me and then down at the letter, as if reluctant to take it from me. Perhaps she heard something in my voice; she raised her eyes to mine again.

'Agnes was the only one who called me Maggie,' she said.

With a shaking hand, she took the sheet of notepaper and stared at it as if terrified of what she might find there. I found her spectacles in her handbag and passed them to her. Putting them on, she slowly unfolded the yellowing paper and I went back over to the window, wrapping my arms around my body. The room felt even colder, although my shivers weren't only from the chilly air. It felt as if I was seeing the real Aunt M for the first time – the words of the inscription and letter were plain – Agnes was far more than a friend and flatmate; of that, I was sure.

After a moment I heard a quiet sob and hurried over to her. The letter and glasses lay in her lap, her eyes were closed and tears tracked their trails down her cheeks. I gently took her cold hands and dropped a kiss on them.

'She didn't just leave you without a word, did she? Agnes didn't want to go without telling you what she was doing but was bound to secrecy.'

Aunt M nodded and opened her eyes, the lower lids red and pooled with unshed tears.

'I *knew* in my heart she wouldn't just have disappeared without saying anything, but I told myself not to be so naïve,' she whispered. She stroked the letter, tracing the signature with her finger, then pushed it away from her in a gesture that spoke of frustration – anger even. 'Why oh why didn't I look in the book? If I'd only picked it up and opened it, instead of shoving it in the drawer out of sight . . .'

She looked at me, pain etched on her face. I had no idea what to say and wasn't entirely convinced that she hadn't just forgotten it was there. It seemed such a strange thing for Agnes to do – why leave the letter in that book? Why not somewhere much more obvious? Did the book have some significance?

'Why didn't you?'

She dropped her gaze, and a blush coloured her pale cheeks. I didn't want to embarrass her by asking directly what their relationship had been, but she must realise I'd grasp the significance of the letter.

'It was too hard,' she said and gave another sob, almost making me lose what little control I had, too. 'We both loved Tennyson, and it was a reminder of what I'd lost.' She took a breath and looked me straight in the eye. 'You read the letter – you must realise that Agnes and I were more than just friends. Does that shock you? It's not something you would have expected from your old auntie, I bet.'

There was a glint in her eye and a defiant set to her jaw. What could I say? Yes, I was shocked, not so much to learn my ninety-year-old spinster aunt had had a love affair with another woman, though it was quite a revelation, but that she had successfully hidden such a fundamental part of herself. And yet, it made sense of so many things I had wondered about over the years. Aunt M's solitary personal life, for one, when she was so vivacious and sociable, and had so many friends. I had never had an inkling, and it made me sad to think she had never felt able to tell me.

'It's a bit of a shock, I admit,' I said. 'I've often wondered why you never married. I guess I know the answer now. It can't have been easy, back then? Society was a whole lot less accepting of same-sex relationships than it is nowadays.'

'Do you know, in some ways, I think the war made it easier than it might have been ten or twenty years later,' she said. 'In a big city like London, where it was pretty chaotic, you could get away with things that would have been seen as unacceptable during peacetime. Everyone lived for today, for who knew what might happen tomorrow. Does that make sense?'

It did. Though how would I possibly know what it was like? Yet I could imagine everyone wanting to make the most of every minute of every day.

'It does,' I said. 'I still don't understand why you never found the letter though. Even if Agnes had gone, didn't she give the book to you? Surely it helped to remind you of her?'

A new tear appeared, forging a trail down Aunt M's powdered cheek.

'Because, when I couldn't find her, I thought she'd thrown me over for someone else. That she had gone into hiding from me.' I could see the pain in her eyes, still fresh, even after such a long time. 'It hurt so much. I was heartbroken, couldn't bear to remember what it was like being with her.'

'She must have thought you'd open the book again, to leave her note there . . .'

'It lay on my bedside table. We would read to each other before we went to sleep. I don't think she could have realised how distraught I was at her disappearing.' Aunt M lifted the letter again, soaking up each word. She dropped it onto her lap and put her hand over it, staring at me. 'And why didn't she come home? The letter says she'd only be gone a few months and we would be reunited after the war. It ended less than two years later – so why stay away? She could at least have written to me, let me know she was safe and well. I still don't know what happened to her. Did she die?' she said. 'Whatever she was doing must have been dangerous, surely?'

'I don't know the answers to all of your questions, Aunt M. But I've been doing some research on Agnes and I've discovered where she went.' Aunt M's gaze sharpened and she leant forward. I dragged a chair across and sat beside her. 'She was sent to France, as an agent, working for an organisation called the Special Operations Executive, helping the French Resistance,' I said, squeezing her hands. 'And this note confirms it. I'm going to keep hunting and hope I can find out more for you.'

Aunt M's face fell and she blinked away tears.

'SOE,' she whispered. 'I remember hearing about them and what they did during the war. Their agents often didn't make it back home; the work was so dangerous.' A sob escaped her, then she took a breath and dabbed at her eyes. 'Is that what befell Agnes, do you think? But surely I would have heard something? Although, I suppose if it was a secret mission, they wouldn't have told me where she was, would they?' She slumped back in the chair, her face pale and drawn with exhaustion.

'If it's any comfort, I couldn't find anything that said she had been killed in action or taken prisoner by the Nazis,' I said, wanting to give her some kind of hope. 'So let's not give up yet. I'll keep searching, and you never know, maybe I'll discover what became of her.'

My heart bled for her. She looked so lost. She'd carried her secret for over seventy years. Well, it might be late in the day, but I would do what I could for her from now on. She held the letter as if it were a lifeline, connecting her to Agnes. It made me determined to find out what happened to her elusive lover, no matter what it might take. The question Aunt M kept asking ran around my head and I had to find the answer.

Why didn't she come home?

Chapter 17

Agnes

FRANCE – 1944

Parachuting in seemed the most surreal way to return to the country of her birth. Agnes shifted in the constricting space of the plane and loosened her scarf a little. The heat and noise invaded her body, making her head thump, and she tried, unsuccessfully, to find a comfortable position and shut it out. The despatcher had advised them to sleep if they could. It would be three hours till they reached the drop zone and who knew how long before they had the chance to rest again after they jumped.

How the hell are we supposed to sleep?

Her mind slipped back, and guilt was a sour taste on her tongue. The letter she had left for Maggie was nowhere near enough to explain what she was doing and why. More of a salve to her conscience than anything else. To hell with the rules – she had to leave some clue as to what she was up to.

The young man sitting next to her lounged in a relaxed manner, his long legs splayed out in front of him. He had his arms crossed and his head lolled backwards, but she knew he wasn't sleeping, just as none of the other three were sleeping.

She was the only girl.

Not a girl; a woman. She needed to keep her own sense of self-belief. The brass had faith in her capabilities, which included the fact she was a grown-up, not a child. She supposed it didn't help she barely made five feet and an inch in her stockings and had the face of a naïve fifteen-year-old. But it was one of the things the recruitment officer said made her ideal for the job. Nobody would suspect a slip of a girl of being an agent and a radio communications expert. She had surprised her instructors with her ability to decipher the most complicated of messages, and the thrill she felt when she discovered the message in a piece of text never lessened.

This. This is what I can do. And if it helps kick the Nazis out of France then I'm proud to do my bit.

She unwrapped the scarf from around her throat. It was the only thing of her own she had been allowed to wear, because she'd had it since she was a child. A reminder of home in the heart of Dordogne. Only four years ago – another lifetime.

Bitterness rose like bile and she pushed the memories away.

Her neighbour stirred and stretched, bringing her thoughts back to the present.

'Are we close?'

His accent was a drawl, which could have been American to her untuned ear. When they'd met at the final briefing, he said he was from some small town near Montreal; she hoped he could pull off a convincing French accent. He reached into his pocket for a smoke and lit it with a gold-cased lighter.

'Put that out. Do you want to blow us all to hell?' The RAF sergeant grabbed the cigarette and put it under his boot, grinding it till there was nothing left. 'I'll throw you out without a chute if you try another stunt like that,' he said, his face up close to the shrinking Canadian.

'Sorry, Sarge. Wasn't thinking. Won't happen again.'

Agnes stared at him. How could this man be so relaxed he'd forgotten smoking was banned on the plane?

He glanced at her and shrugged, a small tight smile giving away his nerves.

'I hope you're going to remember our training more readily, once we're in the field.' She couldn't resist the dig. Her nerves were pulled as tight as a bowstring and she just wanted this part to be over. The ridiculous jumpsuit enveloped her, and the straps of the parachute dug into her shoulders and chest. Tension raced around her body. She prayed she wouldn't freeze and forget her training once she jumped.

'I'll be fine once we're on the ground. I hate flying though. No control, y'know, just relying on this sheet of tin to stay in the air.' The Canadian took his spectacles off and rubbed his eyes.

He's as nervous as I am.

It was comforting in some way. She tried to recall which of the French names he'd been given.

'Are you Gilles? I've been given Céleste Sarraute as my under-cover name.' She tested the unfamiliar name on her tongue. She was no longer Agnes Kerr and needed to remember that. 'We should get into character.'

She spoke in French, the language of her childhood coming as naturally to her as dipping bread into a bowl of hot chocolate.

'Philippe LeConte. Gilles is sitting at the end.'

'I know there are two drop points. Are you jumping at the first?'

'Yeah. The other guys are headed for Toulouse. It's just you and me for Montréjeau, kiddo.'

A warm rush of relief was a welcome change from the nervous tension, and Agnes smiled at him.

'I'm glad we don't have to wait another hour before we jump. I want to get on with it, now we're almost there.'

'Me too, kiddo. Me too.'

The sergeant checked their parachutes one last time, tightened the straps, and hooked on their static lines. The plane began descending, and he opened the trap and stared out into the clear night air. Agnes glimpsed trees swaying in the plane's draught, and the occasional darker shadow of an isolated farm rushing by, as the Halifax dropped lower. The cold wind brought tears to her eyes, blurring her vision, and her stomach clenched.

The despatcher shouted above the drone of the plane's engines as he watched for the drop zone.

'No, no, nothing yet. We're going around again. It should be close now.'

Agnes snatched a look at Philippe, and he winked at her, his expression alert and expectant.

The sergeant leapt up and yelled at them.

'ACTION STATIONS. Prepare to jump.'

She moved to the open trap and stood at the edge, staring into the black void, running over everything she'd learnt in her mind. What to do if the chute didn't open or became entangled; how to land. Her low-heeled town shoes would give her no protection, so her ankles were bound up tightly with bandages to protect them.

When the time came it seemed as if her mind was separate from her body, working unconsciously. The dozen heavy packages had gone out first, and then she was out too, the freezing wind taking her breath, her stomach up in her throat somewhere, until it dropped with a nauseating swooping sensation. She fell fast and straight before her chute opened and she was jerked upwards for a moment, the straps biting into her breasts. Glancing up at the billowing silk, she prayed the lines wouldn't twist and breathed a small thanks as it opened into a beautiful arc, slowing her fall, and allowing a gentle descent, giving her time to pick out a few solitary stars peeking through the broken cloud. For a few moments she felt horribly exposed, naked to anyone who might be watching. She floated above the trees and looked down at the shadowy forested hills below her. It seemed as if she was suspended for an age, desperate to get to the safety of terra firma.

She couldn't see Philippe, but spotted the packages hitting the ground in a clearing of trees, amid dim lights set out to guide their direction. Her training taking over, she prepared herself for the landing, the field racing up to meet her as she bent her knees and hit the ground. Her parachute dragged her over tussocky grass and sharp little rocks, and she dug her heels into the ground and grabbed the lines, pulling with all her strength to stop herself. Coming to a halt when the canopy got caught on a bank of gorse, she stood and found herself staring at a small, wiry-looking man smiling at her.

There was a moment of panic as she wondered if she was in the right place and whether he was, in fact, a French Resistant, or if he might produce a gun and shoot her on sight. What if it was a trap set by the Germans to lure them into the wrong place? She couldn't breathe, her throat closed, and stars pricked at her eyes as she fought to get oxygen into her lungs. Staggering under the weight of the chute, she put a hand out to steady herself, and the man grabbed her arm and spoke. His voice dragged a sigh out of her battered body, the accent a thick local dialect that bore almost no resemblance to the French she'd grown up speaking. Her pulse slowed fractionally, and she smiled back at him.

'Welcome, mademoiselle. My name is Georges Luzent. Here, let me help you. We need to get out of here as soon as possible.'

He gathered up the silk parachute with a brisk efficiency and within a few moments she was following him across to the other side of the field, where a small truck was half hidden in the trees that ringed the open space. Philippe leant against it, holding a dirty handkerchief to his forehead.

'A rock,' he said, grinning. He removed his spectacles from an inside pocket. 'Good job I'd taken these off, before we jumped.'

She stood on tiptoe, took the handkerchief from him and looked at the gash above his right eyebrow.

'You'll live.'

There was activity all around as men gathered the packages from the field and loaded them onto a flat cart pulled by a pair of oxen. Agnes and Philippe climbed into the truck, while Georges issued orders to the rest of the group, then jumped into the driver's seat and they set off on a narrow, overgrown forest track. The ride was slow, and Agnes breathed in the scents of the forest – pine resin, a whiff of woodsmoke, and the occasional earthy stench of a farmyard – the smells of her childhood. It all seemed so familiar, she found it difficult to believe her beloved France was in the grip of occupation and war.

Squeezed in between Georges and Philippe, she relaxed for the first time in what seemed like days. When the truck stopped, she realised with a jolt her head had dropped onto Philippe's shoulder. He grinned at her.

'We're here, kiddo. Sorry to disturb your beauty sleep.'

They had halted outside an ancient farmhouse that looked as if it had grown out of the wooded hillside behind it. In the light of a half-moon that slipped in and out of the clouds, shadows hid the building until they were almost on top of it. Windows on either side of the door glowed with a low light and there was the warm, pungent smell of animals close by. Agnes dragged herself out of the truck behind the two men, the cold deep inside her bones. Trying to shake off her fatigue, she followed them into the old house and was hit by a wall of aromas and warmth. Flames crackling in the enormous fireplace heated a copper cauldron that hung from an iron hook. Saliva flooded Agnes's mouth like a grape exploding on her tongue.

Georges' wife, Florence, a straight-backed, rather severe-looking woman until she smiled, welcomed them into her home, fussing over Philippe's cut head, and the scratches on Agnes's hands from the gorse prickles. Their jumpsuits were bundled up and thrown in a corner, and Florence suggested they freshen themselves in the scullery – a lean-to shed outside the kitchen. Agnes found she had to break the ice in the bowl before she could wash. Splashing her face with the freezing water, she gasped and burst out laughing as she pictured Maggie's horror at something so rustic.

The unbidden thought brought a lump to her throat. She shook her head to dispel it and tried to tidy her hair into some sort of order before returning to the warm fug of the kitchen.

The table was laid with enough food and wine to feed a crowd and soon the remainder of the reception group arrived, reporting they had stashed all the containers and packages from the drop zone. Agnes stared at the amount and quality of the food. After years of living on rations, she could barely believe what lay before her. The cauldron of chunky vegetable soup, with pieces of spicy sausage floating in it, was accompanied by baguettes, an enormous ham, and a wheel of pungent cheese. It was washed down with bottles of *vin ordinaire* and a glass of pastis, which brought tears to her eyes. It tasted like a banquet and within ten minutes of finishing, when everyone had lost their initial reticence and were smoking and sipping from tiny cups of foul black coffee, she slipped away.

Lying down on the pile of jumpsuits, she closed her eyes at last. Images of the past hours chased each other behind her closed lids, and her muscles twitched and ached with tiredness. The low background hum of men's voices and the occasional gruff bark of laughter had a cadence and rhythm to it, and finally she fell asleep to the lullaby of the strange dialect, and an image of Maggie in her mind.

'Céleste. Come on, wake up,' Philippe said, shaking her shoulder. 'We're leaving. Get your stuff.'

Agnes blinked and looked up blearily. Shadows ringed his eyes and his skin had a pallor to it that spoke of too little sleep and too much pastis and cigarettes. She stood, brushing down her skirt and trying to tidy her hair.

'Do you know where we're going?' she asked.

The Canadian shook his head, busy dragging his soft duffel bag out of the pile emptied from one of the containers. Agnes saw the corner of her old suitcase under a leather bag, the case with the radio in it next to it.

It was light outside, a bright, frosty morning that lit up the hoar on the bare trees as if they were hanging with diamonds. In the distance, the snow-covered high peaks of the Pyrenees chain rose above the valley. Agnes screwed up her eyes and shaded them with her hand, glad to be outside and on the move. The few hours of sleep had been so deep she felt as if she'd spent the whole night in a comfortable bed. Excitement bubbled in her stomach. As they climbed into the truck again, she called a heartfelt *merci beaucoup* to Florence, and waved as the farmer's wife raised a hand to them from where she stood in the doorway.

They drove for over an hour by tiny back roads, through villages in the bottom of a valley with dense forest all around, the mountains creeping ever closer. Finally, Georges pulled off the road onto a track that crossed a railway line and a bridge over a river rumbling along a stony bed. They climbed steeply, switch-backing up a hillside before stopping outside a two-storey farmhouse built of stone with a slate roof and green shutters, which stood on the outskirts of a mountain village.

'Here we are,' he said. 'Mademoiselle Sarraute, allow me to introduce you to Monsieur et Madame Espouy.'

Agnes jumped down from the truck. The Espouys had come outside at the sound of the vehicle, along with two small children who hid behind their mother, and half a dozen dogs, including an enormous white beast that bounded over, barking ferociously. Agnes froze, terrified for a moment, until the huge animal stopped in front of her, sniffed her shoes and stalked away to inspect the others. Letting her breath out slowly and trying to appear unconcerned, she went over and shook hands.

'*Enchantée*,' she said. 'I'm happy to meet you. Please, call me Céleste.'

Danielle Espouy – a fair, round-faced woman only slightly taller than Agnes – took her arm and walked her into the house. It was a moment before her eyes adjusted to the warm darkness

132

after the bright, cold air outside. Her host talked nineteen to the dozen, in the same broad accent as Georges. Agnes found it difficult to follow but caught more familiar words as she listened. Danielle showed her the salon and the large, square kitchen with its *fromagerie* at one end, where the milk from their small herd of goats and sheep was made into cheese.

Having exhausted the ground floor, Agnes followed her up the wide, wooden staircase to be shown her bedroom. Danielle pushed open the shutters, revealing a sunny, southern aspect and a view of the mountains that looked much closer than before. It was an impressive and beautiful vista. Agnes turned from admiring the view.

'Thank you for allowing me to stay in your home,' she said. 'I only hope I don't put you in any danger, while I'm here.'

'It is I who should thank you. We must do all we can, as loyal French citizens, to get rid of these Boche devils,' her host said. 'Anything we can do to help, you only have to ask.'

They returned to the outside, where the men were leaning on the truck, smoking. Agnes collected her suitcase and the case containing the wireless. She would scout around the farm later to find a good hiding place for it. Philippe took her shoulders and kissed her on either cheek.

'Look after yourself, kiddo,' he said. 'I hope we bump into each other, sometime. I'll be based at St Antoine, so not too far away – just a mountain or two between us.'

He laughed and ruffled her hair, and she stepped back, irritated at his manner. Why did he have to treat her like a child? This was serious business, not some game, even if she did have flutters of excitement in her belly.

'Take care, yourself,' she said, trying to tidy her hair again.

The two men climbed back into the truck and drove away, slipping sideways for a moment on the icy track, before the wheels bit. The vehicle straightened and shot forward, disappearing downhill and around a corner, leaving a puff of black exhaust smoke hanging in the cold air. Agnes picked up her luggage and followed the Espouys into the house.

She was on her own and there was no going back.

Chapter 18

Agnes

The view from her bedroom window drew Agnes's eye as she unpacked her few belongings after Georges and Philippe left. The mountains altered with every change of light, their distant beauty calming her nerves. Spreading her things around the room she'd been allocated didn't take long. All except the photograph. She'd secreted it under the lining in the bottom of her suitcase, knowing full well if it was found she would be finished as an agent. Now she brought it out of its hiding place and gazed at it for a few minutes, remembering the day by the river when she'd asked Walter to take a photo of her and Maggie. After replacing it with care and putting the case under her bed, she returned to the kitchen, to find Danielle waiting for her.

'Come and meet my mother-in-law,' she said. 'She lives just along the lane and wants to see you.'

Agnes followed her out of the farmyard to a tiny house beside the track up to the farm. They entered through a low door straight into a small living room where Madame Espouy sat beside a bright fire. She was a minute, bent figure who,

Danielle had told Agnes as they walked down the track, still worked alongside her son and daughter-in-law, caring for the two pigs and the poultry that were hidden from the Germans in the depths of the forest. It was plain she was sharp as a pin, as she questioned Agnes thoroughly.

'I don't want you bringing trouble here,' she said. 'You make sure those Boche bastards don't get suspicious about you. There's plenty round here would sell their children, never mind their neighbours.' Then she smiled and patted Agnes on the cheek. 'You seem a good girl. I know you'll do your best. Now then, where's my eau-de-vie, Danielle?'

Her daughter-in-law, raising her eyes skywards, brought a bottle half full of clear liquid and poured a tot into a small glass she placed on the table in front of her.

'Get a glass for this girl, too. It will do her good and keep the chill off.'

'Maman, you know everyone hates your firewater. Céleste, you do not have to drink it. It's Maman's homemade recipe and will take the skin off your tongue.'

'If it's Madame Espouy's own recipe then of course I'll take a glass,' said Agnes, wishing she'd eaten breakfast. It might have lined her stomach.

'Santé,' said the old lady, throwing the liquid back in one go.

'Santé,' replied Agnes, and did the same, choking as it hit her throat. Tears ran down her face and Danielle put a glass of water in her hand.

'I warned you,' she said, laughing. 'Maman, you're very naughty. Poor Céleste won't be able to speak for the rest of the day.'

'Pah. You young things have no robustness. I grew up on this recipe and it's never done me any harm.' She eyed Agnes shrewdly. 'What excuse are you giving those Boche bastards for being here, then, eh?'

'I'm a cousin of Danielle's with a weak chest, recovering from a bout of bronchitis and taking the mountain air.'

Agnes coughed as convincingly as she could and the old woman grinned.

'Aye, well, you'd never get away with being a local with that accent. Where are you from? I don't want to get my story wrong when I'm being tortured by that bastard commandant in St Jean.'

Agnes swallowed hard, not knowing if the woman was teasing her or serious.

'My mother's family were from the Dordogne area, so that's where I'm from as Danielle's cousin. I pray I won't be the cause of you being arrested by the Gestapo, madame.'

The old woman cackled and waved her hand, as if batting away a fly.

'Hah, don't worry about me, mademoiselle, I've evaded the Boche this far, and I don't intend letting them get their filthy mitts on me if I can help it.' Eyeing Agnes up and down, she nodded her head several times. 'You pass for French at least. Though most of the stupid German pigs can't tell the difference between us, anyway.' She hawked and spat into the fire, where the phlegm hissed and bubbled for a moment.

Walking back to the farmhouse, having left Madame Espouy dozing in her chair by the fire, Danielle apologised.

'My mother-in-law is a cranky old lady, these days,' she said. 'But it's the second time in her life that she's lived under the jackboot of the Germans, so you can't blame her for being anxious.' She put her hand on Agnes's arm, stalling her for a moment. 'Please, be vigilant. You're a stranger and will be seen as a suspicious intruder by the locals.'

'I won't let you down,' Agnes said. 'I promise.'

That afternoon she set out to explore the local vicinity, looking for places to hide the radio. It was her only means of communicating with London, and the very thing the Gestapo would give their eye teeth to find. The thought of being discovered with it in her possession made her stomach churn with fear. It was vital she kept it hidden.

The forest that covered the foothills all around the village was wild, with overgrown tracks, fallen trees, and scrub growing rampantly among ancient *granges*. Most had been abandoned for years and were in a ruinous state. There must be plenty of hiding places within easy reach of the farm.

Agnes's legs ached, the muscles twitching with fatigue, after she'd spent an hour hiking up the steep hillside, mentally marking out possible sites to cache the radio in. As the sun fell behind the mountains, she found an old ruin with a young beech tree growing up inside what was left of the chimney. It wasn't far from the farm and well hidden. She made a rough pile of small stones to mark the spot where she needed to leave the track. It was perfect as a first place to hide the radio.

The following day, Jean Espouy invited Agnes to help him take the small herd of goats and sheep to their grazing ground. Each day the animals were taken out of the ramshackle barn hidden in the forest and herded down the valley to a small meadow, where he and his dogs would stay with them while they grazed.

'It'll be better once the summer comes and the sheep go up to the mountain pastures,' Jean said, as Agnes walked beside him at the front of the flock, while the dog herded them from the back. 'Those bastard Boche think our flocks are theirs for the taking. They shot my last dog after he went for one of them when they tried to steal a ewe. He was a good dog too. This one is still young, but he knows his job, and at least he warns me if someone is coming.'

'Is that why you hide them?' said Agnes.

'Yes, but it's so I can keep out of sight as well,' he said. 'You'll have noticed how few men there are around here. Those who aren't fighting in the north are either dead or have been sent off to the German labour camps. Or are members of the Maquis in hiding,' he added, winking at her.

In the evening, Danielle milked the females, showing Agnes how to tease the milk from the teats without annoying the animals, so they wouldn't kick the bucket over and spill the valuable creamy liquid.

'Damn,' Agnes swore, as a black goat with long, curved horns kicked the bucket over for the second time. She glanced at Danielle and saw the grin on her face. 'What am I doing wrong?' she said, rubbing the back of her hand as the animal took an accurate swipe at her this time, the rough hoof raising a weal on the skin.

'You're doing nothing wrong,' Danielle said. 'It's just that the Billy isn't used to having his balls squeezed.'

She burst out laughing, unfastened the rope and let the indignant goat go. Agnes laughed with her, ruefully rubbing her hand again.

'Well, that's a lesson well learnt,' she admitted, and checked the next animal carefully before pulling on its udder.

The milk was covered and left outside in a small shed to keep cool, ready to be made into cheeses by Danielle the following day, and sold at the local market. This was to be Agnes's task and gave her a valid reason to be seen, especially in St Jean Layrisse, where the Grenzpolizei – the frontier police section of the Gestapo – were based.

That evening, two men drove into the farm in a small grey car. Dressed in the same manner as the Espouys and with black berets pulled down low over their eyes, they were introduced as Jacques Comet and Valentine Dupont. Members of the local Maquis group, they stared suspiciously at Agnes. The Espouys had already told her the previous agent had been betrayed to the Gestapo and shot while trying to escape at a roadblock. The maquisards believed it to be a better result than him being captured and giving up the names of those involved. The local commandant, nicknamed *La Cigogne*, 'The Stork', supposedly liked to watch while prisoners were 'persuaded' to talk.

Jacques and Valentine looked at her with a mix of horror and disdain plain on their faces. Agnes's temper flared.

'Mademoiselle Sarraute, tell me please, how do you propose to help us?' asked Valentine, the taller and more talkative of the two. He loomed over her, but she held his eye contact and kept calm.

'My orders are to liaise between you and my chief. He wants the local maquisards to speed up the search for the collaborator before anyone else is betrayed. There will still be *évadés* arriving from time to time who'll need guides to take them over the mountains into Spain. Between us we'll find safe houses for them before they leave,' she said. 'There'll also be messages coming in from London. I'll keep you up to date with what's happening. With the invasion in the pipeline the chief wants us to distract the Boche by any means.'

'We need explosives, more weapons, and ammunition if we're to make an impact,' Jacques said.

He had an impressive moustache that made it almost impossible for Agnes to understand what he said. She caught the gist of it and tried to think what she could do for them.

'Make me a list of what you need, and I'll relay it to the chief. There was a drop of equipment in the same parachutage I came in on. It's down at Montréjeau.'

'*D'accord*,' said Valentine. He nodded and, for the first time, smiled at her, his dark eyes crinkling at the corners. 'You need to change your hair. Look at Danielle: she keeps hers long at the back, not pinned up like you've got yours. If you want to fit in and not be noticed, you must look like a local.'

Agnes patted her hair, heat creeping up her neck, annoyed to have got such a basic thing wrong. London had approved her hairstyle, which she'd chosen because it was how her mother had done her hair. She would let the bosses know they were out of touch with what was the current style. She must pay attention to the smallest of details, as she'd been told in training.

'Don't worry,' Danielle said. 'Tomorrow we'll go through your things and see what we can do. I have a spare pair of sabots you can wear, too. I think they'll be a bit big for you, but they'll do for now.'

She nodded and smiled. 'Thank you.'

Jean Espouy brought out a bottle of pastis and the shrivelled end of a saucisson, and, with business over, they all took a drink to toast Agnes's arrival and the forthcoming invasion, which would chase the Boche back to where they came from.

After multiple glasses of pastis, the two maquisards left, Valentine spinning the wheels of the little car and fishtailing down the hill, while Agnes watched and heard the pair of them roaring with laughter. She wondered how she was going to gain the trust and confidence of these men, with their machismo and bravado.

Later the same evening, when she was dropping with fatigue, there was a cacophony of barking from the dogs. Jean got up from his chair beside the fire and frowned.

'*Putain!* Who can that be?'

He and his wife looked at each other, and Agnes shivered.

There was a quiet knock and, for a second, she thought no one was going to move. Danielle's face had turned ashen, her eyes wide, her breath coming in small gasps. Agnes leant across the table and put a hand over hers, squeezing it lightly. Jean seemed to take an age before he shuffled to the door, unbolted it, turned the old-fashioned iron key, and pulled it open. Outside, his fist raised to knock again, stood a tall, spare-looking man of middle age with a thatch of red hair.

'Good evening, M Espouy. I'm sorry I didn't let you know I was coming tonight. My courier is away on another bit of business for me.'

'*Reynard!* You gave us all a fright and no mistake. I wondered where you'd got to,' said Jean, pumping the outstretched hand up and down. He opened the door wide and brought the visitor inside. 'Céleste, come and meet your patron, Reynard.'

Agnes rose and shook hands with the man who would be her superior officer while she remained in this section.

'Céleste Sarraute, monsieur. I'm pleased to meet you. I can't wait to start my work.' She realised she was gabbling and stopped to take a breath.

The tall man looked amused and switched to English. 'Yes, I'm sorry you've been left in limbo for a couple of days. We've been short of people since your predecessor was killed. It had to be an informer, so we've tightened up on all our connections with the maquisards. It's meant double the hours for most of us.' He patted her shoulder. 'Don't worry, just be sure to remember your training and don't make any silly mistakes. Keep to your back-story, play your part well and don't, whatever you do, speak English in public places. You'll be fine.'

He took the offered glass of pastis from Danielle and sat at the table, where she had placed a plate of bread, cheese and saucisson. Tucking into the simple meal as if he hadn't eaten all day, he continued to speak. 'Now then. Have you had any contact with the local Maquis group?'

'Yes sir. I met Valentine Dupont and Jacques Comet earlier this evening. I don't think I'm quite who they expected – or wanted – as their new agent,' said Agnes. 'They asked for more weapons and ammunition.'

'One thing you'll learn very quickly about the maquisards, is that they always think they don't have enough weapons or ammunition.' Reynard grimaced. 'Everyone is short, but I'll see what I can do.'

'There were containers of weapons and ammunition dropped when I parachuted in. Will they not get a share of that load?'

'Those container loads have to be shared out between all the groups in a huge area. This group is small and some of the other Maquis groups are in much more need. The damned Communists are constantly discovering our caches and stealing them. You would think we'd be on the same side, but they care for nothing and no one but themselves and their precious ideals.'

'I see. It must be very difficult.'

'Well, nobody expects it to be easy, but when we're fighting people who should be on our side, as well as the Germans, it's a blow, I can tell you.' He finished his plate of food and accepted a cup of the disgusting brew that passed for coffee, before fixing Agnes with his pale gaze. 'Please tell me you brought a wireless. We've had no radio operator since Bernard was shot. Silly beggar had his set with him, so he tried to run when he was stopped. We've had to change all our codes in case they manage to crack them. I warn you, you must not, under any circumstances, use the same code more than once. Understood?'

'Understood, sir. I have one of the new transceivers and it's well hidden. Do you have messages you need me to send tonight?'

'Not tonight but expect to receive something in the next week or so. Things are hotting up with the invasion being planned.' He gave her two pieces of paper. 'Now, here's a message I want you to take to this address in St Jean. Memorise it and the address, and then burn them both.'

'Yes sir,' said Agnes, a shiver running up her spine.

'I've also brought you a gift,' the chief said, smiling. 'Come with me. You'll like it, I promise.'

He rose and called a goodnight to the Espouys, who had removed themselves to the salon while the agents talked. Agnes followed him outside to a tiny van and watched him open the back door and extract a bicycle, newly painted and with a large basket on the front. She grinned. It reminded her of the one she'd had when she was a girl, before the war had changed everything.

'It's perfect, thank you,' she said.

'You might find it hard going, with all these hills,' said Reynard. 'But it should make it a little easier to get around. There's only one other thing I must tell you. Your code name is *Claudette*. Do not use it unless you need to prove you're an agent. It'll be how other agents will contact you, so you know they're not fake. I know you will have been told all this before, but it's the most important thing to keep you safe. Goodnight, Céleste. You'll hear from me soon.'

'I understand. Goodnight, sir.'

She didn't know when she would see Reynard again. He was high on the Gestapo's wanted list, and constantly moved from one safe house to another. Agnes wondered how he stayed sane.

Chapter 19

Claire

Aunt M slept all the way back to Stanbury Hall, her head drooping onto her chest, Agnes's letter clutched in her hand. When I pulled up outside the front entrance and tried to rouse her, she muttered something in her sleep, opened her eyes and looked at me. There was no recognition there, as if a switch had been flicked, turning off her cognisant mind. After a moment or two, her head sank forward and she fell asleep again.

Inside, the receptionist tracked down Aunt M's carer, Carole, a tall, capable-looking woman with a warm smile. We went back to the car together, and she gently shook Aunt M's arm to wake her, then helped her out, chatting to her in a quiet, cheerful way, which she seemed to respond to. I might as well not have been there. Once we arrived in her room, Carole guided Aunt M towards the bedroom, closing the door behind her. I stood, looking out at the gardens, my mind miles away, thinking of my days living at the Chimneys.

Happy times, when life was uncomplicated.

I recalled a conversation with her on the day I married Andrew, almost twenty years ago. It was at the reception in the local pub, and both Aunt M and I were more than a little drunk on champagne. She said I made a beautiful bride and would be a wonderful wife and mother, and Andrew was a very lucky man.

I had wept a little – happy tears – and hugged her. Why had she never married? I asked. She was one of the most beautiful women I knew, and everyone adored her. She must have had suitors lining up at the door.

I remembered how sad she had looked for a brief moment, before putting a smile on her face and winking at me.

'I let the right one get away. Wasn't that a silly thing to do?'

Those words came back to me, loaded with meaning, now I knew the truth about her. It made me even more determined to discover what happened to Agnes and why she didn't keep her promise and return to her love.

Back at my old farm-worker's cottage, I fed Betty and myself, poured a glass of wine and sat down to check messages. They were mostly rubbish, except one from a friend, inviting me to her hen night. She was getting married to one of the vets I worked with, and I knew it would look strange if I didn't go. Truthfully, it was the last thing I wanted to do – especially as I knew Helen would be going.

How could I face her? Bad enough I had to work with her, now she and Andrew were a couple. The thought of her giving him the one thing I couldn't was an almost physical blow. Nausea hit the pit of my stomach, and the sensation of drowning grew quickly, a familiar feeling but something I thought I'd managed to beat once my divorce from Andrew was finalised. My heart was a pneumatic drill hammering through my ribs as I rode the waves of panic; trying to breathe, to bring my mind back to the present, as I'd learnt to, years earlier. After what felt like an hour, the attack slowed, and I found myself slumped on the floor, sweat-soaked and shivering.

Exhaustion made my limbs heavy, and my breath came in noisy whoops, fighting to get enough oxygen into my lungs. I didn't want to move but the longer I stayed on the slate floor, the colder I felt, so I dragged myself back onto the sofa. It wasn't the worst attack I'd had, but coming out of the blue, it left me shocked and frightened.

I took the last sleeping pill in the box, drank a pint of water, and crawled into bed, dreading this might be the start of a return to the shattered wreck I had been while trying to conceive. Bed had never been a good place, with nightmares dogging my sleep then. I was a different person now; I wouldn't allow myself to slip back to the shell I'd been then.

I slept without dreaming, waking with a fuzzy head, but a calm mind. I needed something else to focus on, and Aunt M's long-lost lover was the ideal thing to keep me occupied. I phoned the home to check how she was; her obvious confusion and loss of memory the previous day worried me. I was relieved to hear she was coherent and asking for me.

Setting off to Stanbury Hall again, my mind was still full of worry. Was I pinning my hopes on Aunt M being as enthusiastic about looking for Agnes as I was? Using her as a way of burying my own fears and stresses? My heart began hammering again, nausea rose into my throat, and as I arrived at the home I had to sit in the car for a moment, breathing deeply and letting each lungful out slowly, trying to stay calm. I hadn't, until that moment, realised just how important this was to me; how much I was depending on a seventy-year-old mystery to save me from myself.

Chapter 20

Agnes

It was market day in St Jean Layrisse and Agnes rose early to help Danielle prepare her cheeses to sell. The Espouys had a small, ramshackle van, the floor having so many holes you could watch the road going by underneath, which Agnes found alarming until she got used to it and knew where to place her feet. Two kilometres from St Jean a roadblock was set up across the road; soldiers guarded it, stopping everyone and checking their papers.

'This happens every day,' Danielle said. 'Smile politely, make sure you have your papers ready and answer any questions they ask, clearly.'

'Do they speak French?'

'Some do. Usually, it's a case of them shouting loudly in German and throwing their hands about until you get the gist of what they want.'

Danielle smiled at her, obviously unflustered by what had become part of her routine. Nevertheless, Agnes wiped damp hands on her skirt.

The pair of German soldiers manning the barricade were

irritable, the pinch of cold plain on their disgruntled faces. They gave a scant glance at the papers of the two women, poked around in the trays of cheese and waved them on within a couple of minutes.

Agnes found herself letting out her breath.

Danielle glanced away from the potholed road and gave her a twisted smile.

'You'll get used to it,' she said.

It was only a matter of moments before they arrived at the market.

Market day was, traditionally, a day for meeting up with neighbours and friends, as well as selling produce and stocking up on anything needed for the farm. Agnes had fond memories of the market in the town where she'd grown up, but arriving at the *Place du Marche* in St Jean Layrisse, there was no comparison to the days of her childhood. She found it hard to imagine how anyone could still make a living from selling their goods when the Germans took most of what they produced as if it was theirs by right.

Many of the stalls were in place and people were beginning to arrive, anxious to get to the produce first. A man appeared and said *bonjour* to Danielle, then began unloading the boxes of cheese out of the back of the van.

'*Bonjour*, Remi,' Danielle replied. 'This is Céleste, my cousin's daughter. She's staying with us at the farm for a while.'

'*Bonjour, mademoiselle*,' the man said. He wore the same clothes as most of the other men, and had a moustache that would compete with Jacques Comet's.

She gave him a small smile and wished him a good day, then turned to help Danielle. Remi finished unloading the boxes, kissed Danielle on either cheek, nodded a goodbye to Agnes and then wandered away to another stall. Agnes watched him go.

'Does he usually help you on market days?'

'Remi? Sometimes, if he's in town. He works at all the markets around here,' said Danielle. 'He's Jacques Comet's cousin, and

I've known him since we were children.' She dropped her voice. 'He helps the Resistance when he's needed.' She lifted one of the boxes and carried it across to the table. 'Bring the rest of them, will you. I'll start laying these ones out.' While she and Agnes set up the cheese stall, Danielle spoke continuously in a quiet voice, pointing out people and saying a few words about them. 'The woman walking towards us with the blue hat and carrying a basket on either arm. You see her? That's Denise Picard. Stay away from her, she's far too friendly with the Boche. Her husband was taken to work in one of the German labour camps and she'll do anything to get him freed, poor thing. I feel sorry for her, but still, I wouldn't trust her.'

Agnes noted the nondescript woman, mousy hair escaping from under her hat. She looked worn out and defeated.

Danielle continued throughout the morning, pointing out local people and introducing Agnes to inquisitive customers, telling them she was recuperating in the clear mountain air and benefiting from taking the waters in the spa at the top end of the town. Agnes found a judicious cough made people move on quickly.

She felt twitchy and ill at ease, and Danielle eventually lost patience.

'Relax, Céleste. Nobody is taking any notice of you.'

'Sorry. I just want to get the message Reynard gave me passed on.' Agnes took a breath, trying to slow her racing pulse every time a soldier demanded a sample of one of the cheeses.

'Well, it's pretty quiet, just go now, if you want. Which street is it?'

'Rue Gambetta,' she whispered.

'It's in the old town, not far from here. Go; have a stroll around the town, get your bearings. Buy a book from Henri LeGendre, the bookseller on the Allée de Bain. He's a friend.'

'Thank you,' Agnes said, relieved to be doing something at last.

Following the narrow street Danielle had pointed out, she soon found herself in a warren of ancient and run-down houses huddled together in the shadow of the mountainside. Agnes pulled her coat more tightly around her, cold and nerves making her shiver.

Finding Rue Gambetta was straightforward, and she reached the address within a few minutes, discreetly checking the houses until she arrived at number 19. Halting outside, she took a deep breath, made sure she had the message correct in her mind, and knocked on the door with a confidence she did not feel. There was a pause and then she heard the slow tapping of heeled shoes on a hard floor.

The door opened to reveal a woman of indeterminate age, smartly dressed except for the plaid blanket draped around her shoulders. She was thin to the point of being skeletal.

Food is not that short; she must be sick.

She smiled at the woman. 'Madame Duphil?'

'Yes. May I help you?' The voice was a croak.

'My name is Claudette.'

The woman looked at her with surprise. 'Claudette? You're not how I imagined you'd be. How old are you?'

Agnes flushed and bit her lip. 'I may look young, but I assure you, madame, I am old enough.'

She smiled to take the sting out of her words. Mme Duphil had the grace to look embarrassed.

'I'm sorry,' she said. 'It's difficult when I keep getting different people coming to the door. Come in.'

She led the way slowly down a dark hallway with a tiled floor to a small kitchen at the back of the house, the temperature almost as chill as it had felt outside. The room was spotless but shabby, and bare of any ornament, except for a photograph in a silver frame, which took pride of place on a narrow dresser. Agnes recognised Mme Duphil as a younger, healthier version of the ravaged woman who stood in front of her. Beside her in the photo was a tall, well-built man, his arm around her. The pair were smiling, their expressions open and happy.

151

'I believe you have a message for me,' Mme Duphil said.

'The orchestra will be practising in the park at ten o'clock, on the usual day,' Agnes said, passing on the words she'd learnt, a weight lifting as she fulfilled her first task. It meant nothing to her, though from Mme Duphil's frown and how it deepened it had hit a nerve. When she finished the other woman said nothing. She had hold of the back of a chair and leant on it for support. Agnes hoped she wasn't going to collapse.

'Don't look at me in that manner, mademoiselle. I'm dying – I know it. But while I have strength to stand, I will do my bit for France.' She grimaced as if in pain, then conjured up a tight smile and gazed at Agnes. 'Thank you, for bringing the message. I'll see it gets passed on to the right people. Can I get you a drink – a glass of wine or coffee?'

'Oh, that's very kind, madame, but no, thank you. I have another errand and then must get back to the market.'

'As you wish.'

'May I visit again? If you don't mind?' Agnes wasn't sure why she asked the question, only that this woman inspired her, and she wanted to know more about her. She might also be a good contact – must know the local Resistance group and could be a help in tracking down the collaborator. Thoughts raced through her head, as she smiled at the older woman. 'Of course, please don't feel you have to humour me, but I know nobody in St Jean Layrisse apart from my relations on the farm, and I would like to sit and take a glass of wine with you, sometime.'

'You're kind. I would like that. I don't go out much; walking is too tiring. Come and see me when you're next in town and we'll drink wine and talk of happier times.'

Mme Duphil's face softened for the first time as her eyes crinkled in a smile.

'Very well, I'll come soon. Thank you,' said Agnes.

Outside, she continued walking away from the market into the maze of narrow streets that made up the old town. The houses crowded on top of one another, many of them closed up or falling into ruin, with seedling trees and briars growing out of their broken chimneys and gutters. The whole area felt forgotten and dreary, so different from the lively atmosphere around the market.

Five minutes of carefully picking her way along icy lanes brought her out onto the Allée de Bain, the long, straight main street running up to the *thermes*. With the jagged, snow-covered peaks of the mountains as a magnificent backdrop, it could have been a different town to the downtrodden huddle of houses she had just left. Here, the road was wide, with an avenue of trees on either side and shops set back on a broad pavement, allowing people to wander along two or three abreast. Tall, ornate buildings lined the street, and there were cafés and restaurants with tables outside, where – even in February – people sat, drinking coffee, pastis, and wine. Only when Agnes looked closely did she notice the shabbiness of their clothes, their frequent furtive glances to either side. Their baskets held only one or two items of food: some potatoes, a small loaf, a couple of onions and perhaps one of Danielle's little cheeses. Their faces looked pinched, their expressions closed, empty.

There was only one café where the sound of music and laughter could be heard, spilling onto the street. As she passed the door, Agnes glanced inside and saw two tables with soldiers sitting, glasses and half-empty bottles in front of them. One played an ancient, upright piano and they were singing along in German to a rowdy tune. As it finished, they all burst out laughing, thumping each other on the back and calling for more drink. Agnes caught the eye of a young man as he looked up towards the open doorway. He winked and smiled at her, and she put her head down and scurried on past, her cheeks burning as if she'd been caught spying.

Finding the bookshop, she entered, relieved to be out of sight for a few minutes. It was a simple pleasure to browse the shelves and find copies of old friends she'd read as a child. She picked up a second-hand copy of *Les Misérables* and checked her purse to see there was enough money in it.

How apt. Fighting for freedom here in France.

A small, orange, curly-coated dog came trotting over to her from somewhere behind the counter, followed by a man who appeared through a velvet curtain at the back of the shop. Grey-haired and with a pronounced limp, he smiled at her.

'Good morning. Is there anything I can help you with, mademoiselle?'

His light voice had a lilt to it that didn't sound local.

'Good morning. Monsieur LeGendre? My name is Céleste Sarraute, and I'm staying with the Espouy family. Danielle said I should call in to say hello. I'm helping her at the market.'

She bent down to stroke the dog, who smelled appalling but was determined to make friends with her. It stood on its back legs and pawed at her knee, wagging a stumpy tail in delight at the attention.

'How kind of you. Pepi, get down and leave the lady alone. I'm sorry, he has no manners at all, thinks the whole world revolves around him,' M LeGendre said, smiling fondly at the dog for a moment. 'Danielle and Jean are thoughtful people; I don't see them as often as I would like to. It's difficult to get around nowadays, as you know.'

How sad and tired he looked.

'I'll take this book, if I may?' said Agnes.

'Of course. One of my favourites.' He took the volume from her, and carefully wrapped it in creased brown paper, then tied it with string. 'Please, give the Espouys my best wishes and tell them I would very much like to see them soon, if it is allowed.'

'I will do,' Agnes said, as she counted out the correct money. 'Thank you, and good day.'

Making her way back to the market, Agnes's over-riding impression of the people of St Jean was of the strain they were

154

living under. She hadn't noticed it in the Espouys and their neighbours who lived out in the countryside. Here, it felt as if a huge weight was suffocating the people.

She couldn't wait to get back to the farm.

Chapter 21

Claire

My phone buzzed as I set down some food for Betty, the morning after I took Aunt M back to the Chimneys and found Agnes's letter. Stanbury Hall's number flashed on the screen. I hesitated a second before answering, my pulse jumping.

'Hello, Claire McRory speaking.'

'It's Greta Schwartz, Ms McRory.' A pause. 'I'm sorry to tell you that your aunt became ill overnight. We've called an ambulance. I think it would be best if you went straight to St James's hospital.'

My head spun and I dropped onto a chair.

'What's wrong with her? She seemed fine yesterday, a little tired by the excitement of seeing her old home, but otherwise okay.'

'I can't tell you any more than that she became poorly after she went to bed. The doctor will no doubt speak to you after he's examined her,' she said.

At the hospital, I learnt from the receptionist that Aunt M had already been seen and where she was. I found her in a small side ward, alone. Lines snaked out of her arms to various drips. Wires were attached to her then back to a monitor that beeped quietly. A familiar sight I saw every working day. Aunt M looked tiny, her eyes closed, skin the colour of bleached paper. I sat and held her hand, as I had a few days earlier.

A nurse came in.

'Ms McRory?' I nodded. 'The doctor will speak to you now.'

I followed her to a small office, where a tired-looking man sat at a desk, typing something on a desktop computer. He rose to greet me.

'Ms McRory? I'm Dr Sanjeed. Please, take a seat.'

I sat, gripping my bag on my knee, trying to control my breathing. 'What's wrong with my aunt?'

Dr Sanjeed leant his elbows on the desk and fixed me with a kind gaze. I recognised the gesture.

'Miss Scott has had a minor stroke,' he said. 'At the moment she's stable, but she may have another one, or more, over the next twenty-four hours. We've made her comfortable and put her on medication to try and prevent another, but there is little more we can do for her, I'm afraid.' He produced a piece of paper. 'You know she signed a DNR, I presume?'

I shook my head, shocked that Aunt M would know about such things. 'I didn't, no. But then we've been out of touch for a while.' Thinking about it, I wasn't surprised, really. She would want to make things as easy as possible for everyone. 'I saw her yesterday, though, and she seemed fine.' How many times had I been in his position? You never got used to giving bad news. 'My aunt went wandering a few days ago and got very cold and exhausted. Is that a factor?'

'I saw she'd been in recently. It wouldn't have helped, her system taking such a shock.' He rose and discreetly looked at his watch. 'You can stay with her. She will know you're there, I'm sure.'

I wiped away tears. He was a compassionate man, I could see, but he had other, more pressing patients to attend to.

'How long does she have, do you think? I mean, she's not going to die now, is she?'

The doctor raised his shoulders. 'It's impossible to say,' he said. 'She was brought in promptly after the stroke, so we treated her quickly, which helped. She may rally, but this is a reminder that your aunt is not invincible. Are there any other family members?'

I shook my head.

'There's only me,' I whispered. I stood and held out a shaking hand. 'Thank you, Doctor.'

'Go and be with your aunt. Cherish what time you still have together, but be prepared for the inevitable.' He took my hand. 'Then celebrate her long life and remember all the good times you had with her.'

I spent the next twenty-four hours by Aunt M's bedside, fully expecting her to die. She looked so frail; how could her ninety-year-old body withstand such a shock? It seemed inconceivable that just as we had reconnected she might not be here.

'I need you, Aunt M. Please don't leave me alone. Don't go. Not yet,' I whispered, time and again, during those long hours.

Selfish thoughts and wishes, I knew, but true nonetheless.

I thought back to all the times I'd stayed with her; how loving and caring she always was. The fun we had, tempered by her innate sense of right and wrong and a wealth of good sense that never felt forced on me, but that I soaked up nonetheless. How much more of a mother she was over the years, than her sister Jessica ever had been to me.

My own mother, who couldn't wait to offload her only child to anyone who would take her.

I should have known better than to doubt Aunt M's tenacious hold on life.

At the end of the second day, she opened her eyes. I held her hand and smiled at her, but she seemed unaware of me, her gaze unfocused. She was awake, though, and for that I was grateful. The thought of losing her was devastating.

Please, God, let her survive this. Give us a little more time, so I can make it up to her.

I called a nurse, who checked her vital signs.

'She's stable, which is good. We'll keep monitoring her, tonight, and the doctor will see her tomorrow morning.' He smiled at me. 'You look knackered. Why don't you go home for a while? We'll contact you if there's any change.'

He was right; I was exhausted. A shower and a few hours' sleep would help. The amount of coffee I had drunk made my head buzz, and my stomach griped with hunger. I thanked him and left my phone number with reception, who promised to call if Aunt M relapsed.

At home, I fed a very disgruntled Betty, made scrambled eggs and toast and ate them straight from the pan while checking messages. A hot shower, then I crawled into bed and lay, unable to sleep, endlessly berating myself for neglecting Aunt M for so long and then making her overexcited. Now it might be too late to make amends.

Eventually, I must have dropped off, because I woke with a banging head and a mouth that felt like a desert. Glugging down a pint of water and grabbing a banana and an apple to eat in the car, I went back to the hospital.

The side ward where Aunt M had been the day before was empty, and my stomach lurched. They promised they would tell me if she became worse. Where was she? I raced out of the room and almost ran into a trolley being pushed by the same nurse I had seen the day before.

'Whoa, steady on,' he said.

'Where's my aunt? What's happened to her?'

He smiled. 'Come with me, I'm on my way to see her,' he said.

The panic in my chest receded a little, and I followed him along the corridor to the main geriatric ward. In a bed next to the door was a tiny figure. Aunt M lay propped up, looking remarkably alert, considering she had been unconscious for over twenty-four hours.

She smiled at me and put her hand out. I took it, gently holding it between my own two hands, unable to stem the tears.

'Now, dear Claire, there's no need to take on so,' she said.

'I thought I'd lost you.'

I pulled a hankie out of my pocket and wiped my eyes and nose, trying to control my sobs.

Aunt M patted my hand. 'Hah. It takes more than a little stroke to get rid of this old bird,' she said.

She slurred some of her words and her left eye and the corner of her mouth drooped, but her colour had returned, and a plate with toast crumbs on it told me she was eating.

I laughed. I should have known.

I hugged her, gently, and kissed her cheek. Although she was bright and cheerful, I could see she was tired. Leaving her after she dozed off, I went to see if I could find Dr Sanjeed. Almost bumping into him as he came out of his office with a pile of files under his arm, I asked if I could have a quick word.

'I can give you a couple of minutes, that's all, I'm afraid,' he said.

'I only want to thank you for looking after my aunt. And to ask when you think she might be ready to go home.'

'She's a remarkable lady, is Miss Scott,' he said. 'But she's still quite poorly. I want to keep an eye on her for at least a few days until I'm sure the medication is working and keeping her stable. She's not out of the woods yet.'

'I understand. Thank you, Doctor Sanjeed.'

He smiled, and hurried away, his white coat flapping.

Aunt M remained in hospital for the rest of the week, growing more restless and crankier with each day. Finally, she was given permission to go back to Stanbury Hall and I drove her there, constantly taking my eyes off the road to watch her.

'Do you think you could concentrate on driving, instead of me,' she said, eventually. 'I'm not going to pop my clogs between the hospital and the home, you know, and I don't want to end up back in there having been in a car accident.'

'Sorry. You're precious cargo, that's all.'

'Pah. You don't get rid of me that easily,' she said, tartly.

160

It was all very well for her to be so confident, but I took the doctor's warning to heart. She was on borrowed time – and so, I felt, was I. Time squandered, I could never take back.

Chapter 22

Agnes

Winter merged into spring, and Agnes became almost used to living with the fear of discovery. She made a point of calling in to see Valerie Duphil whenever she was in town. The sick woman appeared to have no family nearby and few friends, yet was a mine of information on local families and their goings-on. Rue Gambetta was a route both to the market and, in the opposite direction, to the railway station, and all the world seemed to pass by her window. Drinking a cup of coffee with her, on a break from the market one day, Valerie tapped Agnes on the arm and nodded towards a thick-set man loitering on the street corner opposite the house.

'That's Remi Comet,' she said. 'He's a cousin of Jacques Comet; lives over in the next valley to you.' She frowned. 'Why's he hanging around here at this time of day? If he's not careful, he'll be picked up by the Boche patrols.'

'Oh yes. I met him the first time I helped Danielle at the market,' Agnes said.

Valerie was right: it was a dangerous thing to do. The Germans were always on the lookout for men and boys to round up and send to the labour camps. Was he waiting for someone? Her interest was piqued, and she paid attention to his face, slotting it away in her memory, having not thought about him since she had met him at the market.

As they continued to watch, Remi Comet looked both ways along the street, dropped the cigarette he was smoking and wandered off in the direction of the railway station. A moment later a German officer strode past the window, making the women sit back in their chairs. The flash on his shoulder showed he was Grenzpolizei, and Agnes shivered, hoping M Comet had managed to get out of sight before the Nazi found him.

Reynard ordered an attack on a local factory the Gestapo had taken over to use as a fuel depot and told Agnes and Philippe to work together on it. She cycled to meet the Canadian on a sunny spring morning, down the narrow road alongside the river and railway as they snaked down the steep valley to Cierp-Garin.

Agnes took a seat at a table outside the café where she'd arranged to meet Philippe, enjoying the feel of the sun on her face. Noticing him walking across the street towards her, she stood to greet him. They'd decided to make it seem as if they were a courting couple and she accepted his kiss on her cheek and an embrace that buried her into his chest. Her nostrils filled with the reek of cigarettes and chalk dust from his rough workman's jacket and she stifled a sneeze. Finally, he released her and pushed her back so that he could look at her, holding her shoulders as he gazed at her.

'You're looking well, *ma petite*,' he said, raising his eyebrows.

Agnes regarded him with her head on one side, taking in his skinny length. 'I wouldn't say the same of you. They must either be starving you or working you to death.'

'My hands were in ribbons for the first two weeks. Now look at them – callouses so hard I could cut them with a knife and feel nothing.'

Behind his spectacles, Philippe's eyes were tired. She sat down again, and he sat opposite her, leaning in across the small table, towards her.

'You're good at this,' she whispered, laughing at him.

'Gotta keep up the cover,' he said, taking one of her hands in his.

Agnes stopped herself from pulling back. A man had never held her hand before. Only her father, when she was a child, and Philippe's hand was nothing like his. The rough paw enveloping hers felt strong.

He raised an eyebrow at her. 'Okay?'

She nodded, and smiled to hide her discomfort.

An image of Maggie crept into her mind, and she wondered what she would think if she could see her now. The waiter appeared and asked if they wanted more coffee, interrupting her reverie, and she realised Philippe had been talking and she had no idea what he'd said. He waved the waiter away and stood up.

'Are you actually listening?' he hissed, impatience in his voice. 'Look, *ma petite*, let's go for a walk around the park. You might pay more attention to me, then.'

'I'll pay attention when you pay me some respect and stop calling me "*ma petite*".'

Rising, she walked away, leaving him to throw some coins on the table and follow her. Catching up with her, he took her arm, grinning.

'You're right, and I apologise, um, Céleste,' he said. 'It's just that I'm shocking at remembering names, so I make up a kind of nickname for people to make it easier. It's not meant to be an insult – it's just you're so tiny. From now on I will call you *Tigresse*. You can't be offended by such a fierce name, surely?'

She tried to ease the tightness in her face. Was he still making fun of her? She would just have to prove herself to him as well as to the French. They had to work together; all she could do was back down. She smiled with her mouth, her eyes not meeting his.

164

'Right. Tell me again, and I promise to concentrate this time,' she said, as he linked his arm with hers and they made their way to the small park in the centre of the village.

That evening, once it was dark, she met Jacques and Valentine at the farm. A diversion would help their odds of success, which is what she had to persuade the maquisards to do. However, the two Frenchmen were adamant they should be in the fray. Frustrated with how little had been achieved since her arrival, Agnes knew they blamed her.

'Look,' she said to Jacques, as he demanded yet again to be allowed to join in the raid. 'The more people who know about this, the more likely it is we'll be betrayed. The Gestapo are desperate to find out who's in the local Resistance, ever since the previous radio was discovered, and it's only a matter of time before someone talks.'

'You have no right to stop us being there,' countered Jacques, his huge moustache seeming to have a life of its own, as he spat the words at her. '*Merde!* Why did they send a child to do a man's work?' He turned away with a look of disgust, thumping his thigh with his fist. 'Valentine, can you get through to this . . . this baby . . . that our group must take part in the raid and not just be some kind of sideshow? I'm sick of trying.'

Valentine raised his eyebrows at Agnes, a slight smile lifting one corner of his mouth.

'I can understand you want to keep the raid a secret. Of course, you do – as do we. But, mademoiselle, you forget that you may need us there on the night. For one thing, we have inside knowledge of the factory. It's all very well saying we should tell you – but why should we? Why don't you give us the explosives and leave everything to us? This is our town. The people under the jackboot of the Germans are our people. Why should we give you the satisfaction of kicking them where it hurts?'

'As I've already explained,' Agnes said, trying to remain calm, 'until we know who the collaborator is, we have to keep everything just between us. I trust you both, of course, but there are others I don't know well enough to trust with something as important as this.' She put her head in her hands. 'You'll be doing the most important task on the night by creating a ruckus that'll keep the Boche occupied for a few hours, as well as misdirecting the collaborator,' she said. 'You could provide one hell of a diversion for us. Take the eyes of the Germans off the fuel store while we get in there, set the explosives and get out again. What do you think?'

'What sort of a diversion?' Jacques said.

'What do you suggest? I don't know, you're the maquisards after all – surely you've done such things before?'

The two men looked at one another again, unspoken words seeming to pass between them. Valentine scratched the dark shadow of stubble on his jaw, and then pushed his beret to the back of his head.

'What about a flood through the part of town where Gestapo headquarters is? Would that do it?'

At last.

'How on earth can you create a flood?'

'Don't you worry about that, mademoiselle. It's something we've been working on for a while, and this might be the time to do it. Just tell us when you want the diversion and we'll provide it. The Boche will have webbed feet by the time we've finished with them,' said Valentine, winking at her, while Jacques nodded his head so hard the moustache looked as if it were about to take flight.

Agnes bit her lip. She couldn't quite believe Valentine wasn't pulling her leg, but she refrained from asking again.

The three of them went over timings for the night in question, the maquisards making plans that would fit in with her own.

'We'll need Remi. He knows the system, even if he hasn't worked there since he joined us,' Jacques said.

Valentine grunted and shook his head.

'It makes sense to keep it just between us. We can do without him; I know how it works,' he said, glancing at Agnes.

She nodded.

Perhaps I'm finally getting through to them.

Agnes and Philippe had chosen the night of a local religious festival when there would be plenty of activity in the centre of town. The German troops would be busy either joining in with the festivities or on guard, so it should be quiet enough out on the fringes where the factory was situated. They had five days to get everything in place. She buried a frisson of fear, refusing to allow herself to think of the consequences if anything went wrong.

Philippe met her two days later at the same café in Cierp-Garin, continuing to play the part of her *beau* with an enthusiasm that made Agnes squirm.

They discussed the plan for the attack on the factory. Jacques had relented enough to give her a contact inside the fuel store, who was prepared to leave a side door unlocked.

'How much time do you need to set the explosives?' she asked Philippe.

'I won't know until I get inside the building,' he said. 'It'll depend on how many I need to set and the distance between them. I don't want something going off like a damp squib and all our work being for nothing if the whole thing doesn't go up.'

'I've been to the perimeter of the factory grounds, and there's lots of cover just outside the fence,' she said in a low voice. 'I found a place where we can crawl under the wire near the trees on the south side, and the door is only about fifty yards away. I'll keep lookout for the guard. He takes ten minutes to patrol the outside of the building, and at one-thirty he has a fifteen-minute break in the guardhouse at the main gate.'

'Perfect, that should give me plenty of time,' Philippe said. He smiled at her and took her hand again. She tried to smile back – thinking it must look more like a grimace, but he didn't seem to notice. 'We make a good team, don't we, *ma Tigresse*? Don't look so nervous; it's going to be fine. The Germans won't know what's hit 'em.'

He laughed and she couldn't help feeling infected by his attitude. They were young, on their own and about to give the Boche a bloody nose. At that moment it felt as if they were invincible, and she laughed with him, chinking her coffee cup to his as they raised a toast to each other. She noticed a group of old men watching them. They grinned at her, winking and nudging each other.

She smiled back at them.

If they only knew the truth.

Chapter 23

Claire

Once Aunt M returned to Stanbury Hall, she improved daily. Tired and still struggling to enunciate words clearly – which frustrated her – she nonetheless appeared much better. I visited her daily, but only stayed for a short time, conscious of not exhausting her fragile resources.

I went to see Andrew, dreading having to face him again, after he had told me that Helen was pregnant.

Arriving at the veterinary hospital at the end of surgery, hoping to avoid meeting any of the staff, I parked around the corner and slipped in by the side door. Andrew was in his office and looked up in surprise when I appeared.

'I didn't expect you back until next week,' he said.

'I came to say that I'm taking more time off. I need a month.'

His face tightened. 'A month? You know how busy we are, Claire; that's going to leave us really stretched, especially with Easter coming up, and people on annual leave.'

I shrugged. 'It's not a request, Andrew. Get Helen to sort it out – that's what she's paid for.' *Unnecessarily snide, Claire*, but I couldn't resist making the comment. 'You can hire a locum, or cut surgeries. Whatever; I don't care.'

I could tell he was furious, but he wouldn't meet my eyes, just clicked the top of a pen rapidly, a habit I knew well and a sure sign of stress.

'Helen's off just now. She's got terrible morning sickness.'

I didn't know whether to laugh or cry.

'Poor her.' I turned to leave, pausing at the door. 'It's not my problem. I'll be back in four weeks.'

As Aunt M's strength and mobility improved with the help of a patient, kind physiotherapist, I stayed longer with her whenever I could. We talked, played cards or I read to her, for one of the effects of the stroke was that her eyesight had suffered, and she found reading very tiring.

The boxes of books I had retrieved from the Chimneys still sat on the floor of her small living room, and I suggested we could unpack them and put them on her book shelves. We spent a happy hour sorting through the first couple of boxes; Aunt M directing where to put them – she had a firm idea where they should all go – and me dusting them, checking they weren't damaged, and placing them in the order she wanted.

One of the boxes held the book of poems by Tennyson. It was damaged; water had left marks on the cover and I wondered what had happened to it. Aunt M looked rueful.

'That book was the only thing I was able to rescue from my flat when it was bombed,' she said. 'It must be serendipity that I saved it.'

'Can you remember what happened?'

'As if it were yesterday, dear. Everything is so clear, it's like a film reel in my mind. It's funny how I can remember events, faces, and names from decades ago, yet not what I had for dinner yesterday.'

'I don't think it's unusual, Aunt M, sadly,' I said. 'Do you want to tell me about it? It must have been terrifying.'

'Well, I wasn't there when the bomb hit, thank God. I wouldn't be here today if I had been.'

Her eyes took on a distant look, as she relived the horror of losing her home . . .

I came home from work to find the end of the street blocked by fire engines, police and ambulances. There was a pall of acrid smoke, and the flames licked high above the roofs around the bend in the road. I was held for ten minutes while more fire engines arrived and got set up. I remember sitting on my motorcycle, shivering in the rain.

I asked a policeman, who was putting a rope across the road to keep everyone away, what was going on.

'Bomb blast, we think,' he said. 'Though it might be gas – but there've been a few too many "gas" explosions recently, for my liking. I reckon Jerry is retaliating for the thumping our boys are giving him across the water.' He waved me back. 'You can't come through, miss; the whole building is likely to collapse.'

I argued that I lived there. Wanted to know which block had been hit.

I tried to see past him, panicking; all my belongings were there – all the reminders of Agnes, all her things that I'd never had the heart to get rid of. What would I do if they were all destroyed?

The policeman was momentarily distracted by someone else, and I put the bike in gear and slipped around the end of the rope and down the road, ignoring his shouts, concentrating on dodging the burning debris and reaching home.

A fireman appeared out of the gloom and smoke and stood in front of me with his hands up, stopping me from going any closer, but I could see well enough. The whole of one side of my building had been blasted away and lay in a smoking heap of bricks and glass and household remnants. Bits of furniture, curtains, a bath, poked out of the debris. A water main had fractured, and a spout of water was soaking the rescue teams like a giant geyser. Firemen pointed hoses at the fires, and the flames fizzled and hissed. The smell was appalling.

A line of people had climbed on the pile of rubble and were carefully lifting blocks of masonry and handing them to the next person in the chain. I sat on the bike and stared in horror – the block was three storeys high and there were four flats on each floor – there must be people under there, buried alive. Or not alive. I'd rather be blown to smithereens than lost under all that like a piece of flotsam. Agnes and I used to talk about 'going together' – the reality in front of me was far removed from our imaginations. I had seen the aftermath of bombed houses before; of course I had. Hadn't everyone who lived through the war? But never this close, this personal. It was like I had been assaulted. I felt wounded, traumatised.

The remains of the flats still standing were stark against the glow of the flames. Mine was one of them. The blast had ripped away part of the wall and I could see into my bedroom and bathroom. Curtains flapped and billowed through the shattered windows. It reminded me of a doll's house with the front opened up so the tiny pieces of furniture could be played with.

I couldn't stop the tears, as much from the smoke as my distress. An ARP warden tried to lead me away.

'You need to get behind the cordon, miss,' he said. 'It's too dangerous for you to be here.'

I ignored his words. I couldn't leave.

'Are there people under there?' I nodded towards the pile of rubble. 'They're my neighbours. I need to know. Please, tell me.'

I must have looked like a wild woman. The spray from the broken water main was soaking me and I'd lost my cap.

'We don't know how many were in the building when the explosion happened. Nobody has reported they were going away, but we just don't know. People are far too complacent when it comes to keeping us informed,' he said, wiping his forehead with a large, dirty handkerchief. He looked exhausted. 'Look at that mess. If we know folks are safe, we won't worry about digging for survivors. You live in the block, you say? Perhaps you can help us. Come with me.'

He set off towards a large van parked further down the road and I followed, pushing the motorcycle.

A small group of people were gathered at the back of the van. One man seemed to be directing operations and I was shoved in front of him.

'This young lady says she lives here. I thought she might be able to help us work out how many are missing,' said the ARP chap. He handed me a tin helmet. 'Here, miss, put that on. There's bits still falling all over the place.'

The man in charge gave me a pad and pencil.

'Can you write down how many people you know lived in the side of the block that's collapsed. God, it's like the Blitz all over again. Those bastard Germans – excuse my language, miss,' he said. 'I thought we were done with all this.'

'I'm afraid I don't know everyone who lives in the building, especially the ones on the top floor.'

'Well, do your best,' he said. 'Anything will be a help – and if you know whether they work and might be out of their home at this time of day, that would be much appreciated, too.'

Since Agnes went, I'd been as good as a recluse, and only knew a few of the people in my block. There were others I'd seen often enough and had an idea where they lived, though. I did my best and handed over the list to the officer in charge.

'Thank you. This is a great help. At least we know roughly how many people we need to track down.'

'I hope they were all out of the building when it was hit.'

A shudder started in my legs. I couldn't seem to make it stop and had to lean against the side of the van. The ARP warden noticed me and took my arm.

'You all right, miss? You've gone very pale. It'll be the shock hitting you.'

He led me to the front of the van and let me climb inside and sit in the passenger seat.

'Thank you, I'm fine, really,' I said, trying not to be sick.

'You stay there as long as you need to.'

I gazed over at my flat, hanging by its fingernails on the edge of the devastated building, and asked when I could get in to collect my things.

'No one's going into that building. It's far too dangerous, could collapse at any moment.'

'But I need to rescue my belongings. They won't pull it down before I can get them, will they?'

'All you can do is wait until it falls and then salvage whatever survives.'

I couldn't take in his words; it hit me that I was homeless.

I couldn't bear to look at the ruination in front of me for one more moment. I wheeled my motorcycle back to the edge of the cordon, pushing my way against the flow of gawkers. But the crowd had grown and some of the neighbours had arrived. I got shoved alongside them and we stood together in a huddle. I had nowhere to go, little money on me and not even a change of clothes.

I wanted to make a dash for it and get into the smoking building, race up the stairs and grab a few of my things, but it was a stupid, pointless idea.

I knew I should count myself lucky – I was alive and they were only 'things' – there were others so much worse off than me, but as darkness fell, I remained, watching the teams carefully removing rubble. They wouldn't give up until every single person was accounted for.

Aunt M fell silent, her face sombre and tired. It seemed extra-ordinary that people lived with such dread and fear throughout the war. My life was so easy and comfortable compared to those days. Her story, told in such a calm tone, made me realise just how much I took for granted.

Chapter 24

Agnes

Agnes tried to ignore the water dripping down the back of her neck as she tramped along beside Philippe in the gloom of the forest. The cloud was down almost to ground level and a fine misty rain hung in the air. As they continued the march towards St Jean the darkness deepened, and the rain became a persistent downpour, drenching them both.

'The way this rain's coming down, there'll be no need for Valentine and Jacques to provide a diversion; the town will be under water anyway,' Agnes said, pushing her wet hair out of her eyes. 'I detest this low cloud; it gives me claustrophobia. I can't breathe properly.'

She walked faster to keep pace with Philippe, who was striding ahead along the forest track.

'Don't knock it. It's perfect for keeping us out of sight of the Germans. And if your maquisards can provide a little more distraction for us, then so much the better.' He stopped and checked the fastening on his rucksack, making sure the explosives inside were still dry. 'Come on, Céleste, we need to be there in time for the guard to go on his break. I don't want to have to rush setting the explosives, a few extra minutes will make all the difference.'

Agnes broke into a trot, her feet squelching with each stride, and they kept up a good pace in silence until the track met the main road. Crouching behind a large beech tree, Philippe peered around the trunk, looking up and down the road. The cloud kept visibility down to less than fifty yards, and with the rain pouring down it was impossible to see anything in the dark.

'Well, if we can't see anything, neither can anyone else,' Agnes said, her heart up around her throat somewhere. 'But we have to do the last mile on the road, so if a patrol comes along and we can't hide, we say our car broke down and we're walking into town, okay?'

She felt rather than saw Philippe nod. They slid down the bank and onto the road, brushing leaves and dirt off themselves before starting to walk, holding hands as if it was the most natural thing in the world.

Five minutes later they heard the unmistakable sound of a motorcycle and dived into a ditch at the side of the road, pressing their faces into the mud and dead leaves. Agnes swallowed down hard as the noise of the engine grew. It passed them without pausing but they remained still for minutes after it headed down the valley, away from town. Philippe was the first to get to his feet, his face and clothes plastered in dripping mud and leaf litter, which he tried to brush off with an unsteady hand. Agnes crawled out of the ditch behind him, and rose, her legs hardly able to support her.

Now they were behind schedule and Agnes pushed the pace, the two of them trotting along the road, filthy and shaken by the near miss. Ten minutes later they hid in the trees on the southerly side of the perimeter fence with the side door to the factory in their sights through the gloom. Agnes checked her watch, just able to make out the black hands against its white face and realised that it had stopped. She swore quietly and Philippe stared at her, his eyebrows up in his hairline somewhere.

'It must have got waterlogged when we jumped in the ditch,' she whispered.

'Shit. We'll wait a few moments, see if the guard is still on patrol,' he said.

They crouched beneath a stand of hazel. A couple of minutes later, visible as not much more than a shadow, a German soldier traipsed around the corner of the building, his rifle pointing towards the ground. The dim light set on the gable end of the building barely made a difference to the visibility.

As the guard passed out of sight, the pair of them shimmied under the gap in the fence Agnes had discovered. A shallow ditch, overgrown with briars and thistles, ran under the wire and gave just enough room to crawl through. It only took a few seconds to reach the door Jacques had assured them would be unlocked. Philippe pressed the handle down and cursed as it held firm. He put his shoulder to it and shoved, but it still didn't move. Agnes pushed past him to try herself, but the door held fast; either it was the wrong one or the contact hadn't unlocked it. She wanted to believe there was some logical explanation, but all she could think of was how vulnerable they were.

'Must be the wrong door,' he muttered.

'No. I'm sure this is the right one. South side of the building, away from the road and the main gate,' Agnes whispered, furious he'd doubted her. 'Have you got your keys?'

Philippe nodded, but instead of trying to pick the lock he crept around the gable end and ran along the wall of the building, Agnes following him, cursing under her breath. It felt like time was speeding away in front of them. The guard would be back on patrol in a few minutes and they'd achieved nothing. Why couldn't he accept she was right?

Reaching the end of the building, Philippe stopped, put his hand out for her to get down, and cautiously looked around the corner. Agnes crouched against the wall; a glow from more lights lit the area in front of the building – the main gate and guard house. She peeped out from behind Philippe's legs and saw a vague shape moving behind the steamed-up glass of the guardroom.

It was no use trying to get in at that end; they'd be seen, for sure. She rose, turned, and began to move quietly back the way they'd come.

Stay calm. There's still plenty of time to get the job done.

She heard Philippe following her, swearing under his breath. Returning to the door, he pulled out a set of thin, strange-looking keys from his pack, picked out two and inserted both into the lock. Delicately, he twisted and fiddled with them while Agnes went back to the corner, flattened herself against the wall and kept watch. Glancing at him, the impulse to snatch the keys and do it herself was almost impossible to resist. After what seemed like an age, she heard a quiet sigh.

'We're in,' he whispered, followed by a string of curses as he pushed the door and it still held firm. She ran back to him and watched disbelievingly while he tried again. 'It must be dead-bolted on the inside,' he muttered. They stared at each other for a second. 'We could blow it. Set a quick fuse and then get in and out as fast as we can.'

He unslung his pack and began to undo it.

Agnes grabbed his hand and shook her head.

'It'll never work. I reckon we've only got a few minutes before the guard begins his patrol again. Even if we opened the door, there's not enough time to set the charges and get out.'

'Fuck's sake. How could this go so wrong?' he hissed.

'We need to move, not stand here arguing. Come on, lock that door again. We don't want them to suspect anyone's been here.'

Running back to the corner, she checked to see the guard hadn't begun his patrol, while Philippe relocked the door. He gave a low whistle and Agnes took one last look past the corner.

The rain had eased but the low cloud had, if anything, become denser. Fear spiked as she saw the shadow of a man, indistinct in the gloom.

'Come on,' she hissed. 'The guard's on his way.'

Philippe slung his pack over one shoulder, and they crept to the far end of the building, paused for a second and then set off for the fence in a crouching run. They were halfway across the rough grass when a shout and a volley of barks split the night air.

Why had she not noticed the guard had a dog?

'Run. Don't stop,' rapped Philippe and she raced for the fence, stumbling over the sodden ground, the barking getting nearer. Terror gave her speed and she kept running, the perimeter a blur in the mist and dark. Shots sounded far too loud in the still night air as she flung herself under the gap in the fence. Philippe, on her heels, pushed her forward with a grunt, and she crumpled in a heap below the hazel trees. Scrambling up and not daring to look back, she ran towards the road. It was only after she'd gone twenty yards she realised there was nobody behind her and glanced back to see Philippe holding his side, slowing with each faltering step. She ran back to him, putting his arm around her neck and taking his weight over her shoulders.

'Come on, we must get out of here,' she said, each word a gasp. 'Let's find somewhere out of sight, and I'll look at your side.'

'Bastard shot me,' he said, grunting with every movement. 'It makes more sense for you to keep going, Tigresse, get to safety. I'll hole up and wait till they go past me, then make my way back down the valley.'

He let out a quiet moan as they both stumbled over an exposed tree root. She couldn't hear any sounds of pursuit but there was no doubt the guard would have alerted others. Agnes held Philippe tighter, but she knew her strength would be gone long before they reached safety. When she was as sure as she could be that they weren't being followed, she stopped. Philippe leant against a tree, sliding to the ground, holding his side. At that moment, a siren split the night air, its wail rising and falling, and Agnes almost collapsed with fear. But Philippe laughed, a strange, choked sound, and she realised what it meant: Valentine and Jacques had succeeded. She hoped the Gestapo were swimming in a flood of biblical proportions, but even if they were only a little wet it gave them a breathing space.

'Let me see,' she said, opening Philippe's jacket, slick with the dark stain of blood. Quickly she pulled off her soaking scarf and tied it around his middle, bunching up his shirt tail as a pad to help stem the flow. 'If they bring dogs, your blood will lead them straight to us,' she muttered. 'Let's hope the rain will wash it away, and this'll help it stop.'

'Thanks,' he said, quietly. 'Like I said, you should go. Get back to the farm, while the Boche are being kept occupied. I'll climb up off the track and hide out until morning, then make my own way back.' He grinned lopsidedly at her, his teeth showing as a pale grimace in the gloom. 'With your expert nursing I'll feel better once I've had a rest.'

'Shut up and get on your feet. I'm not leaving you, so stop talking rubbish,' she said, pulling him upright.

He staggered, then leaned on her again as they set off. Thoughts rattled around her head. How could she possibly support him all the way back to the farm? She was almost exhausted and they weren't even back at the forest track; and there was still a mile of open road to negotiate. They reached the junction where the lane turned onto the main route. She could make out the first of the outlying houses on the edge of St Jean Layrisse. The side road leading to the market was fifty yards away, towards the town centre, and Agnes found herself turning left as if her feet had a mind of their own.

'Where the hell are we going? This is leading us towards the Germans, hot away. You've got a funny idea of escape, kiddo,' muttered Philippe.

'For fuck's sake shut up, and stop speaking English,' she hissed. 'I have a plan; just pray the Gestapo already have their hands full.'

Agnes hitched Philippe more firmly under her arm – she was sure she hurt him with every step, but they had to get off the road before anyone saw them. The weather continued to be on their side, the rain falling heavily again as they turned into *Rue du Marché* and staggered closer to her destination. They were halfway along the street when she heard the sound of an engine approaching. Quickly, she pulled Philippe into a doorway. Hardly daring to breathe, they hid their faces while a motorbike and sidecar drove slowly past. The driver scanned the street, and a soldier moved a gun mounted on the front of the sidecar from side to side, his face pale in the gloom of the night.

Twenty long minutes later she stopped at number 19, Rue Gambetta, and allowed Philippe to slide in a heap onto the step. She rapped loudly on the door, praying that Valerie Duphil was well enough to get out of bed and come to let them in. After knocking repeatedly, Agnes heard the shuffle of feet.

A querulous voice demanded to know who was bashing her door down in the middle of the night, and why in the name of all that was holy was that siren blaring – were they under attack? Agnes smiled – poor Valerie must be terrified, but damned if she would let anyone know that.

'Valerie,' she said in a low voice. 'Please let us in, it's Céleste Sarraute. I have a friend with me, and he's been injured. We need your help.'

The door opened immediately, and Valerie's white, fearful face appeared round the edge of it. She looked both ways along the fog-bound street and then pulled the door wide and stood back, leaning on a walking stick. She wore a long nightdress with a shawl over her shoulders, and looked haggard. The older woman helped Agnes get Philippe through into the kitchen. They must look like nothing on earth, Agnes thought, catching her reflection in the hall mirror. Enormous eyes in a white face smeared with rain and grime stared back at her. She could be mistaken for one of the many homeless she had seen cowering in doorways.

'I'm sorry for frightening you, but I couldn't think of where else to go.'

'Think nothing of it. You did the right thing. I don't sleep much anyway and I'm happy to help. Your friend is hurt? What happened?'

'He's been shot.' Agnes glanced at Philippe. His face was grey, a line of sweat standing out on his forehead. He sat hunched over in the chair, eyes closed. 'We were on a raid, but something went wrong and we had to run for it. A guard saw us. The Boche will be looking for us everywhere. We had to get out of sight.'

'Let's get him upstairs. He can go in the spare bedroom. I've got painkillers and some bandages. We can at least make him more comfortable. You go ahead – it's the second door on the left – and I'll follow when I've boiled some water and gathered everything we need together.'

'Thank you. Come on, old chap, can you manage to get up the stairs?'

Agnes put Philippe's arm around her neck again, and he slowly pushed himself up from the table. They made a slow ascent of the staircase, shudders racking him as they staggered up each step.

The bedroom had the musty air of a space not used. A counterpane covered the small bed, and Agnes pulled it back to reveal a cotton sheet and thin blanket underneath that gave off a strong smell of mothballs. Philippe sank onto it and she took off his spectacles and helped him remove his coat and boots. He was soaked through, and she untied the ruined scarf and began to peel off the rest of his wet clothes. Feeling out of her depth, she nonetheless undid his belt and trousers and pulled them off, before pushing him gently backwards onto the bed and lifting his legs onto it so he was lying stretched out, his long white shanks incongruous without their normal covering.

Clothes maketh the man . . .

'Concentrate, this is no time for such nonsense,' she muttered. She fumbled with the buttons on Philippe's shirt and rucked up the vest under it to reveal a ribby torso showing each clearly defined muscle. There was a minimum of body hair – only a thin line, as if someone had pencilled it in – which travelled down from his navel and disappeared into his underpants. Heat swamped Agnes's face.

'Enjoying the view?'

The croak of Philippe's voice made her jump and she quickly covered the lower half of his body with the sheet and blanket.

'Don't be ridiculous – I wanted to check you had no injuries other than the bullet wound.'

'You could have just asked me, Tigresse,' he said, a twisted grin doing nothing to hide his pain, but amusement and something else – a challenge, perhaps – in his eyes.

'I thought you'd passed out.'

Her face was on fire. The arrogance of him, when she had so much else to think about.

Thoughts raced through her mind as she stared at him, knowing she would have to perform another intimate action when she washed and dressed the wound. It looked like someone had hacked a piece of flesh out of his side in between his bottom rib and the bony protuberance of his hipbone. To her inexpert eye, it seemed as if it was a deep flesh wound. There was no bullet hole, no innards spilling out of the wound, and she prayed he'd been lucky, that nothing major had been hit.

'So, did you find any?' he said, the grin still on his face, almost cadaverous amidst the sheen of sweat and the grey tone to his skin.

'Pardon? Find any what?'

'Any other injuries, Nurse. What else were you looking for?'

He was laughing at her again, and stress and fear boiled over in her head. How could he be so flippant? She looked down at him, and without any thought of what she was doing, lifted a hand and slapped him hard across his face. Then she sat on the edge of the bed and put her hands over her face.

Philippe rubbed his cheek. 'I guess I deserved that. "Tigresse" sure does suit you. I'm sorry, okay? I was being stupid.' His words came between grunts of pain and Agnes dragged her hands down her face. There was a red mark where she'd hit him, but his pallor had turned from grey to bone-white and he'd closed his eyes again. 'I would really appreciate it if you could do something for this damn bullet wound,' he said in a faint voice.

His eyelids fluttered and she grabbed his wrist, feeling for a pulse, breathing a sigh when she found it, even though it was fast and weak.

'You've lost a lot of blood. I should try and get you to a hospital.'

'Ain't gonna happen, kiddo,' he whispered. 'Clean me up and get me outta here. I'll be fine by tomorrow.'

'Of course you will,' she said, patting his hand as if he were a child, thinking there was no possibility of moving him so soon.

She needed to prevent him losing any more blood before he became so weak he wouldn't be capable of getting out of bed, never mind making it back to the farm. She hoped that with no bullet to try and remove, once the bleeding was stopped, he would improve enough for them to leave.

The sound of Valerie making her slow way up the stairs gave her an excuse to escape, and she went to help her. There was a box of aspirin, bandages, iodine, and a bowl of hot water with a cloth floating in it, on a tray that was in danger of being dropped. Agnes took it with a smile of thanks, returned to the bedroom and set it down on the bedside table.

Feeling more confident, she poured a good glug of the dark brown liquid into the hot water and rubbed it well into the cloth. Working gently but thoroughly, she checked no tiny threads of Philippe's clothing had stuck to the wound while she cleaned it. He snatched a breath now and then but lay still while she worked. Then she poured neat iodine into the raw flesh, eliciting a word from the patient that shocked her but made her smile – a tiny revenge.

'I wish we had some of those new medicines,' she said. 'You need penicillin. If it doesn't get infected, I'll be amazed.'

185

Valerie had been looking on and passing things to her as she tended to the wound.

'I have some sulphonamide powder if you think that'll help him,' she said. 'I get abscesses on my legs and the doctor gives it to me from time to time.'

'It'll be a great help. Thank you so much for everything you've done for us, Valerie.'

'Phssh, away with you. Any decent person would do the same. And what good will it do me? I'm tired of hanging on; if I live to see France freed of these bastards – excuse my language, monsieur – then I will die content.'

Agnes turned to the French woman and put her arms around her. For all her bravado, she looked ill and exhausted.

'You're an angel,' she whispered.

Valerie patted her back, sniffed, and turned away.

'I'll go and find the antibiotic,' she said, her voice hoarse.

Agnes liberally spread the powder over the wound and then covered it with a clean pad and wrapped a crepe bandage around Philippe's middle to hold it in place. Running back downstairs she filled a glass with cold water, brought it to him and gave him a couple of aspirin tablets to swallow. There was no more she could do.

Agnes stayed in the room, trying to find a comfortable position on the small, upright chair in the corner. Exhaustion dragged at the corners of her mind, and every muscle ached, but sleep was impossible. Each ragged breath Philippe took was loud in the quiet and she knew he wasn't sleeping either.

'Do you want another aspirin?' she asked when he groaned and swore under his breath.

'I think it's started bleeding again,' he muttered.

'Let me see.'

She put the small lamp on and unwound the bandage, sticky with fresh blood. Taking a fresh pad of cotton, she shook some more of the sulphonamide powder onto it and placed it firmly against the raw meat of the wound.

'Fuck,' Philippe hissed. 'Don't take up nursing as an occupation, will ya?'

'Sorry.' She bound the pad again, while the patient bit down on his lip and beads of sweat appeared on his face. He shivered and she put a hand to his forehead. 'Are you cold? Here.' She laid the plaid blanket she'd been wrapped in over him.

Giving him another aspirin and a glass of water, she watched as he swallowed it down. His eyes had sunk back in his head, and under the sheen of sweat his face was grey.

'Thank you,' he said, laying his head back with a sigh. 'That's better.'

'Try and sleep. It's almost morning and we must get out of here before they start searching for us.'

He grunted and closed his eyes. Agnes put the lamp out and went back to her chair, tucking her cold feet under her and wrapping her arms around herself against the chill of the room.

She must have dozed for a while. Movement roused her and daylight diffused through the thin curtains. Philippe was awake, watching her, his face a better colour but pain behind his eyes. He scrabbled for his spectacles, which lay on the bedside table.

'Don't move, I'll get them,' she said, yelping as her foot seized in a cramp.

Hopping across the room, she placed the specs on his face. Sitting on the end of the bed, she massaged her foot; every muscle creaked, her shoulders and back aching and stiff. She stood and stretched out the kinks, feeling Philippe's eyes on her.

'You look a little better,' she said, sitting back on the bed.

'Yeah, your nursing isn't so bad, after all,' he said, a shadow of his normal grin on his face. He tried to sit, grimacing as he pushed himself up.

'Wait.' She took his arm and placed the pillow against the bedhead, then helped him sit against it. 'Okay?' He nodded. 'We need to get out of town as soon as you can move. The Gestapo will be all over the place looking for us. Do you think you can walk, if I help you?'

'Of course. It's only a flesh wound. I'll be fine.' He grabbed her hand, pulling her down beside him. 'You saved me, last night, Tigresse. I owe you.'

Agnes stood up, heat running up her face. 'We're partners, aren't we? I wasn't about to leave you to the mercy of the Boche.'

There was a quiet tap on the door and Valerie entered, fully dressed, with her hair immaculate, as always. Gone was the frightened woman of the previous night. She still looked ill and tired, but the upright, strong person Agnes knew was back in place.

'Good morning. Did you manage to sleep at all?' Valerie said. 'I'm making some coffee and I've some bread from yesterday. I'm sorry I can't offer you more.'

'Good morning. Please don't worry – you've already done more than enough for us,' Agnes said, kissing her on both cheeks. 'We can never repay you for taking us in last night.'

They smiled at each other, and Valerie looked at Philippe, her head on one side.

'You look a little better this morning.'

'Yes, I am, thanks. Are there squads out looking for us, do you think?' His expression slipped for a second and Agnes caught a glimpse of something dark on his face. 'I'm sure our Resistance friends will have done their best keeping the Nazis busy all night. Hopefully, they're too busy drying out to be worrying about us. And after all, nobody saw our faces, did they?'

'Talking about drying out, our clothes are a mess – we look like we've slept under a hedge.' Agnes picked up the ruined shirt with Philippe's blood all over it. His trousers were still soaked and covered in mud, and hers weren't any better.

'Give them to me,' said Valerie. 'I'll lend you something, and there are still some of my husband's clothes in the wardrobe. They'll do, I'm sure.'

'Thank you, Valerie. Even a coat to cover up our dishevelment will do. You're so much taller than me, I doubt anything will fit.'

'We'll see. I'll be back in a minute.'

She went out of the room, and Agnes turned her attention back to Philippe.

'It's market day, so the town will be busy, which should make it easier to blend in. The Germans are used to seeing me on the cheese stall and you can keep up the act of being *mon copain*.' She thought for a moment. 'What about the explosives? We're laying ourselves wide open if we get stopped and searched.'

'We sure can't leave them behind,' Philippe said immediately, catching a ragged breath as he moved too quickly. 'Will your hosts be at the market? Perhaps we could ask them to hide the stuff in among their things?'

'We can't expect them to do that. They risk everything by associating with me as it is. I won't do it.'

'Why don't you let them decide?' said Valerie, coming back in with her arms full of clothes. She dropped them on the end of the bed. 'My dear, you must realise by now, we French want to do as much as possible to help you. Without the likes of you and your friend here, things would be so much harder for us. Being made to feel useful makes such a difference to me and people like the Espouys.' She turned to leave again. 'Try those on for size. I'll make the coffee. It'll be ready in a few minutes.'

Agnes stared at her back as Valerie shuffled out of the room. Her mind raced.

Philippe interrupted her thoughts. 'She's right, you know. They have to make the decision; it's not yours to make for them.'

'But what if they're caught? Their children, Marc and Nicole? How could I forgive myself if it was my fault they became orphans? Make no mistake – they would become orphans – we both know that.'

'Look, kiddo. This is war, it's not a game. The Espouys knew what they were about when they took you in. Do you think the

Germans would believe they didn't know what you were when you arrived? Just by having you in their home, they're putting themselves at risk every single day.' He pushed the cover off his legs, took a breath and swung them over the side of the bed, groaning at the movement. 'Pass me those pants, will ya? They look like they might do, and we need to get moving as soon as possible.'

Sweat popped onto his forehead again as he moved, and he wasn't quick enough to stop a catch of breath. His bravado might fool Valerie, but he was far from well. She picked up the trousers and passed them to him, then left him to get himself dressed.

Chapter 25

Claire

Now I had learnt so much more, thanks to the letter and Aunt M opening up about her life during the war, it was satisfying to make headway with Agnes's story. The basic information was readily available, which in a lot of ways made me sadder on Aunt M's behalf. Seventy years of believing her love was dead or missing and yet I had uncovered her movements back then with a few days' research.

I knew where Agnes was posted to, and the chapter about her in the book on SOE women gave me the name she used while in France – Céleste Sarraute. There was lots I didn't know yet, but if I kept digging, surely there must be more I could discover.

I couldn't find any evidence of her capture or execution, which was some relief. But there was no indication she'd returned to England either, so I didn't feel much further forward in knowing what happened to prevent her returning to Aunt M. It was a frustrating process, but also a satisfaction in every tiny piece of information I uncovered. The notebook I jotted everything down in was filling up.

I researched as much as I could about the Pyrenees region and the war in that area. It was part of Vichy France, and being on the border with Spain, there were numerous escape routes over the mountains. The terrifying ordeals undergone by people in some of the accounts of escapes were sobering. I found myself wanting to see the mountains, appreciate what they were like in reality – not just read about them in a book. With time to fill, visiting the town would be a good way to keep my mind off Andrew and Helen.

Once Aunt M had recovered some of her strength and I was less worried about her, I sat her down and told her everything I'd discovered.

She was outraged.

'So, there were other young women who did the same as Agnes – just disappeared into thin air?'

I nodded. 'Their next of kin were told, but no one else.' I understood her anger. What if someone I was close to suddenly went missing without a word? It seemed unconscionable. 'Did you ask Agnes's family if they knew where she went? If they were the only people she could tell, they must have known, don't you think?'

'Her mother died not long after I met Agnes, and she was estranged from her father, had cut all ties. Didn't I tell you that, already?' Aunt M said. I nodded. She frowned. 'I did contact him – her father – I looked his name up in the telephone directory. I rang every Christopher Kerr in London until I found him, and said I was a friend of Agnes. He admitted they were estranged – he didn't even know she was missing.'

'Gosh, Aunt M – you should have been a detective. That was good thinking.'

She shrugged. 'I was so worried, and I thought they might have been notified if she'd been killed in an accident or something like that.' Sighing, she repeated her words. 'They didn't even know she was missing.' She fell silent. I didn't say anything, hoping I hadn't lost her again. 'Do you really think you'll be able to find her, after all these years?' she said, at last.

Still with me.

I didn't want to get her hopes up.

'I have no idea, in all honesty,' I said. 'But now you're so much better, I've decided to go to the town in France where she was posted. I hope I might be able to discover what happened to her, or at least learn more about how the war affected that area.'

'Goodness, there's no need to go to such lengths on my behalf, dear.' Aunt M's eyes opened wide with surprise. 'I know I said I'd like to know what happened to her, but you must be far too busy to go haring off on a wild-goose chase.'

'To be honest, it's a good excuse for me,' I said. 'I need to get away for a wee while; things with Andrew are . . . difficult.'

She eyed me sharply. 'I knew there was something you weren't telling me,' she said. 'I'm so sorry if you two are having problems, dear.'

She leant across and patted my hand. Her sympathy almost undid me, and I had to blink hard for a second. I really should tell her about our divorce, but felt completely unprepared. I swallowed the sob caught in my throat.

'Where are you going?' she said, oblivious to my reaction.

Glad of the distraction, I pulled a map of the Pyrenees out of my bag and laid it out on the small table between our chairs, folding it to the central area.

'I've discovered she stayed near a town called St Jean Layrisse, which is in the Midi-Pyrenees department. The Gestapo had a base there. I've tried to find out something about it but there's hardly anything about the war. Lots about the town itself, its history and the present day; it seems odd I can't find more about that time.'

Aunt M peered short-sightedly at the map, her eyes still giving her trouble.

'Which is the town – St Jean Layrisse, did you say it was called?'

I pointed it out to her, ringed it in red felt-tip pen and wrote out the name in large letters at the side of the map with a big black arrow pointing to it. Promising to stay in touch and send her a postcard, I gave Aunt M a hug, and left her gazing at the map.

Chapter 26

Agnes

Agnes and Philippe slipped out of the house while the street outside was quiet. Philippe had his arm across her shoulder and hers was around his back, playing the lovers. They wandered down towards the market, taking their time. Agnes was acutely aware of the rucksack on Philippe's back, with the explosives still lying at the bottom.

No one paid any attention to them, apart from Henri LeGendre, who was walking back to his shop carrying a basket with some onions, a baguette, and a small truckle of goat's cheese in it. His small orange poodle trotted along beside him and ran over to Agnes, its stumpy tail wagging nineteen to the dozen. She bent and scratched the dog's head, and Henri stopped and wished her good day, kissing her on both cheeks. He looked at Philippe with shrewd eyes and turning to Agnes, spoke quietly.

'Your friend looks as if he's had a night on the tiles after the festival yesterday. You young things need to keep a low profile for a while. I heard the Boche are hunting for a pair of maquisards who tried to break into a fuel dump last night. They're pulling in anyone who's a stranger in town – and some they just don't like the look of.' He winked at them. '*Bon journée, mademoiselle, monsieur.*' And, raising his hat, he walked on past them.

Agnes and Philippe stared at the old man's receding back for a second and then continued on to the marketplace, their pace slow. It was a relief to see Remi Comet helping Danielle set up her stall in its usual position. Agnes made straight for it, leaving Philippe looking at a stall selling plates and cutlery.

'*Bonjour, mademoiselle,*' Remi said. 'Danielle mentioned you weren't coming to the market today. I hope you're feeling better.'

Agnes swallowed, forgetting the excuse they had made up for the possibility of her not being there this morning. She glanced over at Danielle, who was glaring at her.

'Thank you, Remi. I'm much better. It seemed unfair to leave Danielle with all the work, and I managed to get a lift into town with a friend.' She allowed herself to blush, batting her eyelashes at him and smiling. 'It was kind of you to help Danielle set up.'

He smiled back at her, his eyes lost in a sea of wrinkles.

'That's my job, and Danielle is an old friend. What else would I do?'

He touched his beret and nodded, then wandered away to the next stall, leaving Agnes shivering as the sweat cooled down her spine. Danielle caught her arm and dragged her behind the stall.

'You look terrible,' she said in a quiet voice. 'And he looks worse. What happened?'

'It was a disaster,' Agnes muttered. 'We were almost caught before we even got inside, and Philippe was shot. We need your help, Danielle, please?'

Danielle drew in an audible gasp. 'Your friend is still able to walk, so I'm hoping he isn't too badly hurt?' she said.

Agnes shook her head.

'You don't have to ask, Céleste. You know I'll do whatever I can.'

'The explosives are still in the rucksack Philippe is carrying. Can you hide them in your van and take them back to the farm for us? They never bother you, but we're bound to get searched at the roadblock, especially after last night.'

'I heard Gestapo headquarters got a soaking,' Danielle said, her mouth twitching into a grin.

Agnes tried to smile back at her. It seemed the maquisards had done their work well. She couldn't imagine what Jacques and Valentine would say when they knew how badly the raid had failed. Anger over-rode her other thoughts – it was *their* contact who'd let them all down. If the door had been unlocked as was promised, the following nightmare wouldn't have happened.

Danielle spoke to her again, and Agnes brought her attention back to the other woman's words. Of course, the rucksack could go in the back of the van.

Agnes gazed over to where Philippe still stood in front of the same stall. A pair of German soldiers passed him as they patrolled the area, guns held at the ready. Agnes watched, hardly able to breathe, as they abruptly turned and walked back to him.

Pushing Philippe out of the way, they barked something at the stallholder, who had a display of hunting knives alongside the kitchenware. Gesticulating to him, they flung the merchandise to the ground, grabbed the hapless vendor, and began shouting at him in German, waving one of the knives in his face. The man was obviously terrified, repeating *desolée* over and over, but the bigger of the two soldiers held him in a headlock while the other flicked open the knife and dragged the blade down his cheek. Agnes gagged at the sound of the man's scream, and the marketplace became held in a moment of suspended animation as everyone stopped and stared. It was an act of pointless brutality, and then it was over and the Germans continued their patrol as if nothing had happened. The knife seller crumpled to the ground holding his face, blood dripping through his fingers, whimpering to himself.

A man at a neighbouring stall went over to him and began clearing up the mess of broken china scattered over the ground, watched – Agnes noticed in horror – by Philippe. He said something to the injured man and gave him his hand to help him stand up, by which time Remi had also come to the man's aid, and Philippe stood back.

Why does he have to do that? Why can't he just keep his head down, stay unnoticed?

She was about to go and drag him away when the soldiers arrived at the Espouy stall and started digging into the cheeses on display with their grubby fingers. Danielle smiled serenely at them, pointing out the different types she had with her today – asking if the gentlemen would like to taste anything? All the cheese was made on her own farm and was the freshest in the valley, she could guarantee it. Agnes stood quietly, hoping not to be noticed, although the smaller of the two – the one who had cut the stallholder – she had met before at the market, and he always tried to flirt with her, grabbing her hand and putting his arm around her waist. He made her shudder, but she would smile politely at him and pretend she didn't understand German, which was not far from the truth.

But today they must have been given orders to keep patrolling, and after making the cheeses unsaleable to anyone else, they moved off, licking their fingers – the smaller soldier catching her eye and making an obscene gesture with his finger in his mouth. He winked and laughed when she flushed, then was gone.

Danielle swore under her breath in a long, vicious string of oaths as she changed the cheeses for new ones. Agnes couldn't stop shaking and sat down on a small stool behind the stall. She tried to steady her breathing and after a moment looked up to see Philippe standing in front of her, leaning against the van, holding his side, his face chalk white.

'I'm okay,' she said, trying to stop the wobble in her voice. 'That bastard should be shot for what he just did.'

She was shocked at her own vehemence and the hatred coursing around her. It was as if an electric current had passed through her body. She wanted to take the knife and thrust it as hard as she could into the soldier's leering mouth.

'Not gonna disagree on that one, Tigresse.'

'Please – can you avoid going near stalls that are about to be smashed by Germans? I thought you were going to be arrested, until they started on that poor unfortunate man.'

'Me too, kiddo, me too,' he muttered, so only she could hear. Still, she scowled at him for his rashness. He hobbled away, moving more slowly the further he went.

I must get him out of here. He's going to collapse before much longer.

'Why don't you both come back with me?'

Danielle's voice broke into her thoughts.

Agnes considered her offer. It would be much easier if they had a lift, but Danielle wouldn't leave for at least two more hours, and she wasn't sure he would still be able to walk by then. But getting back any other way seemed impossible, so what choice was there?

'I don't know. It's still early and you have your cheeses to sell. He's lost a lot of blood and needs to be somewhere where he can rest for a while, or he'll be even worse for wear.'

'I've had more than enough this morning, after what those two *cochons* did to poor M Sutro . . . and what they did to my cheeses. I felt like ramming them down their fat, ugly throats and letting them choke.' Danielle's face reddened, her brow creased in a furious frown. 'Come on, help me pack this lot up and we'll go home. I can't bear being here any longer.'

She began putting all the remaining cheeses back into their boxes. Agnes helped her, and within ten minutes everything was cleared away into the back of the van.

Agnes went over to where Philippe had found a seat at a table outside the market café, a glass of water in front of him. His smile was a thin-lipped grimace, his eyes hollow with pain. She took his hand as any girlfriend would and dragged him to his feet.

'Come on, you must meet my aunt; she's heard all about you.

We've been invited for lunch, so we'd better hurry if we want a lift home with her.'

'That's very kind of her,' he said, plastering a grin on his face. 'I can't wait to taste her cheese.'

The pair walked with their arms around each other – her hand hiding the small dark stain on the side of his shirt under the dead man's open coat.

Fitting the three of them into Danielle's tiny van proved difficult, with Philippe lying in the back, curled up among the boxes of unsold goat's cheese. Agnes sat in the front passenger seat as usual, sure that any half-witted German soldier would notice the guilt writ large on her face if they were stopped.

The routine roadblock was in place on the edge of town, and a queue of half a dozen or so vehicles and farm carts were backed up already. Agnes's heart thumped against her ribs and she wiped her hands repeatedly along her thighs in a mindless way, until Danielle snapped at her to stop. The Germans took an age to let each vehicle pass, checking papers from front to back instead of the flick-through they normally did. The rain and low cloud of the previous night had gone, and it was a clear, sunny morning, making the temperature in the interior of the van rise with each minute they had to wait.

'My cheeses will be ruined if these bastard Boche don't let us through soon,' muttered Danielle. 'M LeConte, I hope you're not sitting on one of the boxes. Your large arse will heat them even more.' Philippe hurriedly shifted his position, and Agnes heard a quiet groan. They had barricaded the boxes high enough behind the front seats for him to be out of sight to a casual observer. If the back of the van was opened for a proper search he would be seen immediately, but there was nothing they could do about it. The women had removed their coats and used them and a couple of old sacks to cover him – little enough but all they had to hand.

'My *large arse* is useful for some things, but it's not overheating your precious cheese,' he said, as Agnes turned and raised her eyebrows at him. Exhaustion was written on his face, but he winked and showed her a corner of his pack still with the explosives in the bottom he was using as a cushion.

'I hope your derriere doesn't heat that up too much,' she said, quietly. 'Things might get a bit too hot in here.'

He put his head back against the side of the van, stifling a snort of laughter, and shut his eyes. His cocky confidence was wiped away as Agnes stared at him, his spectacles enlarging the black rings under the closed lids, his mouth a tight line of pain. He looked much younger and more vulnerable than the irritating smartmouth she found so annoying most of the time.

The queue slowly inched forward, until the car in front was ordered to stop, and the two people inside had their papers taken from them.

'*Raus! Geh raus!*' ordered one of the soldiers.

The frightened-looking couple were marched at gunpoint to the guard post. The nondescript car was searched, soldiers almost pulling it apart. Eventually, one of them let out a yell and the others went over to see what he'd found. A bag was pulled out of the boot, where Agnes could see it had been hidden under a false base. The soldiers ripped it open and out tumbled cartons of cigarettes. Picking up their haul, two of the soldiers marched off to the guardroom.

Nausea rose in Agnes's throat. If they chose to search Danielle's vehicle, they would all be in deep trouble. Why had they chosen that particular car, though? The couple must have done something to alert them – perhaps their papers weren't in order – or someone had given them away? She glanced at the other two. Danielle looked like a rabbit caught in a headlight, her eyes staring at the scene in front of them. Philippe seemed to have fallen asleep, hidden under the sacks, a gentle snore the only give-away. She touched Danielle on the shoulder and the other woman jumped, banging her elbow on the steering wheel.

'*Merde*. What did you do that for? You gave me a fright,' she said, rubbing her arm.

'Sorry, I didn't mean to startle you. You looked so fixated on the car in front. They'll notice if you seem too worried, won't they?'

'I've not seen them so strict since they discovered the radio and shot your predecessor. It was hellish for weeks afterwards – every time I had to come to St Jean Layrisse they went through all my papers and searched the van too. I just hope they're happy to have found something in that car.' She rubbed her funny bone again and looked over at the guardroom. 'Poor people. They'll pay a high price for some black-market cigarettes.'

Philippe stirred in the back.

'This is taking forever,' he said. He winced as he moved and shuggled in the small space, looking like he was folded in half with his knees tucked up to his chest. 'What's happened?' he whispered. 'Why do you two look like we're in trouble?'

Agnes told him what the Germans had just found in the other car.

'Shit. Well, let's hope they're satisfied with that and let the rest of us go,' he muttered.

Danielle sat up very straight. 'Right, here they come – get under cover in the back there, and, Céleste, best polite face and smiles for our Boche friends,' she said, batting her eyelashes at the two sentries as they approached the van.

One of the soldiers put his head down to the open window. 'Papers,' he said, in French.

Danielle had already collected the identity papers together and presented them to him in a bundle with a smile. The soldier took his time going through them, putting his head inside the van to stare at Agnes, and giving a small nod of recognition to her.

'What's in the boxes? You're on your way out of town early today? Let me see that there,' he said, pointing to the box behind

Agnes's seat. She prayed he wouldn't want to inspect the whole of the back of the van, wriggling round in her seat to obey his order as quickly as she could while trying not to unbalance the rest of the precarious pile.

'We only stayed for a short while this morning – the market was dead and nobody was buying anything,' said Danielle, as she passed the box through the window. 'It might have had something to do with the patrols beating up innocent people trying to go about their business,' she sniped, glaring at the soldier, as he opened the box, sniffed the contents and put it on the ground beside him.

'Watch your tongue, woman,' the second German rapped, pushing his face into the car with a scowl. 'There was a break-in at one of our depots last night, but we'll find the perpetrators, have no doubt of that. If you see any strangers around, you must inform us or the *Milice*. You understand?'

Agnes almost gagged at the man's rancid breath filling the small space. He glared at her and Danielle, his eyes lingering on her knees where Valerie's borrowed skirt had rucked up. She pulled the rough tweed down as far as she could.

'Of course,' muttered Danielle. The papers were shoved back into her hand and she passed them to Agnes and started the van. The German picked up the box and tucked it under his arm then stepped back and waved them on through the barrier. 'Bastards,' she said quietly as her cheese was taken over to the guard post. 'I hope it chokes you.'

They drove away not daring to look at each other, the silence inside the tiny vehicle speaking volumes.

Chapter 27

Claire

Two days after leaving Aunt M looking at the map, I drove up a winding road in the central Pyrenees between banks of snow piled up on either side of the cleared tarmac. The snow chains I'd rented along with the little car bit and held on the icy corners as I slowly negotiated the hairpin bends taking me ever higher. Breasting the summit, I pulled over and got out to enjoy the magnificent panorama in front of me.

Snow had fallen overnight, leaving a dusting like icing sugar covering the valley ahead. A backdrop of some of the highest peaks in the range brought grandeur, and yet the valley seemed unbowed by its rugged guardians with their steep, rocky buttresses and glaciers, gleaming in the midday sun.

It was a view both ancient and modern. I could see a light industrial site on the edge of the town below, and huge pipes leading straight up the mountainside spoke of a hydro scheme. Pylons carried a line of telecabines up to a ski station above the town. And yet, the villages dotting the valley looked, from this distance, as though they had been there since time began.

Squat stone buildings crowded around squares and tiny churches like something from a painting by a French master. The small, snow-covered meadows were surrounded by beech and pine forest, the russet of dead leaves creating a patchwork with the dark green conifers.

I shivered as a cloud blocked out the sun for a few minutes, and the temperature dropped sharply. There were no other vehicles or people around, and I felt vulnerable; it would not be a good place to get stranded. As if to confirm my thoughts, a snowflake landed on my face, and by the time I got back in my car and had started down the steep, winding road into St Jean Layrisse, it was snowing heavily. I drove slowly, coming up behind a snowplough halfway down the hill, and was relieved to reach the first houses. The mountains all around were now obscured by low cloud and fat, fluffy flakes of falling snow. It was a rapid change from the sunny aspect I'd enjoyed twenty minutes earlier. This was not a climate to take for granted.

The centre of town was busy, with crowds wandering around in bright padded jackets and salopettes, carrying skis on their shoulders. It was lunchtime and, with the weather closing in, the hordes had come down from the mountain. I managed to nip into a parking space as another car pulled away, causing a long and irate blast of a horn from someone on the wrong side of the road, who had obviously eyed up the same spot. I smiled sweetly at him (of course it was a man), laughing at the look on his face. Andrew always said I had shocking manners when it came to driving in town, but I see it as a dog-eat-dog kind of world out there, and who dares wins, right?

Pulling up the hood of my jacket, I went to find the tourist office. Locating it was easy; realising I'd missed it closing for lunch by ten minutes, frustrating. It was shut until mid-afternoon – what kind of hours did the folk around here work? Time to find something to eat then, and see if there was a bed to be had anywhere in the local vicinity.

Lunch was a tasty dish of cassoulet – that most local of dishes to the south-west of France – followed by a piece of good local brebis cheese with a cherry confit, which matched the flavour perfectly. I found some 3G on my phone and did a search for somewhere to stay, while I ate. There were plenty of hotels and *chambres d'hote* in town and around the outlying villages, but finding one with a bed for a few nights took a while. Eventually I came up with a place a couple of kilometres from the centre of town, run by a British couple. Perfect.

Harriet Sargent opened the ancient front door of Villa Sarnaille with a smile and a hand that shook mine enthusiastically. A small, dark-haired woman with multiple piercings and bare feet, who looked a dozen or more years younger than me, she welcomed me into her home and put me at ease right away. Taking my bag, she led me up a wide oak staircase to a small room on the second floor with views, she assured me, of the mountains when they weren't swathed in cloud. The snow had stopped, and a glint of brightness hinted at the sun making a reappearance, which brightened the space. The room was basic but spotless, with polished antique furniture and a cast-iron bedstead filled invitingly with pillows and a thick fur throw.

She talked as if we had known each other for years, asking how I was, if it was my first stay in France, where I lived in Britain and what I did. Did I want dinner and breakfast the next morning? Was I allergic to anything, or a vegetarian? It was no bother if I was – French supermarkets were much better than they used to be so far as labelling things went. It was a little overwhelming. I told her where I lived and what I did – a mistake, as there is always a pet that needs looking at for some minor ailment, and their elderly cat wasn't eating well. I suggested getting his teeth checked.

She said she was from Devon originally, and we swapped stories of places we both knew in the south-west. Her husband was originally from Australia, and they'd moved to the area over ten years ago to run an adventure holiday company as well as to set up the *chambres d'hote*. He was away on an expedition with clients that week, winter-climbing on the Spanish side of the mountains, which was why there was a spare room for a few nights. She would need it back by the end of the week for one of the climbers, when they returned.

I felt swamped by the amount of information I'd just ingested. But if she could tell me as much about the locals as she'd told me about her family life, I may have struck gold. She left me to unpack and freshen up, which took all of five minutes. Checking the time and realising there was still over an hour until the tourist office reopened, I went downstairs to explore the old house.

Harriet was in the kitchen and offered me a cup of tea, which I gladly accepted and took into the guests' lounge. A huge wood-stove blasted out enough heat to make me strip off my heavy jumper. I curled up on a squidgy sofa in front of it, the cat jumping onto my lap and kneading my leg while purring loudly. It made me think of Betty, and I had a moment of homesickness, wondering how she was on her own and being fed by my neighbour, Mrs Curtis.

I drank the tea and spent a while skimming through some leaflets of activities and attractions in the area. St Jean was a well-known spa town, specialising in *les curistes*, people who were sent to 'take the waters' by their doctors. The thought of having a treatment was tempting – perhaps I would have time to try one myself, before I went home.

Harriet put her head round the door and asked if I wanted anything else, as she had to go and collect her children from school in half an hour. I shook my head, and then asked if she had time for a quick chat. She came in and sat beside me.

'Is there something you want to know about the area?' she asked, lifting the cat off me, and putting him gently on the floor. 'You know you're not allowed in here, naughty boy.'

'He's all right. Makes me feel at home,' I said. 'I wondered if you might know anybody who could help me track down the whereabouts of an old friend of my aunt.'

It was hard mentioning Aunt M without a lump forming in my throat, and I stopped for a moment and took a breath before continuing. I explained my reason for being in St Jean, and that I needed someone with local knowledge who could tell me more about the war years. Did she have any contacts who might be able to help?

'Let me have a think,' she said. 'There's someone I suspect might be able to help you, but I'll speak to him first. He's a funny man and doesn't really like strangers, but if anyone knows anything, he will.' She rose and went to the door, where she stopped and turned. 'Was she a Frenchwoman?'

'French mother, British father, I think,' I said. 'She was recruited as an agent by the British and sent here to help the local Resistance.'

'What did you say her name was?'

'Agnes Kerr. Oh, but she will have used her given French name while she was undercover. Céleste Sarraute, I think.'

'Hmm, not a name I've heard, but that means nothing,' said Harriet, and disappeared to get her children.

Chapter 28

Agnes

Philippe stayed out of sight at the farm, sleeping in a tiny room at the back of Maman Espouy's little house. Agnes redressed the wound each day and, with the help of the sulphonamide powder, it healed cleanly. Philippe took full advantage of Danielle's home-produced food and ate prodigious amounts, much to the amusement of the old lady.

A couple of days after the disastrous raid, Agnes walked down to Maman Espouy's house as the sun was slipping behind the western mountains, turning their snowy caps from white to rose. She found Philippe sitting on a bench enjoying the last of the sunshine.

'I'm going to cycle down to Montréjeau tomorrow and see Georges,' she said. 'I need to find Reynard and I'm hoping Georges might have heard where he is. He needs to know what happened the other night.'

'Can you not radio London and get them to pass on the message?'

'I want him to hear it from me, not second-hand. If I can't go to him myself, I'll send a message by one of his couriers – Georges will know where I can contact one.'

'Be careful then, Tigresse; the valley is still crawling with Boche patrols.' Philippe shifted his position, wincing at the movement. 'I'm sorry I can't be more help right now.'

'Someone must have known we were coming, the other night, don't you think?'

Philippe shrugged. 'Maybe, or perhaps it was just one of those things that went wrong.'

'I don't believe that for a minute. And if the Boche were tipped off it must have been someone close to Jacques or Valentine, surely? Or even one of them?' Agnes spat the words. 'If one of them is the collaborator, they should be shot.'

'Whoa, slow down,' Philippe said. 'You can't throw around accusations like that without proof. Those two have been the backbone of the local maquisards since the occupation, haven't they? Calm down. I know how frustrated and angry you are – I am too, but we need to work together and prove who the traitor is, not just make wild guesses.'

Agnes stared at him. She knew he was right, but was surprised at his words. She thought he would have been the first to agree with her. She nodded.

'There is something you can do,' she said, still smarting. 'You can help by staying out of sight while I'm gone – you shouldn't be sitting here for one thing. If any of the neighbours came to the farm, they'd see you for sure.'

He had the grace to look embarrassed and hobbled into the house, muttering an apology. She left, too irritated to put up with him. The sooner he went back to St Antoine the better.

Agnes returned from her trip to the Luzent farm at Montréjeau late in the afternoon, hot, tired and hungry. Georges Luzent had told her Reynard was out of the area but he could get a note to him, so she had written an account of the failed raid. It was frustrating to have to put in writing how badly wrong everything had gone, but no point in glossing over it. Arriving back at the farm she was annoyed at how little she had managed to achieve since being posted to St Jean Layrisse.

Determined to shake off her bad mood, Agnes went in search of a new location for the wireless, constantly anxious that if she left it in one place for too long, somehow the Germans would find it. The forest above the village provided a wealth of hiding places and she knew in reality that the case was unlikely to be found, but there was no harm in being extra cautious. Who knew if one of the villagers was a German spy and might be eyeing her with suspicion? She couldn't afford to be complacent with the collaborator still at large.

Climbing up a tiny deer track she soon found what she was looking for: a broken-down barn, almost buried under young ash and beech saplings and thorny bramble bushes. Wild boar had made a tunnel through the impenetrable mass, and being so small, she managed to crawl through the fetid hole and discovered the remains of a gable end wall with a few rafters still clinging to it. It had only taken her fifteen minutes and would be perfect. After placing a few small sticks to guide her back later in the day, she returned to the farm with the sun on her face, her mood lifting.

Agnes offered to do the milking after she got back to the farm, the routine task comforting after the physical exertions of the day. Her thoughts took her back to London, wondering how Maggie was, missing her laughter and her touch. She tied the last goat to the post, and it stood patiently chewing its cud, while she fetched a clean bucket. She had just sat down when Danielle came into the dairy, slamming the door behind her. Agnes looked up in surprise, and – seeing the expression on the other woman's face – stood up.

'What's happened?' she said.

'Henri LeGendre's missing,' Danielle said, her voice high and strained. 'His neighbour went to see if he was sick when he didn't open the shop this morning. He's not in his apartment, and neither is his dog, Pepi. There's a search going on. Jean has gone to help look for him.'

'Oh, no. I hope he's found safe and well. Is there anything I can do?' Agnes said.

Danielle shook her head. 'No, I don't think so. Thank you for offering, though. I'm very worried, Céleste. Henri is a tough old character, but he's not good on his feet – his arthritis makes him unsteady.' She stood, wringing her hands. 'I can't imagine where he's got to. He never misses opening his shop. Never.'

Danielle left, muttering under her breath. Agnes stared after her, wondering what could have happened to the old man. She sat down to milk the restive goat, her forehead pressed into its warm flank while her fingers teased out the creamy milk, working without thought, her mind miles away. She hoped Jean would arrive home soon, with good news.

Jean came home late that night, looking drawn and tired. He and others had searched all through the evening, and Henri had eventually been found only two hundred yards from his own door, unconscious and very cold, on a track that was little used. Thank God they had found him before night had set in.

'Anyone would have thought he'd slipped and fallen, if it wasn't for the state his dog was in,' said Jean, shovelling in bread and cheese and washing it down with red wine.

Philippe poured him another glassful and topped up his own at the same time. 'What's his dog got to do with it?' he asked.

'That little old orange poodle, do you mean?' said Agnes, noting how Philippe was now moving freely, without wincing.

'Yes. Pepi. He dotes on it. Treats it like it's his most prized possession,' Jean replied. 'It was sitting beside him, cowering in terror. It tried to run away when we got there, but came back when we lifted Henri. Poor little mite was in pain. Looked as if it had been kicked or beaten.'

'You think someone attacked Henri and his dog?'

Agnes could hardly believe what she heard. Anger bubbled inside her.

Jean nodded. 'Without doubt. There's a derelict farm right next to where we found him, and it's plain someone's been there. Cigarette butts, boot prints in the mud, as well as all the nettles and grass flattened down. It looks as if it's more than one person too. A meeting place, perhaps.' Jean shrugged, wiping his mouth on his sleeve. 'All we can hope is the old man regains consciousness and can remember who hit him – if he even saw who it was. It must have been last night when there was hardly any moonlight.'

'Perhaps he saw or heard something he wasn't meant to.' Agnes's mind raced, thoughts tumbling over each other. Whoever it was didn't want to run the risk of being seen. But why hurt the dog? It made no sense to her. 'Is he at home, or did they take him to the hospital?' she asked. 'He'll need someone to look after him, until he's well again. He lives alone, doesn't he?'

'Valerie Duphil had him taken to her house. She has a spare room and has some experience of nursing,' said Jean. 'He'll have better care there than in the hospital.'

'Yes, she was very kind with Philippe when he got injured.' Agnes was amazed at the woman's strength of mind. 'I'll go tomorrow and check how he is when we go to the market. See Valerie has everything she needs and can cope.' She sat and thought for a few moments. 'It's best if no one knows where Henri is. If it gets out he survived, he'll be in danger. Who knows what, or who, he saw.'

'We don't know if he will survive, yet,' said Danielle, her eyes filling with tears. 'I can't bear it. This damned war – it's turned friend on friend, neighbour on neighbour. Is there nobody we can trust, anymore?'

Agnes put her arm around her shoulder and hugged her. Danielle tried to stay strong, to make life as normal as possible for her children, but she bottled everything up. If Henri died from this assault, it would hit her hard. She'd already lost too

213

many friends and relatives. Jean finished his wine, and stood up, clearing his throat.

'You're right, Céleste,' he said. 'We must hope Henri wakes and can tell us who assaulted him.'

'Let's go a step further and put out a rumour that Henri is unlikely to survive – or that he's dead. Make whoever did this think he's safe.'

'Good idea,' he said. 'There were only one or two of us who were there when he was found and know where he was taken.'

'We need to get this bastard before he does any more damage,' said Agnes. 'Maybe he's overstepped the mark this time, and we can finally catch him.'

'Let's hope so,' said Jean. 'Let's hope so.'

Chapter 29

Claire

While exploring the town centre, I called in at the tourist office to ask if there were any clubs or societies associated with the history of the town during the war. The man behind the desk pointed me towards the town hall, saying classes and clubs were organised from there. I bought a large-scale map of the valley and picked up a glossy magazine with St Jean Layrisse plastered across the front and sections in French, Spanish and English.

A helpful woman at the town hall gave me a handful of leaflets detailing courses, clubs, and social events. You could learn chess, Spanish, English, computing, and Gascon dancing, or get involved in numerous sporting clubs. You might choose to play a musical instrument or immerse yourself in the ancient language of Occitan and join the local choir, which specialised in singing traditional folk songs. It sounded like something I'd enjoy doing but wouldn't help me find Agnes. Nothing on local history, which might have been useful.

Wandering along the main street, I passed the local museum – closed for renovations, and unlikely to open in the near future, judging by the state of the building works taking place. So, no help from that source, then – unless they had a decent website I could delve into. I carried on towards the spa, which stood proudly on its own, built into the mountain. There was a subtle smell of sulphur on the air the closer I got to the baths, and – through enormous plate glass windows – I could see people lying on loungers around a circular pool. It looked inviting and relaxing – tomorrow, I told myself, I'd come and spend an hour forgetting about everything, and indulge myself in a little pampering.

Walking back on the opposite side of the road, I passed a small square in which stood the town's war memorial. An ornate bronze sculpture of several soldiers carrying a fallen colleague, with a weeping woman on her knees in front of them, her hands clasped and held up in front of her; it was a dramatic statement. I stopped to read the inscription of all those who had died fighting for their country in three wars – the Great War, the Second World War, and the Algerian War. The names were strange to me – Espouy, Duphil, Comet, and many others – I was sure they would not be pronounced the way I thought they should. I'd already found it difficult to decipher the local accent – it could have been a different language to the French I'd learnt at school.

I was halfway back to the *chambres d'hote* when the car in front of me came to an abrupt halt. Slamming on the brakes I stopped with inches to spare. Trying to see what the hold-up was, I wound the window down and stuck my head out. Hearing raised voices up ahead, curiosity got the better of me and I got out. In front of the queue two men stood in the middle of the road having such a full-blown row that others had stopped to watch the performance.

There was lots of gesticulating and shouting, with some of the bystanders adding their two cents' worth. As I reached the scene I could see a child kneeling on the ground, his arms around something, sobbing his heart out. One of the men stood over him, his back to me, shouting at the other fellow, who was backed up against an old van, smoking and yelling just as loudly.

I threaded my way to the front and saw it was a dog the boy cuddled. I ran over and crouched down. The child looked at me with eyes full of tears, hiccoughing as he tried to speak.

'*Il est mort*,' he said and buried his head into the rough grey fur of the animal's neck.

'Do you mind if I take a look?' I said, my basic French deserting me. The boy ignored my words, clinging to his pet.

I put a hand on the dog's still-warm head, sad for the child and his pet, and rubbed its ear. It twitched under my hand, making my pulse jump, and I lifted an eyelid. The membrane was pale but the eye reacted when I touched the pupil. The animal was alive.

'*Monsieur!*' I yelled, but the man paid no attention, too caught up in the argument. I jumped up and grabbed his arm, making him swing round, his expression fierce. I realised it was the same man I'd beaten to the parking place that morning, and I flushed, seeing the flicker of recognition in his eye. 'This dog is not dead. He needs help. *Il n'est pas mort. Mais vite aider le chien.*' He looked at me as if I was a madwoman, and I shook his arm and pointed at the sorry sight on the ground, shouting in English. 'The dog is alive. You need to get him to a vet. Now!'

The animal was coming round, its eyes flickering. I hoped it didn't have brain damage. I told the man I was a vet in my pidgin French, and he nodded and rattled off something I had no hope of understanding, then yelled a parting shot at the van driver.

I must have looked bewildered because he switched to English. 'Thank you, madame. It is the dog of my son.' He indicated the little boy, who still gave the occasional sob, but looked up at us with a hopeful gaze. His hand stayed on the dog's neck, stroking it over and over again. 'Will it live do you think?'

'I don't know how badly it's hurt. There may be broken bones or worse. Your vet will tell you after they've made an examination.'

He looked at a loss. 'The vet is on the other side of town and my car is at home.'

217

'I'll take you,' I said. 'My car is just there.'

'Thank you. You're very kind.' He looked relieved and said something to his son, who smiled through his drying tears at me.

He lifted the dog, which whimpered, but then gave a weak wave of its feathery tail. The boy comforted his pet, whispering into its ear and sitting close to his father who almost filled the back of the small car. Following his directions, it took only a few minutes to reach the veterinary surgery.

I stayed outside while the man and his son took their dog into the nondescript building. Plastered onto the window was a sign saying *A Vendre*, which I tried to remember the English for but failed. It was almost dark, the sun having gone behind the steep sides of the valley and sending the temperature plummeting. Keeping the engine running kept the car warm, and I swallowed my guilt at helping to kill the planet. After half an hour when they hadn't returned, my impatience got the better of me and I followed them inside the small surgery.

The pair were sitting in the waiting room without their dog, and I guessed the vet had taken it off to do tests or x-rays. I sat beside the little boy and asked his name and that of his dog in my awful French.

'Je m'appelle Luc, et mon chien s'appelle Jurot,' he said.

He looked at his father and said something that made his dad grin and nod.

'He says you speak French very badly,' the father said, and winked.

I laughed. I couldn't deny it. *'Bonjour, Luc. Je m'appelle Claire.'* I put out my hand and Luc hesitantly took it and we shook hands. 'And your name, monsieur? I must apologise for my behaviour earlier when I stole your parking place in town.'

He stared. 'Hah! I was very put out – it's right, no? Put out?' I nodded. 'I was very put out that you took my place. It was a quick manoeuvre, though. I was impressed, I have to admit.' He grinned again, which lit up his dark face. 'My name is Laurent.'

'Your English is very good,' I said. 'Much better than my French.'

He shrugged. 'Luc's mother, she teaches English at the school here. She made me learn.' He looked down at his hands, twisting a signet ring around his middle finger and fell silent.

A grey-haired man in a white lab coat came into the waiting room at that moment. Behind him limped the dog, Jurot, looking sorry for himself. On seeing his pet, Luc jumped up and ran over to him, kneeling down and hugging him, gently. The dog wagged his tail and put his head onto the boy's shoulder, giving his ear a small lick. Luc laughed and kissed him.

Laurent listened to the vet, who had a box of medication in his hand and gave him instructions. I found the dialect and speed of their conversation impossible to understand, though my professional curiosity was piqued. The two men shook hands and Laurent took a dog lead out of his jacket and gave it to his son. Luc attached it to Jurot's collar and led him slowly out to the car.

'Where do you live?' I asked. 'I'll give you a lift home. Jurot should be kept quiet until he recovers – no running around.'

'The vet said the same thing,' Laurent said. 'We live further along the road where the dog was hit by that idiot driver. He shouldn't have been loose, but I know the man would have been going too fast – he always does. It might have been a child he hit.' He stopped his rant and took a breath. 'Thank you for the offer. And you must come in and have an aperitif with us.'

'Oh, that's not necessary, I'm going that way myself. I'm glad I could help and Jurot's injuries are not serious. Did the vet tell you anything more?'

'He said the van must have hit him on his head, a small hit? Is that right? My pardon, I don't know the word in English.'

'A glancing blow, I think is what we would say in English.'

He nodded. 'Thank you, yes. He was thrown onto the road, so bruising everywhere, but no bones broken and no internal injuries.'

He turned to his son and spoke rapidly. Luc nodded, his eyes filling with tears.

'What did you tell him?'

'That he must take more responsibility for his dog. He was the one who let him run off down the road. I've told him a hundred times to keep him on the lead until they're up in the forest.' He shook his head. 'Kids, eh? Drive you mad, most of the time.'

I said nothing. How would I know?

Laurent directed me to a modern house that sat among other modern houses in a small development, close to Villa Sarnaille.

'Will you come in and take a drink?' he said.

'Thank you, but is it rude of me to say no?' I said, fatigue dragging at me. 'I've only just arrived and I'm quite tired, but I'm staying in the area for a few days – perhaps another time?'

'Come tomorrow, then. Six in the evening – *apéro* time,' he said.

'Thanks, that would be perfect.'

I watched as he chivvied Luc up the drive, the dog between them. This was a totally unexpected turn, but I couldn't help smiling at the little group.

Chapter 30

Agnes

'Take care, Tigresse,' Philippe said, holding Agnes's face between his hands and smiling into her eyes. 'I owe you one.' He climbed stiffly onto his bicycle and waved as he wobbled his way down the hill away from the farm. 'Keep in touch, and let me know how the old man is, okay?' he called.

Agnes watched him until he disappeared around the bend in the track. It seemed an eon since she'd helped Philippe to Valerie's house. The thought of Henri LeGendre lying unconscious in the same house brought back the anger she'd felt on first hearing what had happened to him. She allowed the fire of rage to build and keep her warm.

The following day she and Danielle loaded up the little van with cheeses as usual and drove into St Jean Layrisse. Once they'd set up the stall in the marketplace, Agnes left to go and visit Valerie, taking some cheese and bread with her.

The streets were quiet. The clampdown by the Gestapo had kept most people at home. Soldiers patrolled continuously, stopping and searching people without provocation. The atmosphere was a sodden blanket lying over the town, oppressive and dark, which Agnes cowered under, even though the sun shone and the mountains' snow-topped peaks were pristine.

Hurrying through the lanes to Valerie's, she looked around before going to the door. The street appeared to be empty, with windows shuttered on the buildings either side, the quiet making the dread worse. She knocked, feeling vulnerable with her back to the road. Sweat ran down between her shoulder blades.

After an age, she heard Valerie's slow steps coming along the hall. She greeted Agnes with a smile and the habitual kiss on either cheek, but Agnes could see the strain in the other woman's eyes. They shut the door quickly and went straight upstairs to the room that had recently been occupied by Philippe. Now, the spare frame of Henri lay in the narrow bed, covered in blankets and an eiderdown. The old man had a nasty bruise around one eye and looked so pale Agnes thought he must be near death. He didn't move and was obviously still unconscious, his face gaunt, as if all the flesh had been stripped from his head. A hand, curled into a claw, lay on top of the covers, and Agnes, placing her own small brown hand over it, gave it a gentle squeeze. The skin was as dry as paper left in the sun.

'He's not woken, yet,' said Valerie. 'I'm worried if he doesn't come round soon, he never will. I try to get a little water down him and he still seems to swallow instinctively, but it's not enough.' She straightened the covers, though they looked perfectly placed to Agnes. 'Jean Espouy told me he had been attacked, and poor Pepi, too. Why would anyone do such an awful thing to a harmless old man and his pet?'

'I suspect Henri saw something he wasn't supposed to,' Agnes said. 'Who else knows he's here? He – and you – might be in danger, if whoever did this knows he's not dead.'

'Only the people who carried him here, as far as I know,' said Valerie. 'Jean Espouy, Valentine Dupont and Charles Pradel. I would trust any of them with my life.' She wrung her hands together and sat on the end of the bed. 'I can't believe someone I know might be the person who did this. I'll make sure no one else knows he's here and ask the others not to say anything.' She sighed. 'As long as they haven't already spread the word.' Her shoulders slumped for a moment, her eyes losing focus. Then she made a conscious effort to straighten. 'I have a gun, you know,' she said, looking up at Agnes. 'And I know how to use it. My husband made sure of it when the pig Boches first occupied our beautiful country.' Her mouth set in a thin line. 'Let them try and hurt my friend. They will have me to get through first.'

Not for the first time, Agnes was filled with admiration at Valerie's depth of spirit. She hugged her gently, feeling the fragility of her bones.

'You're a wonderful woman,' she said. 'I know Henri is as safe here as anywhere. I just pray he comes round. Now. Let's keep our own strength up – come and eat with me; you deserve a banquet and all I can offer is bread and cheese, but it will have to do.'

While they sat downstairs at the little kitchen table, eating the food she'd brought and drinking coffee, Agnes heard a dull thud from the room above. Valerie was busy with the coffee pot and didn't seem aware of anything, but Agnes flew out of her chair and up to the little bedroom. Henri was fretful, mumbling nonsense, not properly conscious. He tossed and turned, his head moving from side to side on the pillow. His flailing arm must have knocked the little water glass off the bedside table. Agnes put her hand on his shoulder, speaking softly, attempting to settle him, bring him fully awake, if she could. It was as if he was in the middle of a bad dream, trying to get away from someone.

'Henri. Henri, it's Céleste. Try not to move too much,' she said. 'Shhh, quietly now. You're safe here; no one is going to hurt you.'

She kept on, in the same comforting tone, hoping he would wake before he did himself any more damage. Valerie joined her, sitting on the other side of the bed, taking his other hand and stroking his forehead, brushing the thin white hair back from his face.

After a few moments he calmed down and fell back into unconsciousness, although it seemed more like sleep now. Perhaps he was coming back to them and would wake properly the next time. All they could do was wait and hope; for if Henri couldn't identify his attacker, Agnes had no idea how they would succeed in capturing the traitor.

The attack seemed too much of a coincidence for it not to be connected to the betrayal of her, Philippe, and her predecessor. It was well known Henri was a good friend of the Espouy family, and she visited his shop whenever she was in town. If he had seen something he wasn't supposed to, then maybe his attacker had hit him to frighten him, make him keep his mouth shut. But why hurt the dog too? What purpose could possibly have been served by such unnecessary cruelty?

Henri looked peaceful, and Agnes was tempted to shake him to see if he was just sleeping. Valerie would be horrified if she did, but she had to do something, anything, rather than just watch him lying there. She rose and walked about the little room, pacing from one side to the other.

'Why don't you go, Céleste?' Valerie said, a touch of irritation in her voice. 'You can't do anything for him, while he's like this. I'll send word if – when – he comes round.' She stopped Agnes, with a hand on her arm. 'I know you want to find out who did this to him, but only he can tell you that. Go. Help Danielle at the market and pop back here before the end of the day.'

'Sorry. I hate feeling useless.' Agnes patted the hand still holding her arm. 'Can I stay overnight if he's still not woken up by the time I return? You look exhausted and need your sleep. I'll sit with him while you go to bed.'

'Exhaustion is a permanent part of my life, nowadays,' Valerie said. 'But if it's what you want to do, then yes, I'll be glad of your company, and we can take it in turns to rest and watch over him.'

'I'll come back as soon as I've helped Danielle pack up the stall.' Agnes leant over the still form in the bed and squeezed the hand lying on top of the bedcovers. '*A bientôt*, my dear friend,' she whispered.

Sometime after midnight, while Agnes dozed in the small chair in the corner of the bedroom, Henri finally came round. Just as a mother wakes half a second before her child utters its first cry of hunger, so some sixth sense made her open her eyes as the old man moved. He put a hand up to his head and groaned. Agnes went over to him, the light from the small night-lamp just bright enough for her to see his eyes open.

'Sshh, try not to move,' she said, in a low voice. 'You've had a knock on the head. Valerie Duphil's been caring for you.'

Henri groaned again. 'I have an awful headache.' He licked cracked lips. 'I need a drink of water.'

'Shall I help you to sit up a bit?' Agnes piled another pillow behind his head, raising him up a little. 'There, that's better. You've given everyone quite a fright.'

She poured a glass of water and held it for him while he drank. The small action exhausted him, and he lay back, closing his eyes again. A frown deepened across his forehead. Agnes remained quiet, giving him time to gather his thoughts.

'What day is it?' he said, his eyes still closed. 'How long have I been here, and where's Pepi?'

'You've been unconscious for two days, Henri,' Agnes told him. 'The men who discovered you found Pepi beside you.'

'He's a good dog.'

'I'm sorry to say that poor Pepi was hurt too, Henri,' she said. 'He's being looked after by your neighbour. I'll find out how he is, as soon as I can.'

Henri lay still while Agnes talked, and she wondered if the shock of her words had been too much for his fragile state and he'd passed out again. She put a hand on his shoulder and gave it a gentle squeeze, before turning away and returning to the chair.

'Don't leave me. Please,' Henri said, his voice creaking like old leather left out in the sun.

'I'm not going anywhere; don't worry. I thought you might be tired. You've had an awful shock, as well as being bashed on the head.' She sat down. 'I'll be here if you need anything.'

'My poor dog. Why would anyone hurt him?'

'I don't know, Henri. I was hoping you could tell me. Do you remember anything? Who hit you? Did you recognise them? Why were you up the lane in the first place?' Her voice rose with each question.

Henri closed his eyes again. 'I don't know. I can't remember anything.' He put his hand up to his head. 'Wait, I do remember. Pepi had the shits; that was why I was up there so late.'

'So, it was at night. Late at night?'

The old man gave a weak nod. 'Did you hear something? Voices, perhaps?' He looked so frail and small, but she couldn't let him rest. 'How many were there? Did you recognise someone?'

Henri covered his face with shaking hands.

'I don't know. It's a blank. I'm sorry.' There was a catch in his voice. 'Please, let me rest. I'm so tired.'

Agnes relented, biting her lip. Perhaps his memory would return once he was more lucid.

Henri spoke again, in barely more than a whisper. 'Please, stay. Sit with me, at least for a while, until I drop off again. I'm tired, but everything hurts, and I don't know if I can sleep. Getting old is no fun, no fun at all . . .'

Agnes rose again and tucked the bedcovers a little higher over his shoulders. His breathing was light and even, and – as his sleep deepened – a quiet snore came from his half-open mouth. She sat and wriggled in the chair, trying to get comfortable.

Her brain raced and sleep was impossible. Hurting the dog made no sense to her, unless Pepi had done something to warrant it. Maybe he had barked in alarm and the attacker did it to shut him up. Or had he tried to protect his master? Attacked the attacker? Should they be looking for someone with a dog bite? But then, how much damage could a poodle do to a grown man?

Finally, as she slid into a restless sleep, her thoughts turned to the one person she knew could have been relied on to calm her fears and give her the confidence to do the right thing. Sometimes she almost forgot the sheen of skin and the line of hip as they lay like spoons in the narrow bed, and it terrified her. The thought of never seeing Maggie again was too much to contemplate.

The following morning Henri seemed brighter and stronger and complained of being hungry. Valerie hid her tears of relief at seeing her old friend on the road to recovery, sniffling into her handkerchief and complaining it was the start of a cold. Agnes carried breakfast upstairs and the three of them ate together.

She itched to question Henri again. Would he remember anything more? Instead, she curbed her impatience until after they'd cleared the tray away. She sat on the bed and took his hand, patting it in a distracted fashion, as she broached the subject.

'I remember taking Pepi up the lane behind my apartment before I went to bed.' The old man frowned. 'He'd eaten a whole wedge of cheese earlier in the day, and it always gives him the shits. Such a greedy little pig.' He looked at Agnes, anguish in his eyes. Sniffing, he carried on. 'There are some old farm buildings about halfway up the hill, and I thought I heard voices, arguing. It doesn't do to pry nowadays, so I wanted to get out of there as quickly as I could, but Pepi had stopped to sniff something, and I had to wait for him.' He paused, a fond smile on his face. 'I remember now, he'd found something disgusting to roll in. I called him, and suddenly there was a man on the lane, in front of me, wanting to know why I was there.'

'Was it one of those German bastards who did this to you?' Valerie said, hatred in her words.

Henri shook his head, shut his eyes and winced. After a moment he opened his eyes again and continued.

'No. He was French.'

Agnes sat up and exchanged a look with Valerie. Her heart thumped in her ribs.

'Did you recognise him?' she asked.

Henri frowned. After a moment he shook his head, more gently this time. 'No, I didn't know him, but he reminded me of someone, and I'm sure I've seen him before.' He looked at her and shrugged. 'I'm sorry, I've been trying to think where, but it won't come to me.'

Disappointment weighed her down. They were no further forward. A glimmer of an idea came into her head. Pushing the thought away, she smiled and patted Henri's hand again. 'Don't worry – perhaps you'll remember when you stop trying so hard. Can you tell us what he looked like; maybe we can get an idea if you describe him?'

Henri perked up a little. 'He was big. Much bigger than me, and broad, but not fat. And I got the impression he wasn't young. More mature than those boys in the Maquis, at least. It was dark, and the torch beam was in my eyes, so I couldn't see his face properly but he had a moustache and wore working clothes – he could have been any farmer or hunter from around here. That probably doesn't help much.' He sighed. 'I'm sure I heard some German words, and I remember hearing someone else running down the lane when I was stopped.'

He lay back in the bed, closing his eyes for a minute. Valerie tweaked the blankets, so they covered him up to his chest. Agnes thought how pale and thin he was. A smile suddenly crossed his face, as if a thought had amused him.

'What?'

'I've just remembered something. It won't help you, but it makes me feel a little better.' Henri's eyes sparked. 'The man knocked me down and stood over me. I was dazed and frightened. I thought

228

he was going to hit me again, when I heard him yelp and swear. I think Pepi tried to defend me . . . bit him on the leg and wouldn't let go.' He looked up at her. 'That must be why he was hurt; he was trying to protect me. Silly old dog . . .' he whispered.

'Brave little dog,' said Valerie, bending over and kissing Henri on the cheek. 'You need to sleep now; you're exhausted. I'll be downstairs if you need anything.' She looked at Agnes. 'Let's leave the patient to rest, shall we?'

They went back to the little kitchen and Valerie made some more coffee. Agnes sat at the table, mulling over what Henri had told them. It wasn't much, but there were clues that might help them. A big man with a moustache, and – if Pepi had done a good job on his leg – a limp. It could be anyone, but the number of older, fit and able men still in the area was vastly reduced. Any man who had been caught by the Germans had been imprisoned or sent off to the labour camps. Those still at liberty were in hiding in the forests or up in the mountains. Only boys, old men and women were left to keep the town working.

Valerie sat down opposite her and blew on her coffee. She'd been very quiet since Henri told them what he remembered.

'Can you think who it might be?' Agnes asked her.

The older woman shook her head. 'His description could fit any of the local men,' she said, watching Agnes over the rim of her cup. 'What will you do, now?'

Agnes shrugged. She didn't want to explore the thought that had infiltrated her brain. The risk was too great; it was reckless and foolhardy. Yet, like a scab that had to be picked, she found herself wondering if it would work. Because right now, they seemed to be running out of ideas as to how to catch the collaborator and prove he was the one who'd left an old man for dead. Agnes had no doubt the two were one and the same person. Jacques Comet's moustache kept coming into her head – he was a big man and not a boy. He fitted the vague description. She sighed – along with almost all the other local men, as Valerie had said.

'Céleste?'

Agnes dragged her thoughts back to what Valerie was saying. 'Sorry. My mind is miles away. What did you say?'

'I wondered how long we should keep Henri hidden. He might still be in danger.'

'You're right. He should stay out of sight, though it's not safe for you or him, while he's here.' And with those words the plan took flight, and she realised how it could be put in place. All it would take was a word here and there. She got up from the table, in a hurry to get moving. She must speak to Philippe. 'Do you feel safe with Henri if I leave?' she asked, abruptly.

Valerie covered her surprise quickly. The older woman pushed herself up from her chair slowly, wincing as she straightened.

'Of course,' she said. 'Nobody knows he's here, apart from those who brought him to me.' Her gaze sharpened. 'You have a plan. I can see it on your face.'

'I'll be back as soon as I can,' Agnes said. 'Don't let Henri leave before I return.'

Chapter 31

Claire

I arrived back at Villa Sarnaille as the apres-ski hour was in full swing. Harriet had her hands full with guests returning from the *pistes*, cold, tired and hungry. She put out a tableful of cakes, scones, and hot drinks, and took away wet gear to dry overnight somewhere in the back of the house. Most of the other people were French, except for a Dutch couple, who appeared to know Harriet personally. They spoke very good English and I introduced myself as we poured ourselves cups of tea. It was pleasant to make small talk for a change.

Matthieu and Katya were the epitome of Dutchness – I'm not short, but they towered over me, both of them at least six feet tall. Matthieu had the blond, square-jawed look of a Scandinavian, while Katya was a beautiful redhead, fine-boned, with translucent, glowing skin. They both suffered from 'panda eyes', having spent three days skiing and wearing goggles, but looked so fit and healthy I felt decidedly flabby beside them.

I like the Dutch. Those I'd met before were direct, blunt – some might say, to the point of rudeness – and didn't suffer fools gladly. All admirable traits as far as I was concerned. These two were no different, and I soon discovered they also shared a wry sense of humour, making me laugh at their stories of spills on the slopes and the antics of other skiers. Katya was distantly related to Harriet and had known her since they were children. We talked about family and the threads that bind us all to each other. I found myself telling them about my search, and how important it was to me. I mentioned Harriet's possible contact and how much I hoped they might know something that would help me track down Agnes.

'Harriet inhales gossip and information,' said Katya. 'If anyone can help you, she can – and will. It's just the sort of intrigue she loves.'

Her words lifted my spirits and renewed my feeling of confidence, which had slipped away over the afternoon with so little achieved.

'I know Agnes was posted here, but there is hardly anything about the war in this area – that I've found, anyway. I hope Harriet can point me in the right direction.'

'Lots of people will never talk about their experiences during that time. My grandfather for one,' said Matthieu. 'He was a kid in the war, but he refuses to talk about his childhood. I think it's still too painful for him to deal with. I only know his story because his sister wrote an account of it. Her grandson found the book after she died and showed it to me a couple of years ago.' He fiddled with his mug. 'My great-grandmother was sent to a concentration camp. She was Jewish and her whole family died in the gas chambers. The family managed to get my grandfather and his younger sister out of the city hidden in the back of a cart. They were taken to his father's family in the countryside, and lived there in hiding, until the war was over. He wasn't told what happened to his mother and her family until much later. He was never the same afterwards. Suffered depression, mood changes, black rages. His whole life – even now, as an old man.'

Katya put her hand on his arm, gently rubbing it.

Matthieu placed his own hand over hers and gazed at me. 'Kat's the only person who knows, apart from my family. Your search may provoke strong feelings in others, besides yourself, Claire.'

I stood, lost in thought for a moment. His story was not so unusual, but deeply affecting.

'I'm sorry you lost so many of your family. Thank you for telling me,' I said. 'I guess I haven't considered the impact my questions might have on others.' I put down my cup. 'It's nice to meet you. Please excuse me – I'll see you at dinner.'

I made my way quickly out of the room, and passed Harriet in the hall.

'Hello again, Claire,' she said, then, seeing something on my face, she stopped. 'Are you okay? You're as white as a sheet.'

I managed a smile. 'Thank you, I'm fine, just a little tired.'

'It's too busy during the evening, but I'm intrigued to know more about your search,' she said. 'Shall we have coffee together, tomorrow morning? After everyone has gone out – say ten o'clock?'

'I don't want to put you to any trouble,' I said, feeling like a prying busybody, after hearing Matthieu's family tale. 'I hate the thought of dragging up old memories, opening old wounds, you know.'

'I thought that was the whole reason you were here?'

'It is,' I admitted. 'But I've just had a conversation with someone who made me realise I can't go trampling over people's memories and family tragedies without a care.'

'Have coffee with me in the morning and tell me where this is all coming from. You were so enthusiastic, earlier. It would be a shame to give up, now,' she said. 'And the guy I told you about is willing to meet you. What harm can it do?'

I couldn't come to a decision, swithering one way then the other. In the end I decided to take Harriet up on her offer of coffee the following day. It might help to talk it over with her, and I was interested to meet the person who might, for the first time, be able to shed some light on the wartime activities in St Jean Layrisse and, possibly, Agnes.

I went to bed early. Curling up under the warm duvet, I opened the magazine I'd picked up. I must have read all of three sentences before my eyes drooped and I turned off the light.

The next morning, I had coffee with Harriet.

'It's true some people will never speak about the war,' she said. 'But I know some who love spinning yarns about the "old days" – once they start it's hard to get them to shut up.' She grinned. 'You'll find folk around here tell it as it is. If they don't want to talk to you, they'll say so.'

'That makes me feel better.' I took another cup of coffee and sipped it slowly. 'When did you say your friend could meet me?'

'He said he could come this evening, but he rang last night and said something had come up, so he's coming tomorrow morning,' she said. 'Is that okay with you?'

'Oh, that's fine. I have an invitation for this evening, so it works for me, too.'

'Gosh, you work fast. Is it to do with your search?'

'No. I gave a guy and his child a lift yesterday. They were stuck so I helped them out. I've been invited to have aperitif with them.'

'Oh, well, that's worked out for both of you, then,' she said. 'I must get on. Have a good day.'

'Thanks, you too.'

I spent the day touring around St Jean Layrisse, exploring the neighbourhood. Taking the telecabine up the mountainside to the ski station above the town, I marvelled at the views of the surrounding mountains and the whole Layrisse valley below. The sun was warm and I sat for an hour or more, people-watching, and wishing I'd brought my ski gear with me. The conditions were perfect and I envied the crowds enjoying themselves on the slopes.

Returning to town as clouds descended and it began to snow again, I went back to Villa Sarnaille and warmed up beside the fire.

I took out the magazine I'd fallen asleep over the previous night and flicked through it. The centre spread caught my eye. A superb photo of an old building in a mountain valley, surrounded by enormous peaks. In front of it a monument being unveiled, a memorial to those who had helped escaping men and women over the border to Spain during the Second World War.

My attention sharpened. This was the first thing I'd found that even referred to the war, apart from the memorial in town. I learnt it was local people who led the escapees by tiny, forgotten tracks, to safety. The photo showed a group clustered around the huge block of stone with a brass plaque on one face. The men were all related to the *passeurs* – the guides – an important part of the Resistance movement. The town was proud to honour its sons and daughters who helped others evade capture by the German invaders.

A frisson of excitement ran through me. At last. Here was something I could use. I squinted at the caption to the photo, and there, in the middle of the group, his name in print, was Laurent, the man I'd helped the previous day. I caught my breath and read the article again, heart thudding. It seemed too much of a coincidence. That same feeling I'd had during my search at Kew, of someone directing me in my search for Agnes made the hairs on my arms stand up.

Perhaps I would find some answers after all.

Chapter 32

Agnes

Agnes found Philippe at the quarry in St Antoine. He spied her lurking outside the main gates and came to meet her. Taking her arm, he bustled her away and began walking along the road towards the town, glancing back at the gate house where a German guard stared after them.

'What are you doing here?' Philippe hissed. Before she could answer he stopped while they were still in sight of the guard, grabbed Agnes and kissed her. She struggled briefly, but his arms held her and he whispered in her ear. 'We're being watched. Kiss me back.'

She did as he asked and glanced over Philippe's shoulder, hating that the guard had a broad grin on his face.

Continuing along the street and once they were alone, Agnes halted in the middle of the road again and faced him.

'Henri LeGendre has woken up.'

'And? Was he attacked by a patrol?'

Agnes shook her head. 'No. It took some time for him to remember, but he's certain it was a Frenchman, and someone local.'

Philippe's eyes widened. He continued walking, his pace slow.

They came to a small café with a couple of tables outside, and he sat down at one, nodding at Agnes to do the same.

'Is this safe? Isn't there somewhere a bit more private we can talk?' Agnes looked around.

Philippe gazed past her, his eyes flitting from one side of the street to the other.

'I don't have long, and if anyone sees us, I want them to think we're a couple, not up to no good.' He leant in to her. 'How is Henri? I hope the old man is all right.'

'He's recovering, although he was unconscious for over twenty-four hours after he was found.' Agnes fought her anger. 'He didn't recognise whoever attacked him, but is sure there were two of them, and one was German.' She grabbed his arm. 'You realise he must have disturbed the collaborator, don't you?'

Philippe said nothing for a moment, looking over her head at the decimated hillside behind them. When he eventually brought his gaze back to her, his eyes were sharp.

'If he didn't know who it was, we're no further forward in discovering who the traitor is.' He rubbed his face, stone dust streaking his cheeks.

'I have an idea to as to how we can flush him out,' she said in a low voice. 'It's why I came to you, first. I want to run it past you.'

'Go on then,' he said, shading his eyes from a beam of sunlight as he stared at Agnes.

'Well, nobody, apart from the men who carried him there, knows where Henri is, or whether he's alive or dead. I want that information to leak out.'

Philippe's eyes narrowed as he took in her meaning, and slowly nodded. Agnes laid out the rest of her idea, and they discussed it in whispers for a few moments.

A waiter arrived and they fell silent. Agnes realised how hungry she was. 'Is there any food?' she asked.

'We have some cheese,' said the tired-looking, elderly man. 'Will that do, with some bread and a little wine, madam?'

'Thank you, it sounds perfect.' She smiled at him, and he shuffled away.

The two of them continued to talk through Agnes's plan, their heads close together. Philippe added one or two suggestions of his own.

'You know you're not fit enough to help, don't you?' she said, speaking quietly as they shared the plate of food the waiter laid in front of them.

'There's no way I'm missing it. You'll need me – you know you will.'

Fierce, immediate, brooking no argument.

'How useful can you be if he puts up a fight, or tries to make a run for it?'

'That's my problem, not yours. And the more the merrier, eh, Tigresse?'

He grinned at her, lights in his eyes dancing. She realised with a jolt this was what he'd come to France for. He loved the thrill of it, pure and simple; the danger, the excitement and the risk-taking were his lifeblood.

Philippe cycled back up the valley with her. Agnes kept a keen eye on him and noticed he was much stronger already, though he was panting by the time they'd pedalled their way up the long pull to the Espouy farm. He agreed to remain there while she set the plan in motion, although Danielle didn't seem too pleased to see him again so soon.

'You eat too much,' she moaned. 'How can I feed you all? The hams are nearly finished and there'll be no vegetables other than leeks until the summer.' She poked at his stomach. 'You'll have to make do with bread and cheese; it's all I have.'

'Bread and cheese will be fine,' said Philippe, kissing her on either cheek. 'What can I do for you this afternoon? You look exhausted and at least I can earn my dinner.'

'You can muck out the pigsty. Maman's leg is bothering her and I don't have time.'

Agnes winked at him and grinned at his expression.

She made it back to St Jean under cover of darkness. Valerie must have been looking out for her because she opened the door almost before Agnes had chance to knock.

'How's Henri?' she asked, as soon as she was inside.

'He's a strong old devil, and he must have a skull of iron,' said Valerie, smiling. 'Come and see for yourself.'

She led Agnes through to the kitchen, where Henri was sitting reading a newspaper and drinking a glass of pastis, looking very much at home. The wound on his head still looked nasty, and the bruising around it was a mix of dirty yellow and purple, but the old man greeted her with a smile.

'I'm so happy to see you looking better,' she said, bending to kiss him on either cheek.

'Oh, I may not be as young as I once was, but I'm still made of tough stuff. Don't you worry about me,' he said. 'Now. What have you been up to all day? Valerie and I have been on tenterhooks wondering where you went in such a hurry.'

'I went to see Philippe,' she said. 'We're going to set a trap for your attacker.' She paused. 'You two are the bait.'

The two old friends looked at each other and nodded.

'You know you can count on us,' said Henri. 'That *cochon* hurt Pepi, and he deserves everything that's coming to him.' Colour flooded his face, and he thumped the tabletop with his fist. 'Valerie, am I right? This is your home, after all.'

Valerie nodded, her mouth a grim line, eyes cold and hard.

'I would like to pull the trigger myself if I could,' she said.

'You'll be joining the queue. So, the first thing is to get the news out that Henri was attacked and left for dead, but he's survived and thinks he knows who hit him.' Agnes looked at Valerie. 'You could drop a word here and there, just a little chat to your friends, making out how you're the one nursing him, that he's sick, but recovering his memory of what happened.'

Valerie nodded again.

'We'll be watching the house, but you won't see us. I hope we'll get a result without delay – you know what this place is like for gossip. Once the word is out, whoever did this will show his face. He can't risk Henri identifying him.'

Agnes ran through the plan she'd discussed with Philippe. There wasn't much time; the quicker they acted, the sooner the collaborator would be caught. She could almost feel her blood pumping through her veins, every sense on high alert. It wasn't fear exactly, more an expectation and a frisson of underlying excitement.

Perhaps she wasn't so different to the Canadian, after all.

Agnes and Philippe arrived at the empty house opposite Valerie's before dawn. Philippe took his skeleton keys out and picked the lock while Agnes kept watch.

'I hope you're more successful than the last time we tried to break into a building,' she whispered, not able to resist the dig.

'That was not my fault and you know it,' he muttered.

Tension sang in her veins, making it impossible to keep still. She stalked the street while Philippe worked, her eyes on the junction with the road to the station, as well as scanning the street they were on. Nobody was about, and when a low whistle told her the door was open, she hurried back to the house.

Agnes checked they could see Valerie's door through the window of the small, drab front room, and they settled in, taking it in turns to keep watch on number 19, Rue Gambetta.

They saw Valerie leave the house to spread the news of Henri's attack in the morning, making her way towards the market, leaning on a walking stick. The bookseller was well known and liked; people would be shocked by the news. There was nothing they could do but wait and hope.

The day dragged, and nobody went near the house, apart from a couple of old friends of Henri's, who came to see how he was. Agnes was running on nothing but adrenaline, her eyes gritty, stomach griping with hunger, mouth dry. The lack of sleep over the past few days made her limbs heavy and filled her brain with a fog.

Philippe leant against the torn wallpaper next to the front-room window, peering out past the edge of a dirty net curtain at the door opposite, behind which Henri and Valerie waited. He seemed immune to his own fatigue, his concentration focused on the house. Agnes watched him surreptitiously from time to time, noticing the way his face had changed since he'd been shot – the lines at each side of his mouth and the pallor of exhaustion ageing him beyond his years. He might have been made of stone – no more underlying excitement, just a sense of wanting to get the job done.

At a few minutes after six o'clock, when the sun had dipped behind the mountains and the street was filled with deep pools of shadow, a man walked down the road, hands in his pockets, beret pulled low over his eyes. He wore a dark, rough woollen jacket, breeches, and working boots, and could have been anybody. He stopped outside Valerie's house and Agnes's pulse jumped, just as she heard the intake of breath from Philippe.

'Wait until he gets inside,' she muttered. 'We need to be sure it's him.'

The man looked up and down the street, knocked on the door and stood back a step. Taking his right hand out of his pocket he removed something hidden behind his back under his jacket.

'Fuck.'

Philippe hissed the expletive. Glancing at him, Agnes could see his gaze was fixed on the shadowy figure, his knuckles white as he gripped the ragged curtain. Blood pounded in her head.

The door opened a crack, and the man moved forward as a pale face appeared. The two spoke a few words and then the door opened enough to allow the stranger to enter. Before it was closed Agnes saw Valerie's anxious stare at the house opposite.

'Now!'

They ran swiftly across the street. Reaching the front door, Agnes turned the handle and they stole into the hall with her leading.

She found it hard to breathe. All her senses heightened – picking up voices from the kitchen, the chill of the empty hall and stairs, a waft of lavender from the potpourri on the hall table. Philippe's breathing was as loud as a steam engine and she wanted to tell him to hush, for surely everyone could hear him. She tasted her own fear, and took her gun out, finding comfort in its cold, hard grip.

Philippe halted beside Agnes as they heard Valerie speak, her voice high and tight, fear in every word. Then another, loud and rough, demanding to know where Henri was. She strained to recognise who it might be, but it was muffled by the closed door and impossible to tell.

Oh, Valerie, we're coming.

They moved on, following the sounds down the hall. Valerie's voice, louder now, telling the man he had to leave, Henri wasn't up to visitors yet.

Keeping his attention on her and not on the silent pair creeping up behind him.

Her courage giving them time to push open the kitchen door and witness the scene ahead of them.

Agnes's first impression was of a broad-backed, tall man, looming over Valerie. His rough working clothes and powerful body odour filled the small space and the few sticks of furniture seemed to shrink to doll's-house size beside his bulk. She might have been looking at a tableau.

She spoke first, the gun in her hand pointing at the man's back. 'Raise your hands and turn around, slowly.'

The stranger stiffened and turned. Agnes scanned his face. He looked familiar, but with his beret pulled low over his face and in the dim light of the kitchen she couldn't make out who he was. Itching to rip the beret off and discover his identity, she kept her eyes fixed and her gun trained on him, sensing Philippe was doing the same. Valerie stood on the other side and she motioned for her to join them, wanting her out of the firing line and safely behind them.

242

The man began to raise his hands, then dropped one and grabbed for something in his jacket. Before anyone had a chance to move there was a crack. The man yelled and collapsed, his left arm hanging useless from the elbow, a dark stain beginning to bloom through the rough material of his jacket. His gun dropped to the floor, skittering across the tatty linoleum, and Agnes grabbed it. She stared at Valerie, and the Frenchwoman shrugged, placing the small handgun carefully on the table in front of her.

'I told you I wanted to be the one to put a bullet in him,' she said, and gracefully slid in a heap onto the rocking chair in the corner.

For a second everything seemed to stop. Agnes blinked, came to her senses, and went to Valerie. The old lady's hands shook and her face was white. Agnes poured her a cup of water from the jug on the drainer.

Everything seemed to be happening in slow motion. Once she knew Valerie wasn't going to faint, Agnes crossed to where Philippe had grabbed the injured man by the collar and dragged him to a chair, shoving him roughly onto it. The man's breath came in grunts of pain. He struggled, hanging on to his broken arm, but Philippe showed no mercy, forcing his arms behind the chair back, raising the moans to a scream of agony. Finding no pity in her heart, she stepped up and pulled off the man's beret. Shock made her gasp.

'Remi Comet. You? You're the collaborator? Why man? Jesus, Jacques is going to want to kill you himself.' Fury ignited in Agnes's breast. All she saw in her mind's eye was Henri lying in the bed upstairs, close to death. Before she thought about it she smacked him across the face with the butt of her pistol. 'How dare you turn against your own people, your own family?'

He flinched and hung his head, unable to look her in the eye.

'Who is this?' Philippe said.

'Remi Comet – Jacques' cousin. He works at the markets,' Valerie answered, her eyes never leaving the man cowering in the chair.

'Is he one of the maquisards?'

'Yes, though he doesn't live in the valley. Wait until your cousin hears it's you who's betrayed the group all these past months. You'll wish I'd put that bullet through your black traitorous heart.'

Agnes barely recognised Valerie's voice. It could have cut steel.

Remi Comet looked around at the people in the room, and through the pain on his face he showed an arrogance and disdain Agnes found disconcerting.

'I was only looking out for my family,' he spat. 'The Germans are winning the war, and when it's finally over, I'll be the one who has a job and money and respect from the new government. What will you lot have? You'll be the ones who are strung up, your homes burnt to the ground, your families dead or living like pigs in the forest.' He shut his mouth with a snap.

Philippe stared at him, saying nothing. He shook his head, as if the man was deluded, but Agnes's stomach twisted. She'd never let herself believe the possibility of the Germans being the victors, and the ramifications if such a thing happened.

'Well, you can explain all your reasons to your cousin. I think he'll have a few things to say to you before he hangs you,' Philippe said.

Dragging the prisoner through the hall and out into the street, Agnes went ahead and watched for patrols while Philippe kept his gun pressed into the man's back and marched him through the warren of alleyways and tracks that took them out into the forest and the mountains.

As it grew dark, Agnes led the way to the Maquis camp, relieved, but unable to relax. She could see the tension on Remi Comet's face, and knew that though he was injured he would do anything to escape. He might moan and cry, but whenever she glanced at him, she saw his eyes darting from side to side or fastened on the gun she carried. Their success would all be for nothing if he got hold of it. She gripped it more tightly, and though her body ached with fatigue and her head swam, she ignored everything and focused her attention on their prisoner. Philippe maintained a menacing presence behind him, his gun constantly digging into Comet's back, shoving him forward to his fate.

A young maquisard keeping watch jumped down onto the path in front of them, startling Agnes. She whispered the code word and he led them to the camp, his young face alight with excitement. He walked with a cocky step and stood tall; only the trembling of his hands gave away his fear.

Jacques and Valentine met them as they entered the camp.

'What's happened?' asked Valentine. 'Why is Remi with you? He's hurt. How did that happen?'

'Better ask him that.' Philippe's face was a grim mask. 'This is your collaborator.'

The two maquisards looked with horror at the man who had betrayed them for months.

'I don't believe it,' Jacques said, emphatically. 'Remi? I know you, man. You'd never turn against your own. These people don't know you like I do. They're mistaken, aren't they?'

Agnes saw the moment Jacques' words broke his cousin. Shame crept over Remi Comet's face and he began to shake. The rough bravado leaked out of him and he fell to his knees.

'They made me do it,' he whined. 'The Gestapo. You have no idea what they're like. They would eat their own mothers if they were ordered to.'

Jacques turned away, disgust plain on his face. Then suddenly he spun around and launched a flying kick at his cousin, his boot landing squarely in Comet's face. The man screamed, his nose smashed and spurting blood. Jacques kicked him again and watched as he fell forward, hitting the ground hard.

Agnes could stand no more. She shivered and turned away as more of the maquisards came to take their own revenge on the man who had caused so much terror and hurt. The sight of him whimpering as he lay in the dirt trying to protect his head made her feel sick. Summoning up the memory of Henri lying so close to death did nothing to help. She was relieved they'd caught him; that was all.

'I'm going back to town,' she said to Philippe, as Remi Comet was dragged into a makeshift cabin. 'I don't need to see what they do to this man. I don't blame them for wanting retribution, but I'd rather not watch.'

He looked quizzically at her. 'Are you okay?'

'Yes, fine,' she said, too quickly. 'Relieved we've finally got him.' She rubbed her face, the skin rough and gritty under her hand. 'I want to check on Valerie and Henri. I'll see you back at the farm, later.'

He nodded, his eyes already on the wooden shack.

Retracing her steps down the tiny path to St Jean, Agnes found Valerie and Henri remarkably calm and unflurried. The bookseller looked with pride and affection at his friend.

'Isn't she a marvel?' he said to Agnes. Valerie blushed and smiled at him. 'You're a force to be reckoned with, Valerie Duphil. The Boche had better watch out.'

'I hope no one heard the gunshot,' she said, batting away his compliment. 'It was a bit stupid, but I was so angry – and afraid.'

She looked at Agnes, a shadow behind her eyes.

'Your house has thick walls, and it's a small gun,' said Agnes. 'It wouldn't sound more than a pop from outside.' Valerie seemed relieved and smiled at her. She turned to Henri. 'Have you never met Remi Comet before? I've met him a few times with Danielle at the market, and remember Valerie pointing him out to me a while ago.' She sighed. 'He always seemed a quiet fellow. Didn't say much.'

'I thought he reminded me of somebody I know,' said Henri. 'It's his father, Jacques' uncle.' He shook his head. 'I've not seen Remi since he was a boy, when Bruno would bring him to my shop occasionally. I didn't recognise him but he has a look of his father. I should have seen it.'

'If you hadn't been bashed on the head perhaps you would have remembered,' said Valerie.

Agnes caught an air of satisfaction about her, a brightness that had been missing. There was something between the two as they sat together in the small kitchen. Of course, they were old friends and looked out for each other, she thought. And yet . . . she caught a glance between them, a hand held for a moment longer than necessary . . . she felt a pang, a longing to know that feeling again.

Chapter 33

Claire

It wasn't far to Laurent's house from Villa Sarnaille, so I left the car and walked, my boots crunching on the snowy road as it fell to freezing again. I was a little nervous. I knew nothing about these people other than they had a dog and the family had a connection to the Resistance during the war. As I stepped gingerly along the icy road, I wondered how I could broach the subject of Agnes. Would Laurent be as sensitive about his family history as Matthieu's grandfather was? Would I be stirring up memories long buried, or – as someone like myself who had never experienced anything so terrible – would he be willing to talk about it?

Laurent filled the doorway when he answered my knock. I'd been so preoccupied with the dog I'd not really noticed his stature the previous day. Standing well over six feet tall, of dark complexion, with a bushy black beard containing a sprinkling of grey, and deep-set, green eyes, he looked like the sort of man who should be striding over mountains hunting bears or wolves or something.

He welcomed me in, his voice deep, with a resonance that seemed to come from far within him. Even when he spoke in a normal tone, I got the impression of a power that could command anyone within earshot to listen to what he was saying.

As he took my coat, Luc came running downstairs and stopped in front of me. 'Thank you for helping with Jurot, yesterday,' he said, in English.

He glanced from me to his dad, a questioning look on his face. 'You're welcome,' I said. 'I'm happy I could help and Jurot is okay. Your English is better than my French.'

He giggled, looking at Laurent again, who nodded his head towards the stairs. Luc turned tail and ran back the way he'd come, obviously relieved to have done his duty.

'He insisted on sleeping in the kitchen with the dog, when I wouldn't let him take Jurot up to bed with him,' Laurent said, chuckling. 'He's a good boy.'

'He obviously thinks the world of him,' I said. 'How's Jurot doing?'

'I've kept him quiet today. He's sore and stiff, but he's eating and I think he'll be fine in a few days.' He looked at me and smiled. 'Thank God you were there yesterday. I'm not sure what we'd have done otherwise.'

'Someone else would have stepped in and helped, I'm sure,' I said. 'Poor Luc looked so upset. I had to help. It's my job, after all.'

'That dog is his world,' admitted Laurent. 'I don't know how he'd cope if he lost him. Jurot's helped him such a lot since his mother and I split up.'

I dropped my gaze. I'd noticed the way he'd said 'Luc's mother' the day before at the surgery. Not 'my wife', or her name . . . so that was the shadow I'd seen in his expression.

I followed him into an airy living room warmed by a modern woodstove. The gable end was filled with a huge window that looked straight up to the mountains, shining silver in the rising moon. It seemed wherever I went they loomed like magnificent guardians over the town. He offered me a seat on a large corner sofa that faced the window, then went over to a side table with glasses and bottles on it and poured something into a wine glass.

'This is a local aperitif. It's made with herbs from the mountains. I hope you like it,' he said, offering it to me.

I took a sip and savoured the unusual flavour. It was rich and dry, almost like a sherry. Not what I'd expected. I smiled at him and he filled a glass for himself, bringing small plates of sliced dried sausage, olives and pieces of cheese, and placing them on a coffee table in front of where I sat, before joining me on the opposite end of the sofa. A silence fell for a few moments, as we ate and drank, but it didn't feel uncomfortable. He seemed a man who was used to being quiet, didn't expect small talk.

'This is such a nice room. The view is beautiful,' I said, looking around me.

Laurent smiled. 'I was lucky to get this plot. It has the best aspect and I could build the house to get that view of the mountains.'

'Did you build this?'

He grinned. 'Well, it is my job. I run a construction company.'

'Aah, well that would make sense, then.' I laughed. Looking around, I appreciated the workmanship in the beams and general finish of the place. 'It's a lovely house.'

'It suits me – and Luc. He can walk to school when he's staying with me, and it's not too far from his mum either, now he's old enough to go by himself.'

'Have you been on your own for long?' As soon as the words left my mouth, I could have bitten off my tongue. 'Sorry. That's none of my business.'

'Oh, don't worry. My wife and I split up just over a year ago.' His smile was crooked as he added, 'She's with someone else now.'

'I'm sorry,' I said again.

'Don't be. We hadn't been happy for a long time. We persevered for the sake of the boy, but in the end, it was the right thing to do.'

'I understand,' I said. 'Sometimes you just have to admit things aren't working, and give in.'

'You too?' he said.

I nodded and looked at the faint indentation where my wedding ring used to be.

'Anyway,' I said, brightly, 'I'm very pleased to have discovered this beautiful corner of France. I shall make sure to come back again.'

'How long will you stay, this time?'

'Only another few days, sadly,' I said, twiddling my empty glass, wanting to broach the subject of the article but not sure how to.

'Not nearly long enough to explore the area,' he said, rising and taking it from me. 'Let me get you another drink.'

He went over to the table and refilled both glasses. Taking my replenished glass from him, I mentioned I'd read the article, and wasn't it a coincidence just after we'd met?

'Oh, that,' he said. 'They did it back in the summer, as a commemoration ceremony.'

'So, your family were involved in the Resistance?' I asked.

He nodded.

'Grandfather was a *passeur* – one of the guides who took escapees over the mountains to Spain. There were routes all along the Pyrenees chain.' He pulled a face. 'It's why there was a Gestapo post in St Jean.'

'Goodness, it must have been terrifying,' I said.

'Yeah. Not everyone got out.' He fell silent, his face sombre.

I didn't know how to keep the conversation going. This was such a good opportunity, and it might be my only chance to find out about Agnes. He seemed to have shut down though, obviously didn't want to discuss the war with a stranger.

I swigged my drink, the wine warm in my throat. Laurent remained silent and I gazed around the room again, appreciating its comfort and warmth. Above the fireplace was a mantelpiece, full of photos of Laurent, Luc and a thin, dark woman. On the wall at the far end of the room was a collection of old black-and-white pictures in frames. They looked interesting, and I rose.

'May I?' I said, indicating the photographs. 'I love old photographs. It's so fascinating to see how people lived back when they were taken.'

Laurent looked a little surprised. 'Of course.' He gave a small laugh. 'Though I don't think my family has anything extraordinary about it.'

'But every family is unique, don't you think? Each has its own story to tell. Skeletons in cupboards, romantic alliances, rags to riches, all that sort of thing.' I rose. 'It's why soap operas make such good TV, isn't it? Everyone loves to know what's going on in their neighbour's house.'

He laughed again. 'You're right. I guess it's human nature to be nosy about other people.'

He sat back and I felt his eyes follow me as I went across and inspected them.

The photos were all old, family-type portraits of past generations. Some were taken outside what looked like a stone farmhouse. Most had children and dogs in them, which made me smile. One caught my eye, as it was completely different to the rest. The same shiver I'd experienced in the archive centre at Kew ran through me again. My stomach did a flip as I realised I had seen it before. It was the same one Aunt M showed me of her and Agnes in uniform.

The one I had brought with me.

Chapter 34

Agnes

The town was quiet when Agnes left Valerie's house, but she was jittery after the drama of the previous few hours and jumped at every leaf that moved, every shadow in every doorway. On leaving the town, her nerves settled as she pushed her bicycle up a steep, rocky track that would eventually bring her out just above the farm lane.

The night was mild and humid, with clouds building behind the high peaks, meaning a potential storm later. Sweat trickled down the inside of her blouse. Fatigue dragged at her muscles and she was tempted to abandon the heavy bicycle. But who knew what the next day would bring? She might need it and the thought of having to come and retrieve it before starting off on another arduous journey persuaded her to keep going.

She realised she'd overshot the little path that would take her to the farm. Swearing under her breath she heaved the bike around and backtracked, staring into the darkness for the small cairn that indicated her way home. The night sounds of the forest were all around her, but she couldn't relax. Foreign noises, such as the sound of metal scraping on metal she'd just heard, made her pulse leap. Pulling the bicycle off the track, she crawled down a bank and lay still, slowing her breathing, acutely aware of every tiny sound. There it was again, something not in tune with the natural order of the world around her.

In her mind an age passed, during which she lay, stiffer, damper, and colder by the minute. At last, she steeled herself to go back onto the track and get home as fast as possible. Putting her hands flat on the earth beneath her chest, she was about to push herself up when the unmistakable sound of a rusty wheel protesting at the uneven ground reached her. The noise was very close now, and she held her breath and slid further down the bank, burying her face in her arms.

The squeaky wheel and scrapes of metal on metal diminished, as the cyclist passed her hiding place and continued along the way. She dragged herself back up the slope to the rim of the track and risked a glance at the shadowy body moving away from her. The familiar shape made her smile; immediately followed by intense irritation at his sloppy procedures.

She picked up a rock and threw it after him, watching as he leapt off the bike and threw himself and his machine off the path. She stifled a giggle at his reaction, hysteria not far away, tension bubbling under her skin. Sneaking up as close as she dared – for she wouldn't put it past him to shoot first and ask questions later – she whispered a few words about the need to keep one's wheels oiled if one wanted to remain unseen and unheard.

A head slowly rose above the rock he'd hidden behind, and he stood up stiffly, one hand holding his side, annoyance plain, even in the dark. Lifting his bicycle out of the bushes, he pushed it towards her and stopped a couple of yards away.

'You passed the path down to the farm,' Agnes said, quietly. 'And that bike is a disgrace. I could hear you coming a mile away.'

'You must have missed the turn-off too if you're this far along the track,' Philippe countered. 'And I hit a rock back along the way;

it's done something to the front wheel – I don't normally make a habit of giving away my presence, I assure you.'

He came closer, his face mirroring her own exhaustion and his steps slow and halting.

'What happened with Remi Comet?' she said.

Philippe squared his shoulders. 'Do you really want to know?' he said. 'You saw Jacques' reaction when he was told his cousin was the collaborator. Can you imagine how he must feel, discovering that the man he's known all his life was passing on all the plans the maquisards were making?' He rubbed his face, as if to erase what he'd seen and heard over the past few hours. 'Remi Comet is dead. I won't bore you with the details.'

Agnes dropped her head. Images of the violence she'd witnessed flitted through her mind. How much worse to see a captive, a man unable to fight back – even if he was a traitor – being subjected to more brutality.

'Let's get back to the farm,' she said. 'I must send a message to Reynard tonight, via London.'

'Surely you can leave it until tomorrow,' he said. 'You've done enough today.'

She shook her head. 'The Gestapo will soon start wondering where their informant has disappeared to. Even if they don't suspect he's been caught, the whole valley will be locked down while they look for him. I can't wait until tomorrow.' They walked along the track, looking for the cairn at the head of the final path to the farm. 'I take it you'll want to stay with the Espouys tonight?'

He nodded.

'In that case, I could do with a hand to carry the radio equipment up to the new hiding place I've found, where it'll be safe to send a message. I didn't have time to do it, what with Henri being attacked and everything. Unless you're in too much pain. You look exhausted,' she finished.

'You don't look too hot, yourself, Tigresse,' he flashed back at her. 'Of course I'll help you – just point me in the right direction.

It's been a long day; the sooner we get the job done, the sooner we can get some sleep.'

They walked on in silence, until Agnes saw the pile of stones at an outcrop of rock and heather, where the tiny path down to the farm began. The sky had lightened enough for them to make out the fields and small farms on the valley floor. Birdsong filled the air, and the sky became streaked with pink as the rising sun appeared above the peaks ahead of them, turning the snowfields a soft shade of rose. They stood for a moment, and Philippe turned to her and very gently brushed her lips with his.

Agnes stepped back in shock, as much from the electricity shooting through her as from a sense of indignation at the act itself. She pushed him away and in the next instance pulled him back to her and kissed him hard. She broke the clinch and turned her back to him, wiping her mouth with a shaking hand. Tears threatened, and she blinked them away, guilt bringing anger with it.

Flinging her bike along the path, she set off down the steep descent, not caring where she set her feet. She heard Philippe behind her, keeping pace, not saying anything, as if he knew he'd crossed a boundary. Five minutes later she arrived at the edge of the village, out of breath, an ankle burning from twisting it on a loose rock. She slowed and limped between the houses to the farm lane and arrived at the Espouy farm with relief. Philippe moved with just as much pain by the look of him, but still she said nothing. They parked their bicycles against the side of the barn and Agnes went inside the semi-dark building to where a ladder led up to the loft. She had hidden the radio temporarily behind a false partition on the end wall.

She wearily climbed up and pulled the heavy case containing the radio transmitter out of its hiding place. Lugging it back to the top of the ladder she struggled to hold it under one arm while she descended the uneven rungs, hanging on with her free hand, her ankle in danger of collapsing under the extra weight. Philippe steadied her with a hand on her back and much as she hated him touching her, it was as if his hands stoked a fire in her belly that had been ignited by their success in exposing Remi Comet.

For all her exhaustion, the pain in her ankle, hunger and thirst, she felt more alive than ever before. This was why she endured the hardship, the loneliness, the guilt and heartbreak of leaving Maggie. The thrill of making her plan work and catching the collaborator made everything else worthwhile. Every nerve in her body fizzed, her senses so heightened she imagined she could hear the bats squeaking to each other as they returned from their nightly hunt.

She recognised then this was what made Philippe do what he did, and that she was far more like him than she had been prepared to accept. Did he see it in her? That they were, in essence, the same?

Before she had time to think about what he was doing, he took the case from her, placed it on the floor, and kissed her again. This time his lips were warm and insistent, searching hers until she could withstand him no longer. She kissed him back, every fibre of her body on fire. He pulled her into him and kissed her once more, his passion overwhelming.

'Stop. Not now, not here,' she said, pulling back, her mouth tingling, her body turned to liquid. Aching for more and hating herself for it. What was she doing? Another body lying close to hers passed through her mind and, closing her eyes, she tried to blot out the image of Maggie's face and turned away.

'Yes, here. I want you, Céleste. Now.'

He put his hand on her neck in a caress, his voice low and thick, sending a shiver through her, and her treacherous body responded in a way she'd not felt before. This was not the same loving passion she had known with Maggie, but lust and a need she didn't recognise and hadn't realised she had. She let him lead her, the dark recesses of her mind regretting her actions, yet not caring, not wanting him to stop, his lips and hands gentle but demanding, her body aching for release. When it came, she cried out and he held her, stroking her hair, and kissing her eyelids. Heat filled her, and a sweet heaviness that begged her to stay lying in his arms, to sleep and forget the horror of the day.

But after the heat came a tremor she couldn't stop. She felt chilled to the bone, scoured and empty, and she turned her head away, the double-edged sword of shame and guilt slicing through her. The act was as much of a betrayal as those of the man who'd been executed as a traitor.

Climbing the steep path back up into the forest seemed to take forever. Agnes was exhausted, her ankle ached, her belly cried out for food, and guilt dogged her footsteps. Low cloud had covered the early sun and a mizzle of rain fell, making the path treacherous underfoot and difficult to see in the gloom under the trees.

She hoped the markers she had placed to help guide her back, when she'd discovered the ruined barn, hadn't been dislodged by passing wildlife. Trying to remember the way, stressed and tired, would have been impossible. Even so, they had to backtrack a couple of times. By the time she saw the tangle of scrub and saplings she was dizzy with fatigue. Philippe looked puzzled.

'Is this it?' he said. 'I thought you said it was a barn?'

Agnes looked at him; the sheen of sweat on his cheeks, his eyes sunk deep in their sockets. Their short liaison in the barn might have been a lifetime ago. She pointed to the cave-like entrance.

'I need you to keep watch, while I send my message. It could take a while. London may not send a reply immediately,' she said. 'You'd struggle to get through this hole, but I'll be able to hear you from inside. Whistle if you see anyone, and I'll cut the connection.'

Fear folded itself around her. Radio signals were routinely picked up by the Germans and could be pinpointed to within a small area. Moving the radio from place to place could only keep her safe for so long. In the end, it was almost inevitable she would be discovered.

Philippe handed her the bulky case, unslung the Sten gun he carried on his shoulder and checked the magazine. Climbing above the thicket where he'd have a wide view of the small clearing and the forest around it, he chose a mess of large trees ravaged by some forgotten storm, their trunks and branches a gigantic bird's nest of timber. Watching him clamber into the midst of the rotting wood, Agnes could barely make him out. He was almost invisible.

'I'll be as quick as I can,' she said, her voice low.

She crawled inside the tunnel, pushing the case in front of her, getting it caught on tree roots and briars a couple of times, her arms burning with the effort, nerves frayed at the noise she was making. Once inside the ruin, she found it was almost dry, the overhanging branches providing protection from the persistent rain. Working as quickly as her fumbling fingers would go, she set up the radio and climbed precariously up the gable wall to get the aerial as high as possible. Once everything was set up, she put on the headphones, and her tired brain went into automatic mode. She knew what she needed to say, and the code to use, based on a Tennyson poem. Tears pricked her eyes as it reminded her of Philippe's hands on her body, and her betrayal of Maggie's love.

She pushed aside her exhaustion and guilt, and concentrated on what she needed to do. She kept an ear out for a warning from Philippe, fear giving her fingers speed. Still, tapping out the dots and dashes took a while and sweat ran down inside her clothing. Finished at last, she sat back, rubbing her ankle, and easing the crick out of her neck. Now all she could do was wait, and hope London replied without delay.

She sat on the mossy ground, leaning back against the ruined wall, the quiet giving her thoughts full rein to make her even more wretched. The sound of a message coming through brought her to attention in an instant, and she rolled onto her knees to see the reply. It took her exhausted mind a moment or two to work out what it said.

CONGRATULATIONS STOP
BIRD CRASHED NEAR M STOP
6 DEAD 1 SURVIVOR STOP
CARGO RETRIEVED STOP
LIAISE WITH G FOR PICKUP AND EXTRICATION
STOP
END

Agnes checked her decoding. A downed plane wasn't unusual. Survivors were rare though, and she wanted to be sure. She'd not had much to do with the Freedom Trails; the Murphy Line did that work. Why did they want *her* to get this survivor out? Shrugging, she took the aerial down and began packing away the radio when the sound of voices made her freeze.

Germans.

She prayed Philippe was out of sight and wouldn't precipitate anything. The soldiers might keep moving; there was nothing to indicate her presence. Barely breathing, she tried to pick out words, her ears tuned to gauge the number of men coming ever closer.

It sounded as if there were only a couple of them, but she couldn't make out what they were saying. One of them laughed and another said a few words that might have been a joke. Perhaps Philippe would stay hidden and let them pass. What did a couple of rag-tag Boches matter in the greater scheme of things?

Don't do anything, you crazy Canadian. Just let them go . . . They've not seen us.

She willed him to stay hidden. She was so tired, and so sick of violence and fear, all she wanted was to go down to Danielle's and sleep.

Then Philippe spoke and her heart jumped into her mouth.

She crawled through the tunnel until she was at the opening into the clearing, keeping her head down. She couldn't see much, being so low to the ground, but she could hear the exchange between the men.

In atrocious German, Philippe told the soldiers to drop their weapons and put their hands behind their heads. Looking to her left, Agnes could just see him, leaning against a tree, his Sten gun in one hand. He was relaxed, a twisted smile on his face, and reminded her of a cat who'd cornered a mouse and was playing with it. The light glinted on his spectacles, hiding his eyes, and she could smell smoke as he took a drag on a cigarette.

A clatter as the soldiers' guns hit the ground made her jump, and she wriggled a bit more to see if she could get them into her eyeline. Two pairs of tatty boots, one with a broken lace, came into view. It was a banal, pathetic sight.

The soldiers weren't brave. They begged Philippe not to shoot them – all they'd been doing was hunting for game, trying to augment their meagre rations.

'What do you think the French families have left to live on, after you Boche bastards have stolen all their food? Fresh air?'

Their pleas fell on deaf ears. Agnes saw Philippe's expression harden, and he lifted the gun and shot the two Germans where they stood. She clambered out of her hiding place. Both were young, and one was still alive, shot twice in the stomach, his hands clutching at the mess of blood and shredded uniform. His eyes bulged from the lids, and he stared at her as she gazed down at him. He looked no older than Pierre, and she had to bite down hard on her lip and stop herself from weeping at the brutal reality of it all. These boys were someone else's brother and son.

'*Bitte . . .*' he whispered.

She shook her head, trying to dispel the guilt at what she had been party to. At that moment, it all seemed so pointless.

Philippe walked over, took out his handgun and shot the man in the head, the sound reverberating round the clearing and into Agnes's brain. She looked away from the thing that was no longer a man, and out of the corner of her eye saw a movement in the trees, heard the crack of a twig. Probably a deer, she thought, uneasy that something had witnessed what they'd done.

261

'You didn't need to do that,' she said. 'They hadn't seen you, so why? Why bring even more danger to the valley when the Boche discover two of their soldiers have been gunned down?'

'I'd have thought, after all that's happened in the past week, you would understand. If I have to tell you then you're not the person I thought you were,' he said, his voice cold. He put his gun back in its holster. 'Come on. We need to bury these two.'

Her head swam. 'How the hell do we bury them? We've nothing to dig with.'

'Go and get the radio, and then we'll shove them inside the thicket. With any luck, the boar and vultures will get rid of the bodies for us. These two will just go down as another AWOL statistic.' He shook Agnes's shoulder. 'Céleste, wake up! We haven't got time to waste. Let's move.'

Agnes wormed her way into the barn again, and finished packing up the radio with hands that shook so much she could hardly fasten the case. Crawling backwards out of the tunnel, pulling the case after her, she stood up, brushing leaf mould and twigs from her breeches. The rain had stopped, and steam rose from the damp ground, bringing with it the scent of leaf litter and wet moss. Philippe took the German weapons, hiding them under the scrub at the base of the pile of twisted and uprooted trees he'd been standing behind.

'I'll send one of the lads to pick these up,' he said. 'Help me get these two into the tunnel.'

They dragged the bodies into the space Agnes had crawled out of. They had to pull the scrub away to make the hole big enough to hide them, then did their best to repair the damage and brushed over the area to erase any signs. Blood stained the mossy ground where the men had fallen.

'It just looks like a hunter's kill, and the next rain will wash it away,' he said, picking up the radio case and his gun. 'Let's get back to the farm. It's been a long night.'

Chapter 35

Claire

I stared at the framed photograph, my mind struggling to make sense of what I was looking at. How could the photo of Margaret and Agnes be here in Laurent's house? Why would he have the same picture? I pointed at it, my hand not quite steady.

'Who is this?'

My voice sounded strange, even to me, and Laurent frowned. He came and took it off the wall, gazing at it. He pointed to Agnes. 'Céleste Sarraute. The other, I think, is someone she knew in England. I forget her name.'

'Margaret,' I whispered.

How on earth did Aunt M's photograph end up here, in this house? Of all the strange things I had discovered, it was the most extraordinary. Did Laurent's grandfather know Agnes? If he was in the Resistance, he must have done, surely, for the photo to be here.

'What?' Laurent said, seemingly oblivious to my turmoil.

I cleared my throat. 'Margaret Scott is the other woman. My aunt.'

The green eyes drilled into mine. 'What?' he said again.

I stared back, unable to make sense of the coincidence that had led me to this moment. Perhaps Agnes had had a hand in it after all, guiding me from beyond the grave. A strangled laugh forced its way out of me; I had to hand it to her, she'd played a blinder. Excitement bubbled up, along with a hundred questions. Laurent had a look of utter confusion on his face.

I pointed to Agnes. 'I've come here to try and discover what happened to this woman seventy years ago.' I shook my head, trying to think straight.

'Why? What was she to you?'

Was. Past tense. I avoided his question. 'Did she know your grandfather during the war?'

He nodded. 'She stayed with my grandparents, while she worked as a radio operator for the Resistance.' He gazed at the photo again, a slight frown creasing his forehead. After a moment his eyes met mine, the frown deepening. 'Look, why should I tell you about my family history? I have no idea what your interest is in Céleste.'

I didn't know where to begin. How could I tell him she had a love affair with my aunt before she was posted to France? I explained she'd been a friend and colleague of Aunt M's and had disappeared without a trace during the war. It had bothered my aunt ever since, and I wanted to see if I could solve the mystery.

'My aunt . . . her mind wanders. Sometimes she believes she's still in the war. She and Agnes . . . Céleste . . . shared a flat. She keeps asking where she is.'

I faltered, Aunt M's pale, terrified face when I first found her coming to mind.

This wasn't what I envisaged when I began my search. I imagined looking through dusty records, hunting in graveyards, speaking to those she might have fought alongside, not turning people's lives upside down with outlandish revelations. I had the same feeling I'd had after I'd talked to Harriet's guests about the war – that I had no right to go stomping all over their memories.

'How did you track her down to St Jean?' Laurent asked.

'Her old records are all still there, in London,' I said. 'It was pretty straightforward finding where she was posted. But then the trail went cold. I couldn't find out what happened to her once she was here.' I shrugged. 'I hoped – hope – to find someone who knew her and can tell me.' Another laugh forced itself out of my throat. 'After I read the article that had you in it, I hoped you might be able to . . .'

'Wait. Are you staying at Villa Sarnaille?' he asked. I nodded, surprised at his sudden change of tack. 'You're not the one Harriet wants me to meet?'

It was my turn to stare. This was surreal.

'Yes. I asked if she knew someone who could tell me what happened here, during the war. She said you were interested in local history and might be able to help, or at least introduce me to someone who could.'

'Harriet loves to involve herself in everything going on around her,' Laurent said with a wry smile. 'And she's very hard to say no to.'

'I can imagine.' I rose and gave the photo back to him. 'I should go. I need to think – it's all a bit much to take in.'

'True,' he said. 'But I want to know more, and you should come and meet my mother and grandmother. They can tell you more about Céleste.'

His mother and grandmother? Had Agnes survived the war if she had known them well? Why the hell hadn't she come home to Aunt M, then? The more I learnt, the more confused I felt.

Laurent's eyes sparkled as he looked at me. He seemed as excited as I was.

'That would be fantastic, as long as they don't mind meeting me.' I needed some space to think about everything. We walked back out into the hall, and Laurent gave me my coat. Putting it on, a thought crossed my mind. 'Can I see Jurot before I go?'

'Of course. He's through here.'

I followed him into the kitchen and there was Jurot, lying in a basket, his tail thumping in greeting. I bent to him and gently stroked his head, checking his eyes and carefully feeling for any pain. He licked my hand, seeming unfazed by my prodding.

'He's recovering well, isn't he? Give him a couple of days and he'll be good as new.' I gave him a final pat. 'You're a lucky boy, Jurot. It might have been much worse.'

'He was lucky you were there, and so were we,' Laurent said. 'I don't think I can thank you enough for your help.'

His eyes crinkled at the edges when he smiled. I mumbled something about being in the right place at the right time. We left the patient snoozing in his bed and Laurent led me to the door. I put out my hand.

'Thanks for the aperitif,' I said.

He ignored my hand and kissed me on either cheek. 'I'll pick you up from Harriet's place tomorrow morning. *À demain*, Claire. Goodbye.'

Laurent shut the door behind him, leaving me with a head full of scrambled thoughts and impressions. I walked back to Villa Sarnaille feeling as if Agnes was once again steering me forward, wanting me to succeed. I looked up at the star-filled sky and hoped that somewhere, out in the ether, she and Aunt M would meet again one day, and be as much in love as they had been seventy years ago.

I couldn't wait until tomorrow.

Chapter 36

Agnes

Agnes slept for eight hours. Sleep that was filled with nightmares of being buried alive, and waking to find she was sharing a grave with the two dead soldiers. She woke in a tangle of bedsheets, cooling sweat chilling her aching body and her head filled with cotton wool.

Exhaustion dulled her senses as she swung her legs over the side of the bed and tentatively put her injured foot to the floor. It was stiff and sore, and there was a bruise blooming on the ankle, but she could bear weight on it.

Pulling on the same clothes she'd taken off before falling into bed, she wrinkled her nose at the stale smell of sweat and dampness clinging to them. After making a rudimentary toilette, she hobbled down the wide staircase, meeting Danielle halfway.

'I wondered if I should wake you. Your friend has been up for hours.'

'You should have. I didn't mean to sleep so long,' said Agnes. 'It was a very long day – and night. Did he tell you the good news?'

'Yes. I can't believe it was Remi,' Danielle said. 'I've known him since we were children. We went to school together.' She looked close to tears. 'Why did he do it? I don't understand.'

'He believed the Germans are winning the war, and it's better to be on the winning side.'

Agnes couldn't contemplate the possibility he might be right. And even if he was, she knew the maquisards would never lay down arms and surrender.

But it won't come to that. The Allies are preparing for D-Day. It won't be long until they retake France, and all the other countries Hitler's armies have invaded.

She had to keep telling herself that, otherwise what would be the point of it all?

'You're hurt,' Danielle said.

'It's only a twisted ankle. I got a message from London last night, and I need to go and see Georges. A plane crashed near where he is, and there's a survivor. I've got to get him over the border.'

'Borrow my van. I managed to scrounge some fuel yesterday so the tank's full.' Danielle carried on up the stairs. 'I'll find a bandage to bind up your ankle, in a moment. Jean will guide the *évadé* if you want. He's sick of being in hiding. A bit of a walk will be good for him.'

She smiled. The haunted look in her eyes gave away the lie.

Agnes went in search of food and coffee, finding the remnants of dinner still on the table. She carved off a large chunk of bread, and a piece of cheese, and poured herself a cup of coffee from the pot keeping warm on the stove. Taking her food with her, she wandered outside to find Philippe, walking down to Mme Espouy's cottage. Her ankle felt stronger the more she moved it. She found the old woman sitting on a rough bench outside her front door. Hunkered down on his haunches beside her was Philippe.

'So, I hear there was some excitement last night,' said Mme Espouy. 'And there are two less Boche pigs to worry about.' She spat on the earth between her feet. 'Good riddance to them. I hope they rot in hell, along with the coward Remi Comet.'

She shut her mouth with a snap, and Agnes glanced across at Philippe, her cheeks hot. The thought of his hands on her body made her flesh crawl.

'I've got to go and see Georges Luzent,' she said. 'I could take you part of the way to St Antoine.' She blew on the scalding coffee and took a sip. 'Thank you for helping last night – this morning. God, it seems like an age ago, already.'

'My pleasure,' he said, grinning. 'Any excuse to stick it to the Germans. I'll accept a lift, gladly. It'll shorten the journey on my bicycle.'

'I'll wait until sunset before leaving.'

'What? Are you leaving us again, young man?' said Mme Espouy. 'I think we need to have something to commemorate your successes. Where's Jean?'

'He's keeping out of sight, in case the Boche come calling,' said Philippe.

'Go and find him and tell him to bring that camera of his. I want a photograph of you two – you make a perfect couple.' The old woman winked.

Agnes blushed again as Philippe rose and did as he was bid. Had Mme Espouy guessed? It was impossible – she was just teasing them; she must be. The sooner he went back to St Antoine, the better.

Jean appeared, muttering, from the direction of the farm, Philippe beside him, carrying the camera.

'I don't see why we need to do this,' he grumbled. 'After all, you two were just doing your jobs.' He pointed to a flat area of grass behind the cottage. 'Right, stand there. Link arms, and you'd both better have a gun in your hands, to suit my mother.'

Philippe picked up his rifle, took Agnes's hand and drew her over to the place Jean had indicated. She pulled back and stopped.

'This is ridiculous. What if we're seen posing like this? The Boche could be crawling all over the place at any moment, and we're having a photo taken.'

She walked away, trying to keep her temper in check.

'What's got into you, Céleste? It's only a photo.' Philippe stepped in front of her. 'It'll take two minutes. A keepsake for Mme Espouy. And it'll look like we've been out hunting, nothing more.' He grabbed her arm. 'Come on. What harm will it do?'

She gave in. Perhaps he was right; she was too tired to argue. Still.

'I don't have my gun with me,' she said.

Philippe pulled his handgun out from its holster, swung it round and presented the grip to her.

'Here, take this.'

Agnes stared at it. The last time she'd seen the piece it was being used to shoot someone in the head. The image was burnt onto her retinas and for a second her stomach heaved. Swallowing, she took the offered gun and stood as Jean had directed. Philippe slipped his arm through hers.

'Is this right?'

'Yes, it'll do. Right, don't move, while I take a couple of shots.'

Agnes stood rigid, the feel of Philippe so close making her flinch. He caught something in her body language, and turned to look at her, just as Jean took the picture.

'Relax, Tigresse,' he said, then bent and whispered into her ear, 'Perhaps you're remembering what happened last night, eh?'

She jerked her arm out of his, brushing the front of her jacket. Handing him the gun, she turned to leave. 'Are we finished, Jean? Yes? Right, I must find Danielle.'

Tired as she still was, Agnes found it impossible to switch off while she waited until the sun slipped behind the western ridges and shadows deepened in the valley. She washed, changed her underwear and blouse, noticing bloodstains on her breeches as she put them back on. She rubbed at them with a cloth, but the marks stubbornly remained.

Wanting some meaningful activity to blot out the thoughts running on a loop in her head, she helped Danielle with the milking and setting the cheese for the market in a couple of days. Keeping her hands occupied might stop her seeing the corpses of the Germans in her mind's eye, and the fleeting glimpse of something running away. The more she replayed it, the more her brain became convinced it was another person – not a deer, not a boar, but a man, his white face the flash she'd seen and at first assumed was a deer scut.

Dusk filled the valley by the time they'd finished clearing up the *fromagerie*. Agnes went to find Philippe and tell him they should leave in half an hour. She noticed flashing lights down near the valley road, as if torches were being swung this way and that. The sound of voices wafted up the hill, blowing away on the breeze. It was hard to hear what was being said, but it wasn't French; she was sure of that. Philippe came running up to the house.

'Germans, coming this way, banging on doors, shouting about something,' he said. 'I couldn't make out what they were saying, but I'm guessing they're looking for us. We'd better get up into the trees, stay out of the way, until they've gone.'

Danielle came out and ushered them inside the house.

'If they have dogs, being in the forest won't save you,' she said. 'Get down into the cellar. I've sent Jean down there already. Céleste, you know where to go.'

Agnes pushed Philippe down the ancient, worn stone steps of the cellar, telling him to keep walking to the far side, feeling her way in the dark. The air was heavy and cold, and there was an overpowering smell of onions and garlic.

Jean's voice came out of the blackness. 'Quick, you two, over here,' he said.

'Here' was a small room, built into the rock of the mountain, with a stone wall blocking it off from the rest of the cellar. Once the door was shut from the inside, it looked as if it was just a stack of old shelves leaning against the back wall. With the three of them shut inside together, it quickly became claustrophobic, as if there wasn't enough oxygen for them all. The room was barely high enough for Philippe's lanky frame, and he chose to sit on the one rickety chair rather than stoop. The only other furniture in the space was a small square table and a cot bed with a blanket over it. Jean had a small torch that gave him enough light to hold a match to a stub of a candle in a jar on the table. Once the torch was off, the tiny luminescence threw grotesque shadows on the walls, like some huge puppet show.

Agnes's senses sharpened in the darkness. The rank smell of the men too close to her, the drip of water somewhere, and the sound of voices getting louder until they seemed to be right above them. Danielle spoke, her voice high and sharp, so close she might have been in the room with them.

'No, there's been nobody else around,' she said. 'But, if you want to search my farm, who am I to stop you?' Her voice wavered. 'It's just me, my old mother-in-law, and my children, now. All the men are either dead or gone, thanks to the glorious Third Reich. Who are you looking for, anyway?'

Agnes heard the German's rough reply, his French basic, but understandable.

'Two of our brave men were gunned down in cold blood early this morning. A third, who was able to get away, saw the whole thing. We're looking for a man and another – possibly a young boy,' the soldier said. 'If you or anyone else is harbouring these murderers, there will be a heavy price to pay, you understand?'

Agnes's head spun and she sat down on the cot, her legs buckling. She'd been right – it was a man she'd seen.

'Whoever they are, they're heroes in my book,' the voice of Mme Espouy, strong and unafraid. 'Two less of you bastards to worry about.'

Agnes imagined her spitting on the boots of the soldier, and held her breath. Danielle muttered something, trying to hush the old woman. The man raised his voice telling her to shut her mouth followed by a thud and a shout from Danielle.

'She's an old woman. How can she be a threat to you?' Danielle cried. 'Maman, Maman, are you all right?'

'Tell the old bitch to mind her manners next time,' said the German.

Jean paced the small room, muttering oaths. Agnes couldn't tell whether he was cursing the German, or his mother for being so outspoken. Terrified he would be heard from outside, she put a hand on his arm and stilled him. He sat on the cot and put his head in his hands.

The German ordered his men to search the house and buildings. Thank God she'd not put the radio back in the loft. She hoped it was safe inside the hollow tree above the farm.

The three of them sat, listening to the search going on outside and in the house. Philippe seemed turned to stone, tension vibrating off his body. Agnes frantically tried to remember if she had replaced the photograph of her and Maggie in its hiding place at the bottom of her suitcase. Everything had happened so quickly over the past few days she hadn't looked at it since before Henri had been hurt. Had she put it away? Fear clawed at her gut. A picture of two women in British uniforms was a death sentence for everyone if the Germans found it. She held her breath and listened for the triumphant shout as it was found. But she heard nothing, only the sound of boots clattering on the stairs and stamping through the house.

The cellar was ransacked, and Jean blew the candle out so they were sitting in pitch blackness. The sound of the shelves that hid the door being emptied of the cans and jars that stood on them made Agnes want to retch. She was sure the soldiers must be able to hear her heart thumping, but after a few minutes they moved on to look elsewhere. Time dragged on, and even with terror still running through her like a hot wire, fatigue dragged at her muscles, her eyes gritty and dry from lack of sleep.

Finally, there was a rap on the door. It was a code, and Jean pushed the door open, allowing in a little light that made them all blink. Danielle waited on the other side. The cellar looked as if a tornado had gone through it. Jean hugged his wife, who cried on his shoulder.

'Maman?'

'She's dazed and has a cut on her head where that bastard hit her with his rifle. She's lucky he didn't kill her. Stupid old woman, risking her life like that,' she sobbed. 'What will we eat? Those pigs have ruined everything.'

Agnes righted the shelves where preserves were stored. Strings of onions lay scattered and trampled on the floor, and a bag of flour had been thrown against a wall, looking as if someone had splattered a tin of paint there. She picked up the pieces of a coffee pot from the floor and placed them with care on a stone shelf. If this was what they'd done to the cellar, how much worse was the house?

Jean was still comforting Danielle. 'Sshh, we'll survive. We always do.'

He held her, patting her back as if she were a small child, and looked over her shoulder at Agnes, his eyes cold and hard.

Chapter 37

Claire

I slept badly, my mind full of everything I'd learnt, and the impression Laurent had made on me. He was an interesting man, and I looked forward to meeting him again, along with his mother and grandmother.

I'd barely spoken to Harriet, who was busy with her guests. When she walked into the guests' lounge with Laurent following her and introduced him, we both laughed.

'What?' she said, looking from him to me. Laurent told her how we'd met, and her eyes grew wide. 'Wow, that's a funny coincidence.'

'It gets weirder,' I said. 'The woman I'm trying to find lived with Laurent's grandparents during the war.'

'No way? How did you find that out?' Harriet's excitement was infectious. I laughed and told her. 'Gosh, it's a small world, isn't it?' she said.

Laurent shrugged. 'You know how small a community we have here in the valley. It could have been any one of a dozen families.' He smiled at me. 'Shall we go? I phoned Maman and said I was bringing you to meet her.'

'I'm ready,' I said, and: 'See you later,' to Harriet as we left.

We said little as Laurent set off and drove along a small road that twisted and climbed through a steep forested hillside. The snow became deeper the higher we went, but the road had been cleared, leaving huge drifts at the sides and a narrow track in the middle. My mind buzzed with questions, though, and I couldn't stay silent.

'Last night you said Agnes – Céleste – knew your grandmother and mother. Past tense. I take it she's no longer alive?' I said, after a while.

'Céleste Sarraute died before I was born,' he admitted.

Perhaps there was the reason Aunt M never heard from Agnes again. Perhaps she always meant to get in touch, or go back and see her, but died before she got the chance.

'Is your grandfather still alive? The one who was a . . . *passeur*? Is that the right word?'

He shook his head, glancing at me then back to the road as he negotiated another hairpin bend.

'It is the right word,' he said, then added nothing, a frown on his face, as if he was weighing his words. I watched him, and after a moment he seemed to make up his mind and continued. 'He died up in the mountains during the war, helping a British pilot escape to Spain.'

'Oh, that's tragic, I'm so sorry.'

Laurent shrugged. 'It was his job and his choice. I would have liked to know him, though.'

'You say Céleste stayed with your family. Did she never go back to England?'

I still couldn't see why Agnes had remained in France.

'She died two years after the war ended, of pneumonia, I think. Perhaps she would have gone back, eventually.' Laurent smiled again, a soft look in his eyes. 'She had grown very close to the family; I know that much. Apparently, my grandfather used to call her *Tigresse* – Tigress. That tells you something about her, don't you think?'

It did. She was obviously a force to be reckoned with. A different side to Agnes from the one Aunt M knew and loved, it seemed. I digested what he'd told me. In many ways it was the simplest of stories, and yet it threw up so many unresolved questions. The one foremost in my mind was *why?* Why had Agnes decided to stay in France? I had read her letter and seen the words, promising to come back to Margaret as soon as she could. What had changed so much that she was prevented from fulfilling that promise? And why had she not, at the very least, sent Aunt M a letter saying she was safe and well, but had a new life and she should forget about her? It seemed such a cruel thing to do and didn't fit with the kind of person Aunt M remembered Agnes being.

Perhaps, Aunt M had developed rose-tinted specs when thinking about that time in her life.

Laurent turned off the narrow mountain road onto a track, still covered in snow. Slowing to a crawl he drove until we came to a farm at the edge of a village, pulled in and stopped.

'Does your mother speak English?'

'A little, though I'll help,' he said. 'Come and meet her.'

Chapter 38

Agnes

Later that night Agnes and Philippe set off in Danielle's tiny van with his bicycle in the back. As they approached the junction where she was to drop him off, Philippe suggested she let him accompany her to the farm near Montréjeau.

'Why?' she asked.

She didn't want to have him sharing another tiny space with her. It was enough that she had to take him as far as Cierp-Garin.

'I haven't seen the Luzents since that first night, when we arrived,' he said, with a shrug. 'And if I go straight back to St Antoine I'll be seen. I know I'm being watched. After everything that's happened it might be best if I stayed out of sight.'

Agnes nodded reluctantly, keeping her eyes on the dark road ahead. The silence grew. Philippe squirmed in the passenger seat and tried to get her to talk to him.

'Fuck it,' he said, when she continued to ignore him. 'If you want to act like a child, it's no skin off my nose.'

He leant his head against the door of the van and closed his

278

eyes. Agnes drove on down the valley, her hands relaxing on the steering wheel the further they went.

The ancient farmhouse where she and Philippe had first been taken after they parachuted into France felt like a second home to her now. Georges and Florence like the grandparents she barely remembered. They greeted Agnes as if she were family and were reserved but polite on meeting Philippe again.

'This is an honour, having both of you here,' Georges said. 'Though perhaps travelling together is not the wisest thing to do, from all I hear.' He raised an eyebrow and Agnes flushed. How did he know? Georges continued, clapping Philippe on the shoulder and smiling at her. 'Unmasking the collaborator was good work.'

Covering her confusion with a cough, she got straight down to business. 'I received a message from London, saying there was a survivor from a plane crash, and to come and see you,' she said. 'What happened?'

Georges' expression sobered.

'It was a Halifax bringing in more weapons and a replacement for someone who'd been captured up near Tarbes. The cloud cover was low, and the pilot didn't see the mountain in time, we think. He flew straight into the side of it. One of the shepherd boys heard the plane go down and went to see if he could help, but the only survivor was the tail gunner. The back of the plane broke off on impact, which saved him. He's hurt but fit enough to make it out. We must act quickly; the Boche will have heard what happened, no doubt about it.' He rubbed his face with a gnarled hand, the flickering flames of the fire giving him a grotesque look for a moment. 'The locals managed to retrieve the bodies of the dead, as well as the guns. They are well hidden, so all the Germans will find is a wreck. We'll bury the men together in a temporary grave for the moment. I hope, in time, they can be laid to rest in a proper cemetery, God rest their souls.'

Florence refilled his and Philippe's glasses with pastis. Agnes cupped hers, swirling the liquid within. She'd barely touched it, the warmth of the kitchen and aroma of the liquid making her head swim.

'The families of those poor men will be grateful they've not fallen into the hands of the enemy, at least,' she said. 'Where's the injured man, now? I need to move him. The sooner we get him over the frontier the better.'

'He's safe, hidden in a house near here, but will need a few days before he's fit enough to travel on foot.'

She told the French couple about the search for them and the killing of the Germans.

'The frontier guards will be everywhere, on the lookout for whoever shot the soldiers.' She sighed. 'It'll be a tough journey for an injured man. They'll have to take the least-used paths over tougher terrain to get to the border.'

Georges raised his glass at her and Philippe.

'You did well, the two of you, not only capturing the collaborator but taking out two Boche pigs, as well,' he said. 'Ach, it's a shame one of the bastards escaped, though. If he recognises either of you, you'll have to hope you can make a run for it.' He took a drink and lit a cigarette. 'Perhaps, my Canadian friend, you should get out too. You've stirred up quite a hornet's nest while you've been here, and if they catch you, the Gestapo will do their worst.'

'That's why I'm here. And a risk we all take,' Philippe said, shrugging, a brief smile tightening his face.

'Of course. But if you have to spend your whole time in hiding, you're no use to anyone. You'd be better served by going to a different patch, where you're unknown,' Georges said. He dragged his hands through his thin hair, so it stood out as if an electric charge had passed through it. He softened his tone, but his words were uncompromising. 'There are others who could benefit from your skills. The north is desperate for more men of your calibre.'

Agnes nodded her agreement. Philippe glanced at her, his eyes bleak, opening his mouth as if to argue the point. Perhaps he saw something in her expression, for he dropped his gaze and shrugged for a second time, then shook his head.

The thought of not having him working alongside her brought a moment of despair. For all her loathing of what they'd done to the two young soldiers, she'd got used to working as a team and would feel lost without him. But Georges was right – the St Jean group couldn't afford to have someone so dangerous in their midst. Their success was built on stealth and the ability to stay hidden, and he'd attracted too much attention.

'I'm not going to apologise for doing the job I was sent here to do,' he snapped, suddenly, rising from where he sat at the table. He threw his hands up. 'What am I meant to do? Sit on my arse and let the rest of you do everything? Hah! Not my style, Tigresse – you know that.'

'You're a great asset, we all appreciate the work you've done,' she said. 'But you're no use to anyone with a bullet through your head, and the Boche won't rest until they've found you.'

God, she was sick of constantly having to massage the egos of these men. Why couldn't he accept what was obvious to the rest of them? But she needed to keep him on her side, at least for the moment.

In his usual mercurial way, he barked a hollow laugh and gave her a lopsided grin. 'Better to go down fighting though, eh?'

She couldn't help but smile back. 'I'll get a message to Reynard and see what he recommends. It's his decision,' she said, straightening her face.

'But he'll be here in an hour,' said Georges. 'He wants to see you – I thought you knew that.'

'Does he? It wasn't in the message I received from London.'

Why did Reynard want to meet with her? The brief elation buoying her up after the capture of Remi Comet sank without trace.

* * *

281

Agnes woke, confused and unsure of where she was for a moment, the blanket Florence had given her slipping off her shoulders. She shivered in the chill of the kitchen, now the fire had died to embers, and stretched the kinks out of her back. If she hadn't been so exhausted, she'd never have been able to sleep in the ancient chair. Philippe still sat at the table, a tumbler of pastis in front of him, along with an ashtray full of butts. He ground out another one as someone knocked at the door.

Georges went to the door and said something in a low voice. He was answered immediately and Reynard entered and shook his hand. He looked even thinner and more worn; the red hair faded, his eyes bloodshot. But he seemed as sharp and decisive as always, greeting Georges in a few words, before approaching the table and addressing Agnes.

'Céleste. I'm pleased to see you again,' he said. 'You're doing a good job up in St Jean, and I wanted to congratulate you on your success in catching the collaborator.'

'Thank you, sir,' Agnes said, her spirits lifting. 'The local maquisards were furious when they discovered who it was. One of their own turning out to be the collaborator was a massive blow.' She took a sip of the pastis Georges had put in front of them both, trying to clear her muzzy head. 'I suppose someone else will be targeted and persuaded to turn their coat, now. We must be on our guard.'

Reynard nodded. 'True,' he said. 'The enemy are always trying to find a way inside our network – as are we, with theirs.' He paused. 'Has Georges told you about the plane crash?'

She nodded.

'Good, so you know we have an injured man who needs to be helped. Speed is important but we must give the poor fellow a bit of time to recover so he can make the journey over the border. I want you to get him out in three days, at night, of course, and use the route from Col des Ares. It's the least used, and most remote. As far as I know, the Germans aren't patrolling that area

– with the way things are going in the north, they've lost some of their troops to the fighting there, which is in our favour.' He took a slug of his drink. 'I'll leave it to you to liaise with the French and have a guide ready.' She nodded again, having no idea where Col des Ares was, but knowing Jean Espouy would. 'There's another who will go with the airman,' he said, turning to Philippe. 'M LeConte, it's good to see you again. I hear you've made a mighty nuisance of yourself since you arrived. It's been duly noted. You've done good work here, but London wants you back so they can send you into Paris. There'll be plenty to keep you occupied there.'

The surliness Philippe had shown earlier disappeared, or was well hidden, as he acknowledged his new orders. 'I'll do my best to make life difficult for those Nazi bastards, sir,' he said.

Reynard smiled. 'Good man, you'll be an asset to the Paris Resistance.' He turned back to Agnes. 'Céleste, I know you'll carry on the excellent work you've been doing, without the help of our Canadian colleague. I hear you've made a good team, but we don't have enough people to keep two of you in one area. It's up to you from now on.'

Agnes sat up, the prospect of dealing with Valentine and Jacques on her own not as daunting as she expected. Perhaps it was the success of the past few days.

The Englishman broke into her thoughts. 'I need a word with you in private. Let's take a breath of air, shall we?'

'Of course, sir.' She followed him outside to a bench beside the wall of the house. They sat, the darkness enfolding them, and she felt rather than saw her chief looking at her.

'The name of the injured airman – the rear gunner – is Sergeant Edward Kerr,' he said, without preamble.

Agnes felt herself physically knocked backwards, shock at hearing Edward's name making her head swim. She put her hands over her face and then dragged them down her cheeks and stared at Reynard, shaking her head.

It couldn't possibly be her brother; there must be a mistake. It must be someone else with the same name.

'It can't be.' Then: 'Are you sure?'

'I'm afraid there is no doubt; it is your brother,' he said. 'I didn't want to tell you in front of the others. I understand your relationship with your family hasn't been the closest. I thought you might need a moment alone when you discovered who you were taking out.'

Agnes thought back to the last time she'd spoken to Edward and Pierre at their mother's funeral. Bile stuck in her throat at the memory. Cutting herself off from Christopher Kerr meant losing touch with them, tainted as they'd been by her hatred of her father. She'd almost convinced herself she didn't miss them.

She wrapped her arms around her midriff. The thought of seeing Edward terrified her. How badly was he hurt? What would she say to him? What if he didn't recognise her? It was an inconceivable coincidence that he was the injured airman – she had no idea he was even in the RAF.

Reynard put his hand on her shoulder, making her jump. She'd forgotten he was still there.

'Are you all right?'

She shook her head. 'Not really sir, no,' she said. 'I need to see him. Now. Please, take me to him.'

The short journey to the cabin, high above the forested foothills, was a distraction by its very nature. She had enough to do to keep the van on the rocky track; there was no time to think about what lay ahead. But when they arrived at the small stone building, she was rooted in her seat, hands gripping the steering wheel, unable to bring herself to leave the vehicle, her mind churning.

'Céleste? Come on, we can't hang around. We're compromising this place and the safety of your brother every minute we're here.'

Reynard's voice jolted her back to reality. She stepped out of the tiny van and was glad of the fresh night air filling her lungs, clearing her head. She followed him to the hut and waited while he tapped on the rough planks of the door, the sound loud in the stillness. Agnes heard the scrape of wood against stone as someone pushed a chair back, the door opened, and a man dressed in local working garb peered out. He looked no more than a youth, his eyes wide with fear, and his voice cracked when he spoke.

'Who are you? What do you want?'

Reynard was quick to put him at ease, using a code word. The young maquisard pulled the door wide and they followed him into the rough, bare room that made up the cabin. Agnes could see a small sleeping platform at head height in the dimness of the lamplight. There was no fire in the grate and the room had a cold, musty smell about it. Sitting in one of the two rickety-looking chairs was a second man of slight build with a bandage around his head and one arm in a rudimentary sling. His face was white with pain and fear, and Agnes's throat tightened at how like their father her brother now looked. He pushed himself up from where he sat and came over, peering at them in the dim light of the lamp on the rough table in the middle of the small cabin.

Reynard spoke. 'Sergeant Kerr, I'm pleased to meet you. This is Mademoiselle Sarraute, who is going to help you get out of here in a few days, once you've recovered enough to make the journey. It's an arduous trek, and you'll need to get your strength back before you make it.'

The chief spoke quickly and firmly. Edward looked from one to the other of them, incomprehension clouding his face. Now she was finally standing in front of him, all Agnes wanted was to put her arms around him. It had been so long since she'd allowed herself to think of him or Pierre, knowing it wasn't them she should hate, but unable to separate her rage against their father from her feelings towards her brothers.

So much wasted time . . .

Her chief spoke again, switching back to French, asking the young maquisard to step out of the cabin for a moment – there was a message he wanted the youth to take to his fellow Resistants. He caught her eye as they went out, and she nodded a thanks to him.

'Agnes? Is it you?' Edward's voice sounded hoarse and strained, but he had enough sense to speak French rather than English.

'Who else would it be?' she said. 'Teddy, I didn't even know you were in the RAF.' Moving closer, she put a shaking hand up to his bandaged head. 'I hope you aren't in too much pain. You had a lucky escape, by all accounts.' She lowered her hand and whispered, 'You know the rest of your crew didn't make it?'

He dropped back down into his chair and put his head in his hands. After a moment he nodded.

'Yes, I know they bought it. I wish I'd been killed too.' He looked up at her, and she could see the torment on his face. He cleared his throat and blinked a few times. 'They were a good bunch of lads. We'd flown together for months, got into a few scrapes but always made it home. It's unfair that a bloody mountain killed them in the end.' A sad, twisted smile appeared on his face and he stared at his hand, blood caked under his fingernails and grime embedded in the skin. At last, he shook his head. 'I guess you can't take anything for granted.' Taking a breath, which made him wince again, he looked up at her. 'And how, in the name of God, did you end up here, and why?'

Agnes sat in the other chair and tried to think how much she should say. Nothing. She knew that. But the desire to tell him everything was overwhelming, and she feared once she began, she'd not be able to stop.

'We only have a few moments, not nearly enough time to tell you everything,' she said. 'This war has thrown up so many strange things, made people do things they never imagined they could or would.' On the verge of tears, she realised how close she'd come to never seeing her brother again; perhaps not even knowing he was one of the bodies buried in a shallow grave, somewhere close by. It made her bitterness and anger seem childish. Spending so much time with the Espouy family, seeing them working together each day, and their love for each other, brought home the desert of her own family life. 'Teddy, we've never been close, but you know I'll always be here if you need me, don't you?' It sounded so weak, but she couldn't bring herself to say more.

He smiled at her. 'I never doubted it,' he said. 'We Kerrs have always been a strange mob, eh? I blame Father. He's a chauvinist of the first order.' Her expression must have told him something, as he added quickly, 'Oh, have no doubts, Pierre and I always wanted you to join us, when he coached us in all those boring sports, but he would have none of it. "A young lady's place is in the drawing room or the bedroom".' Edward mimicked his father's voice, and Agnes couldn't help but smile. Her brother covered her hand with his. 'It must have felt as if you were invisible . . . and then what he did to Maman was unforgivable.'

'I could never face him again afterwards. Her death is on his head.' Her rage towards Christopher Kerr surfaced and she stood, striding around the small room. 'It's his fault she killed herself. I'll never forgive him. Never.'

Edward came and put his good arm around her shoulders and pulled her close. She forced back the tears that threatened to overwhelm her. She couldn't give in to them; there was too much at stake.

The sound of the door latch drew them apart, and Agnes sat down abruptly. She struggled to regain her composure, pushing her hair back from her forehead and surreptitiously wiping her wet cheeks at the same time.

'Mademoiselle Sarraute will come for you in three days, Sergeant Kerr,' Reynard said. 'Do you think you'll be strong enough to make a tough march by then?'

Edward nodded. 'Of course, sir. I'm grateful to you all for helping me.'

'Think nothing of it, young man. It's why we're here. Céleste, we should go before it's light.'

Agnes rose again.

'I'll be back in a few days and bring some clothes for you – you'll need to look like a local,' she said. 'Don't leave the cabin in case you're seen. Rest while you can. You're going to need all the strength you have for the trek over the mountains.'

Edward stood to attention and gave them a clumsy salute. As they left, Agnes looked back at him and saw the grief and fear behind the smile he gave her. She hoped they'd have time to heal some of the scars they both carried and thanked the gods or fate, or whatever else had thrown them together.

Chapter 39

Claire

Stepping out of Laurent's car, I turned and stopped momentarily, amazed by the grandeur of the view in front of me. The whole of the St Jean valley lay ahead, with the snow-capped peaks of the Pyrenees rising above the town. From this altitude, I could see fold on fold of ridges disappearing into the distance. It was awe-inspiring. Who could fail to be impressed by such a sight?

I followed Laurent towards the house. It was slate-roofed, stone-built and had bright green wooden shutters at each window. Pots on either side of the ancient-looking wooden front door had been cleared of snow and showed off spring pansies and early-flowering bulbs. Facing south towards the mountains, the house took advantage of the sun. At this elevation, the snow was at least a foot deep and a path had been dug out across the yard, which we now followed.

Laurent shouted in his booming voice as he opened the door and ushered me inside the dark hall. Leading the way into a large, warm, and aromatic kitchen, he bade me wait while he went to find his mother. Nerves made me jittery, unable to stay still, and

I wandered around the room, admiring a sideboard filled with traditional copper pans that gleamed in the low sunlight coming through the window, opposite. The wood shone with years of polishing and had a depth of patina that could only have come from decades of care. This was no built-in modern furniture – all the cabinets looked as if they'd been hand built, and most of them had red and white checked curtains in place of doors. The table was huge, scarred and stained by the generations who had made meals and eaten at it. It was as if I'd stepped back to a past time, and I wondered if I was seeing exactly the same setting as Agnes had looked on when she had first arrived at the farm. I had no doubt the large fridge-freezer beside the traditional range-cooker was a modern addition, as were the spot lamps set into the wood-panelled ceiling. But the meat hook with a ham hanging from it must be original, as was the deep-set sink with its wooden drainer and copper taps.

Laurent came stomping back into the room, followed by a tall dark-haired woman. I stood and went to meet her.

'Bonjour, madame,' I said, extending a hand to her.

She smiled, and – ignoring my hand – took my shoulders and kissed me on each cheek.

'*Enchantée,*' she said. 'Call me Marguerite, please. Pardon me, I don't know your name.'

She looked over at her son, raising her eyebrows at him. I could see how alike they were, although she had none of Laurent's stature. The dark complexion and deep-set eyes were the same, but her face had a fineness in the bone structure which, coupled with her height and carriage, gave her a look of elegance, even though she was dressed in rough work clothes.

'My name is Claire. Claire McRory,' I said in my schoolgirl French, smiling back at her.

My anxiety floated away; Marguerite had a relaxed manner that put me at ease. It had been the same with Harriet. What was it about this place and its people?

We sat at the table, and Marguerite put a huge old cast-iron kettle onto the range and prepared a coffee pot, grinding the beans and putting them in the top of the base, ready for the water to bubble through. Laying out a plate of madeleines, she brought everything to the table and, once we had all taken a cup and a cake, she sat too.

We nibbled the cakes and sipped coffee in awkward silence for a couple of minutes, until I complimented her on them, saying I was no good at baking. Laurent translated for me, and his mother looked a little sheepish and then admitted she'd bought them from the local supermarket. She laughed, and the ice was broken. Laurent said his mother's madeleines were far superior to the ones we were currently eating, and I must come back and sample them sometime.

'Now,' Marguerite said, when the coffee and cakes were finished. She spoke in halting English. 'Laurent, who is this English lady who comes with you and looks so uncomfortable? How do you English say it? Like a fish out of the river?'

'Like a fish out of water, madame. That's how we say it, but you're right in its meaning,' I said, speaking slowly in English, not confident enough to try and explain in French. 'I've come to France to try and discover what happened to a close friend of my aunt, a very long time ago, during the war.' Laurent sat at the head of the table, his expression unreadable, saying nothing. 'The woman I'm looking for was an agent for the British Special Operations Executive and was sent to the Pyrenees to help the local Resistance fight the Germans. Her real name was Agnes Kerr. Her French code name was Céleste. Céleste Sarraute.'

I hadn't taken my eyes off Marguerite while I spoke, not sure if her English was good enough to follow what I said, watching for any reaction. Her face was impassive, except for a small frown, until the name Céleste was mentioned. She sat up straight, looked at Laurent first, then stared at me, her mouth open. She and Laurent spoke rapidly for a few minutes.

Eventually, he snapped something and stalked out of the room, leaving me with Marguerite.

'Please excuse my son,' she said. 'He didn't tell me why he brought you to meet me, and it's a shock. Please explain how you know that name.'

I sat for a moment, wondering what the spat had been about and why my being here was such a shock. What should I say?

What the hell. I've come this far; I can't go back now.

Chapter 40

Agnes

The evening before Agnes and Philippe were due to go back to collect Edward, the Espouys brought out one of the few unbroken bottles of eau-de-vie and toasted them both. Her awkwardness made Agnes's head ache, and a celebration was the last thing she wanted. Philippe drank glass after glass of the fiery liquor, becoming more morose with each mouthful.

Mme Espouy had dinner with the family and saved the day, relishing her role of having stood up to the Germans, the grubby bandage around her head a badge of honour. The old lady held court, her stories becoming wilder and more exaggerated with every glass of eau-de-vie she consumed. Eventually, when she was nodding off in her chair, Jean got her up and walked her back to her tiny house. They heard her singing as she weaved her way home, carrying her precious bottle of firewater.

Danielle said goodnight and disappeared upstairs. Agnes picked up the last few glasses and cups from the table, but Philippe put a hand over his and poured himself another shot of pastis. Irritation prickled like old sweat on her skin.

'Don't you think you've had enough?' she snapped. 'Tomorrow's going to be a very long day, and you're still not properly fit. This stuff will make it worse.'

He grabbed her wrist, catching her off balance so she almost fell and ended up sprawled across his knee. Pulling her into him he kissed her hard on the mouth. He tasted of alcohol and cigarettes and she recoiled. For the second time since they met, she slapped him, the sound of her hand on his cheek shockingly loud.

'Go to bed, Philippe.'

He let her go, not meeting her eyes, a red bloom rising on his face. She felt dirty, wanting to wash away the taste of him.

'I'm sorry,' he said. 'I'm not sure what I've done to make you dislike me so much, but whatever it is, I apologise.' He rubbed his cheek and smiled sadly at her. 'You're quite a woman, Tigresse, and I'm gonna miss you like crazy.'

She couldn't meet his gaze, and felt a pang of guilt. She was an imposter, playing a role with him, just as much as she was playing a role as an agent. It was far too late to tell him the truth about herself, and she didn't want him to know the real Agnes. Letting her lust get the better of her had been the biggest mistake of her life and what she'd done made her skin crawl. The sooner he left the better for all of them. The glasses chinked against each other as she dropped them into the sink, her hands shaking. Holding on to the side of the wooden drainer, she cleared her throat, trying to find the words to pacify him.

'It was wrong, what we did,' she said, eventually, looking out of the window into the darkness. 'And I'm as much to blame as you. It's for the best that we won't see each other again.'

Muttering goodnight, she escaped to her room.

The next day Agnes returned to the small cabin to pick up Edward. She drove Danielle's van and Philippe sat beside her, silent and morose.

Edward looked pale and tired, but said he felt better. The bandage had gone from his head, revealing a long, jagged cut that ran from the side of his forehead back into his hair, still matted with blood. Agnes inspected it for signs of infection and was relieved to see the cut looked to be healing cleanly. His arm was still immobilised, but she noticed he was able to move without wincing. The three of them shoehorned themselves into the tiny vehicle, Philippe folding his long limbs up around his ears in the back, while Edward was allowed more comfort in the passenger seat.

There was so much Agnes wanted to say to her brother, but with Philippe there it was impossible. She had no orders to accompany them on their journey past the drop-off point, but couldn't bear the thought of saying goodbye so soon. Who knew if either or both of them would survive the war, or if they would get the chance to meet again? The decision was easy to make, in the end. She would walk with them, at least for part of the way.

Jean Espouy had given Agnes directions to the jumping-off point of the trek, and though she hadn't recognised the name when Reynard told her where to go, she knew where they were to meet. It was outside the exclusion zone of the valley and not so heavily patrolled, which should make it easier to disappear into the mountains. Thickly forested with few tracks, it was a place to lose your bearings. Jean was one of the most experienced guides; she was glad he was the one taking her brother out. Still, it would be a tough and dangerous journey.

Jean met them at the beginning of the path, appearing out of the evening twilight as if he were a ghost. He was unhappy when Agnes told him she'd decided to walk with them, and said if she began the trek, she'd have to go the whole way to the border, as she would never find her way back on her own.

'I thought you had an injured ankle? And now we have food for two days. I only brought enough for three of us.'

Agnes shrugged. 'I don't eat much, my ankle feels fine, and

I'm as fit as I've ever been,' she said. 'Please, Jean, I want to go with you. It's important to me.'

His gaze sharpened. 'Why? What's so important that you need to come too? Don't you trust me to do my job?'

She shook her head, not sure what to say to him. All she could do was tell the truth.

'Of course, I trust you. You're one of the best, to my mind.' She took his arm and drew him away from the other two, lowering her voice. 'The pilot is my brother. And I'm not supposed to let anyone know, but if it helps you understand why I want to go, then so be it.' She shrugged. 'And who knows, it might help in the future if I have to make another trip with an *évadé*. You can show me the ropes.'

Jean threw a glance at Edward, then back to Agnes. His shrug was so quintessentially Gallic that she almost grinned. 'It's up to you,' he said. 'I'm only the guide, here. But if you complain of being tired or hungry, I will leave you at the side of the path until I've done my job of getting these two out of here. Understand?'

She nodded, hoping she'd be as capable as she promised.

'Well, get the van off the road and out of sight. There's no point signposting where we've started from by leaving it there,' he grumbled.

The small path they took rose steeply into the thick beech forest. Darkness had fallen and with the trees in full leaf, it was almost pitch-black. Agnes had no idea how Jean could see the track, but he was unerring and walked with a confident stride, even though the floor of the forest was covered with a thick layer of the previous year's leaves. Here and there she could make out the remains of a retaining wall or a broken fence post and knew they must be following one of the ancient stock routes, now mostly unused except by hunters.

In places the track broadened enough to walk two abreast and she came up alongside Edward, talking with him in a quiet voice, desperate to make up for lost time.

'How is Pierre? Does he live with Papa?'

Edward shook his head. 'He signed up as soon as he was old enough, and is a sub-lieutenant in the army. The last I heard from him he'd been posted to North Africa and was driving tanks in the desert.'

Agnes felt sick at the thought of her younger brother being in uniform. She dropped back as the path narrowed again, and said a silent prayer for Pierre. She tried to imagine him in charge of other men, and couldn't. All she saw in her mind's eye was the little boy in short trousers she'd grown up with. Even at their mother's funeral he'd seemed so much younger than her, and that was only a few weeks before his birthday.

The forest engulfed them in its dark security as they progressed, climbing steadily. Agnes felt as comfortable as if she was down in the valley, stopping to allow a pair of deer to cross the path, watching them disappear into the beech trees within a moment. Edward waited for her when the track widened again, and they walked side by side.

'You've changed,' he said, stumbling over a tree root. She grabbed his arm and steadied him. 'Thanks. It's as if you've found your confidence. You seem so at home in this terrifying place.'

She smiled. 'There's nothing terrifying about the forest,' she said. 'It's people who are terrifying.' They walked on for a few minutes in silence. Agnes had a thousand questions, but there was no time to ask them all. 'Did you know he wanted a divorce?'

She felt her brother hesitate.

'No. But I knew he wasn't going back to Maman. If I'd known how badly he had treated her . . .' He fell quiet and slowed his pace. 'I knew she hated England, and where he'd decided she should live, but to do what she did . . . she must have been so desperate.'

Agnes felt his grief, just as strong as her own. Her vision blurred and she wiped her eyes.

'Now is not the time to have this talk,' she said. 'Promise me, when the war is over – and one day, it will be over – we will sit down together with Pierre and celebrate Maman's life. It's the least we can do for her.'

'I promise,' he said.

She walked on ahead of him then, tears filling her eyes, hating the fact that in a couple of days she would have to let her brother go, with no idea if she would ever see him again.

After an hour or so the moon appeared fitfully through the tree canopy, giving more light to pick out the path. Agnes could see her brother struggled to keep up on the steep incline, although the months of cycling and hiking around the valley had hardened and strengthened her, and she found the climb easy. Two hours into the journey, they came to a hairpin bend and for a moment the trees cleared, and a rocky outcrop allowed them a view into a small valley below. Above, the mountains rose, lined up like sentinels shining in the moonlight, their snowy peaks reflecting silver against the black sky. A pair of owls called to each other lower down the valley, their hooting eerie in the darkness. Edward sank onto a rock, his breathing ragged.

'Gunnery training doesn't prepare one for such physical labour,' he said, stopping between words to suck in lungfuls of the cold, clear air.

'Once we're above the trees it'll get easier,' Agnes said. 'We'll begin to traverse the mountain rather than continue to climb.' She pointed at a gap between two peaks. 'You see that pass? On the other side is Spain.'

'So near and yet so far,' Edward muttered, his head dropping between his knees. Agnes put a hand on his good arm and squeezed it.

'You'll make it; we'll take it slow, give you time to rest.'

Philippe lit a cigarette, the match flaring in the night, illuminating his features for a moment. The sharp, phosphorus tang of it felt foreign in this place. Agnes was aware of him watching them as he smoked, his expression stony. As they started walking again, he set off close behind her, making her uncomfortable, feeling as if he was pushing her to move more quickly than she could go.

'Go in front of me, if you want,' she said at last, as they forded a stream swollen with meltwater. It rushed over the edge in a waterfall that dropped into the darkness below them, the spray making the air chill and coating her face. She stepped up the bank to let him past.

'I prefer the view from here,' he said, his tone mocking her. 'What's with you and the airman? Do you prefer the flyboy to me? Is that why you've given me the brush-off?'

He stood in front of her, preventing her from continuing, and she glanced along the path, anxious to keep Jean and Edward in view. The last thing she wanted was to get separated from them and be left with him. He took hold of her wrists, pulling her into him.

'Don't be ridiculous,' she hissed. 'Strange as it may seem to you, I don't go running after every man I meet. And just because I don't want to be with you, doesn't mean I'm looking to be with anyone else. Now let go of me, and let's move.'

'Well, you sure are up close and personal with someone you've only just met. Seems to me you're kidding yourself.'

'Oh, for fuck's sake, Philippe. He's my brother, damn it. Okay? Now leave me alone.'

The admission was out of her mouth before she could stop it. She wanted to lash out, rage at him for his arrogance and presumption, but her anger could only be expressed in whispers. He dropped her hands and she jumped off the bank, shoving him backwards as she passed him. He swore, but she ignored him, her heart thumping in her ribs, leaving him standing staring after her.

The others were already fifty metres ahead and she hurried to catch up to the barely visible shadows moving in the gloom. Philippe caught up with her as she strode up the track. She felt his presence behind her but kept walking, determined not to let him needle her into another row.

'Céleste, stop a minute. Please.'

Gritting her teeth, she paused and turned. 'What now? Haven't you said enough?'

'I'm sorry, Tigresse. I didn't mean those things. I guess I'm jealous, is all,' he said.

'Philippe, in less than two days you're going to be in Spain, and I'll be going back to the farm. There's no point in this, is there?' she said. 'We'll probably never meet again. You've got to forget about me.'

'It's hard to forget someone you're in love with.'

He took her arm, and with a resigned sigh, she softened. Putting a hand up to his face, she smiled at him, sadly. Her conscience was a weight around her neck as she thought of Maggie; betraying her just added a stab to her heart. And now she'd broken another heart – wasn't one enough? What was wrong with her? Why couldn't she tell him the truth?

'Believe me, I know.' Giving him a soft kiss on his cheek, she turned away, hoping he didn't notice the tears in her eyes.

As dawn leached the darkness from the sky and night became day, Jean found a group of young pines near the path, which gave shade and cover from any planes that might pass overhead. The forest was beginning to thin out, and they'd already passed through open spaces, which was a relief from the dense darkness of the trees but made Agnes aware of how vulnerable they were.

Jean handed out a little food, and they all drank from a stream that crossed the track close to where they sat, and refilled their water bottles.

'Sleep, while you can. We'll need to get moving in a few hours if we have any hope of reaching the rendezvous in time. We're way behind where we should be,' Jean said. 'Make sure you've no buckles or other metal showing. If the sun reflects off it and a spotter plane notices, we'll be in trouble.'

He moved away a little and lay down under a small pine tree with his head on his pack.

The prospect of spending daylight hours on the open mountain was a frightening one, but if it helped Edward to keep up then they must do it. Agnes knew how dangerous it would be, had heard the stories of German pilots hunting escaping Allies like hawks after a rabbit.

Philippe got up and wandered away to find somewhere to lie, and she spoke quietly to her brother.

'How are you holding up? It's a tough climb for someone who's just walked away from a plane crash.'

'I'll manage,' Edward said, quietly. 'I can't say it's the easiest thing I've ever done, but after a bit of sleep, I'll be fit to go again.' He nodded his head towards the Canadian, who had lain down a little distance away. 'What's between you and him? You can cut the tension between you with a knife.'

Agnes gazed over at Philippe. 'He's jealous,' she said. 'I didn't tell him you were my brother, and he thought I was being overly familiar with you. I've put him right.' She grinned. 'It would be quite amusing if it wasn't so stupid.'

'So, have you two got a thing going on then?'

'No.' The denial was instant. 'He's a bit overprotective; that's all.'

Edward raised an eyebrow at her, and heat filled Agnes's cheeks. She looked down, fiddling with her bootlace; what would he say if she told him the truth about herself?

'Get some sleep,' she said, brushing off his comments. 'You'll need it.'

Turning away, she found a flat spot in the shade of a gnarled juniper bush and lay down under its fragrant branches.

Agnes woke to find the sun had moved around and was now full on her face. Hot, with her head thumping, she sat up and looked at the others. Jean was awake and putting on his boots, while Philippe and Edward still slept. Checking her watch, she discovered it was mid-afternoon. Jean glanced across at her and nodded his head at the others.

'Wake those two, will you. We need to get moving.'

Philippe stirred at the sound of his voice, and Agnes went over to Edward who was laid out still sound asleep. She felt reluctant to disturb him; he looked so peaceful, lying curled up on his side. But they had to get going, so she crouched down and gently shook his shoulder.

'Edward, come on, we've got to go.'

He mumbled something and then opened his eyes, a frown creasing his forehead. 'Ugh, I thought I was in the middle of a bad dream,' he said, sitting up. 'It seems I was right.' He smiled lopsidedly at her. 'Not that seeing you is a bad dream, of course.'

Agnes grinned at him. 'Come on, you idiot. Jean will leave you for the bears if you don't shift yourself.'

She took his good arm and helped him up, and they went over to where Jean had doled out a little of the food he had left in his pack. Hungrily munching on stale bread and dried saucisson and washing it down with more of the icy cold water from the stream, Agnes felt revitalised. After topping up their water bottles again and hoisting their packs, the small group set off.

The forest gave some shade from the sun but after an hour it thinned out until the trees gave way to stunted bushes and a few gnarled pines and oaks. Jean stopped and they rested for a few minutes looking at the narrow trail that skirted the side of the mountain. Ahead was a vast slab of rock and rubble rising steeply to the pass Agnes had pointed out to Edward. Their path traversed an enormous hanging valley that looked as if it had been carved out by some kind of gigantic spoon, the valley floor a stomach-clenching distance below.

As they set off again and left the security of the trees, a cool breeze rose, and she lifted her face to it, glad of the fresher air, after the sticky heat of the forest. She stared at the tiny path winding its way around the side of the mountain, thinking it was more of a goat track than a footpath. Keeping her left hand out, hugging the hillside, she decided walking in the middle of the night had its advantages – she couldn't see the terrifying drop below them, for one thing.

Jean's decision to start earlier than he originally planned meant they were still walking in daylight when they left the forest. The path was not as steep, and they made good time; Edward seemed to have regained some strength and kept up well. The trail then began a number of switchback turns up another slope, and Agnes could tell he was struggling to maintain the pace Jean set. He gradually lagged further and further behind the group, and stopped often, bent over as if in pain. Philippe and Jean seemed oblivious that her brother was being left on his own.

'Jean,' she called quietly. 'Edward can't keep up this pace on such steep ground. Will you please slow down a little?'

The two men stopped and turned to look back down the trail. As they did so Agnes heard the drone of a plane, panic making her crouch down and flatten herself against the rock wall she was passing. Glancing back, she saw her brother stop and look up, and Jean yelled at him to get down. The plane flew below them and seemed to be quartering the hillside, following the contours only yards away from the rough terrain.

It was strange to watch it pass by and look down on the pilot through the Perspex hood of the cockpit. She noticed her brother standing where he was, too tired perhaps to comprehend Jean's instructions, saw the pilot turn his head as he flew past, much closer to her brother than to the rest of them, higher up. She shouted to Edward to hurry and saw Philippe run down the path towards him, stopping to help the exhausted airman, saying a few words to him, though Agnes couldn't hear what they were. Edward staggered on and caught up with them as they continued up the mountainside, his face drenched in sweat and his body trembling with fatigue.

'I'm sure the pilot saw you,' she said, taking his arm as he stopped in front of her, barely able to remain on his feet.

'He's bound to return for a second pass,' Jean said. 'We need to find somewhere to get out of sight.' Rapping out orders, he pointed up the hillside. 'That rockfall will do. Come on, stay low and pray he doesn't come back before we get there.'

They scrambled up the scree-covered hillside above the path and were halfway to the safety of the rocks when Agnes heard the ominous sound of the plane's engine, again. Panic pushed her on, knowing how vulnerable they were.

'Hurry,' Jean yelled. 'Get to the rocks. It's our only chance of not being seen.'

Agnes pushed and pulled her brother with her, trying to get to cover before the plane came back. Fear gave her strength and speed she didn't know she possessed. Within a minute or two, just behind Jean, she shoved Edward over the lip of the corrie where the rockfall had come to rest, telling him to get behind one of the boulders and keep down.

It was only then she realised Philippe wasn't with them and looked back to see him running back down the track, making no attempt to hide himself.

'What the hell does he think he's playing at?' muttered Jean. Cupping his hands around his mouth, he yelled, 'Philippe, you fucking idiot, come back. You'll be spotted before you get anywhere near the trees.'

Agnes saw him pause and look up at them.

Don't. Please, don't.

She knew, then. Saw the flash of a grin on his face as he gave them a quick salute, before turning and setting off at a run again along the flatter part of the track, just as the plane came into view.

Afterwards, she thought it had been like watching something in slow motion. Philippe kept running, the trees too far away to get to in time, but leading the pilot further away from them, giving them the chance to escape. The plane closed in on him and she heard the stutter of a machine-gun, saw the dust kicked up by bullets hitting the ground all around the running man, and the plane pass so low over his head, he fell to the ground. Then he was up and running again, and for a moment, she dared to believe he would make it, be invincible – his luck holding – using up yet another of his nine lives. Living to tell the tale.

She couldn't breathe, just fixed her eyes on him as he ran again, willing him on, praying he would make it before the pilot could turn the plane and return for another go. And he almost did – was within fifty yards of the safety of the first trees when the German came back, and she heard the spit of the gun once more.

At first, she thought he'd stumbled; the path was so rough, it was a wonder he'd not fallen before then.

Get up. You're nearly there . . . you can make it. Get up and run!

And he did get up, dragging a leg he kept going, doggedly covering the final yards in a lurching hobble, staggering forward, not looking back.

The pilot put the little plane into a steep dive and banked to turn and finish off his prey. Agnes saw Philippe pull himself upright, face his enemy and look him in the eye as the bullets finally found their mark.

The three of them waited, cowering under the cover from the rock fall, until the plane disappeared along the mountainside. A tremor ran through Agnes that she couldn't stop, and all she could see in her mind's eye was Philippe's last defiant stare at his enemy as he was gunned down. He couldn't be dead; she would not, could not believe it of the man she had shared so much with. She tried to run back along the path, but Jean stopped her, hanging on to her while she struggled to get away.

'Let me go to him, Jean,' she cried as he wrestled with her. 'How can we leave him lying there? He's not dead; he can't be. We must help him.'

'*Putain!* No, Céleste, no. We must wait – make sure the plane doesn't come back. The pilot won't believe LeConte was on his own. He'll know there are more of us somewhere close by,' Jean said, shaking her by the shoulders. 'We'll wait until dark, and then go to him.'

Agnes fought against him. The reckless courage she'd always known was part of Philippe's character had been his undoing. The thought of him lying alone, perhaps not dead, but seriously wounded and dying, was more than she could bear.

'We must go to him – he might still be alive,' she begged, again.

'He'd be the first to tell us to wait. His sacrifice would be for nothing if we move too soon.'

Jean's words finally got through to her.

Of course.

Philippe had known exactly what he was doing, was anything but reckless. He didn't expect to reach the trees, but tried anyway, to give the rest of them a chance of evading the German. To rush out now would be sacrilege after what he'd done for them.

The plane returned to prowl along the side of the mountain. The group made themselves as small and still as they could in the corrie, and the pilot passed over them and moved on. As night fell the temperature dropped, and Agnes stretched muscles grown cold and stiff. Once it was almost dark, Jean rose, and they climbed back down to the path and retraced their steps until they found Philippe. He lay on his back, his eyes open behind cracked spectacles, staring unseeing at the stars. The trees were only yards away.

'You almost made it, you mad Canadian,' Agnes whispered, crouching down, gently removing the specs and closing the lids over his eyes. Tears dripped onto his face as she bent and kissed his cheek. 'We can't leave him here, Jean,' she said. 'What if vultures or bears find him?'

'We can't do anything for him now,' Jean said. 'We'll pull him under the trees there; he'll be out of sight. We must keep going, Céleste, if we're going to get this man to safety.'

'He said something to me when I was struggling on the track,' Edward said. He seemed in a daze, fear and exhaustion written on his face. 'He said to tell you he understood. That he had no regrets – and to say it was a privilege to have worked with you.'

His voice cracked and he cleared his throat. 'I didn't realise what he meant to do. He saved my life.'

Agnes went and put her arms around her brother, buried her face into his shoulder, and allowed herself to give way to grief for a moment. He held her, his chin on her head, patting her back as she cried. After a while she took control of herself, knowing she couldn't afford to fall apart completely. They still had to get to the border and deliver Edward safely.

I can't let his death be in vain. I owe him that . . .

The three of them dragged his body to the first of the trees. There they laid him beneath an ancient, wizened oak, covered with his overcoat.

'He'll be all right here until we return,' Jean said, quietly. 'Come on, we still have a long way to go before tomorrow morning.'

It was late into the night when the trio eventually reached the pass Agnes had pointed out to Edward the previous day. The cloud descended in the last hour, obscuring the moon, and they could only see a few yards ahead. It slowed their pace, as Jean made a careful ascent of the final switchbacks. The rocky landscape of limestone slabs still had snow and ice covering most of it, making the path even more treacherous, and the concentration required was exhausting. Agnes's eyes stung with the strain of staring ahead, fatigue weakened her legs, and her ankle ached. She didn't allow herself to think of the body lying a thousand feet below them. There would be time enough for that, once Edward was safely in Spain.

He'd not said a word throughout the past couple of hours and she knew he had reached the limit of his reserves. His face was a grim mask of pain, placing one exhausted foot in front of the other, an automaton slowly winding down.

The pass itself was achieved by stepping through a narrow port in the rock face, and as she followed the others into the gap, Agnes discovered the mist and low cloud had disappeared on the southern side, and in the moonlight she could see a vast, sprawling valley far below them. Arid and sparse, it was a very different landscape to the one she'd become familiar with on the French side. Jean allowed them to rest for a moment or two and take a drink, then set off again, following a much clearer trail that descended between huge boulders and short, stunted thorn bushes that dragged at their clothing as they passed.

'We are now officially in Spain,' he said. 'The guide will be waiting for us a few miles from here along this track; there's a shepherd's cabin where we'll meet him. If you have more to say to each other, do it now – there'll be no time for lengthy goodbyes when we get there.'

He strode on ahead and left them to follow more slowly.

Agnes wondered how they could make up for all the lost years. She didn't know what to say, and it seemed Edward felt the same, as he trudged along in silence, his head hanging, stumbling occasionally.

'You know you can't try and contact me again, even though you've discovered where I am,' she said, at last. 'Nobody here knows my real name, remember. But I promise you as soon as I can I'll be in touch. I don't ever want us to be estranged again.'

She stopped and took his hand then wrapped her arms around him, needing to feel his physical presence before he left her again. She inhaled the smell of him, the aroma of dried sweat and the underlying maleness. He patted her shoulder awkwardly.

'If ever there was a higher power at work, this has been testament to it,' he said, his voice rough. He cleared his throat and she released him. They stood for a moment, the silence stretching ahead of them, before Edward spoke again. 'I've been wondering one thing, about your work here. Why did you not tell us what you were doing?' He took her chin in his hand and scanned her face. 'You know a friend of yours – Margaret something, I think – contacted Father, asking if he knew where you were? She seemed pretty distraught – said you worked together and shared a flat? We didn't even know you were missing.'

He walked on, leaving her standing in a daze, her mind spinning. Despair threatened to overwhelm her. After all that had happened, the hope that her love waited for her, knowing she would come home, had kept her sane. But realising Maggie hadn't found the letter was soul-destroying. What must she have thought, when Agnes disappeared without word and left no trace behind, no clue as to her whereabouts? She wanted to scream, to tear her hair, rend her clothes – it was too much to bear, and it doubled the guilt she carried, already.

How could she get word to her, let her know she was alive and hadn't forgotten her? What a mess it all was. She chased after Edward.

'I was only allowed to tell one member of my immediate family, but why would I want to do that, after everything?' She stumbled over the words, realising how petty they sounded. 'I wanted to let Maggie know where I was going but couldn't.' Saying her name out loud after so long was almost too much. Agnes gulped in a breath, steadying her spinning thoughts. How to explain in the time she had left with her brother? 'Papa's never shown any interest in me; I can't imagine he was worried about me. And you know how much I hate him for what he did to Maman.'

'I understand, I really do. But Pierre and I are your family too – don't forget that.'

Grabbing Edward's arm, she stopped him on the track.

'Could you let Maggie know I'm okay, when you get back? She must be worried about me.'

The words came out as a plea, and Edward frowned.

'Sounds as if you're more concerned about your friend than about us,' he said. Then he sighed, and stroked her cheek. 'Give me a note and I'll see what I can do.'

How could she possibly make him understand? She leant into him and they stood for a second or two before moving on. Edward held her hand and they walked the final part of the trail in silence, keeping step with each other. There was so much Agnes wanted to tell him; about Maggie, especially, but it would have to wait until they met again. And they would meet again; she knew it in her heart. For now, all she could hope was that he'd get back to England safely, and this filthy war would soon be over; must surely soon be over. With the big push imminent, the Allies would have the Nazis on the run.

By the time they reached the shepherd's cabin, Jean and the Spanish guide were drinking coffee and smoking cigarettes outside the rough stone building. Edward collapsed onto the ground, and leant against the wall. He closed his eyes. The sling was tattered and stained, the hand poking out of the end of it, filthy, and his face looked as pale as a ghost in the moonlight. Agnes didn't want him to go, wanted more time with him, bereft already at the thought of him leaving.

Turning away, not able to look at him, she unslung her pack and sat on a rock, relieved to take the weight off her feet. Pulling a tattered bit of paper and a pencil out of her bag, she hastily scribbled a few words, telling Maggie not to worry. Folding it in two, she wrote the address on the back and gave it to Edward.

'Please don't forget,' she said.

'I won't. She's obviously someone important in your life.'

He put the scrap of paper into the top pocket of his jacket and shut his eyes again.

Jean and the guide were involved in an animated conversation. Agnes couldn't follow a word of the thick dialect they were speaking. She caught Jean's eye and raised her eyebrows at him in a silent query. He stubbed out his cigarette and came over to her.

'He thought you were the second *évadée*,' he said. 'I told him the other one couldn't make it – no point in telling him otherwise in case he goes blabbing his mouth off to the wrong person.'

For a moment, the chance of carrying on with Edward dangled before her, the temptation to keep going almost too much to resist. Then she nodded and turned away.

The Spanish guide said something in the same unintelligible

language, hoisted his pack on his back and picked up a rifle in one hand and a stout stick in the other. Edward dragged himself off the bench and squared his shoulders.

'Well, this is goodbye. I know I'm damned lucky to be getting out of here in one piece; I just wish it was under different circumstances,' he said. 'Jean, thank you, old chap, for getting me this far. Please, look after my sister for me.' He stretched out his hand and Jean shook it, muttering something about Céleste not needing to be looked after. Turning to Agnes, who was doing her best not to cry, Edward took her in a bear hug, leaning his head into her shoulder. 'We have a lot to catch up on, and I hope we get the chance to carry on with our reunion before too long. Stay safe, okay?'

'I will.' She managed a watery smile and hugged him back. 'I'll be home soon, I promise.'

'Goodbye then . . . Céleste, I'll see you in London.'

'In London,' she whispered, watching him stumble along behind the guide, until the darkness swallowed them up and they were gone.

Chapter 41

Claire

I told Marguerite everything I knew about Aunt M and Agnes, and how much Agnes's disappearance had blighted my aunt's life. She sat with her eyes on mine, saying nothing, her face impassive. I wondered if she even understood what I was saying, such was her non-reaction. I would have expected someone listening to a total stranger say that their mother's long-dead fellow Resistance fighter had a love affair with my aunt would be shocked, but Marguerite remained silent until I stuttered to a halt. I spread my hands on the table and looked down at them, grief catching me off-guard for a moment. I took a long breath and raised my eyes to hers, blinking back tears.

'All I want to do is discover what happened to her and why she never contacted my aunt again. It seems cruel to me, and not the kind of thing someone who loved another would do,' I said. 'I'd like to understand why Agnes – Céleste – discarded Aunt M without a backward glance.'

Marguerite stood up abruptly, and I thought for a moment my words were too harsh. She went over to the enormous sideboard and opened a drawer, rifling inside it until she found an old-fashioned folder, tied with a ribbon. She lifted a small photograph off the plate rack and brought them both back to the table. From the folder, she took what looked like a couple of airmail letters, faded and creased with age. Carefully, she spread the ink-covered sheets on the table. I'd seen that writing before and noticed the name on the front – why would she have letters written to Margaret? Marguerite gently stroked the thin blue paper, smoothing the creases with her fingers.

'These are all our family have left of Céleste,' she said, softly. 'They were letters she sent to England just after the war finished. Months later they were returned to her. I think the address was unknown or wrong or something.' She looked at me. 'They're addressed to someone called Margaret Scott. Is that your aunt?'

Realisation of what I was being shown hit me, and I flushed, embarrassed and ashamed of my tirade. Marguerite obviously knew at least something about Agnes's relationship with Aunt M. My throat closed and I couldn't speak for a moment, but I nodded, staring at the letters. So, Agnes hadn't forgotten about the woman she'd left at home. But why didn't they find their way to Margaret? I knew things had been chaotic after the war, but I didn't know they'd been so bad letters got sent back to the sender's address.

'Do you mind if I have a look at them?'

'Not at all. Please take as long as you want to read them.'

I picked up the first one and looked at it closely. I didn't know aerogrammes had been around for so long. Turning the letter over to examine the exterior, I discovered the reason for it never finding its way to Margaret. It was addressed to a place in London, and I remembered a conversation I'd had with Aunt M when she said she'd moved out of the city after her street was bombed.

If Margaret had found Agnes's first letter hidden in the poetry book; if Agnes had known their flat had been bombed; so many ifs and buts, keeping them apart and not knowing what had happened to the other. It was heartbreaking for both of them. Fighting tears, I flattened out the first blue sheet of writing and began to read.

Chapter 42

Agnes

At twilight, Agnes and Jean set off for home. Agnes's ankle ached from the steep downhill slope, but it took far less time to reach the trees where they had left Philippe than the uphill trek.

When he reached the trees, Jean waited for her. She sank down beside him, trying not to think of what lay just a little distance off the track. Putting her head onto her knees she cradled her arms around herself.

'How can we get him off the mountain?' she whispered.

'*We* can't,' Jean said. 'I'll take his papers back with me now, and then return with some of the Maquis as soon as I can.'

'Jean, we can't just leave him there. Won't the Germans come looking for him?'

'I doubt it. It's too remote and difficult to reach,' he said. 'Let's cover him with something. There are lots of dead branches around – they'll do. When we come back, we'll find a spot to bury his body, until it's safe to move him to a proper burial place, like they've done with the crew of the Halifax that crashed.'

'Do it soon, won't you? What if he gets eaten by something? Vultures or wolves or something?'

'There are no wolves around here,' Jean grunted, and muttered the Canadian was past worrying about such things.

A black cloud hit Agnes. All she could see in her mind was Philippe's face as he grinned and saluted them, before running for his life. She found it hardly believable he'd died after all they'd gone through together. Worst of all, she could never repay him or even thank him for the sacrifice he had made in saving Edward, Jean, and her.

Two days after returning to the farm, Jean and two of the maquisards went back to retrieve Philippe. Jean told Agnes that they had carried his body down to a hidden spot in the forest. There they buried him in a shallow grave and placed an unmarked stone over him, so it could be retrieved and buried later with full honours at a proper ceremony.

Exhaustion finally caught up with Agnes and she slept for the best part of two days, before waking with a nausea that made her body weak and washed out. Food made her retch, and fatigue dogged her. She still had work to do though, and with D-Day approaching, the maquisards had more raids planned on the local railway and bridges. Her days were filled with organising the logistics for where and when and how they would be carried out, as well as sending and receiving messages from London. Her relationship with Valentine and Jacques improved; the men now viewed her as one of their own.

Making some cheeses for Danielle one afternoon, with a scarf over her face to block the smell, which threatened to make her vomit, Agnes heard Jean and his wife talking in the kitchen. Jean quipped that perhaps there'd been more to the relationship between Céleste and the Canadian than they'd known about.

'What are you talking about?' Danielle demanded.

'The girl looks just like you did when you were carrying our two.

Surely you've noticed?' he said. 'Mark my words, he's left more than his memory behind.'

'That's a terrible thing to say,' Danielle snapped. 'She never showed any affection for the man; yes, she's upset he's dead, but aren't we all? Maman has cried every day since we heard the news – but to accuse her of having an affair with him, and worse, to be carrying his child, is nonsense.'

'Well, we'll know soon enough. Then you'll see I'm right.'

Agnes heard him stomp away down the steps into the cellar, and Danielle begin scrubbing the table, her irritation plain in the short, sharp repetition of her strokes. Cold sweat made Agnes shiver. She leant against the wall. Surely Jean was wrong? She was suffering from some kind of food poisoning – that was all. It was a common enough complaint, the water on the mountains probably the cause. What did he know? She couldn't be pregnant; she had too much to do, especially now Philippe wasn't there to help her.

Determined to ignore what she'd heard, putting it down to Jean's disdain for anyone who succumbed to any kind of illness, Agnes pushed the conversation out of her mind. The possibility he was right was too terrifying to contemplate.

It was another ten days before Danielle tackled her.

'Céleste, this malady you're suffering from, have you any idea what's causing it?' she asked, when she took her a homemade herbal tea.

Agnes was curled up on a chair with her favourite jacket wrapped around her after a day of sending and receiving messages from London and circulating instructions to the maquisards. She had cycled to Montréjeau and liaised with Georges' group on a plan to blow up the railway between them and St Jean. The details were coming together and as it was a new moon in three days, everything was set to go ahead then. She was light-headed with exhaustion.

'I suppose it's something I've eaten, or maybe the water was bad when I went with Jean and the others,' she muttered.

She didn't want to think about what had happened on the trek to Spain, although her mind insisted on flipping between the last time she'd seen Edward, as he struggled to keep up with the Spanish guide, and the vision of Philippe running down the mountainside.

'Are you sure it couldn't be ... something else?' Danielle wouldn't look her in the eye, playing with the wedding band on her left hand. Agnes gritted her teeth, not wanting to hear the words she knew must come next. 'Did you and Philippe have an affair?'

Agnes dropped her head, letting her hair hang like a curtain. Anything to hide the flush setting her face on fire. 'What? No, of course we didn't,' she said.

'Céleste – be honest with me. Is it possible you're pregnant?' Danielle took her hands, the work-hardened skin of her palms feeling rough against Agnes's.

She pulled them away and wrapped her arms around her body, holding her sides, refusing to think the unthinkable. 'It was only once,' she whispered. 'We were on such a high, after discovering who the collaborator was, and ... it just happened.' She shuddered. 'I knew it was a mistake, but Philippe – well, you know what he was like.'

'I can imagine,' Danielle said, her mouth a grim line. She took hold of Agnes's hands again, squeezing them for a moment. 'Don't worry, we'll work something out. And you're so tiny you won't show for a while, so nobody else need know.'

Agnes's mind froze, still refusing to acknowledge what she knew was the truth. What would she do now? A pregnant agent was not something the brass would accept. All she could hope was to keep her condition secret for as long as possible. She looked at Danielle's kind face through a blur of tears – all she seemed to do lately was cry. Wiping her eyes, a surge of rage ran through her at her predicament, the unfairness of it all.

She made a vow to herself that she could – and would – get through this. She put a hand on her belly, a brief feeling of wonder hitting her at the tiny being already growing inside, protective instincts she didn't know she possessed surfacing.

'Please,' she said. 'Don't tell Jean or any of the others. The brass will send me back to London if they find out. I want to stay here with you and carry on. There's so much still to do.'

'You know you can stay as long as you want to,' said Danielle. 'Like I said, it'll be months until you show, and we can find some looser clothes, later on.' She tugged at the front of Agnes's jacket. 'And in the meantime, this Canadienne has plenty of room for you to grow, and no one will notice.'

Agnes pulled the rough garment around her body, as if it could protect the tiny being growing inside her. A memory flitted through her brain of a sunny day in London, not long before she'd been recruited, when Maggie had joined her and Pat at the river, and the photo she cherished was taken.

Oh God. What have I done?

Chapter 43

Claire

My darling Maggie,

It's been so long since I left you, and I miss you each and every day, my love. The war is over, thank God, and I hope you are well and happy. What a time it was, wasn't it? I've seen and done things I would never have dreamt of and I'm not sure I will ever be the same again. The last two years have ripped part of me away and it feels as if the scars will take forever to heal. Oh, not that you can see them – I was fortunate and escaped physical injury. Inside, I'm not so lucky, and not so different to many around here, who carry their wounds deep within. We don't speak of them – of course we don't – but we all know each other's pain. So many gone who won't return, so many families in ruins, and for what? All at the behest of a man who, in the end, took his own life rather than face the consequences of his actions.

This letter is so hard to write, my love, it's so difficult to find the right words, but you deserve to know. For I'm not coming home to you – at least, not yet, not now.

There was a man, a Canadian, who was an agent I worked
with. I didn't like him – he was so sure of himself and made
fun of me for being small and young, when he was tall and
felt himself so much older. But we had to make the best of
it because we had to rely on each other, and after a time we
became close, forgot our differences. He was persistent in his
pursuit of me, and in a moment of madness I relented to his
passion, though hated myself for my weakness afterwards,
knowing I had betrayed you and the love we had.

He was courageous but too bold and the Gestapo marked
him out. They hunted him, and he had to get away, over to
Spain. He was killed while trying to escape, drawing enemy
fire away from our group. Afterwards, I found out I was
carrying his child.

I'm so sorry, my darling. I know you'll find it hard to
accept, and I don't understand it myself, even now, but the
war made us do crazy things, and my beautiful Marguerite
is the one bright star in the darkness of that time.

It fills me with dread, not knowing if you've found another
to love. Not knowing if you're even still alive. All I can do is
wait, and hope you can find it in your heart to forgive me
and respond to this letter.

You are, and always will be, my one true love.

A

My head snapped up and I caught Marguerite watching me,
her expression inscrutable. I read it again, scarcely believing the
words, shock washing over me like a wave.

Agnes had a child? Of all the reasons for her not to return to
Margaret, I had never dreamt this might be the one. Thoughts
and questions spun in my head and my vision blurred at the
thought of how this would affect Aunt M.

I swiped a hand across my cheeks, and carefully folded the letter.
I wasn't sure if I could face reading the second. Marguerite said

321

nothing, giving me the chance to gather myself. I could feel her eyes still on me, and looking up I gave her a watery smile, and she smiled back in sympathy.

'Agnes – *Céleste* – was your mother?' She nodded, sitting down beside me and patting my hand, gently. 'It's silly, really,' I said. 'I didn't know she existed until a few weeks ago, and yet I feel so close to her, because of my aunt. I was prepared to feel angry when I found out she'd survived the war, but reading this, my heart aches for the pair of them.' Glancing at Marguerite, I gave her the first letter. 'You know what this says?'

'Yes. Danielle, who lived here and let Maman stay after the war ended, had it translated for me, after Maman died. She thought I should know as much about my mother as possible, once I was old enough to understand.'

'So, you knew about her relationship with my aunt even before I arrived today?'

She nodded. 'It's not something we've spoken about in the family. But yes, I knew about her affair in England.' She shrugged. 'Whether she would ever have taken me back there, if she'd lived, who knows? She was half French and had spent most of her life in France. After the letters were returned, it must have seemed impossible to go back with a young child, when there was nobody there waiting for her.'

'May I read the second letter?'

'Of course, help yourself. I'll make some more coffee.' She rose from the table and gathered the cups.

The second letter was much shorter and had an air of desperation in the choice of words.

My Dearest Maggie,

    I wonder if you received my first letter, and why you don't reply? I wait each day in hope, wishing that something will arrive to let me know you're safe and well.

    Or perhaps now you know the truth you hate me; your love is dead and you want to forget me and everything we shared.

If that is the case then so be it; I understand. I'm not sure I can forgive myself either. But what's done is done, and if you want nothing more to do with me, I will continue here in France with my beloved Marguerite and make the best of it. My daughter's wellbeing is the most important thing in my life now and I thank God every day for her.

Know this though, you are and will remain my one true love.

Your A

I sighed. Such small things kept them apart, and for Agnes to die only a year or two later, after surviving everything she'd gone through in the war, seemed far too cruel. I felt no sense of accomplishment in completing the task I'd set myself. Just grief for Aunt M, waiting for so many years in vain.

Marguerite placed the replenished cups of coffee in front of us.

'Do you want to take the letters back with you? Your aunt must want to read them,' she said.

'But don't you want to keep them as a memory of your mother?' I'd hoped to copy them, but having the originals was more than I'd expected. 'If you allow me to copy them, I'm sure my aunt will be more than grateful.'

'It seems the right thing to do – they will find the right person in the end.'

'Then yes – and thank you, it's most generous of you.'

'I hope they give your aunt some comfort.'

I wasn't sure what to say, but felt I needed to have some kind of conversation with her. Discover how she felt about her mother's history. She would hardly remember her, surely, it was so long ago. She must have only been two or three when Agnes died.

'Does my being here and dredging up the past upset you?' I asked.

'Not really. It was a very long time ago,' she said, with a small smile. 'I have no memory of my mother. All I have are things like pictures in my head, you know? I remember one of my birthdays, and she'd made me a cake, and Danielle laughed because it was just about the first thing Maman had ever made.' She smiled again, her eyes losing focus for a moment. 'Or at least, I think it's a memory. But then again, perhaps I've heard the story so many times I just think I can recall it.'

She seemed so unfazed by everything this morning that I had nothing but admiration for her.

She passed me the photo she'd taken off the sideboard. It was a picture of Agnes, her head and torso, looking older than in the one I had. She was unsmiling, her face more mature, the eyes more serious, the hairstyle different. She was wearing a short, heavy jacket that looked too big for her, a scarf around her neck, and a beret that sat at an angle on her head. She looked very different to the photo of the laughing young woman I had. This Agnes looked tough, determined, and slightly scary.

'When was this taken?'

'At the end of the war. The Canadienne was her favourite coat,' said Marguerite.

I thought I'd mistaken what she'd said. 'Canadian's coat?'

Marguerite laughed at my expression. 'No! The style of coat is called a Canadienne. Nothing to do with my unknown father,' she said.

That brought me back to a question nagging in the back of my mind. I'd hesitated to ask it; it seemed far too personal, but Marguerite was so relaxed and open about everything I decided to, anyway.

'Have you ever tried to trace your parents' families, find out where they were from? You may have cousins, aunts, and uncles.'

'*Bofff!* Why would I do such a thing? I never felt the need. The Espouys have always been my family. They're all I need.'

I nodded, wondering if Laurent was just as uninterested in his family history as his mother. She pulled another photo out of the file and handed it to me.

'This is the only picture I have of them together.'

I gazed at a grainy, black-and-white image of a man and a woman who was dwarfed by him, both dressed in rough work clothes, gaiters, boots and berets. The man held a rifle and had crossed belts of ammunition over his chest. His eyes were obviously on Agnes, and he had one arm over her shoulders. She held a handgun and stared straight at the camera. Marguerite pointed to the man.

'That's Philippe LeConte, my father.'

I scrutinised the picture. Agnes's expression was solemn, but there was little I could glean about her. I was fascinated to see her with the man she worked with on a daily basis and who she must have fallen for. I wished there was a close-up to see the faces more clearly, but the quality of the picture was poor and enlarging it would have made the image even more blurred. I rubbed my eyes, gritty after staring so hard at the picture.

'Who took the photo?' I asked.

'Danielle's husband, Jean, under sufferance from his mother, who insisted on it, apparently,' Marguerite said, grinning. 'She was besotted with Philippe. They would sit outside her house and he'd tell her stories, while she plied him with drink. It was taken just before he left.'

It seemed it wasn't only Agnes who fell under the Canadian's spell.

'Is there anyone who still remembers them? Any of the local maquisard group, perhaps?'

'I think one or two might still be alive. But the person who knew my parents better than anyone lives just along the lane.'

My pulse jumped, and I stared at her, raising an eyebrow.

'My mother-in-law, Danielle, lives in the small house you passed on the way in; we can go and see her now if you like?'

I frowned, confused at her use of 'mother-in-law'.

'You married Danielle's son?'

'I did. When Maman died, Danielle and Jean raised me alongside their own children, Marc and Nicole.' She laughed. 'He used to think of me as an annoying little sister until we hit our teens, then we fell in love.'

'Won't she mind us arriving on her doorstep without invitation?' I asked.

'Danielle is almost a hundred years old – she's very deaf but loves an audience to tell her stories to. I know she won't mind at all.'

Marguerite got to her feet. I picked up the photograph and rose quickly. I could hardly wait to meet the person who had known Agnes all those years ago.

As we walked the fifty metres down the lane to Danielle's cottage, Marguerite told me the little house was where each grandmother went to live when their husband died, and the next generation took over the farm. It seemed to be a family tradition, the women outliving their men. I guessed two world wars and slavishly hard work wouldn't help.

'Laurent said his grandfather died during the war. That was your father, I guess?' I said, thinking aloud, trying to make sense of the two families and how they connected. Marguerite nodded. 'Was his other grandfather, Marc's father, killed then, too?'

'No,' said Marguerite. '*Pappy* Jean survived the war. He died of cancer about twenty-five years ago. It was very sad – happened so quickly. One minute he was a strong, capable farmer, the next he became a walking skeleton.' She looked at me, sadly. 'I took over the farm completely at that time. I'd always made the cheese and done the markets with Danielle, but I look after the goats and sheep now, as well.'

'You must have your hands full,' I said.

She shrugged. 'Marc has always been a teacher, and anyway, we couldn't survive on what the farm brings in nowadays, even with subsidies from the EU. Laurent comes over and helps at busy times – haymaking and so on. I doubt he'll keep the farm when we're gone, though,' she said, as we reached the door of the cottage. 'He's not interested at all. He'll probably sell it to an incomer who just wants a holiday house with a pretty view.'

I wondered how hard it must be to know she wouldn't be the next matriarch living in the tiny house.

Laurent joined us as Marguerite led me into the cottage through a low door. He gave me an enquiring look. I tried to smile and appear calm, even though a storm raged in my head from all I had learnt. He had to duck as we entered the house and put a hand on my elbow as I almost missed the step down just inside the door. Our eyes met as I looked up and thanked him.

'Okay?' he said, quietly.

'Yes,' I said. 'Your mother has told me everything. It's a lot to take in.'

He smiled. 'It wasn't my story to tell,' he said, looking a little sheepish. 'I'm sorry if it's been a shock. Come and meet my grandmother.'

Sitting in an ancient armchair, beside a roaring woodstove that belched out enough heat to drive a steam engine, was a small, ancient woman, who appeared to be sleeping. Marguerite went over and crouched down in front of her, taking her hand and gently patting it to wake her. The woman stirred and opened her eyes, looking a little bewildered to see a stranger in her home. Collecting her senses, she struggled to sit up and smiled, saying how delighted she was to have visitors.

Danielle Espouy was tiny, with a face as brown and creased as a well-ripened walnut, framed in pure white hair pulled back into a straggly plait. Her eyes were extraordinary, deep-set in a sea of wrinkles, they looked as keen and sparkling as those of someone seventy years younger. She seemed to only have a couple of teeth and had a habit of smacking her lips onto her empty gums, as if she expected them to suddenly reappear.

I took to her immediately, and we spent half an hour talking about her time in the war, and Agnes's part in it. Her memory was as clear as if it had all happened a week ago, instead of more than half a century, and when I showed her the photo Marguerite had produced, she smiled fondly at it, stroking the faces of the two young people.

'What was Philippe like?' I asked after she'd been talking for a while, Laurent translating for me. 'He and Céleste must have had a good rapport to be able to work together.'

'He was a charmer, that one, and this one is so like him,' said Danielle, nodding at Laurent, who flushed under his tan. 'He could talk anyone around to his way of thinking, and he was bold, almost reckless. He got shot, you know. Yes, he did, he did,' she said, nodding her head vigorously, like a small bird. 'Céleste and I had to get him out of town right from under the noses of the Boche through a roadblock, with him hiding in the back of my van, underneath a load of my cheeses. They were ruined, by the way.'

She smacked her lips several times in quick succession, as if to emphasise the point.

'Is that when he had to escape over to Spain?'

'Oh, no. That came later, after the collaborator was caught, and Philippe killed a couple of German soldiers. He was seen and knew the game was up.' Her eyes lost focus, as she relived her memories. After a moment, she came to and continued. 'He didn't make it to the border though, did you know? Germans shot him from a plane.'

I was hypnotised by her words, amazed at her recall, and wanted to keep on asking questions and listening to her stories. I didn't want to outstay my welcome though, and raised an eyebrow at Laurent.

'Do you think that's enough? I don't want to exhaust your grandmother.' Danielle, in truth, seemed as fresh as a daisy, but it felt rude to keep badgering her. 'You must need to get back. I've taken up enough of your time, today.' A thought struck me. 'Would you mind if I took a photograph of you all, to show my aunt? I know she'll want to know who you all are.'

Marguerite spoke quickly to Danielle, who smiled, nodding vigorously. Laurent looked less impressed, but agreed to sit with his womenfolk for me to take a few shots with my phone.

'Thank you. I have another day or two before I leave for home.

Could I return tomorrow and talk with Danielle some more, if it's not too inconvenient?'

I crossed my fingers and hoped I wasn't presuming too much on their hospitality and kindness.

Laurent spoke to Marguerite for a moment, then turned back to me. 'She's happy for you to come again tomorrow.'

We said our goodbyes to Danielle and walked back up to the main farmhouse. I thanked Marguerite and followed Laurent to his car. It was a hair-raising ride down the mountain road to the valley and Villa Sarnaille.

'I'll pick you up in the morning,' he said.

'Thanks so much.' I kept my hand on the door handle. 'Can I take you out for dinner – as a thank you for all your help?'

The words were out before I could stop them and sounded far too casual to my ears. What was I thinking?

'I'd like that,' he said. 'See you tomorrow.'

And he was gone.

I spent the evening gazing at the photos of Agnes I'd taken copies of on my phone, and thinking about the letters she'd written that had never reached their destination. I wrote down everything I could remember from the conversations I'd had with Marguerite and her mother-in-law, and noted down anything I wanted to ask, the next day. I was impatient to speak to Danielle Espouy again, and learn more about Agnes. It felt as if I was almost at the end of my search; there were only a couple of things I wanted to tie up.

I should be looking forward to going home. I should be thinking about getting my life back on track. But my mind was constantly pulled back to Agnes's story and how she and the Canadian had been drawn to each other. If his grandson was, as Danielle had said, very like him, I thought he must have been difficult to resist. Laurent was not someone I would easily forget, even though I had only just met him.

I looked forward to meeting him again.

* * *

Laurent picked me up again the next morning and drove me back up to Marguerite's house.

'My mother had to go to town, I hope you don't mind me being your host, this morning?' he said.

'Not at all,' I said, relieved I wouldn't have to work so hard at conversing in French.

He prepared coffee, and we sat on a bench outside the front door, enjoying the sun that warmed the wall at our backs, while we drank.

'Have you never been curious about your grandparents' backgrounds?' I asked, voicing my thoughts, after we'd sat in a pleasant silence for a few minutes.

'Why do you ask?' Laurent frowned.

'Just curious, I suppose,' I said. 'This search on my aunt's behalf has made me interested in the whole family thing.' I shrugged. 'I was never close to my own family, apart from Aunt M, but yours seems very close, even though you know nothing about your mother's side.'

He frowned again, turning the small coffee cup round and around in his huge hands.

'I want, very much, to discover who my mother's family were,' he said, at last. 'She is against it, though. We argue about these things, all the time. She says our family here is all we need, so why dig around for answers to questions about people we've never known?' He went back to staring at his cup, as if the answers were in the coffee grounds swirling in the bottom. 'You know Luc's mother and I aren't together anymore, and he lives with her, so I only see him at the weekend. I want to be able to tell him where he comes from. Who his ancestors were, you know? You have opened a door for me, Claire, and for that I'm thankful. I hope your questions might persuade my mother to change her mind. I don't want to go behind her back and find out about the past without her approval, but if I have to, I will.' He nodded in a decisive manner, staring at the view of the valley below. 'I know I must do this thing, now.'

I glanced at his profile surreptitiously. He had a strong bone structure, visible beneath the mat of hair on his face, the lips full and well defined. I hurriedly looked away, embarrassed he might think me rude for staring. He caught my eye and smiled.

'Shall we go and see my grandmother, now?' he said. 'Have you finished your coffee?'

I nodded, and he took the cups and set them inside the kitchen before leading the way down to Mme Espouy's house.

Danielle Espouy greeted me as if I was an old friend, welcoming me into her home, and bidding me to come and sit beside her.

'Do you want some coffee?'

'No, thank you. We've just had a cup,' I said.

'Laurent, bring me that bottle of eau-de-vie that's in the cupboard.' Danielle smiled widely. 'I don't get many visitors these days. We must celebrate.'

Laurent shook his head at me, in some sort of warning, as he handed me a small glass of clear liquid. At the first tiny sip I understood why – I felt as if half my throat had been ripped out, the liquor stronger than anything I'd ever drunk before. Blinking back tears and trying hard not to cough, I praised the spirit, gasping that, sadly, I had to drive later, so couldn't take any more of the excellent vintage. Danielle laughed.

'Too strong for you, eh, girl?'

I nodded, still too overcome to be able to speak normally. When I'd got my breath back, we continued our chat about Agnes, and Danielle's memories of her. She stopped mid-sentence, as if a new thought had come to her.

'You knew Céleste's brother was here during the war?'

She made everything sound as if it was something I should have known and had forgotten.

'No, I didn't know that.'

'Why yes, he was. She had two brothers. One was in the air force, and his plane crashed near here. The crew all died but for him, and Céleste had to get him to the border.' Danielle took a strong swig of eau-de-vie as if it was purely water, and then continued. 'It was the same time the Canadian was killed. Poor thing, she was distraught – her lover dying, her brother injured, and disappearing almost as soon as they were reunited. They were hard times for everyone.' She seemed far away for a moment. 'I think she'd not spoken to her family for a long time, but meeting her brother again meant a lot to her.' She shook her head, sadly.

I sat and digested this. Aunt M had said Agnes was estranged from her family. But how bizarre that her brother ended up here, and they found each other again. It made it even more strange that she never went back to England.

'Did Agnes – sorry, Céleste – never go back to see her brother, after the war was over? If they mended their relationship, it surprises me she didn't want to see him again.'

Danielle nodded her head vigorously.

'Oh, but she did, she did. She made a short visit to him. Came back with the illness that killed her, poor thing.'

Her words stopped me in my tracks. So, Agnes *was* in England after the war, but didn't go and see Aunt M? Did she even try? Perhaps, because her letters had been returned, she presumed the worst – that her love was dead, or didn't want anything to do with her? How could I ever know what happened all those years ago – it just made me sad for both of them.

Danielle interrupted my thoughts. 'I have something to show you.'

From a small table beside her chair, she took a photo frame that had been lying face down. Lifting it, she passed it to me, and I saw it was the same photo I'd recognised in Laurent's house that I'd brought with me. I smiled at it, so familiar to me now, then handed it back to her.

'This is your aunt?'

'Yes, this is Margaret. She has the same photo. They look so young and happy, don't you think?'

She nodded in agreement. 'You look like her, you know. Yes, you do. I knew you must be a relative when I saw you for the first time, yesterday.' She sat, gazing at the picture. It wasn't the first time I'd been told I resembled my aunt, although I am not nearly as beautiful and chic as she was when she was younger. 'Céleste thought she must be dead, you know. Yes, she did. She was so unhappy and missed her terribly. I'm glad you came, and you can give your aunt some sort of comfort, after all these years.'

'Did you know about their affair?'

Danielle shook her head. 'Only when her letters were returned. She was so distraught, she couldn't hide it from me.' She shrugged. 'I was surprised at first, but love is love, eh? And I know she loved your aunt – you can be sure of it.'

It was tragic that so much had conspired against them at the end of the war, and they never found their way back to each other. I guessed it wasn't such an unusual story – there must have been thousands of unhappy endings at that time.

Laurent and I left the old lady dozing in her chair and walked back towards the farmhouse. Another thought occurred to me.

'Is Agnes – Céleste – buried here in the village?'

'Yes. I can show you the cemetery if you have time,' said Laurent.

We retraced our steps along the lane, passing Danielle's tiny house and turning into the village. The church sat above the houses, on a rocky knoll, with the graveyard below it. Laurent took me to a corner at the back, under the high perimeter wall, and I gazed at the grave of Céleste Sarraute. A simple stone had her French name and the date she died etched into it. I took another couple of photos to show Aunt M.

To me, it seemed perfect as a last resting place: peaceful, simple, and with an awe-inspiring view of the valley far below. Above, the snow-covered peaks shone and a red kite glided by, its head dipped forward searching for prey. I lifted my face to the sun and closed my eyes for a moment. My search was over. I had kept my promise to Aunt M, and there was nothing more keeping me here.

'Where's Philippe LeConte buried?' I asked.

'They put him in a graveyard with other Allies who were killed in this area,' he said. 'It's a way down the valley, on a hillside, overlooking the mountains.'

'Perhaps, one day, I'll come back, and you can show me where it is,' I said, lightly.

'I'd like that,' he answered, with a smile.

He looked at me, the brilliance of his eyes cradled in small lines that spoke of too much time in the sun. For some reason I couldn't explain, my stomach did a backflip when he smiled at me.

We drove back to Villa Sarnaille. He got out of the car and we walked up the drive together.

'Let me take you for dinner tonight as a thank you.'

'I've a better idea,' he said. 'Come to my home and I'll cook something. You can check Jurot's doing okay.'

'But it should be my treat. I want to pay you back for all your help and kindness.'

'Look, we can argue about it all night, but nothing can repay your help with Luc the other day.' He smiled. 'You can bring the wine.'

I laughed. 'Red or white.'

'*Comme tu veux,*' he said, laughing with me. 'I can only make one decent dish. It's called *Tartiflette*, and is full of potatoes, cheese and ham, so you'd better bring your appetite with you as well as the wine.'

'Sounds delicious. Seven o'clock?'

'Perfect. See you then.'

He took my hands, leant in and kissed me on both cheeks again, his lips warm on my skin.

'Bye,' I said, watching him walk away.

Harriet met me in the hall as I closed the front door and took off my thick coat.

'How did it go?' she said.

'Very well. Old Madame Espouy is marvellous, considering her age. Her memory is pin-sharp, though she made me drink some foul home-brewed liquor.'

'Hah! That would be the famous local eau-de-vie the farmers make,' she said, laughing. 'It strips paint, so I've heard.' She looked at me, her head on one side. 'More importantly, how did you get on with Laurent?' My smile must have given me away, for she laughed again. 'Oh, that good, eh? He's a lovely man.'

'I don't know what you mean,' I said, knowing my face had turned scarlet. 'I'm going to supper there tonight,' I blurted out.

'To his house? You must have made a good impression. Half the local singletons would give their eye teeth for an invitation from him.'

'Oh stop. He's just being kind.' I didn't need her teasing; I was confused enough already. 'Anyway, it means I won't be here for dinner. I hope that doesn't put you out.'

'No problem at all. Seriously. I hope you have a lovely evening.'

I smiled at her and made my way to my room, wanting to get everything Danielle told me down in my notebook. I also needed time to compose myself before I met Laurent again. I was leaving tomorrow and would probably never see him again; there was no point in encouraging any more familiarity between us. He was a nice man, and by luck we'd discovered a connection between our two families. That was it.

I found a small wine seller in one of the back streets of St Jean, and bought a five-year-old bottle of Bordeaux, which was recommended by the owner. I'd have preferred a rioja, but when in France and all that; I hoped it was acceptable. I also bought a *tarte au citron* as dessert.

Arriving a few minutes past the hour, butterflies did loops in my stomach as I knocked on Laurent's door. He kissed me again on both cheeks – I wasn't sure I'd ever get used to it as a greeting – my English reserve found it far too familiar. I gave him the wine and the lemon tart, and he led me through to the same room as before. A table was laid for two, and he told me to sit while he opened the wine and finished making a salad.

'Oh, let me help, please,' I said. 'Is Luc not with you, this evening?'

'No. He's at his mum's. You can put the salad together if you like.'

I followed him and was greeted by Jurot, who jumped up and came over with barely a sign of the sorry state he'd been in a few days earlier. I bent and stroked his head, happy he'd made such a good recovery.

'Does Jurot stay with you all the time? I thought he was Luc's dog?' I said, as he leant into my leg.

'Luc's mum doesn't have room for a dog, and she's out all day at work. It's easier having him here. Luc usually comes and walks him after school – which was when the accident happened. And then he's here at weekends.' He sighed. 'It's not perfect, but you know, nothing ever is.' He shrugged and turned to the stove, where a delicious smell rose from the oven. 'There's salad, tomatoes and all that stuff in the fridge. Help yourself to what you like. This is ready.' He lifted a shallow casserole dish from the oven. Its contents bubbled and hissed. My stomach growled.

'Oh, excuse me. I'm starving,' I said, trying to cover my embarrassment. 'It looks and smells wonderful.'

'I hope it tastes as good.'

He passed me a dish and I quickly put the salad together, then asked for some olive oil and a lemon for a dressing. We took the food through to the table, and Laurent brought bread and the wine.

The Tartiflette tasted as good as it promised, and the wine passed muster. We ate and drank slowly, talking non-stop, changing subjects at random, as something sparked our interest, discovering things we both liked, disagreeing about things we didn't. The lemon tart was sharp and creamy, and Laurent served some pungent local cheese with a wonderful nutty flavour.

I helped him wash up, and we took coffee back to the living room and sat beside the dying fire.

'This has been a lovely way to finish my stay here,' I said, stretching my feet out to the hearth and gazing at the view. 'I wish I could stay longer. I'd love to see this place in spring – the trees and meadows must be beautiful.'

'You must come back; this place is different at every season. I would like to show you around. Say you'll come again.'

I looked at him. His eyes were on mine, serious where they'd been full of fun for most of the evening. I put a tentative hand up to his cheek, his beard soft under my palm. He leant towards me and we kissed: a promise that we would meet again. I leant into his shoulder and we sat in silence, watching the moon climb above the high peaks. I said a silent thank you to Aunt M and to Agnes for leading me here. It was the last place I expected but I knew this was where I was meant to be – it felt like I'd finally come home.

Chapter 44

Claire

Greta Schwartz and I had stayed in touch while I was in France; I checked in each day and she knew to phone me immediately if Aunt M had a relapse. I was terrified she might have another stroke and I wouldn't be there for her.

As soon as I got home, I went to Stanbury Hall, finding Aunt M in a complete flap anticipating my visit. I wanted to break the news to her gently, worried the shock might be too much for her, but she was agitated and full of questions, demanding to know everything I'd done and discovered. I found myself recounting my whole experience in one go, getting things out of order, trying to keep up with her, as she interrupted constantly, so that I jumped ahead of myself to answer her.

When I had nothing more to say, I showed her the photos I'd taken and she shed more tears at seeing Marguerite and Laurent.

'She has a look of Agnes. Her eyes are just the same,' she said, squinting short-sightedly at the images I'd printed off. 'But she's so tall. Agnes was tiny, you know.'

'I think Philippe LeConte was tall,' I said. 'Perhaps that's where she gets it. Her son is the same.' I gave her the letters. 'Marguerite gave me these for you. Agnes wrote them.'

She looked at them in confusion. 'Why did she not send them to me?'

I showed her the address on them, and a tear trickled down her cheek.

'Oh, no,' she whispered.

I handed her a magnifying glass, patted her hand, rose and kissed her. 'I'll leave you in peace to read them and come back in a while.'

She was in tears again, when I returned.

'She came to London after the war, you said? Why didn't she come and find me then?'

She sounded bereft, as if this was the deepest cut after all the years of not knowing anything.

'I don't know. Perhaps she did – perhaps she went back to your old flat and saw it had been destroyed – wouldn't she think the worst?' I clutched at straws, trying to give her some kind of comfort. 'After her letters were returned, she must have tried to find out what happened to you, surely? If there were no answers, perhaps she decided to remain in France.'

'Well, everything was in a terrible state of confusion, and I moved to another place without telling anyone where I was going,' she admitted. 'My flat being bombed was such a terrible shock. One got used to seeing people being made homeless, all their possessions destroyed, and I dreaded it happening to me. I suppose the longer my home escaped being hit, the more I hoped I had got away with it. Afterwards, I tried to get my life back in order, but I think I lost my way for a while.' Gazing at the blue aerogrammes on her lap, she seemed far away. 'It was always the thing that terrified me the most – the thought of being buried alive and nobody knowing I was there. Agnes knew that and we promised each other we'd always be together at the end.' Her face was bleak. 'At least I know she didn't forget me. It's some comfort.'

After she'd had time to digest everything, it seemed Aunt M was finally at peace. The one thing she regretted more than anything was never having the chance to know Agnes's daughter.

'I would have loved that child, if Agnes had come home, you know, dear,' she told me. 'I always wanted a family of my own. I think of you as the child I never had and was terribly jealous of Jessica, and furious with her for being such a distant mother. When she and your father split up and she disappeared off to Australia with that horrible man, I was very glad to have you stay with me.'

'You were always more of a mother to me than she was.'

I empathised so much with her, and for the first time I told her about the problems Andrew and I had faced, which, ultimately, had broken our marriage.

'I knew there was something. You've always had an aura of sadness about you, even though you do a good job of hiding it. I thought it was because of your parents,' she said. 'My poor, dear Claire. Life has dealt you a tough hand. I hope you find happiness, my dear. You deserve it, after everything that's happened.'

'Thank you,' I said. 'Some things are just not meant to be, I guess. And we tried our best to make our marriage work. In the end it was better to let it go and try to get on with our lives.'

I didn't tell her I had decided to sell my half of the veterinary practice. I knew I could never reconcile myself to working alongside Helen now. If Andrew wanted to buy it, all well and good, otherwise it would go on the market. I had no idea what I would do but St Jean Layrisse called to me like a siren and I knew I would be back there as soon as I could.

For the first time in as long as I could remember, I was excited about my future.

Chapter 45

Agnes

LONDON – 1946

Agnes climbed up the last few steps onto the pavement, and breathed in the smoggy air, coughing as the acridity caught the back of her throat. People pushed past her, hurrying about their business, and vehicles of all shapes and sizes moved up and down the road in a stilted dance, stopping and starting to an unheard tune. The noise assaulted her ears; it seemed inconceivable that she used to think this was normal.

Standing for a moment, she put her bag on the ground and hitched Marguerite more comfortably onto her hip. After adjusting the scarf around her neck, she picked up the bag and set off along the street, following the instructions she'd memorised from the letter. It was cold and raw after the heat of the Underground, and she shivered in her thin coat, regretting not bringing heavier clothing with her. The toddler held a grubby teddy bear in one hand and the thumb of her other one was plugged firmly into her mouth. Dark curls stuck damply to her forehead, and Agnes pushed them back, kissing her lightly on the cheek, extracting a giggle as her daughter tried to squirm out of her reach.

The address was a tall, elegant house in the middle of a row of similar homes. Agnes banged the wrought-iron knocker, then stood back, gazing up at the three floors with their tall windows, trying to slow the hammering in her chest. The door opened, and Edward was there, his arms held out in welcome. She walked into his embrace, and they stood for a moment, locked together. Relief and happiness filled her that, after so long, they'd found each other again. Marguerite broke the clinch when she dropped her teddy and let out a squawk of distress.

Edward picked the toy up, along with Agnes's case, and led them inside, leaning heavily on a cane. A lump rose into her throat at what he had gone through during the war. Surviving a plane crash, escaping to Spain thanks to Philippe's self-sacrifice and then almost drowning when the ship he was on hit a mine. It was a miracle he was still alive, and Agnes wanted to feast her eyes on him and keep her arms around him to make sure he was real.

'There's someone else here to see you,' he said, as she followed him along a wide hall with a high ceiling. For a moment, she imagined Maggie might magically be waiting for her. It stopped her in her tracks for a second as her brother went through an open door. What would she say – how could she explain? Edward lost everything except his life when the ship went down, so her note had never found its way to her love.

When her letters were returned, she'd explored every avenue, needing to know where Maggie was; the Red Cross had no record of her, so had she been posted somewhere new, or left the WAAFs, or fallen in love with someone else? With no answers to any of her questions she imagined her love must be dead and had grieved for months.

But she had to carry on for her daughter's sake and had locked the sadness away. The thought of meeting her again now, with a child in tow, was enough to send a blend of hope and fear rocketing through her body.

Marguerite dropped the teddy again – it had become a game with her in the past few weeks when she thought her mama wasn't paying enough attention. Agnes quickly retrieved it and straightened, changing the child to her other arm. Her daughter was quite capable of walking by herself, but it gave her something to do with her hands. Taking a breath, she entered a large, airy drawing room. Edward stood, talking to another man, and her spirits dived into the depths of her stomach, then soared as she realised who she was looking at.

'Pierre!' Placing Marguerite on her feet, Agnes strode across to her younger brother and hugged him. 'Why didn't you tell me he was here?' she demanded, searching for the words after so long only speaking French.

Edward wore a broad grin, looking ridiculously pleased.

'Well, I wasn't sure I could get here in time for your arrival,' Pierre said. 'My work is erratic. I never know when I'll be called away, so it was better to say nothing in case I couldn't make it.'

'Oh, my dears, it's so wonderful to see you both.' Agnes couldn't keep the smile off her face. Joy bubbled inside her, and she turned to lift the impatient child pulling at her skirt, demanding to be included. 'Edward, Pierre, I'd like to introduce you to your niece, Marguerite.'

She planted a kiss on her daughter's forehead.

'*Mama, faim!*'

'*Oui, chérie, je sais.*' Agnes turned back to her brothers. 'Sorry. She's always hungry. I don't suppose you have a piece of bread she can have, do you?'

A tall, red-haired woman entered the room at that moment and walked straight over to Agnes.

'Hello. I'm Barbara, Edward's wife.' She stroked the top of Marguerite's head. 'And this must be your daughter. She's a beauty, and so like her mother.' She smiled and offered her arms to the little girl, who, with a serious face handed her teddy to her.

'*Teddy faim*,' she said.

'Sorry,' Agnes said, trying to shush her. 'I'm very happy to meet you.'

The two women kissed each other's cheeks, then Barbara took the toy and thanked the impatient child. 'I guess we're all hungry, aren't we? Shall we go and have tea? It's ready in the kitchen.'

Over seed cake and cups of weak tea – a drink Agnes hadn't tasted since she'd left England almost three years earlier – she and her brothers tried to catch up on all the time they'd missed together. Barbara, meanwhile, kept Marguerite busy with games and food, entertaining her with shadow puppets and songs.

As the afternoon light dipped, Pierre glanced at his watch and stood up. 'Ah, I wish I could stay longer, but I have a meeting at six. I need to get moving if I'm going to make it in time.'

'You will come again, before I have to leave, won't you?' Agnes said, hugging him. It was inconceivable that this would be the only time she'd see him. 'Please, Pierre. I've hardly heard anything about what you do – or even where you live nowadays.'

'Oh, you won't get much out of him,' Edward chipped in. 'He's a close sort, our brother. Keeps himself to himself.'

Pierre smiled but looked a little uncomfortable. 'My life is far too boring to warrant discussion,' he said. 'But of course, I'll come and see you again. How long are you staying?'

'I'm here for four days.'

Everyone followed him out to the hall, where he wrapped an expensive-looking scarf around his neck.

'I'm not working on Sunday, so why don't we go for a walk somewhere? Along the river, or Hampstead Heath, perhaps? I'll ring you, Edward, and we can arrange to meet somewhere.'

Pierre shrugged his shoulders into his overcoat and put on a hat, checking the angle in a mirror, and Agnes thought how debonair he looked. So unlike Edward, who was much less formal in a pair of old corduroy trousers and an open-necked shirt. Marriage suited her older brother, she thought. There was still so much she wanted to know about their lives – she'd missed too many years because of her hatred for her father. Wasted time she could never reclaim. Hugging a struggling Marguerite to her, she waved as Pierre strode away down the street, barely recognising him for the same small boy she remembered from their days in France.

The following day, after Edward had left for his office, Barbara offered to take Marguerite off her hands for an hour or two. Agnes must surely have other old friends she wanted to see while she was in London? And it was very cold for the little one to be out and about.

'You're going to be such a good mother, one day.' Agnes smiled at her. Barbara had bonded with her daughter already, and Marguerite was used to being looked after by a variety of surrogate aunties and cousins. Edward's wife blushed and looked down at her hands. 'Oh, my dear. You're expecting, aren't you?'

Barbara nodded, her red hair falling over her face. She raised her head and Agnes saw the sparkle in her eyes. 'I'm pretty sure I am, but I've not said anything to Edward until I've been to the doctor and it's confirmed. Please don't mention it to him.'

'Your secret is safe with me. What wonderful news for you both.' She hugged her sister-in-law, feeling the happiness radiating from her. So, her daughter would have an English cousin. It was another reason to keep connected with her family. Perhaps they would come over to visit her in France, once everything was more normal. Her reluctance to come back seemed childish, now she was here. There was just one more thing she must do; something she dreaded and yet yearned for.

Standing in front of what had been the flat she'd shared with Maggie, Agnes wiped tears away from her cold cheeks. Icy rain fell, stinging her face, but she continued to stare at the piles of rubble and rubbish that lined both sides of the street. Was this the answer to her questions? Did Maggie endure the thing she dreaded most – being buried in the aftermath of a bomb blast? At least she knew now why her letters were returned; the worries she'd had that her love had found someone else, had forgotten her, could be put to bed. Grief choked her, and she closed her eyes, blocking out the physical evidence of so much pain.

A man pushed past her. Pulled out of her memories, she shivered as rain dripped down her neck. It felt unconscionable to leave, disloyal that she hadn't been there to share the fear and pain with Maggie. Didn't they always say when their time was up, they would go together? They'd be drinking champagne and making love while the bombs fell? And she'd failed her, wasn't there to hold her and comfort her in their last moments. The war had beaten them, in the end, just as it had beaten so many people.

All she had now was her daughter. She turned back the way she'd come. Marguerite was enough; a reminder of her time with Maggie every time she said her name.

'Au revoir, mon amour.'

Chapter 46

Claire

Over the following year I spent all my spare time with Aunt M, taking her out and about, or sitting with her, reading to her or playing cards. She gradually became frailer and more forgetful, yet never lost her wicked sense of the ridiculous. Between us, Greta and I managed to keep her out of hospital until the end. She died peacefully, in her own room at Stanbury Hall.

Her funeral was filled with people I'd never met before, who all had stories of their time spent with my aunt. She was loved, respected, and admired, and would have enjoyed such a good send-off. I could imagine her sitting, dressed to kill, holding court and sipping champagne – in her element.

That night, I went home, opened another bottle of champagne and got horribly drunk, while looking at photos of us together over the years. I cried and laughed, and knew I would miss Aunt M more than I could imagine.

* * *

In the weeks following Aunt M's death, my days were filled with meetings and paperwork as I attempted to get my head around the fact I was wealthy. She'd left me the Chimneys and the majority of her money – I was astounded at how much she had squirrelled away in various share portfolios and bank accounts. I didn't know what to do with her inheritance; the amount was overwhelming and the last thing I wanted was to fritter it away. She had made bequests to her favourite charities, and I considered setting up something in her name – a scholarship for a writing course, or something similar she would have approved of.

The thought of selling the Chimneys appalled me – it held so many fond memories, and the essence of Aunt M was ingrained within its walls. Eventually, I took advice, and had the old house renovated after its long years of neglect, finding a passion in keeping it as original as possible. It took six months to bring it back to life, and then I rented it out at an extortionate rate to an American professional polo player who wanted a base while he played the season in England.

Andrew bought my share of the veterinary practice, and we parted on friendly terms. It felt as if a black cloud that had followed me around for years had suddenly disappeared. I didn't need to work to survive, and enjoyed the feeling of freedom it gave me for a while.

I travelled to France whenever I could, staying with Harriet and exploring the area, often with Laurent, as he showed me his favourite haunts in the mountains. We met for the occasional drink, in between times, keeping things casual. We remained in touch when I was back in England, and our friendship gradually deepened into something more.

We were both wary about falling for someone new, but Luc became the catalyst. He was a mini version of his dad, and had a passion not just for Jurot but for horses too, and kept a small, cheeky pony at the farm. Being a vet gave me kudos, and we developed a strong rapport. He found my attempts at French hilarious, so I challenged him to teach me – not realising at first all the new words I learnt from him were profanities.

After a while, when I was paying for a room at Villa Sarnaille but not spending any nights there, it made sense to stay with Laurent. For the first time in almost as long as I could remember, I felt happy and content.

Early in spring, eighteen months after Aunt M died, and while I was in France, I received a message from Harriet with a link attached. It was a For Sale notice of the veterinary practice I'd gone to the first time I met Laurent and Luc. I remembered the *A Vendre* sign. We met for coffee the next day, and she didn't stop talking about her idea. The town needed a new vet, she pleaded, and I was perfect for the post.

'Harriet, I may be a vet, but I can hardly string two sentences together in French,' I said. 'How on earth do you think I could cope with running a mixed practice, here?'

She laughed. 'Claire, you're more than capable of making a go of it. Hire someone French to help you. Sign up for French language lessons. I'm sure you'll think of something.' She paused. 'And think of all the ex-pats who will come flocking to your door. They are going to love you being their vet.'

She sounded so positive, I laughed too.

'Promise me you'll think about it?' she said.

'I will, I promise.'

Terrified it might scare off Laurent, I tentatively asked him what he thought of me moving to France permanently.

'Who do you think showed the For Sale notice to Harriet?'

He grinned at me.

'Why didn't *you* talk to me about it?'

Under his tan his face reddened. 'I was worried you might back off: that you'd think I was being too pushy, wanting you to leave England and move here.' He smiled. 'I was wrong, wasn't I?'

'St Jean has felt like home since the day I arrived, looking for Agnes.'

Moving into his arms, I rested my head on his chest. I belonged here, with this man, in this place. There was no doubt in my mind.

I signed the final document and put the pen down on the solicitor's desk. He took the papers from me and shook my hand, then turned to M Huget and shook his hand too.

'I wish you every success in your new venture as proprietor of the St Jean Veterinary Clinic,' said M Huget. 'This town needs new blood, and I think you'll serve her needs well.' He pulled out a bottle of whisky from the large bag he'd set down beside his chair and opened it with a flourish. The solicitor took three glasses from a cupboard under his desk, obviously well used to this ceremony, and the old vet poured a large glug into each of them. 'A toast. To new beginnings – *Santé!*'

'*Santé!*' I replied, relieved everything was, at last, settled.

M Huget was a wily negotiator, and he'd driven a hard bargain, but the vet practice was now mine, and I couldn't wait to reopen it.

I took the keys and left as soon as was polite, impatient to get away and digest the fact I was now the owner of a business, in a foreign land, speaking a language I was still learning. It had been a long road, but I couldn't be happier.

I said a silent thankyou to Aunt M, sure she would approve of how I'd spent some of her money.

Later the same afternoon, Laurent and I walked up from his mother's farm to the cemetery. The day was bright and early summer wildflowers filled the mountain meadows, turning them into a colourful carpet on the other side of the cemetery wall. The hum of bees was an undernote to the song of a blackbird sitting in a young chestnut tree at the gate. Overhead, a pair of red kites wheeled and soared in a graceful dance, the sun turning their feathers a deep gold.

Carrying the urn with care, I made my way over to the far wall where Agnes lay. Laurent walked beside me, his arm across my shoulders.

'Are you sure about this?'

'I think it's the perfect thing to do,' I said. 'They can be together again, after all this time.'

Unscrewing the lid, I carefully tipped out Aunt M's ashes onto the gravel that covered Agnes's final resting place. A lump forced its way up into my throat as I rose, and we stood in silence, gazing at the well-tended grave.

After a while we turned, Laurent took my hand, and we walked slowly out of the cemetery.

A Letter from Corin Burnside

Thank you so much for choosing to read *Her Forgotten Promise*. I hope you enjoyed it! If you did and would like to be the first to know about my new releases, follow me on Twitter here: https://twitter.com/write_corinmd

I hope you loved *Her Forgotten Promise* and if you did I would be so grateful if you would leave a review. I always love to hear what readers thought, and it helps new readers discover my books too.

Thanks,

Corin

A Letter from Camp Douglas

Acknowledgements

There are so many people I want to thank who have helped to bring *Her Forgotten Promise* into the world.

First, I want to thank Audrey Linton and the rest of the team at HQ Digital, who took a chance on me and this story and made my dream of being a published author come true. Audrey is a wonderful editor whose enthusiasm, keen eye and ideas helped put the polish on my rough diamond. I also want to thank Helena Newton for her inciteful copy editing skills and Michelle Bullock for her proofread.

Having only written short and flash fiction, I learnt a huge amount about writing in long form from two courses – the PRH Construct a Novel course, where I had the best of tutors in Barbara Henderson, who gave me the confidence to keep going, and where I met some wonderful writers who have become friends as well as writing comrades. CBC's Three-Month Novel Writing course followed a year later and Suzannah Dunn helped bring this fledgling book to life. I was then fortunate enough to have Liz Monument as a mentor and I learnt from her how to take the story to the next level and make it sing.

During that time, I was persuaded to join the writing community on Twitter, and here I met the fabulous group of writers who make up Virtual Writing Group #VWG. Without their help, humour and wisdom I would not be writing this today. They continue to be a bottomless well of support, love and friendship and I cannot imagine life without them.

Agnes, Claire and Margaret came to life in the first instance as a short story, which the lovely team at Virtual Zine published. Thank you, Laura, Mark, Danielle and Simon for believing in the story and suggesting the idea had the legs to become a fully formed novel.

Several drafts benefited along the way from some excellent eagle-eyed beta readers, whose advice and feedback proved invaluable. Anita, Julia, Neema, Sarah, Mark, Kate, Carolyn, Katrina and Deborah, I cannot thank you all enough for your time and expertise.

Her Forgotten Promise owes a huge amount to the wonderful area of France where I have lived for the past ten years. The Midi-Pyrenees, with its rich history and friendly people provided inspiration every time I trod the forest tracks and mountain paths which feature in the story. With Princess Lexi at my side, who is always a willing listener to any knotty plot problem, there is no better place to invent stories.

My family have put up with listening to my latest ideas for stories with patience and good humour, and have provided a wealth of love, support and inspiration along the way. My fabulous sisters, Maeve, Shonagh and Gail, your families, my wonderful mum, Ann, plus Lily, Maureen and all the Burnside clan, I thank you for everything you do for me.

Thanks also to all my friends who have been so supportive and enthusiastic about this adventure. It would not be half as much fun without you guys being there.

Finally, John, Gemma and Michael, you have been unendingly patient, encouraging and supportive. To know you have my back and are always willing to listen to me moaning when things are not going the way I want them to means the world. I could not love you more.

Team Burnside, this is for you.

Dear Reader,

We hope you enjoyed reading this book. If you did, we'd be so appreciative if you left a review. It really helps us and the author to bring more books like this to you.

Here at HQ Digital we are dedicated to publishing fiction that will keep you turning the pages into the early hours. Don't want to miss a thing? To find out more about our books, promotions, discover exclusive content and enter competitions you can keep in touch in the following ways:

JOIN OUR COMMUNITY:
Sign up to our new email newsletter: http://smarturl.it/SignUpHQ

Read our new blog www.hqstories.co.uk

https://twitter.com/HQStories

www.facebook.com/HQStories

BUDDING WRITER?
We're also looking for authors to join the HQ Digital family!

Find out more here:

https://www.hqstories.co.uk/want-to-write-for-us/

Thanks for reading, from the HQ Digital team